Retired journalist and academic **Suhit Sen** writes fiction and political commentary as well as researches and writes on India's postcolonial political history. He is the author of *The Paradox of Populism: The Indira Gandhi Years, 1966-77*. He lives in Kolkata.

THE HUNTER OF LALBAZAR

SUHIT SEN

SPEAKING TIGER

SPEAKING TIGER BOOKS LLP
125A, Ground Floor, Shahpur Jat, near Asiad Village,
New Delhi 110049

Published by Speaking Tiger Books 2022

ISBN: 978-93-5447-298-5
eISBN: 978-93-5447-304-3

10 9 8 7 6 5 4 3 2 1

Typeset in Arno Pro by SÜRYA, New Delhi
Printed at HT Media Ltd, Greater Noida

For Ma and in memory of Baba

Contents

Part One

Lalbazar, Calcutta, December

Tanya parked parallel to the kerb about a hundred metres from her destination. She was driving her own car, not her official vehicle. A parking attendant ran towards her, his arms flailing like the blades of a windmill. She flashed her identity card in his face. He scarpered, deflated. Parking attendants generally don't hassle cops.

Tanya had not only driven her own car, she had dispensed with the services of her driver and her bodyguard, 'personal security officer' (PSO) in cop jargon. Sheonath Singh had objected to her haring off on her own. If anything happened to Tanya and the shit hit the fan, his ass would be on the line, not Tanya's. Sheonath was also a conscientious guy, genuinely loyal to and concerned about his boss, having been at her side since she moved from the districts to Calcutta many moons ago.

Tanya had assuaged his apprehensions. 'I'm not going hunting a serial killer,' she had assured him. 'I'm just going to meet a friend.' Sheonath had capitulated, but not before reminding her that his cell phone would be switched on, and the driver and the car would be in readiness. If there was even a hint of trouble she must call immediately. Tanya gave him her word. Sheonath took his job seriously, but he didn't take himself too seriously as many conscientious people are apt to do. It was a code instilled in him since childhood.

In accordance with convention, Tanya wore her khaki uniform on Mondays and Fridays whether or not she was checking into Lalbazar, the headquarters of Calcutta Police. 'Kolkata Police' actually, ever since the city had been rechristened Kolkata. But Tanya, now past the milestone of forty, had been unable to reconcile herself with the new name, of the city and the force she served. To her, the city remained Calcutta and its police force, consequently, Calcutta Police. Other than in official communications. Today was different. Although it was a Friday, she wasn't reporting to headquarters. She was meeting a journalist in a café.

She'd been to Lalbazar in the morning, where she had received an oracular call from one of the few journalists she almost liked. Raina Aqeel, a bright young reporter with *The Times of India*, had called, seeking an urgent meeting. This afternoon, she'd insisted. Tanya had asked her to call back and, checking her schedule, found that there was no ineluctable call of duty to prevent her from saying yes. When Raina called back, Tanya had tried to sound as brusque as possible, just to keep matters businesslike.

Tanya had gone home and changed out of uniform before proceeding for the rendezvous. The brief Calcutta winter had not really arrived, though it was getting on to mid-December. So, getting out of the stiff uniform was a bonus. Out of khaki, she usually dressed 'sensibly'. Sometimes she thought she'd been a cop for too long. She hardly ever wore a sari. Her usual get-up was either a nondescript *salwar-kameez* (loose trousers and loose tunic) or trousers with semi-formal tops or shirts. When she was really letting her hair down, she'd opt for jeans and a T-shirt. Make-up minimal. That had been drilled into her by a senior colleague in the bureaucracy. She hardly wore any jewellery either. The only piece she had always worn was her wedding ring, but that had come off after her divorce and been converted into a pair of ear-studs. She regretted it as little as she missed her former husband, the shithead who'd cheated on her serially.

On this uncomfortably warm day, she had pared down her accoutrements even further. She wanted to be as inconspicuous as possible. But however hard she tried, she couldn't really go unnoticed. At five-foot-eight, Tanya towered over practically all Indian women. She was taller than some of her male colleagues too. And with her trim figure, thick, shoulder-length hair and not-hard-to-look-at face, she got the second glance more often than not. She also got hit on sometimes, before the men realized she was a cop. Then, they usually beat it.

Tanya's footwear was utilitarian like her clothes. Today, she was especially happy to be wearing floaters because the potholed streets and broken pavements had been puddled by a short, sharp squall, following a monsoon-like downpour in the early hours, making the day uncomfortably humid. She stepped around the water because she hated to get her feet wet. Eventually, she reached Wise Owl, the laidback café where she was to meet Raina. Tanya still wore a watch all the time unlike the increasing number of people who checked the time on their cell phones. She felt naked without her watch. It not only told her the time without the inconvenience of scrabbling in her tote bag for her phone, it also doubled as a bracelet because it had been made for that express purpose. It was a gift from her parents on the occasion of joining the Indian Police Service (IPS). Tanya had been wearing it for almost two decades and took good care of it. It was accurate and it looked good. This was the only piece of 'jewellery' she always wore.

When Tanya found a table, her watch-bracelet told her she had reached ten minutes early. Plus, she thought, Raina's going to be late. Indians were practically always late for appointments and, in her experience, journalists inevitably so. Tanya could steal a few minutes for herself, which she could almost never do. Her job and Shaman, her twelve-year-old son, kept her on her toes. He demanded attention and got it because Tanya had to double up for her unceremoniously booted-out husband. She didn't mind, but these few minutes were an oasis. She had the place almost to herself. Come 6 o'clock, it would be tough to get a table, with the young crowd descending on it.

Waiting for Raina, Tanya's mind went back to the call. Raina had been uncharacteristically evasive, almost enigmatic. When Raina had called her back, Tanya cut the crap. 'I'll meet you,' she said. 'But be warned, I won't have anything for you. I can't talk to you about the two cases I'm actively working on. And you know I don't give anything away on cases I'm not working on myself.'

'I'm not sniffing,' Raina had replied, sniffing. 'If I'd been, I'd just have met you in Lalbazar. This time, I want to give you some information. On one of your sensitive cases. I know more than you'd guess.' That had grabbed Tanya. She thought she'd kept it under wraps. Just goes to show, she'd thought. Bloody Lalbazar. It was like a bleeding colander, with some extra holes thrown in. No hidden charges.

'What sensitive case would you be talking about, Ms Aqeel?' Tanya had asked, in a sufficiently withering tone. 'And what information can you give me?'

'Can't do it over the phone.' Raina was emphatic. 'And can't do it in Lalbazar. You know better than me what your HQs like, don't you? Let's meet at the Wise Owl in Gol Park. The coffee's good. The place is quiet. And cops and newshounds don't go there. It's too civilized.'

Tanya hadn't pushed; she knew Raina was right, as also the price of whatever information she'd get. If it was useful, Raina was sure to get an exclusive, probably on Page One, with a refulgent byline. If it was a dud, she'd get the pleasure of Tanya's company, which on a good day could be pretty entertaining, and a cup of Wise Owl's decent coffee.

Tanya started thinking about the case. It didn't merit being bumped up to the city's elite investigation unit, the Detective Department (DD), and still less the attention of the senior-most officer in the department. In this case, Joint Commissioner of Police (JCP) (Crime) Tanya Samanta, the ranking officer in DD. She hadn't been too happy that the commissioner had dumped it on her desk, but hadn't been surprised. Kolkata Police Commissioner Ajoy Chanda didn't have a high opinion of women in the force, especially the ones who'd cracked the same entrance exam he had. The greater the seniority a woman earned, the more he patronized her. Commissioner Chanda was no great cop. But he knew how the game was played, within the force and with the political bosses, which was why he was the Commissioner and in line to become Director-General of Police (DGP), West Bengal. And, as with most female colleagues, he was not particularly fond of Tanya Samanta.

What had landed on Tanya's desk was a hooch-death case. Four people had died and a dozen-odd more had fallen critically ill after consuming illicit liquor at a shack next to the tracks near the Bagha Jatin railway station in south Calcutta, or Kolkata, whatever. Hooch deaths had been common a couple of decades ago, but their incidence had decreased, perhaps because licit country liquor had become more readily available. When the case had landed on her desk, Tanya had no difficulty recalling the last time a major hooch tragedy had hit Calcutta's immediate environs.

It was, she remembered, in the adjoining district of South 24 Parganas towards the end of 2011, months after the Trinamool Congress had come to power, ending thirty-four years of Left Front rule. One of the worst-ever hooch-death tragedies in Bengal. Around 175 dead. Such cases were normally dealt with by the local police station. Everybody knew who the bootleggers were. Theoretically, it was just a question of raiding the hooch shack, collecting samples and shutting the place down. Show raids would follow, perhaps across the district. Liquor dens would be destroyed. The toughest part of the operation would be apprehending the culprits, who would have absconded.

That was the theory. In reality, the illegal vends would soon be up and running elsewhere, depending on how long it took for public outrage and media attention to fade. The kingpins would seldom be arrested because they had political and police patronage. Hell, they could be influential leaders themselves, with ties to one or more members of the state legislative assembly. Or even a minister. In that case, it wouldn't really matter whether the investigation was headed by officers from the local police station or a hotshot joint commissioner from Lalbazar.

Tanya had no difficulty joining the dots. Assigning her this case was Chanda's way of harassing her. It wasn't particularly subtle. The hooch case would take up valuable time and increase her workload doing routine shit that anyone could have done. Them's the breaks, she thought. But Tanya was resilient. As one of four women IPS officers in Kolkata Police, she had learnt to deal with male colleagues, bosses and underlings. And she knew she'd have to reconcile the daily attrition with her ambitions.

So, Tanya had gone to work on the case in all seriousness. Going to the spot, supervising the demolition of illegal vends within a two-kilometre radius—to hell with the local cops and politicians who protected the racketeers—and talking to the families of the victims and locals. It was routine shit. She could have her team do it, but she didn't. In fact, she got a buzz out of going to the spot. She didn't get a chance to go into the field very often because her duties were largely administrative and supervisory.

The spot where the hooch shack had stood was like

countless others. A fundamental feature of the area along the railway lines in the vicinity of stations was slums. In Calcutta, as in other Indian cities, there are slums and then there are slums. Some are somewhat habitable, but not the ones along the railway lines, which are makeshift hellholes. A universal fixture of these slums is the hooch den. It is to the slum what a temple is to a village, or a tea shop to a city neighbourhood. Here, the denizens gather to get hammered, discourse, complain, and often, quarrel and fight. If they are unlucky, and the ethanol they are supposed to be drinking turns out to be methanol, they die or go blind. It's not just the hooch. Chasing smack, low-grade heroin, complements the hooch. Children could start on either or both in their early teens. Or before.

When JCP Tanya Samanta landed up at the offending hooch den in the Bagha Jatin slum, she was immediately repelled. She was out of touch with some of the realities of urban life. At the same time, she got a distinct buzz, because from the moment she started the investigation at the 'spot', she got the feeling that something was out of kilter. The main accused—the bootleggers who 'owned' the liquor shack—were two brothers: Ghiasuddin and Shamsuddin Mollah. They were nowhere to be found, which was hardly surprising. The people in the shanties knew nothing. They were like the three monkeys who saw no evil, heard no evil and, sure as hell, spoke no evil. The Mollah brothers' home was near Baruipur town, around twenty kilometres south of the vend if you walked along the tracks. But the villagers and family members, again unsurprisingly, hadn't seen them in a long time. How long? Difficult to tell, a neighbour said. Long enough for me to lose track. At least six months? There had been a question in his voice. You tell us, a member of the police team had said, truculently. Don't know. The man had clammed up. Routine.

But what wasn't unsurprising or routine was that Tanya and her team weren't getting anything through the underworld grapevine either. Nobody seemed to know where the Mollah brothers were. Or, at least, they weren't saying anything. Not a peep. And that was surprising, given the vast network of informers Lalbazar ran and the large number of people who were willing to swap stories for immunity from past, present or future crimes. And that was what made Tanya smell, if not actually see, a rodent in the sewers.

That the Mollah brothers had a political patron, or a bunch of them, was obvious. It took Tanya a few hours to get up to speed. The patron-in-chief in this case was the Jadavpur MLA Shila Nandi. Jadavpur was the state assembly constituency, part of the larger parliamentary constituency of Jadavpur, in which Bagha Jatin was located. Till eight years ago, she'd been a housewife. Her husband Chhoton Nandi had been a municipal councillor for years, before contesting the assembly elections from Jadavpur. With the army of goons and thugs and patronage network he had assembled, he won easily. And the three following elections.

Chhoton was much older than his wife and he cashed in his chips at the age of seventy-two, a year or so before his fourth term was to come to an end. The wise heads of the party then decided that his freshly minted widow would be the ideal candidate for the by-election. Chhoton's private army would just have to switch loyalties from late husband to widow. Shila was unwilling. 'I know nothing about all this,' she had told the wise heads. 'I have a household to run; two children to look after. I can't do it. I would be hopeless.' That was eight years ago. Since then, she had won two more elections, first, under the Left Front banner and then, on a Trinamool Congress ticket. Now, she ran the Jadavpur area like a medieval warlord.

She got a cut from everything illegal that went down in her fief: prostitution, drug-peddling, bootlegging, human trafficking, extortion, construction, legal or illegal, the supply of building materials and labour gangs, theft, robbery—everything was grist to her mill. The party got most of the money, but Shila did quite well for herself, thank you. Enough to keep the home fires burning. It was all for her daughter's wedding and her son's education, the uncharitable said slyly. After all, she was a widow. Shila didn't give a flying. The uncharitable could say anything. And the charitable too.

In Lalbazar, however, none of this explained the wall of silence that Tanya had crashed into. Shila, she thought, could be the queen of Jadavpur. But she'd be eaten for breakfast if she so much as went for a walk in Ballygunge, a few kilometres north. Or Garia, a few kilometres south. So why were the hoods doing the *omertà* crap all over the city? When in doubt, talk to Garcia. Inspector Clayton Garcia was the longest-serving officer in her department. Tanya picked him in her team first, whenever she headed an investigation. He was a tall, wiry man. Taciturn. His experience, networks and intelligence made him an invaluable investigator. And like Sheonath, he had contracted the rare disease called conscientiousness. His easy-going manner made him an ideal colleague.

Unlike many cops, he took time off to think through a case. Three days into this one, with the Shila Nandi saga digested, Tanya called him for a one-to-one. 'There's something going on here Garcia, which we're not getting,' she said. 'And it's not the hooch. It isn't any of the standard things either. I can sense that. It's something bigger.'

Garcia agreed. 'I think you're right, ma'am. But I can't understand it. I think it's time to break some heads. Can you give me twenty-four hours?' He didn't say 'a day'.

'Take forty-eight,' Tanya had told him. 'But come back with something.' So, Garcia disappeared for twenty-four hours, no questions asked.

Garcia prided himself on his punctuality and his ability to deliver. He was back in his one-bedroom pad in Bowbazar, a street lined with optical stores and jewellery shops, which was walking distance from Lalbazar, roughly sixteen hours after taking his semi-authorized leave of absence. There were some things Garcia tried not to compromise on: time in the gym; a proper breakfast, since he never knew when his next meal could be grabbed; and at least five hours of the dreamless and blameless, preferably at night.

This day, he slept from five in the morning, after a snack. When he woke up at 10 o'clock, he was ready to take on the day and still had a couple of hours in hand before meeting JCP Tanya Samanta, ma'am. So, he went for a run, even though pre-winter warmth was refracting from the streets, the solid concrete blocks and the masses of human bodies, which he had to continuously dodge. Garcia barely noticed. He got home forty-five minutes later, showered again, had breakfast and a cup of coffee before heading out to meet his boss. He was early, so he rolled a cigarette outside the gate, smoked it and went in.

Tanya was waiting. Nothing had broken in the twenty-four hours since Garcia had left and Tanya was getting restless, though not really desperate, because she *knew* he would bring something. She was sure of it. Garcia knocked on her door at noon—exactly twenty-four hours. There was the usual hush in the room which set in when Garcia returned from a solo flight.

'They are in Bangladesh,' he began. 'But I don't know where. And you were right. It's not drugs and hooch, it's bigger. I'll need to go undercover to find out. Between us, ma'am, we could be beating our heads against a brick wall here.'

'Who's pulling the strings, Garcia? We've broken a few hard heads in this department. We have the equipment, the knowhow.' No one called Inspector Clayton Garcia, Clayton; always Garcia. No one knew why, because first names were more common among colleagues.

Garcia remained silent for a while. 'It's a motley crew,' he finally volunteered. 'There's Aurobindo from Bansdroni; Kalua from Topsia; Kaleem from Kidderpore; Lyangda Jayanta from Sonarpur; and Mahesh Yadav from Burrabazar. There are others, I'll need some time to get all the names. But I'm not sure who's pulling the strings.

It seems to be Shila Nandi. But she's daft. She couldn't run a really big operation outside Jadavpur.'

'We could take her network out. But it would be pointless, wouldn't it, if we can't get the guys behind her?' Tanya said.

Garcia nodded. It had occurred to him and he'd done some basic planning.

'Any guesses?' Tanya asked. 'What's the shakedown? Can we get the Mollah brothers without going through the proper channels?'

'We need to sit tight for a while, ma'am. I know you're itching for action, but this isn't the right time. We need to know more. But the higher we go, the less we'll learn. Can you give me a few days? Today's Friday. I'll be back on Monday. I think some head-banging cannot be avoided. I'll spare you the details, ma'am,' Garcia said.

Though Tanya hadn't said a thing, Garcia knew the deal was done. He also knew that if the shit hit the fan, his boss would cover for him. Not that he anticipated any situation. He was about to leave, when a thought struck him. 'Could you please keep Ishita on standby, ma'am? On a strictly emergency, need-to-know basis.'

'Ishita?' Tanya's tone gave away her misgivings.

Constable Ishita Pal had been seconded to DD about a year ago. Tanya found her bright and enthusiastic, but also inexperienced and impetuous. Tanya had included her in the team because she thought the young woman had potential. She needed a break. But Tanya certainly didn't want to involve her in a Garcia-inspired covert operation.

***

Ishita had got herself a Bachelor's degree in Commerce, with the idea of becoming a chartered accountant. When she finished college with a below-average degree that betrayed a lack of interest rather than ability, she was pretty sure she didn't want to become an accountant of any stripe. Accountancy was way too boring. Her father was a clerk in the city's criminal court. So, Ishita decided to become a lawyer. She enrolled in a law course, during which she met Mrinal Mallik, an assistant sub-inspector (ASI) in the Kolkata Police. They began dating and Mrinal's stories about his job convinced her it was far more exciting than her father's uneventful one.

She applied for the job of a constable, without informing her parents, and got it. Her parents were less than happy, but did not stand in her way. Ishita was assigned to the traffic police. She enjoyed her job, the uniform and the authority it gave her. Her boyfriend was in DD. He had a mentor called Gopal Barui, an inspector, to whom he would regularly talk about Ishita's potential as an investigator. Gopal had finally taken the hints and helped get Ishita into DD, where she had impressed her superiors with her intelligence and industry, though she tended to take the initiative in inappropriate situations.

***

Tanya had observed Ishita's work and was reasonably impressed. But she didn't think her mature enough to handle difficult situations. 'Ishita?' she asked again.

Garcia nodded. 'She'll be involved only if absolutely necessary. And, ma'am, she won't get to know more than she must. She won't be in the line of fire, I assure you, because she won't see the rough stuff. Won't even sniff it. Her safety is my responsibility.'

Tanya nodded reluctantly. And her phone rang.

Garcia walked out of the room just as Raina ventured a tentative hello. And a few hours later, JCP Tanya Samanta was sitting in the Wise Owl, waiting for the reporter, wondering what the hell she wanted to tell her. She was brought out of her reverie by an irreverent voice.

'Hey, you,' it said. 'What are you up to in this nice cafe? Want some company?'

Raina Aqeel had arrived. All five feet and three inches of wiry good humour. Raina had been a champion gymnast in school and it showed. She went for judo classes and whenever her job and romance afforded her some time, she'd either go swimming in or jogging by the Dhakuria Lake, that vast expanse of water and greenery, which was called the lungs of south Calcutta.

Raina had begun her meeting with Tanya facetiously, but the moment she sat down, it became obvious she hadn't brought Tanya out of the office for a laugh.

'What will you have?' Tanya asked. 'And quit looking like you're carrying the Pentagon Papers in your hip pocket.' She ordered coffee for both of them. Cappuccino.

Tanya could make out that the girl was worried, almost scared. There was a brief, but fraught, silence and Raina handed Tanya an envelope. On it was typed: **Read the paper inside**.

The tables next to them were unoccupied and Tanya said so. 'What's with the cloak and dagger?' she asked.

Suddenly, Raina's face turned grey. In a brittle voice Tanya had never heard before, she said, 'Just read it.'

Tanya slit open the envelope and extracted a piece of paper from it. On it was typed:

I have a video shot on a mobile phone. It will be of great interest to you and your department. It should help solve your sensitive case. But I can't show it to you here. I could be in danger. My partner, who shot the video, will be in danger. You might be in danger. We need to have a private screening, just the three of us. Somewhere safe. Until you see the video, don't tell *anyone* it exists. After you've seen it, we'll talk. Where can we go? Write it down on the paper.

Tanya thought for a while. This was too theatrical, but she'd never known Raina to be melodramatic.

My house, she scrawled. But let's finish our coffees and talk about the weather. You'll leave first. Follow my car as discreetly as you can. She pushed the paper back to Raina, who read it and nodded. She was glad she'd come to Tanya, who was sensible and enterprising. Raina finished her coffee and left. A man was waiting some distance away, astride a motorbike. She went up to him. 'She'll be out soon,' Raina told him. 'We are to follow her at a distance, discreetly.' Tanya drove away in a few minutes. Raina and her friend waited for a beat and followed.

~

They parked on a parallel street and walked up to the building in which Tanya lived. It was in Golf Green, an upper-middle-class housing development in south Calcutta dating back to the mid-70s. Not gated. Tanya ushered them in when they reached her door, banishing Shaman to his bedroom. He went, under protest. Raina introduced her friend as Arpan. Then, Tanya offered them tea, which was refused. 'So, what's this cloak-and-dagger stuff all about? And who are you exactly, apart from being Raina's friend?' she asked Arpan.

'That doesn't matter,' he replied. 'What matters is the video clip.'

Tanya let it pass. For the moment. 'Right, let's have a look then,' was all she said.

Arpan booted up his mobile. After some fidgeting, he opened the clip and handed Tanya his phone. The video was grainy and illuminated only by streetlights. But there was no mistaking what it showed: a woman and a man entering a house. The woman was petite, the man tall and lithe. He had his arm around her waist; she was leaning against him. It was shot from behind, but to Tanya it was completely clear. The man in the video had left her office on an undercover assignment a few hours ago. And the woman was someone whom Tanya had been studying for the past few days. The pair was: Clayton Garcia and Shila Nandi.

For a few moments, Tanya felt like she was falling through a bottomless pit of darkness like in a dream. Her vision blurred and she felt nauseous. She made an effort and stood up to get herself a glass of water. She felt like having something a little stronger, but decided against it. She needed a clear head.

Tanya snapped out of it when Arpan spoke. 'Are you all right, ma'am?' he asked. 'I think I'd better explain.'

Damn right, about time, Tanya thought through a jagged hole in her mind.

'I'm a photographer. I do freelance work. News, features, photo essays. I've worked for newspapers in Calcutta. Magazines in India and abroad. Agencies.' Arpan paused to catch his breath. 'I wouldn't mind a coffee, ma'am.'

On tenterhooks, Tanya went into the kitchen and Raina tagged along. 'I wouldn't mind a cup either,' she said. 'I think you should have something stronger.'

Tanya stopped dead in her tracks. 'Why?'

Raina didn't try to be gentle. 'What you saw was just a curtain-raiser. Arpan has more to show you.'

Tanya set about making three cups of coffee. This was one of many jobs she never entrusted to her live-in governess-cook-housekeeper, or benevolent autocrat, Moni*di*, who looked after Shaman, who, in turn, ran a spirited campaign against being looked after. Tanya called him Muddy, after her favourite singer. Waters, the blues legend.

Coffee mugs in hand, they reconvened. And Arpan picked up the thread. 'When I read about the *cholai* (hooch) deaths, I thought I'd be able to get a few shots I could sell. Huts and shacks being razed, people protesting, the cops out in force. Then I heard the details the papers don't always print from Rini.' He pointed at Raina. 'And I got interested in Shila Nandi. Homemaker-turned-MLA-turned-organized crime boss. She doesn't look the part, does she?' That was obviously rhetorical. 'So, I started tailing her. I may not be a cop, but I'm pretty good at following people because I sort of blend in.' Which he does, Tanya thought. Wouldn't stand out anywhere.

'For a couple of days, it was boring. She went to party meetings, met constituents. Shopped. I thought I'd call it off. Earn some money. But then came the assignation. I knew something was up and talked to Rini. She agreed I should follow it up. Shila met this tall, wiry man in Kwality's in Ballygunge Phari. I was a couple of tables away, with my back to them, nursing a plate of sandwiches and a beer. I heard them talk. The place was empty. They were planning a trip to Shantiniketan and were obviously an item. I followed them there. I wasn't really worried about being spotted. You know Shantiniketan on a weekend, half of Calcutta lands up there.'

Arpan stopped and drained his coffee mug. 'I tailed them. I was a free agent and I could help Rini break something. But they weren't up to much. Most of the time, they were shacked up in a small guest house. With plenty of booze. I got some good shots of the two. A gangster and his moll, I thought. Or, a gangster and her toy boy. Big deal. I showed Rini the pictures and she almost fainted.'

Raina took up the story. 'I couldn't believe my eyes. I recognized Inspector Garcia of course. Shit, I've been on the crime beat long enough. And here he was, shacked up with Shila Nandi. I was trying to figure whether Garcia was just a flunkey and Shila's squeeze, or whether he was the boss and she was his squeeze. Jesus! My head was spinning. Next morning, I was still in shock. So, I took the day off.'

I don't know what the hell is going on and what I should do, Tanya thought. But whatever it is, it has to be *today*. I can't bloody take the day off.

Raina went on. 'By the time I was up, Arpan had left. I tried calling all day, but he'd switched off his bloody cell phone. I was so scared. And Arpan returned pretty late. With the video clips. You have to see the rest of it.'

Tanya was back in control. She turned to Arpan. 'Show me the rest. I have to act fast.' Arpan handed his phone over. Tanya was expecting the worst and got it: Shila walking towards the open window, practically naked. In the background she saw Garcia undress and get into bed. And then Shila shut the windows and drew the curtains. Tanya practically exploded. 'How the hell did you get that shot?'

'I climbed a convenient tree; wanted a smoking gun.'

Tanya was getting grimmer by the minute. 'You know what you've got into, don't you?' she said. 'I'll have to confiscate your phone and tell my bosses where I got this stuff from.' She turned to Raina. 'You are not writing a word about any of this. Until we dump the two of them in the dungeons. But you'll still be in danger because we don't know how many cops Garcia has suborned. And you know how leaky Lalbazar is.'

Suddenly, Tanya jumped up. 'Ishita.' It sounded almost like a squeal. Raina and Arpan sprung up as well. Tanya was wondering where Ishita fitted into all this. Was she a co-conspirator or a cat's paw? Or even worse, a potential hostage? She'd have to call. Which she did right away. Ishita responded at the first ring.

'Ma'am?' she said.

Tanya didn't hedge. 'Don't take calls from office or from anyone in the police force. On duty?'

'No,' Ishita said. 'I was cooking dinner.'

'Who do you live with?' Tanya asked, making a mental note. She ought to have known by now. The girl was on her team.

'I share a flat with a couple of friends, when I'm not in the barracks. My flatmates are in the force as well.'

'Stay at home until I give you the all clear.'

Tanya turned to Raina and Arpan. 'You're safe until I break this to my boss. After that, I'm not so sure. You'll have to watch your step. I'll try to arrange some security.' She thought for a while. 'Maybe I can keep Raina out of this. After all, she has had no role to play.' She turned to Arpan. '... Except being your girlfriend and the go-between.'

'Partner,' said Arpan and Raina, in the same breath.

'Whatever.' Tanya was almost getting monosyllabic the closer she came to having to make a decision. 'Give me your phone,' she told Arpan. 'Do you have another one? If you don't, get one. And don't tell anyone, that is *anyone,* anything. And go straight home.' She turned to Raina. 'Good job. But no more playing detective. It's our business now.'

Arpan looked uncomfortable. 'I've got a lot of stuff I need on that phone. I can mail you the clips.'

Tanya exploded. 'Mail! You guys are supposed to be tech-savvy. You know how secure email is?'

Arpan looked abashed. 'Sorry,' he said. 'I can put the clips on a pen drive.'

Tanya wasn't great with technology. She barely

managed Facebook. Twitter was mysterious, impossible to master. 'Okay, transfer the clips on to a pen drive. Then transfer all your stuff on to another one. We'll keep your phone. It's just become evidence. I'll buy you a new one. Get cracking on the transfers. I have pen drives I don't need. And don't delete anything.' As Arpan started working, Tanya turned to Raina. 'I know you are a tough, sensible girl. But this is not in your league. Take care.'

Raina was scared, but tried not to show it.

Tanya went to fetch Shaman from his bedroom, where he was playing a game on the computer. 'At it again,' Tanya said, half-heartedly.

He didn't even look up. 'Finished with homework.'

'Shut that thing off,' Tanya said. 'And come and get dinner. I have important work to do.'

Shaman looked up. 'It's called a computer,' he said, before packing it in.

Tanya smiled and left the room. Arpan was just finishing up. She took the pen drive and the phone, which she switched off, as Raina and Arpan headed out. 'You don't need to watch your step just yet,' Tanya told them. 'But from tomorrow, things will change. Look after yourself.'

***

Dinner over, Tanya packed Shaman off to bed. Then she poured herself a small vodka, squeezed some lime juice into it, packed it with ice and sat in her favourite chair. She really had no options. Whatever her opinion of her boss, she would have to drop it in his lap. She'd have preferred to go to the DGP, but he didn't have jurisdiction over

Kolkata Police. It was late, but it couldn't wait. Not with Garcia out there, wherever he was, doing whatever he was doing. He'd be up to no good. That much she was sure of.

Commissioner Chanda took the call at the seventh ring. Tanya counted. 'Commissioner Chanda,' he said, not recognizing the number because Tanya was calling from her landline.

'Sir,' Tanya said. 'All hell has broken loose. I need to keep you posted urgently. I could go to HQ and wait.'

'What's this about?' Chanda asked.

'Sir, we can't discuss this over the phone. It has to do with the hooch case, but it's very sensitive, sir.'

'Come to my residence,' Chanda said. Not place, not house. Residence. The Police Commissioner's Official Residence.

Tanya set off with the clips right away. The residence was on Loudon Street in one of the posh parts of the city, near the centre, known for its restaurants and bars. By Calcutta standards it was late—almost 10. She made it in well under half an hour.

~

At that very moment, Garcia was lying in bed, supine, but not metaphorically. Not the least bit. He was feeling on top of things. Completely. The bed was in a house owned by an associate. It was, he felt, in *every* sense, a safe house. No one could track him there, unless he allowed it, because no one knew that its owner was his associate. In fact, no one knew, Garcia thought, that his associate was involved in organized crime and racketeering on a colossal scale. Tapan Talapatra was the laundered face of his subterranean organization—a respectable businessman who owned a chemicals factory and a couple of units manufacturing plastic goods. Apart from that, he had a trading company that was doing well. And a chain of kindergarten schools. He was a member of a well-regarded club in south Calcutta, and known to be something of a philanthropist.

Garcia started thinking of Shila and felt even better. She wasn't a twenty-something. The good thing was that she didn't try to be. In her mid-fifties, she was a firecracker, especially in bed. And she would be here. As soon as she could get away without being noticed. Garcia had made all the arrangements. Now, however, he was just a little tired. He had got to Madhyamgram, beyond the northern outskirts of Calcutta, without attracting attraction. But before that, he had had to organize a hell of a lot of things.

The place was well connected, densely populated and far enough from the centre of Calcutta to be a good staging post. He was a good twenty-five kilometres from police headquarters. Soon after Shila arrived, they would leave for Bangladesh, stopping only for a steamy session of sexual calisthenics. Not Chittagong, obviously. That had been misdirection for Tapan's consumption. They had bought a place near Rajshahi town. That would put over 350 kilometres between his workplace, and him and Shila, including an international border.

Their passports were ready and thus a new set of identities. The house they would live in had been bought by 'Ashrafullah Mian' and 'Shahnaz Biwi'. Their combined fortunes had been transferred to new accounts in five private banks in Rajshahi district. Everything was sorted out. All that remained was to make it to Rajshahi safely and even that had been arranged. A car with genuine Bangladeshi registration. The new number plates would be screwed on after they entered Bangladesh. Till then fake Indian plates would do the job. The only problem was crossing the border. Garcia had organized that as well. They would travel with minimal baggage, literally and metaphorically. Garcia was a bit of a monk anyway. Shila would have to leave a lot behind. Her membership of the legislative assembly, her children and household. And her extensive wardrobe. But what the hell! They'd replenish that. The biggest problem was leaving the children behind. Shila had had to make a choice and she'd chosen 'Clay'.

The only outstanding issue was Garcia's empire, of which Shila's penny-ante operations in Jadavpur were a small part. Garcia had taken care of that. Lieutenants had been appointed to oversee different parts of the operations. It was a complex structure that blended functional and territorial jurisdictions. Garcia would obviously run the labyrinthine network, with his associates functioning on a need-to-know basis. Staring at the ceiling, Garcia was thinking: goodbye Kolkata, goodbye Kolkata Police and goodbye Tanya Samanta. And then Garcia, with his preternatural sense of hearing, heard the deep throb of a diesel engine in the distance. Shila was arriving—in a taxi, as planned.

By the time she had her finger on the doorbell, Garcia was already behind the door. It opened with a suddenness that had her falling over. Garcia caught her, not by luck, but by design. And carried her up to the bedroom. He was wiry but powerful. Shila was a slip of a woman. 'My bag,' was all she managed to say.

'Taken care of,' Garcia said. 'Don't worry about the details.'

Shila was only too glad not to. She was happy to be running away from the day-to-day management of the rackets, her constituents, the onerous duties of a legislator, including remaining up to speed with the rules and procedures of the house, which, even after all these years, managed to surprise her with their protean complexities. She was also happy to junk the responsibility of running a household comprising two teenage children and having to worry about their future, but was conflicted about leaving them.

'In Rajshahi, you'll be the Queen Bee and I'll be the Chief Drone,' Garcia had told her. 'There'll be plenty of worker bees around.' Shila had since been dreaming of the small house something like twenty-five kilometres out of Rajshahi town, surrounded by its own thirty-acre patch of farmland, ensconced in hectare upon hectare of rolling, verdant countryside. Their farm and household would be tended by the worker bees, while she would help Garcia run a criminal empire considerably larger than her kitchen garden in Jadavpur.

***

Garcia and Shila had met for the first time six years ago. The encounter, in the very nature of things, had been adversarial. Garcia had been transferred to DD two years ago, when, coincidentally, Shila had become a member of the legislative assembly. Given that she was a political ingénue—though only as innocent as the wife of Chhoton Nandi, many times municipal councillor and MLA, could possibly be—it had taken her about a year to cut her teeth, grow her fangs and take over all the rackets within the bounds of the Jadavpur assembly constituency, from which she was the honourable member.

She had been helped by Chhoton's two closest lieutenants—Bittu and Abhi. The price they had exacted for delivering Chhoton's election and extortion machine to Shila had been greater operational freedom and a bigger share of the take. Shila hadn't been able to object. But after she was on top of things, she started chafing at her lieutenants' presumptions.

In the period Bittu and Abhi were helping their new boss to come to grips with her new situation, Garcia was stepping into the world of organized crime after his transfer to DD following just over two decades in service. Like most cops he'd started in a *thana* (police station) and been transferred around quite a bit. In every police station he worked in, whether in Calcutta or in the districts, he'd cultivated the tough guys and the criminals, giving out clandestine favours when he could. He'd avoided taking bribes and favours and had, thus, accumulated a large pile of IOUs. It was these that had stood him in good stead when he started discreetly putting his criminal network together, around five years before his move to DD. It had been slow going, because of the constraints of working in a *thana* and being shunted around. All that had changed when he became a 'detective'.

Garcia's potential field of operations had widened immediately and he hadn't been slow at seizing the opportunity. Still unobtrusive, Garcia had put together a state-wide network in a year or so, encashing most of his IOUs. Though he'd managed to infiltrate most of Calcutta, sometimes as a junior partner to established and powerful interests, but often by dislodging or eliminating them, some pockets had stubbornly resisted his blandishments or threats. Jadavpur had been one of these. After just over a year in his new job, Mona, one of his lieutenants, had come to him complaining that Abhi and Bittu were proving too tough to break down. 'Who's their boss?' Garcia had asked.

'Shila Nandi, boss, the Jadavpur MLA,' Mona had said.

'I'll take care of it,' Garcia had said, confidently.

But it hadn't been that simple. Garcia had engineered a meeting with her using the plausible pretext of an investigation he had been on. It went badly. Shila had arched her eyebrows when Garcia had told her that he had a network that would be useful to her if she let him begin some operations on her turf. The arched eyebrows had been a dismissal, which had, however, followed the trenchant suggestion that if Garcia were to push his case, she might be compelled to have a word with the commissioner of police. Garcia had left, humiliated. But he bided his time. And opportunity had knocked in a year or so, by which time Garcia's operations in Calcutta had become formidable.

The two crime lords had met by chance at a seminar on the relationship between the public and the constabulary. Garcia had walked up to Shila, introduced himself, given her a card and told her to get in touch if she ever needed help, noticing in the process that the Jadavpur MLA was quite an attractive woman. That Garcia was quite physically attractive was a thought that had almost simultaneously passed through Shila's mind, but she'd brushed it aside. It was only later, while preparing to go to bed that she'd remembered Garcia, and in a flash, thought that he could help her cut her two lieutenants down to size.

She called Garcia the next morning. They brainstormed the next day and Garcia got the opportunity of inserting the thin end of an operational wedge into Jadavpur. It had taken Garcia a month or so to ruthlessly strip Bittu and Abhi of their power and territory. And he'd gifted the overlordship of Jadavpur to Shila, on the condition that it would be a part of his network, on the first night they slept together, after a circuitous getaway to a guesthouse in neighbouring Dankuni town. What had started as a mutually advantageous relationship in which Garcia judiciously used Shila's political contacts to strengthen his network and Shila used Garcia's backing to keep her 'boys' in line, became a partnership, dominated albeit by Garcia.

In the course of working together, they fell in love. In many ways, their partnership in crime had become a sideshow in their relationship. Shila, troubled by the thought of sex outside wedlock, even suggested that they get married in a temple, so that in the eyes of the almighty at least they'd be man and wife. But Garcia demurred. 'Only when we get matters sorted out,' he said. At all times, of course, they had to be careful.

***

In the meanwhile, however, Garcia had urgent business in mind. He grabbed Shila and got her into bed. She protested for form's sake. As matters became steamier, her protests faded away. A good time was had by both. God, Garcia thought, she's better than she has any right to be. Shila was stretched out, almost purring. And then, breaking into the post-coital torpor, Garcia's cell phone chirruped. 'Convoy's left looking for you, boss. Don't know the details. Just picked up bits and pieces.' He scrambled out of bed. 'Shila, up,' he shouted, frantic. 'Get dressed, we're leaving. Don't bother to pack.' He was dressed in minutes and had scooped up a small bag containing essential papers, cards and cash. The call had come from Lalbazar. The cops had cracked someone, they were coming for him.

Shila was struggling to get dressed. 'What's the matter?' she asked. Garcia hissed, 'Hurry.' In a few minutes, she was dressed. 'We have to move, now,' Garcia said, before they barrelled down the stairs. There were two associates waiting outside, near the car, now boasting fake number plates. Garcia and Shila stepped into the car. 'Move,' he shouted, as their henchmen got into the car, a second behind. And they were off within ten minutes of Garcia receiving the call, with a head start that he hoped would take them across the border. Safe haven's hours away, he thought, trying to curb the rising panic.

Just over half an hour after Garcia and Shila had taken

off, a convoy arrived at the house. It was immediately surrounded by armed officers, Tanya choreographing the show. The moment she arrived, she sensed the emptiness of the house. They had cut and run, she knew it. But the house had to be searched, dusted for prints, and the rest of the routine. The ground floor revealed nothing useful: a functional living-cum-dining room, a bedroom with an attached bathroom and a kitchen. Not disturbed in months, if the thick layers of dust were anything to go by.

She went to the first floor, other officers in tow. There were three bedrooms. The team split into three groups. Tanya's team hit pay dirt. The bed was a mess. It didn't take much imagination to guess the reason. And there were two suitcases. The officers snapped on rubber gloves and jimmied the cases open. One was large and full of women's clothing and other accoutrements. The smaller one was functional, neatly packed with essentials. No papers in either case. Unravelling this bit of the story was the easy part. It was almost spray-painted on the walls: Clayton and Shila were here. The difficult part would be catching the pair. Cop and MLA; gangster and moll.

The two other bedrooms had yielded nothing. How had Garcia tumbled to their raid? Tanya wondered. Tapan was in custody after spilling his guts. The police had been careful. Tapan had rung home and the office leaving messages to say he had been called out of town on work. No one else was supposed to know, except the members of the team and the commissioner. Lalbazar must have sprung a leak again. She'd have to identify it. And there'd be hell to pay, Tanya thought grimly. He'd got out just before they reached. But where was he headed? Another round of interrogation beckoned. All that Tapan had let on was where Garcia had holed up. He had disclaimed knowledge of anything else: future plans; final destination; zilch.

Back at headquarters, Tanya set in motion the next round of interrogation. There were three officers in the room with Tapan, who had started perspiring even before his interrogators began sweating him. Tanya kicked off the proceedings. 'So,' she said, ominously. 'You know nothing of Garcia's plans. Where he's headed, who's with him, what he's carrying.' More statement than question. Tapan sweated a little more, while his interrogators remained silent, waiting. She'd turn him inside out, Tanya thought.

'I told you all I know,' Tapan volunteered. He was still wondering how the cops had tumbled to him. Though the cops hadn't known about his connection with Garcia, they'd long suspected his involvement in organized crime. Tanya had had him picked up pretty much on the off chance.

Indeed, thought Tanya. 'If we don't get the information we want,' she said, 'all the guarantees will be withdrawn. We'd have put you in jail anyway. But now we'll make sure that everyone in your network knows why you are in jail. The ones already inside and the ones who will soon be. And as you know, prison isn't the safest place to be, if someone wants to get you.'

Tapan sweated, but remained silent. His interrogators remained silent as well. Tapan wasn't exactly a hotshot dude. A successful businessman, true, but not of the untouchable kind. So, he didn't merit an air-conditioned room, comfortable chairs and a cup of tea; he was being questioned in a cramped room. The fan creaking overhead was just agitating the warm, moist air. Tapan was feeling very uncomfortable, physically and psychologically. That was the whole idea, anyway. Tapan's throat and lips were dry. He asked the cops for a glass of water. Lukewarm water arrived and all the cops left. Obviously, they didn't fancy being stuck in the room.

An hour later, Tapan was still sweating. Profusely. His throat was still parched and his lips dry. He wanted more water, but there was nobody around to ask. After what seemed an age, the cops returned. The first thing Tapan asked for was water. But no one paid attention.

Tanya just asked, 'Remember anything?' Tapan nodded desperately. Tanya sent a cop to fetch water. Everyone remained silent until it arrived and Tapan drank. Gratefully, with relief. And Tanya asked again, 'What do you remember?'

No one followed up. Everyone was sweating it, but none like Tapan. He knew the stakes better than anyone else. If he didn't squeal, he'd be in jail. He would also have to be produced in court, where all the facts would become public knowledge. Tapan also knew that Clayton Garcia's reach was long enough. On the other hand, Tapan thought for the first time, if he squealed and was released, he could go home and start living a normal life. *His* normal life. He guessed he could cook up a story that would sound convincing enough to let him off the hook on all fronts. No one had to know that he had been picked up by the cops. He knew Lalbazar was leaky, but he'd been picked up discreetly; in transit. He had no record; wasn't generally known to the police. There was a chance he could swing it. Still, he hesitated. Sat on the hard plastic chair, sweated and weighed his options. After what seemed like an interminable silence, he nodded. Then said, slowly and clearly, 'Okay, I'll tell you everything I know. But it isn't much.'

Tanya said, 'Start.' And she switched on the recorder.

'He's planned to run to Bangladesh,' Tapan said. 'He and Shila have bought some property there. He told me they were headed for Chittagong. But I'm not sure that's true. He arranged all the transactions from the Bangladesh end. Obviously, he and Shila now have Bangladeshi passports and other documents. No one here knows his new name. They'll cross the border in a car with fake Bangladeshi number plates. I don't know which check-post he's going to use. He'll probably ditch that car in Bangladesh and get into a legitimate vehicle. The other car will return with its original plates. I don't know either the make of the car or its registration number. I know he's got two men with him. I think they are Bangladeshi hoods. That's it.' Tapan exhaled noisily as if to show he'd got a load off his chest.

The cops remained silent for a few moments, then Tanya turned to Inspector Gopal Barui, 'Sound a border alert. You are running the chase. Take anyone you think you'll need.' Barui said, 'There's nothing we can do now. He's long gone.' Tanya glared at him and he scurried. She turned to Tapan. 'That's all you know, huh? So, what's Garcia going to do about money? Who's going to look after his operations? Don't tell me he's retiring to Bangladesh.'

Knowing he'd committed himself, Tapan nodded. 'I don't know the details, but they've transferred all their money to accounts abroad. Bangladesh and other countries. I think they've sold all their properties, except for Shila's house, which she's left for her children. She must have made financial provisions for them, but I don't know what the arrangements are.'

While Tapan was sweating it out in a small, muggy room in Police HQ, Garcia was perspiring in an air-conditioned car, thinking hard. The police were on his trail; someone had sold him out. At that moment, he couldn't be bothered to figure out who it was. He'd sort that out after figuring out how to get to Rajshahi safely. Or after he reached there safely. The problem was deciding on which checkpost to cross when entering Bangladesh. He asked his two associates—Bangladeshi hoods, indeed, who he hoped would become his new aides—for advice. 'The police will soon be after us,' he told Khaled and Mudassar. Garcia was edgy, Shila was terrified, but Khaled and Mudassar were just impassive. Pondering.

After a while, Khaled said, 'Whether the police are after us or not, we should take the most obvious route. We have to cross at Petrapole. Everything's been arranged. And we can be in Bangladesh in a couple of hours. A few more hours, you'll be home.' Shila's heart skipped a beat. And involuntarily she thought of Patuli, her home for so long. She thought of her children and how on earth they were going to manage. She'd left a home for them; plenty of money in joint accounts. She'd left a note explaining not very much. She could send them money from Bangladesh. But they were kids. One in college, the other still in school. Who the hell would look after them? But Shila was too addicted to Garcia for her to have made any other choice. She loved him and loved to have her brains fucked out by him. She had made her choice and she knew it. But that didn't stop her from worrying. After a while, she consoled herself that someone from the extended family would do whatever parenting was required on her behalf.

Garcia was also doing some thinking. Would the obvious crossing be the best one? The advantage they would have, was speed. As his associate had pointed out, they'd be in Bangladesh in a couple of hours. Would the police discover his plan fast enough to catch him at Petrapole? On the other hand, the other crossings were a long way off. He should assume the cops would find out by then and circulate the information to all border posts, airports and ports. Should they try to hire a boat or a steamer and sneak into Bangladesh? Khaled told him it wasn't a particularly good idea; Petrapole was their best bet.

Garcia fell silent. 'Fine,' he said, after a while. He hadn't brought them along just for the ride, nor just as muscle; they were here because they knew all about illegal border crossings and the people who manned the border posts on both sides, the Border Security Force (BSF) in Bengal and the Bangladesh Rifles across the border. They would take him and Shila across to their new home. And they'd stay for a few days, until the two of them settled in. They had been recommended as efficient, unscrupulous and ruthless when necessary. Just the way Garcia liked his close criminal associates.

Things went smoothly at the border post. They were through with virtually no fuss. Relief flooded through Garcia and Shila. Shila started laughing. Garcia reclined and closed his eyes. Khaled continued to drive. Mudassar remained impassive. The Bangladeshis had danced this particular dance too many times for it to mean anything. After a while, Shila stopped laughing and leaned against Garcia, who remained reclined, eyes closed. He just put his arm around her waist.

From the border, Khaled told Garcia and Shila, it could take six to eight hours. They'd also have to stop and eat something on the way. But Garcia and Shila were not bothered how long it took. They'd got away, that was all that mattered. They'd hole up for a few days, establish a routine and get to know the area. Set up house. Then they'd start working; try to recruit Khaled and Mudassar.

While Garcia and Shila were planning their new lives, Tanya hadn't been watching paint dry. She hadn't let Tapan go, but made him call home to tell his wife he'd been detained and wouldn't be back until tomorrow or the day after. Tapan suspected his wife was probably thinking he was bonking some woman's brains out. At that moment, Tapan couldn't be bothered. All *he* was thinking about was satisfactorily answering the questions put to him and getting the hell out of Lalbazar as fast as possible. He was being given a respite for being a good boy; the cops had had a bottle of cold water and hot food sent to him. The food wasn't half bad.

Tanya and the team were taking a break they badly needed. They'd been at it for over twelve hours. Tanya was figuring out the angles, reclining in her chair, eyes closed. All of them knew the way they'd have to go; the question was how. Tanya didn't want to involve too many people, because there already had been a leak; she couldn't even begin to guess how many cops Garcia had suborned, in her department and elsewhere. Clayton Garcia had been a trusted member of her team and she had failed to see through him. She wasn't really to blame, her colleagues had reassured her. Still, she didn't want too many people to know about this particular manhunt. The only way forward was to follow the money trail and her team lacked the skills to crack that. Unless they got very lucky, which was unlikely because, additionally, another country was involved.

Even if they somehow managed to uncover Garcia's new identity and all the details of his bank accounts, they'd still have to persuade Bangladeshi banks to cooperate. She'd have to involve DD's Economic Offences Wing (EOW), which wouldn't be able to do much until her team unmasked Garcia and Shila. Her team would have to find out what aliases they were living under and where they were living, at least roughly. A full address would be a bonus. All that sniffing around wasn't part of EOW expertise. Just the aliases wouldn't be enough. EOW could run into many accounts held by people with the same names.

Unfortunately, however, it was time for her to meet Commissioner Chanda and update him. She would also have to plot the course of future investigations and inform him that EOW would have to be drawn in at some point. She wasn't relishing the meeting because she was pretty sure that Chanda would try to trip her up somehow. Maybe he'd insist on bringing EOW right away. Just to hem her in; piss her off. He knew she couldn't do much about it.

Until then, they'd have to plug away. How many times had she been told during her training and as a rookie that police work was mostly drudgery? Following the routines, making sure all angles were covered, going over the same ground again and again, processing mountains of paper and interviewing countless of suspects and witnesses. There was room for the sudden flash of intuition, but it didn't light the bulbs all that often. As for sitting in a room and figuring things out through a pristine process of deductive logic, forget it! It hadn't ever happened to Tanya, or to any other cop she had ever met, and she'd met a shitload of cops. She and her team would just have to follow up on every tenuous lead, interview busloads of people—just in case. They'd have to go through the paperwork. And deal with the added complication that one of the absconding suspects was an MLA, elected on a ticket provided by the ruling party. Double damn, Tanya thought, also reflecting on the need to compose herself for next morning's meeting with the commissioner.

She was at the commissioner's office at 11 a.m., bang on time. 'So,' Chanda began abruptly, even before Tanya had settled into her chair. 'No progress to speak of.'

Tanya refused to be baited. 'We know Garcia and Shila Nandi are somewhere in Bangladesh. They've transferred most of their assets abroad. And we've turned one of Garcia's close aides.'

Chanda was noncommittal. Tanya continued, 'I think we'll have to get EOW in. Not right now, but after we uncover Garcia's new identity and discover his whereabouts. It can pick up the money trail and we'll get them. We'll need cooperation from Dhaka though.'

Chanda frowned. 'Getting a little far ahead, aren't we, Samanta? Shouldn't you be saying if we uncover his new identity?' When Tanya had been a junior officer, she had been Tanya to Chanda, after she became head of DD, always Samanta. Probably his way of saying he disapproved of the appointment. 'No reason to be pessimistic, sir,' she said. 'We've got a very good team. We'll just have to plug away, we'll get through. Isn't that what they still teach the rookies—don't let up, be thorough, don't ignore any lead? And intuition isn't our default option.' A polite homily to a not particularly respected boss. Tanya felt good.

But Chanda got back; he always had the last word. 'Look, Samanta, you can't throw everything into this one. I know an ex-cop and a ruling party MLA are involved, but you can't put murders, robberies and snatchings on the backburner.' Homily for homily. Chanda was satisfied and nodded, this time in dismissal. Tanya got up unhurriedly and headed out.

Back with her team members, she drew them the picture. 'We can't concentrate too much on this case, forget exclusively. We all want to get Garcia, but we'll have to work on other cases as well. We'll continue to work on this. Keep pulling in his associates. We have some idea about his network, so, for the moment, we have to pull it apart. We'll focus on the gambling, extortion, prostitution, trafficking, drugs and bootlegging sides. Regular briefings will be held.'

Everyone nodded. It wasn't exactly true that none of them had encountered bent cops before. Hell, it wasn't even true that no member of the team had ever accepted illegal gratification. But what Garcia had done was on a different scale. A scale that made his actions a betrayal of the force. He could be directly responsible for the death of the people in the hooch tragedy perpetrated by the Mollah brothers. And who knew, he could have been behind the 2011 case as well.

Conferring with Chanda the next day, Tanya said, 'We don't have much to go on, sir. All we know is that Mrs Nandi and Garcia are probably together. At this point, we can't be sure whether she went with him willingly or whether she went under duress. We don't know what name he's using in Bangladesh or where exactly he is. Once we establish his new identity, if we can, EOW can run him down following the money trail. But that's only after we've established his identity and found out where he lives.'

She stopped for a while and DGP Roy, who had dropped into Chanda's office, motioned her to go on with a barely perceptible nod. 'We have a high-stakes strategy in mind,' Tanya continued. 'Since Garcia disappeared, we've located a number of his associates and mapped some of his network. Since we don't know how big it is, I can't say how large a portion we've uncovered. But what we have uncovered is pretty big—drugs, bootlegging, extortion and prostitution. We have indications that his operations include human trafficking and gun-running.'

Tanya stopped, drew a deep breath, and said, 'I propose to turn on the heat. Dismantle the network. We need coordinated raids over one or two nights, once we've got a concrete plan. My team will lead the raids and local *thana*s will be involved. If we shut down a significant part of his network, we might be able to smoke Garcia out. At least, the more of these goons we get in, the more information we'll get. And a higher chance of uncovering the Nandi-Garcia identities. Then we can get EOW in and try to get Dhaka's cooperation.'

Silence descended on the room. Chanda did not want to speak, because the case was sensitive and he wanted to know what the DGP was thinking, just as an indication of which way the wind could blow, before committing himself. He asked DGP Roy what he thought. Roy was considering the merits of Tanya's case, but was also thinking about political fallouts, diplomatic angles and public reaction. This wasn't his baby. But he was a cop, who also needed to think like a politician. Finally, he took a position. 'Okay, Tanya,' he said, 'you've made a good case. But Ajoy needs to think about this.' Tanya went back to her office, not quite sure whether to feel encouraged or discouraged. It was time to leave, anyway, so she took off. She'd get some time to spend with her son, she thought, if she could get him off the computer and whatever game he'd be hooked on when she got home. Maybe cook something special. It had been a while since she'd done that.

Tanya got home a little before 7, showered, made a cup of coffee and headed for her son's room. She was in for a big surprise. He wasn't playing a computer game; he was reading. She made a brave effort to not look surprised and said, 'Since I've come home early, would you like me to make you something special for dinner? Or, would you like to go out for a bite?'

Shaman barely looked up from his book. 'Whatever,' he said.

'Okay,' she replied, 'We'll eat at home. I don't really want to go out.'

Shaman shrugged, 'Nor I.' Grammatical to a fault.

Tanya left him to his book and sat down in the living room to enjoy her caffeine fix. And, of course, the phone rang. It was a senior member of her team, Inspector Jadunath Majumdar, who was holding fort at headquarters. 'Madam,' Majumdar said, almost choked with excitement. 'You have to come right now. We've caught Ghiasuddin.' For a moment, Tanya didn't register the name. Then she caught on. 'Right,' she said, 'Get as many of the team together as possible. I'll be there soon.' She rushed to her son's room. 'I'm sorry, Muddy,' she said, 'but I have to go. There's an emergency.'

Shaman was used to emergencies. He shrugged and asked, 'When will you be back?'

'No idea. But you should have dinner and go to sleep on time.'

'Try to be back soon,' he said, to his mother's retreating back.

Tanya was a careful driver, but that evening, she sped, stopping short of crashing a light. Ghiasuddin Mollah, she thought. One of the two brothers wanted for the hooch tragedy. Garcia had told her they had escaped to

Bangladesh. If Garcia had been telling the truth in the first place, Ghiasuddin must have bet he could evade the police, thinking the heat would be off by now. If that had been the case, he'd lost the bet. Tanya pulled into Lalbazar and ran to her department. Ghiasuddin was in a cell. Five members of her team were already there. They could take turns breaking Ghiasuddin down.

Tanya told Jadunath and Gopal that she would kick off the interrogation with the two of them. 'Where was he picked up?' she asked.

'Sealdah station,' Gopal told her. 'He was waiting for a train. A railway policeman recognized him from the photographs we had circulated. Quite a stroke of luck.'

Tanya then asked for Ghiasuddin to be parked in the room in which Tapan had sweated and squealed. He would be left to stew for a while, getting into a frame of mind appropriate for an interrogation. The choice of Jadunath and Gopal was not random. Jadunath was a bull of a man. Big, mostly muscle. Over the years, he'd collected some alcohol-related fat around the middle, but not much. He stayed in shape. Jadunath was a bulldozer of a cop. His reactions were instantaneous and often fearsome. Gopal was a beanpole, who looked more like a teacher than a cop. He acted that way, too, always trying to coax information out of a suspect (or informant), while Jadunath would throw the kitchen sink almost before an interrogation started. They made a classic good cop-bad cop team.

Ghiasuddin had stewed, almost literally, for a couple of hours in the claustrophobic interrogation room, before the first shift visited him. Tanya, Jadunath and Gopal. They made themselves comfortable, barely noticing Ghiasuddin, who sat on a hardbacked chair. Each of them had a file, which each proceeded to read, though their contents had practically been committed to memory. Ghiasuddin remained seated, glowering at them. No one spoke. After about fifteen minutes, he broke the silence. 'Why have you brought me here?'

'So, how was Bangladesh? Hope you had a good holiday. You won't have another one in a hurry. Unless, of course, you consider jail time a vacation,' Tanya answered.

'You can't send me to jail. I haven't done anything and I've never been to Bangladesh. I want a lawyer.' The three cops looked at each other and nodded, as if dealing with a delinquent child. More in sorrow than in anger. They remained silent. Ghiasuddin was looking fit to explode. Even at the best of times, his temper was volatile. At this point, hardly among his best moments, he was in danger of tipping over. Shamsuddin was the brains of their operations—a cool customer. Ghiasuddin handled the rough stuff. 'I want a lawyer,' Ghiasuddin shouted.

Tanya looked up from her file. 'Lawyer? You've just been brought in for questioning. You'll be our guest for some time. You won't get hilsa from the Padma River, but we hope you'll enjoy your stay.'

Ghiasuddin was struggling to control his temper, though he knew he had to. He knew he was in custody, whatever the cops said. Motherfuckers, he said silently, fuming. The cops could beat the shit out of him.

'I know you're not the intelligent type, but why did you return from Bangladesh? You would have been safe there. Isn't that so?' Tanya asked, trying to be friendly. Ghiasuddin made a noise that could have meant anything.

And Jadunath stepped in, always the bad cop. He was looking pretty mean and he sounded it. 'You know how many people died from the hooch you sold that day? Four. You know what that means, don't you? Multiple charges of culpable homicide. And then there are the laws you've broken selling illicit liquor. We'll make sure you get consecutive sentences. You'll get your lawyer in good time. But fuck him, he won't be able to save you. Only you can do that. How about a free and frank disclosure of all that's happened since you ran? Who used to protect you, who did you pay off? The whole shooting match, pal. And we don't have all day to spend with pissant scum.' He looked at Ghiasuddin evenly. It wasn't encouraging.

Ghiasuddin glared back defiantly. But to the interrogators it was clear that he was losing his moxie. Ghiasuddin was actually penny ante. Out in the boondocks of South 24 Parganas, before moving to Bagha Jatin, he had been a big noise, especially with the backing of local hoods and the patronage of local politicians. He knew they wouldn't cut the mustard in Lalbazar, especially with Shila Nandi, MLA, absconding. And that cop, Kila. Ghiasuddin wasn't a genius. But he wasn't dumb either. 'I'll tell you about cop Kila and Shila Nandi, if you let me go back to Bangladesh,' he told his interrogators, discovering his singing voice.

Tanya gave him the stare now. 'No deals until we know what you are hawking. If it's worth anything, we'll see what we can do for you.'

Ghiasuddin took a deep breath. 'We used to run our still in Bagha Jatin with the protection of Sadhu. You know Sadhu?' Gopal and Jadunath nodded. Sadhu was a thug patronized by the ruling party. His areas of operations spanned extortion, protection and the supply of inferior construction material at inflated costs and labour gangs to building sites, euphemistically known as the 'syndicate' business. He was patronized by Shila Nandi and at one time, used to hang around at her Patuli house. Extra protection or show of fealty. Whatever. 'We used to pay him. Only him. And no one ever bothered us. Then Sadhu disappeared. And a cop came to our *theka* (booze joint) for money. He was just a *thulla* (constable). Later, I met his boss, Cop Kila. Just once. We told the *thulla* we'd pay him and only him. It would be his job to make sure that no one bothered us. He said we had Shila*di*'s guarantee on that one. And that was that. For the next few months, there was no problem. We paid up in time and no one hassled us.

'Then this disaster happened. We usually distil the drinks we sell ourselves. But that day, we couldn't and we got supplies from Sonarpur, not far from our *theka*. It was bad booze. The moment people started saying they were feeling unwell, we knew we were in trouble. So, we took all the money we had and ran. On the way, we called home and told them what had happened and that we were headed for Bangladesh. We have relatives there. But we are poor people, without passports and other travel documents. So, we called the policeman we used to pay. He told us to keep our heads down and not to call him again. He'd do the needful.' Ghiasuddin stopped and asked for some water.

After a long draught, Ghiasuddin continued. 'We went to Sealdah. It was around 10 p.m. and we were hungry. So, we ate at a roadside shack. After that, we tried to lose ourselves in the crowd. Someone called us at around 1 a.m. and asked us to go to Barrackpore, first thing in the morning. We slept at the station, took the first train and went to the place we had been told to go to. In two days, we were given Bangladeshi passports—in the names of Taufique and Kamran Ahmad.

'We were given instructions on how to cross the border post, and some Bangladeshi currency. And the man who was helping us told us to keep our cell phones with us, but switched off, unless we had to make a call. We were also asked to get new Bangladeshi phones and ditch the old ones. He gave us a number which we should call to give our Bangladeshi mobile numbers. Then we were off. We did as we were told.'

Ghiasuddin paused again. The scrappy underworld shitbag was finally scared. Tanya and her team knew in an instant that they had their man. He was shitting because he was getting to the business end of his story. Tanya merely nodded and said, 'Go on.'

Ghiasuddin nodded as well. 'After we had been with our relatives for a month or so in Pabna, helping out with the farming and fishing, we got a call. It was from the fucking crooked *thulla*. He told us his boss, Kila, was coming to go to Bangladesh on some work. He wanted a couple of reliable people to help him cross the border without leaving any trace. He said his boss had rented a place, they should be able to take him there and help him settle in. We didn't have that kind of contacts in Bangladesh. We were living a quiet life, trying not to draw attention to ourselves. But we knew that the policeman wasn't making a request, he was fucking twisting our arms.

'We made discreet enquiries and were given a phone number for a person in Dhaka. We called that number and went to Dhaka with a cousin. Then we got in touch with two men, who turned out to be acquainted with our cousin. They were involved in smuggling and other illegal activities, probably human trafficking. They were familiar with Bengal, travelled to India often and knew the ropes about illegal border crossings. They agreed to talk to the people concerned and we passed on the number.'

Ghiasuddin stopped. 'The cop Kila is a snake. He'll kill me, my brother and my entire family,' he said, finally.

Tanya unwound from her chair. 'If you don't go on, I'll have to send you to custody. I'll have to brief the media because your case made the headlines. What do you think will happen in jail? Outside, you can run. Inside, you're trapped. Don't be afraid. You help us, we'll help you.'

Ghiasuddin started to talk again. 'After we had put the boys in touch with the policeman, we got scared. We didn't want to have anything more to do with him. We shifted to another relative's house in Munshiganj. We changed our numbers and decided that as soon as we could, we'd try to get our families to Bangladesh, where all of us would be safe from the policeman. Of course, we gave our new number to the relations we had been living with before.

One day, my cousin called. He wanted to meet us in Dhaka, to have a good time. We went to the capital and found that he was with Khaled and Mudassar, the two boys who had helped Kila, and we became quite friendly. We were bar-hopping. All illegal joints. We didn't have permits to drink. We got very drunk. Mudassar especially. He told us they had dropped our friends in a place just outside Rajshahi town, not far from Pabna, where we'd been staying. "Ashrafullah Mian" and "Shahnaz Biwi". Khaled clipped him over the head and he shut up. We pretended we hadn't realized that Mudassar had been indiscreet.'

A collective exhalation fogged up the room. Tanya said, 'All right. We'll keep you in custody for a few days. Then we'll see what we can do.' She called a constable who took Ghiasuddin to a cell. 'Make sure he gets water and food. Give him a cup of tea and some biscuits now,' she ordered. Then she told Gopal and Jadunath to assemble the team and went to her room. The case had cracked wide open, it was time to get EOW in. She called Chanda and gave him the lowdown.

Tanya briefed her team and told them she intended to push for permission to dismantle Garcia's network and get EOW in. 'Finalize the plan on how and when to launch coordinated strikes by tonight. However long it takes.' Nobody groaned, nobody moaned. You could smell the adrenaline in the room. They worked in small groups, coordinated their efforts and came up with a plan around midnight. Tanya had been moving from group to group, making suggestions and smoothening wrinkles. More than one subordinate thought that evening that their boss was the best at what she did. Tanya was a good cop. When the final report was ready, everybody headed out, except the two officers on the graveyard shift.

The next morning, she was at Chanda's office before 11 a.m. There was another officer present: Vivek Singh, Assistant Commissioner of Police (ACP) in charge of EOW. Tanya was his boss.

Tanya cleared her throat, edgy from exhaustion, and began her briefing. 'Garcia and Nandi have escaped to Bangladesh,' she began, without a preamble. 'We've got this information from the prime accused in the Bagha Jatin hooch case. He and his brother had also fled to Bangladesh, but Ghiasuddin came back and was picked up. He says Garcia and Nandi are living not too far from Rajshahi town. We know the day the two gave us the slip and now Ghiasuddin has given us names to match the false Bangladeshi passports they used for their escape. All we have to do is ask the BSF to cross-check their records at the Petrapole post for those names and we'll get the confirmation we need to proceed.

'Garcia and Nandi are in Bangladesh under the names Ashrafullah Mian and Shahnaz Biwi. My team is already liaising with the BSF. We've been informed that before they ran they converted all their assets into liquid form and parked them outside the country. A large portion has been parked in Bangladesh because they are living there. Vivek has to crack that ASAP. In the meantime, I want to bring down the Garcia-Nandi network in a coordinated operation.' Tanya handed a copy of the plan each to Chanda and Singh.

Chanda intervened for the first time. 'I'll need to study the plan,' he said. Tanya shrugged. Singh remained expressionless. 'But we'll clear it today. Meeting here at 5. We'll have to wait for the BSF response, though.' He looked at Singh quizzically, then said, 'You too. After that we'll have to get cracking on the bank accounts. You'll need help from the Government of India.'

Tanya returned to her office and called Ishita, to whom she had given the task of confirming Garcia and Nandi's border crossing. 'They are getting in touch with the people in Petrapole and looking through the records. After I told them that a rogue cop and a sitting MLA were the suspects, the officer I spoke to said it wouldn't take long. They kept quizzing me. I told them that I was just following orders.'

The plan for the raids was worked out, and the officers tweaked it here and there. 'I'm sure I'll get the go-ahead for the raids. The only question is when they will let us off the leash,' Tanya said.

Just then Ishita's phone beeped. She left the room to take the call and was back in minutes. 'That was the confirmation we needed,' she said. 'Ashrafullah Mian and Shahnaz Biwi crossed the Petrapole that evening at around 5 p.m. They've sent me a WhatsApp picture of the page with the entry,' Ishita said, as she crossed the room to show Tanya the message. 'Brilliant,' Tanya said, a big smile creasing her face. 'The green light just flashed.'

At 5, Tanya pre-empted everyone with her 'breaking' story. 'Sir,' she said, 'we've corroborated Garcia and Nandi's identity. The BSF have sent us the page from their log, showing Ashrafullah Mian and Shahnaz Biwi leaving the country. We're circulating photographs of the two at Petrapole to see whether anyone can give us a visual ID. But it's open and shut now. Virtually.'

Chanda nodded and smiled, unexpectedly. 'Good,' he said. 'Singh should take over from here, while Tanya concentrates on taking down the Garcia-Nandi network. Get cracking. We don't have time to lose.'

Singh turned to Tanya and said, 'Can you give me a detailed brief, ma'am?'

'Tomorrow 9:30 a.m.'

~

The next morning, Tanya briefed Singh and gave him all the necessary material. After that she and her team prepared for the night's raids. The team had swollen for the day, with cops from other departments joining in, sworn to secrecy. Tanya needed more eyes, hands and boots on the ground. Eleven locations would be raided. Four of them were storage facilities—for drugs and illicit liquor; two were brothels; three were brothels-cum-transit houses for girls and women incarcerated prior to being trafficked; and two were warehouses for all kinds of contraband and 'safe houses' for tough guys coming into town from the mofussil or villages, who didn't have a place to sleep in Calcutta.

The raids were going to kick off simultaneously at 11, or 2300 hours as Jadunath preferred to call it. Tanya would be in charge of the control room. Spirits were high but everyone was hoping that just this one time, Lalbazar should surprise them by not springing a leak. Many of the people who'd be out raiding were seriously pissed off. Angry because of Garcia's betrayal—quotidian corruption was one thing, but organized crime in cahoots with an MLA? No shit!

With Tanya coordinating the show, the eleven teams hit the eleven locations at 2300 hours on the dot and took them out. Around 300 women and girls were freed. Five activist groups and non-governmental organisations (NGOs) had been alerted. These groups would provide shelters to the women and girls, before they could be sent home or alternative long-term arrangements made for them. Twelve goons, hit men and assorted undesirables, were arrested. A cache of drugs—cannabis, smack and meth, mainly—was recovered, along with thousands of cases of illicit liquor. The cops hoped the new arrests would help identify the rest of the network and bring it down. Unless the politicians and brass thought this was enough. Tanya and her team knew, in any case, that crime abhors a vacuum. And new punters would step into the void created by Garcia's undoing. But that would come later. In any case, that wasn't a compelling argument to allow Garcia's network to remain.

Garcia was in bed after a productive day working the phones and passing instructions to his associates. Some payments were due. He was assured they would be made through established channels before the week was out. Khaled and Mudassar had dropped by to discuss cross-border cooperation. The discussions had been productive and the brothers had promised to set up talks with the other principals. Garcia and Shila had inspected their fields in the early evening, after lunch and a post-prandial nap. Even though between them they knew fuck-all about agriculture, it gave them a pleasing sense of ownership. The rest of the evening had passed as days and evenings are wont to. And finally, they were in bed.

While Garcia and Shila were playing, in that order, underworld honchos, country squire and domesticated couple, Suleiman was having the usual hard time of it. He ran a roadside tea stall on Bowbazar Road, not far from where Garcia had had his lodgings. Garcia had given him the money to set it up. Suleiman had never been involved in Garcia's criminal activities. He had been the crooked cop's devoted gofer, running errands, cleaning his flat, and cooking, when Garcia didn't feel up to it. Suleiman was a free spirit. He had the run of the streets in and around the Bowbazar-Lalbazar area since he was a child and knew practically everyone in the neighbourhood. He'd grown up in the area, orphaned and just a little simple-minded. As a result, he managed to pick up all kinds of gossip and news from the street, which were usually of very little interest to him but often proved to be very useful indeed for Clayton Garcia.

Suleiman usually shut shop by 10, washed, dined, roamed the streets for a while before turning in at around 11. Of the eleven locations raided, two were in the Bowbazar area, not so ironically spitting distance from the police HQ. Suleiman had just gone to bed when the raids began. Scared, he closed his eyes, pretending to be asleep. But, as curiosity overcame fear, he sat up and saw vans transporting a large number of women away and police cars doing the same for a handful of men. Suleiman may have been a bit of a simpleton, but he had grown up on the streets. He knew, without ever being told, that his cop master was involved in stuff cops were usually not involved in. He also knew that Kali*da*, or Clayton Garcia, had something to do with the two buildings that were being raided right in front of his eyes.

Suleiman was someone Garcia had always trusted. His gofer would never let him down. Although Garcia didn't want to involve Suleiman in his criminal activities, he used the information and street intelligence Suleiman provided. Which is why Suleiman was one of the few people in India who had Garcia's emergency Bangladeshi number. Suleiman was beside himself with excitement and anxiety, but he knew it was too late to call Kali*da*. He'd call first thing tomorrow.

And he did. At 6 a.m. Garcia was up and about and took the call with apprehension. Why would Suleiman call so early? 'Kali*da*,' Suleiman began, voice quavering, 'they've raided number 15 and number 23 in Bowbazar.' Garcia cut in, 'Who's raided the houses, Suleiman?' 'The police,' Suleiman replied. 'They took away many girls and some men. I was about to go to sleep, when the raids started, at around 11.'

Garcia swallowed, feeling the panic grow inside him. 'Listen to me very carefully. Try to find out whether other raids have been conducted or not. Don't make it obvious. Just pick up the gossip from your tea shop and the streets. And call me in the evening at around 6.'

Garcia disconnected and exhaled. If he didn't move, they'd get him. Something told him that JCP Tanya Samanta would not let him rest in peace, unless he got her first. But first, he'd have to find out what was going on. He didn't dare call people in case they were compromised. But he didn't want to wait for Suleiman's call. He connected to the Internet: 'Kolkata police late night raids', he typed into the Google browser. And immediately got a number of hits. He opened the *Times of India* page and found a brief story, which gave him little more than what he had learnt from Suleiman. He browsed the other reports and found precious little. Why hadn't they reported more extensively? After a while, the answer came to him. The raids had begun at 11. By the time they had ended, it must have been well past midnight. The papers hadn't had the time to report in detail. He'd check the Internet later.

Feeling a little nauseous, Garcia wandered around what Shila and he liked to call their *zamindari* (landed estate). He hadn't broken the news to her. She'd freak out. Controlling her would be a full-time job. Wouldn't leave him much time to think, to deal with the problem. Impatient, he soon headed back for the house and his laptop. Garcia hungrily devoured the Internet for more news, but found nothing. Then, just to keep alive the pretence of normality, he showered and lunched with Shila, trying hard to give nothing away. After lunch, it was time for sex followed by a siesta. Though his heart wasn't really in it, Garcia went through the motions as best he could and then dozed off.

After he woke up, it was just a matter of winding down the clock, waiting for Suleiman to call, which he did, precisely at 6. The news he got hit him like a shotgun blast from close range. Eleven of his bases had been raided; around 300 women and girls had been freed; a dozen of his men were in custody; and hundreds of thousands of rupees worth of contraband had been seized. No one was willing to hazard a guess at the street price of the drugs and hooch captured. Shit. Garcia's hands had started shaking. 'I'll call back soon. Be near your mobile at all times,' he instructed Suleiman. He poured himself a glass of water. Fuck, he told himself, got to tell Shila. May as well get it over with. He went looking for her. As usual, she was outdoors, admiring the vegetable patches and the fruit trees and the pond, full of fish. Garcia called out to her, 'I've got news for you.'

When Shila got back in, Garcia sat her down and told her the news. Shila was so stunned that she forgot to get hysterical. She had always thought they were an invulnerable couple; she with her membership of the assembly and her position in the party, and he with his police job, contacts and first-class brain for scheming. For quite a while, she was gobsmacked. Finally, she whispered, weakly, 'What do we do now?'

Garcia was silent for a while. Then he said, 'They'll be after us, there's no doubt about that. Tanya Samanta won't let go. She's behind all this. I'll get her, may she rot in hell.' Uncharacteristic. Garcia belonged to the don't-get-mad-get-even school. 'For the moment, however, we'll have to run. Either somewhere else in Bangladesh or some other country. But we can blend best here. We'll sell the property and move to a city. Rent a place. It'll be cheaper and more anonymous. I'll have to get in touch with Khaled and Mudassar. And I need to call Suleiman.' Shila nodded, her face white with apprehension. 'Don't worry,' Garcia said. 'We'll be fine.'

He called Suleiman. 'Keep your eyes and ears open. Don't call me. I'm ditching this phone. I'll get a new one, just to make calls. Never save my number.' Then he called his guy in Lalbazar. 'What's happening?' he asked, voice distorted by fury.

'Didn't know, boss,' came the reply. 'The raids were kept secret. I got to know the next morning, from the papers. I've been trying to get details. Which is why I didn't call.'

'Stay alert. I'm ditching this phone. I'll call when I need something. And, there's been a leak at our end. How did they know where I was in Madhyamgram before I came here? How did they get details of our operations? What the fuck am I paying you for?'

'I've been on it, boss. But nobody seems to know. I'll let you know as soon as I can get the details.'

Garcia hung up.

Then, Garcia called Khaled. 'There's a problem at my end,' he said. 'I can't tell you anything over the phone. We have to meet, the sooner the better.' Khaled remained silent for a while, calculating how much he and Mudassar could make helping solve Garcia's problem. Arriving mentally at a satisfactory figure, he said, 'We'll be there first thing in the morning. Around 9.'

Khaled and Mudassar were punctual. Shila let them in and asked, 'Would you like a cup of tea?' They nodded assent. 'Have you had breakfast?' she continued.

'Yes, we've eaten,' Khaled replied, eager to get on with the job. Garcia joined them at that moment. Everyone was silent until the tea arrived. Not one of those comfortable silences, however. The brothers could make out that Garcia was under pressure. 'We're having some problems with our operations in Bengal,' Garcia began, struggling to keep his voice steady. 'The police have become a little proactive. It's nothing serious.' Khaled and Mudassar were impassive. It was what they did. Required no effort, but sent a message. 'I have reason to believe that sooner or later Kolkata Police will manage to track us down. Our aliases, where we live and what bank accounts we have. Maybe *through* our bank accounts. We need to split. I want to sell this property and move to rented accommodation in Dhaka. Always more difficult to trace people in a city. I should know, I've hunted enough people down.' He paused. The brothers remained impassive.

Shila was silent. So, Garcia continued. 'Can you help us sell this place and find a nondescript pad in Dhaka? We'll chuck our SIM cards and get new ones. We'll also need fresh passports, new identities.' No response. Khaled was waiting for the whole package to be unwrapped before opening his mouth, except to sip the tea Shila had given him. Ditto Mudassar, who didn't speak in such situations anyway. Not unless Khaled asked him to say something. Feeling even more uncomfortable, Garcia continued.

'Where are Ghiasuddin and Shamsuddin?' he asked. 'I tried to call Ghiasuddin, he didn't respond.'

Finally, Khaled spoke. 'I don't know. We hardly know them.' Which wasn't the truth, the whole truth and nothing but the truth. But what the hell, Khaled thought, he wasn't testifying in court. It was Khaled, as a matter of fact, who had advised Shamsuddin to follow his brother back to India, sensing something big was in the works. Shamsuddin, out of his depth in rural Bangladesh and without his brother, had immediately agreed. Khaled and Mudassar had helped him return on the Maitree Express, a train between Dhaka and Calcutta. Shams had let his brother know. His brother, lodged in a safe house, had let the police know. The police had picked him up and dropped him off at the safe house. Tanya and Ghiasuddin had struck a deal. The charges against them would not be dropped. Could not be in practical terms, actually. But if they left Calcutta to seek their fortunes elsewhere, Kolkata Police would shelve the case.

Gopal had asked him then, 'Is there anything you're good at, other than brewing hooch and creating mayhem?'

'My brother and I are skilled masons,' Ghiasuddin had replied, with a touch of asperity.

'Fine,' Gopal had said, 'go and make use of your skills in Gujarat or Gurgaon or somewhere. I suggest you get your brother to come back and leave together. When the shit hits the fan, he might find himself in a tight spot in Bangladesh.' That's how Shams and Ghias were reunited and, indeed, left town in search of work outside Bengal. Shamsuddin, always pragmatic, told his brother that things had turned out for the best. Making a decent living legally beat running from the cops all the time.

Of course, Garcia and Shila were not aware of these developments. As a matter of fact, when they were having the morning conference with the Bangladeshi brothers, the Bengali brothers were still in Calcutta, making preparations to beat it as soon as possible. So, Garcia ploughed on, 'They don't know that I've moved to Bangladesh, they think I came here on work. And they don't know our new identities. But they are a loose end. Still, if they are in India now, nothing can be done. If they are still in Bangladesh, can you take care of them?'

Khaled looked at Garcia for a couple of seconds more than strictly necessary. 'We're mobsters, not killers,' he said. 'You'll have to take care of your loose ends yourself. We'll supply you with new passports. Kosher. We'll also help you find a good price for this property and look for a place in Dhaka. You can count on us to open new bank accounts in the city. You pay us; half upfront—that means now—and half when everything's been sorted out. Then, you're on your own.' Both Khaled and Mudassar had been thinking, 'nothing serious', my ass, you are not a milch cow anymore, you are a fucking liability.

Garcia nodded. 'When can we start?' Khaled was not the sort who wasted words or time. 'Now,' he said. Within four days, the house and farm had been sold; and a flat rented in Dhaka. And, as good as their word, the brothers had organized new bank accounts with HSBC and Standard Chartered. Garcia figured it would help having accounts in multinational banks in case they had to hightail it out of Bangladesh altogether. Once all this was done, Khaled and Mudassar disappeared. Their message was clear, 'Don't call us…'

In Lalbazar, Singh wasn't having a particularly good time. Tanya had cracked the case wide open. She was the 'hero' for the moment. He didn't really mind. He got along pretty well with his boss and he wasn't envious. But her success had piled the pressure on him to deliver soon, which he couldn't because matters were not in his hands. He was preparing a report on the basis of which the Indian government would approach the Government of Bangladesh for cooperation in confirming, first, that Ashrafullah Mian and Shahnaz Biwi were indeed resident in Bangladesh; second, that they were in the country on false passports; third, with the help of Kolkata Police, that they were Indian citizens called Clayton Garcia and Shila Nandi; fourth, that they were wanted in India on suspicion of having committed a number of crimes; and, fifth, that they were operating bank accounts under their aliases. Once these hoops had been jumped through, the Bangladesh government would have to be convinced (the task Singh was involved in at that moment) that these accounts contained the proceeds of a number of crimes and should be frozen. And, finally, the government in New Delhi would have to seek the extradition of the 'couple'.

If that wasn't a large enough list, the report Singh was writing would have to travel to Delhi, through the desks of Commissioner Chanda, home secretary (HS) to the state government, a gentleman called Angshuman Datta, and the chief secretary. This, in itself, would take time. Even if this process was expedited through Datta's good offices, the file would still have to run the gauntlet of the bureaucracy in Delhi. Datta's good offices would cut no ice in Delhi, forget Dhaka. This rigmarole could continue for years.

But Singh had to write the report as conscientiously as possible, which he did before sending it on its voyage, first to Commissioner Chanda's office, where Singh guessed it would remain becalmed for a while. In the meanwhile, pressure on him would mount to do the critical something that it was not in his power to do. So, after getting rid of his report, Singh took a detour. He called a senior police officer in Dhaka with whom he had become friends while on an official tour to Bangladesh. He explained his predicament to Tahir Hussein, who immediately caught on since Bangladeshi bureaucracy wasn't that different from Indian bureaucracy, the penchant for red tape having been inherited by both countries from the British, their erstwhile colonial masters. The triplicate culture.

Hussein promised to do what he could quickly, leaving Vivek Singh a much-relieved man. Hussein called his friend back in three days, with bad news. Ashrafullah and Shahnaz had been living on the outskirts of Rajshahi town at a farm. But a few days before Singh's call, they had sold their property and moved. No one knew where. They had closed their bank accounts in Rajshahi. The banks didn't have any idea about what they had done banking-wise after that. In other words, to mix metaphors, the birds had flown, leaving behind a distinctly cold trail. But Hussein would continue to make discreet enquiries and call Singh if anything significant transpired.

Singh disconnected, discomfort washing over him. Showtime. He'd have to report these developments to Chanda and Tanya, whom he did not want to disappoint. He felt as if he'd let her down. It was a load of bollocks actually. There was nothing he could have done to change the outcome. When Singh went across to her room, Tanya could tell that things were not going according to plan. 'What's the matter?' she asked. And Singh recounted his conversation with Hussein. Tanya frowned. 'Bastard's given us the slip. He must have got to know about the scale of the operations here and taken evasive action. He has an impressive radar.' The two officers sat in Tanya's room, wracking their brains for a way around this unforeseen hurdle. Tanya called up Ishita. 'Come to my room. Right now. And bring your phone,' she said. Bhan glanced quizzically at Tanya, who suddenly looked energized.

'Ma'am,' Ishita walked in, a little apprehensive.

Tanya cut in. 'Do you have the photograph of the page from the BSF log they sent you? I want to see it, pronto.' Ishita pulled up the page and handed the phone to Tanya. She inspected it closely, then said, 'Okay, get back in touch with the guy who sent you this page. Ask him some specific questions. First, do they enter the number of the cars that cross the border? Obviously, they do. Do they keep records of the occupants of each car? In other words, will they be able to tell us the registration number of the car Ashrafullah and Shahnaz were travelling in and the names and passport details of any other passengers in that car?' Singh grinned, finally getting the plot. Ishita still looked a bit mystified, but she didn't know the context. 'As fast as possible,' Tanya said, and Ishita scampered off.

Singh broke the silence. 'If they were using Bangladeshi thugs with bona fide Bangladeshi passports, Hussein will be able to locate them. If they were using fakes, we're lost. If Garcia was using thugs from these parts, and they were using bona fide Indian passports, we'll get them. Otherwise, we're back to square one. If they were using Indian thugs, chances are they would have returned to India and wouldn't know about the second switch anyway. And we'll be back to square one. We'd better hope that the guys Ghiasuddin supplied crossed the border with our loving couple.'

'Yes, they do record the vehicles crossing the border and their occupants. They can give us the information we need, but it's going to take some time,' Ishita reported to Tanya the following day.

'What does "some time" mean?' Tanya quipped. 'Did you ask?'

Ishita smiled mischievously. 'Yes, ma'am,' she said, 'in a couple of days.' She seemed to have all the answers.

After lunch, the day after the day after, Ishita knocked on Tanya's door, beaming. 'There were two other men in the car—Khaled and Mudassar Shaikh. I have the addresses on their passports. When I pressed for a little more information, the BSF men told me that they crossed the border quite often. Probably small-time smugglers and racketeers. Definitely not thought to be involved in terror-related activities.' Khaled and Mudassar. Tanya remembered that Ghiasuddin had mentioned these two names. She'd allowed a lead to fall through the cracks. She kicked herself. It was her job to keep her eyes on all the balls that were in the air.

Later, Singh called his Bangladeshi friend. 'We've got the names of the Bangladeshi boys who helped our couple cross over. We have an address for them as well, the one on their passport. Of course, they might have been travelling on false passports, in which case we'll hit another blind alley. Can you please try?' he asked.

'I'll call when I have something,' Hussein replied, not sounding optimistic. Singh informed Tanya of the developments, who, in turn, kept the commissioner in the loop. 'We'll just have to wait till Vivek's friend gets back to us. Until then, of course, we can concentrate on continuing to dismantle Garcia's empire,' she said. Chanda grunted assent.

For the next ten-odd days, that's exactly what happened. The police kept chipping away at the network as revelations were pulled out like healthy teeth. Other crimes were committed in the fair city of Calcutta. Some of those needed to be investigated as well, so Garcia and Nandi started to recede into the filing cabinets. Then something broke. Hussein called Singh, bearing news. He was truly going out on a limb. 'I've got interesting stuff for you, Vivek,' he started. 'We located the Shaikh brothers. They helped your Garcia sell the Rajshahi property, find a flat in Dhaka and change banks. They told us new accounts were opened with HSBC and Standard Chartered. They also gave us the address for the flat in Dhaka and told my men that they had left Garcia to his own devices and refused to remain in touch because they thought he was going to create way more trouble than the Shaikh brothers wanted. Khaled, who seems to be the smart one, told the officers that he thought something was wrong with Garcia. So, I sent some officers to the flat. It was locked. The landlord said Alamgir and Farzana Muhammad had paid six months' rent in advance because they'd be in and out of the country. We've found no record of two people by these names leaving the country legally. I'd guess they've slipped across the border back into India or slipped into Myanmar. They could have left the country by sea as well. In which case they could be anywhere. I'll try to keep an eye on the flat, but don't get your hopes up, my friend. As for the bank accounts, you know I can't do anything until the paperwork gets done.'

Singh thanked him effusively and invited him to Calcutta. And then hissed, 'Shit. Got away again', to the walls.

He gave Tanya the news. For now, both agreed, Garcia and Nandi were gone. Heck knew where...

Part Two

Park Street, Calcutta, May

It's the middle of the unforgiving month of May. Calcuttans are tired of trying to figure out which month is crueller: April or May. The city is getting its taste of the heat and humidity that conjoin to send the discomfort index soaring past limits of endurance. It's a cauldron and everyone is pissed off all the time. Except those who inhabit air-conditioned spaces all day. But in the early hours it's kind of bearable. Say, from 2 to 6. But despite the warmth, Gloria is shivering violently. She's lying on the grass verge of the lake that constitutes 90 per cent of Minto Park, or Shahid Bhagat Singh Udyan, if you will. Practically no one uses the mouthful the new name is. Gloria has been unconscious and is coming to; the more conscious she gets, the unaccountably chillier she feels. Finally, she surfaces. Disoriented, uncomprehending of where she is, what time it is and what she's doing lying on a patch of grass next to a lake. She looks at her watch—4:30—and it takes her a while to reconstruct a timeline for last evening. How has she landed up here? And what is 'here' anyway?

She gets up gingerly, her whole body hurting. And looks around—at the lake, the trees, the grass verge where she'd passed out and the track for morning and evening walkers. She looks beyond the park, trying to make sense of the hulking shapes in the half-light. And finally, the penny drops—she's inside Minto Park. She tries to spot Belle Vue Clinic, and does. Finally, she knows where she is. She still has to figure out how she came to be here at this unearthly hour, instead of being at home with her two children and her mother. Shit, she thinks. They'll have freaked fucking out. But before she does anything she has to reconstruct last evening's events. She sits down on a bench and thinks. 'Okay,' she tells herself, out loud, 'I was at Sugarloaf drinking myself silly and dancing all by myself.' She tries to remember how much she'd drunk and when she'd left the club. And fails. She wracks her brains, but her memory bank refuses to give up the information. She leans back and feels the pain course through her. And through the pain in her whole body, she feels the extra sharpness of a pain between her legs. And it unlocks her memory in a flash.

The five young men who'd been drinking at the next table. One of them, he'd called himself Soumitro, had joined her. He was polite; obviously well-bred. He'd bought her a drink. The memories kept flooding back. She'd drunk some more, danced some more. Alone, and with Soumitro. What the fuck had she been thinking! She was furious at herself. And scared. It was past midnight when she'd decided to leave. And Soumitro had offered to get her to a cab. The memories became fuzzy, but she remembered clearly enough that she'd been raped. They'd raped her. Yes, she remembered. After that, she remembered nothing. Not where they took her, not when they dumped her inside Minto Park. She started weeping. After a while, she walked to the water's edge and washed her face. She had to get home. She called the person she trusted most—the friend she knew would stand by her, no matter what. Nilanjan.

It was around 5, but Nilanjan replied after two rings. 'Gloria,' he said, 'anything wrong?' She started crying again. 'Shit,' Nilanjan said. 'Where are you?'

Choking back her tears, she said, 'Minto Park. Please come and get me.'

Nilanjan lived on Southern Avenue in the southern reaches of the city, near a much larger lake. At that time of day, it would take him no more than fifteen minutes to get to Minto Park. 'Hang in there,' he said. 'I'm on my way.' In a couple of minutes, he was on the road, full of foreboding. Gloria's been dry for five years, he thought, how in fuck's name had she landed up at Minto Park at 5 in the morning? He reached Minto Park in twelve minutes. The gate was locked and he could see Gloria in there, slumped on the bench. He jumped the gate and was beside her in moments. 'Gloria,' he said, and stopped, thinking that this was not the time for a barrage of questions. Gloria stood up and threw herself at him, sobbing. He held her for a while and finally asked, 'Glo, can you jump that gate?' She nodded, hesitant.

'Want to go to my place?'

'Yes,' she said.

'We'll have to let your mom know you're safe and sound. I guess she doesn't know?' Gloria nodded. 'Okay,' Nilanjan said, 'We'll go home and take it from there.' In the car, Gloria realized for the first time that her clothes were torn. She'd borrow something from Nilanjan.

As soon as they reached Nilanjan's place he made tea for them. While she was sipping it, he asked, 'Hungry?' Gloria nodded. He disappeared into the kitchen and emerged with two plates: omelettes and toast. 'You'd better call your mom,' he said gently. 'You need to get your story together. Keep it simple and vague. Just like in the bad old days.' Gloria tried to compose herself. And then she called her mother, who she thought would be still asleep. But her mother answered after a few rings. Gloria told her she was at Nilanjan's and would be back soon. 'Sorry for not letting you know last night, Mom. I'm fine. Go back to sleep.'

Nilanjan brought her another cup of tea. Gloria knew he was the only person in the world she could tell this story to at this point of time.

Gloria Stevens had been sober for five years through the good offices of Alcoholics Anonymous (AA) and her own strenuous efforts. For the first three years, including in the aftermath of her husband leaving her, she had attended AA meetings religiously, no pun intended. Then, work, the pressures of single parenthood—bringing up two children who got more demanding as they grew older—took a toll on her time. She still attended meetings, but couldn't do it every day. From five days a week it fell to four, and then to twice or thrice. But the urge to drink had been diminishing for quite a while and Gloria had felt safe. Until the fateful day.

Gloria had met Nilanjan at her first AA meeting. From then on, he'd been a pillar of strength. Generally speaking, the AA ethos is to help. Anybody, but especially newcomers, who are expected to go through bad times when they join and try to keep off the sauce. It was not unusual, Gloria discovered, for other members to casually walk up and offer to exchange numbers. In case either party needed help. Many 'old-timers' had told Gloria to call whenever she needed help—call before you take the first sip, they'd say, then we can really help; we're not saying you can't call even after a relapse, but it's more useful to call before you've sipped and slipped.

Nilanjan had been sober seven years when Gloria joined the programme. And he'd been the first to take her under his wing. Despite being suspicious of his intentions, Gloria had realized pretty soon that his help was unconditional. In the beginning, there had been an element of duty inscribed into his overtures: I'm an alcoholic in recovery, it's my duty to help all other alcoholics, especially those in recovery and those who have just joined the programme and need to find their feet. That duty-inspired help had bred mutual affection, unconditional on both sides. This was why Gloria had instinctively turned to Nilanjan.

~

They sat sipping tea. Nilanjan a touch meditatively, and Gloria stretched out on a rack inside herself, near breaking point, but unable to get the words out. How many times had she been told in her early years in AA that the only way to lighten your burden was to share? How many times had she repeated the same to others? But the torrent of words was catching in her throat. Unable to vocalize, Gloria kept sipping her tea not because she wanted it, but because it helped put off telling her story. Nilanjan waited patiently. With every minute that went by, he realized with greater certitude that something had gone badly wrong. It wasn't just Gloria chucking five years of sobriety and deciding to go on a binge and somehow landing up in Minto Park. That could happen. Did happen. Any number of recovering alcoholics relapsed. There were minor relapses, not-so-minor relapses and the big ones that erased months, even years of sobriety. The ones that were either terminal relapses or, at least, forced people to start from scratch. The same cycle: binge, withdrawal, recovery. But, like shit, it happened. Nilanjan's experience told him this was not just a relapse, partly because he was almost sure that Gloria had not had a single drink since the day she had walked into the AA meeting room, five years ago, and counting. Not counting any more, though.

Gloria got up from the dining table and paced for some time and suddenly, the torrent of words forced its way out of her throat. She sat down. Through her tears, she managed to say, 'I was raped last night.' Nilanjan went completely still, not trusting his ears. He didn't know what he'd been expecting, but it hadn't been this. 'Fuck,' was all he could say. 'When? Where? What happened?' he managed to ask finally, head spinning, a black wall of rage building inside him. Gloria buried her head in her hands, still crying. Finally, Nilanjan walked up to her. 'Glo,' he said, 'whatever happened, however it happened, just remember it wasn't your fault. People might try to give you that message, but that's only because your average Indian Johnny is a completely fucked-up, cock-sucking piece of shit. The only person, or people, whose fault it is, is the guy who did it. Or guys. Look into my eyes. And tell me what happened. We'll get the scum if it's the last thing we do.'

Gloria looked up and at him. Stopped crying but her eyes were still brimming. 'It's been a bad month or so, Nilu,' she began. 'Stress at work, managing the house and Mom not feeling up to scratch. I was under a lot of pressure. And, you know, working in a hotel in Park Street is not the ideal situation for an alcoholic, recovering or otherwise.' She smiled wanly. Nilanjan nodded. He knew exactly what she meant.

'Yesterday was a particularly terrible day at work. When I left the hotel at about 8:30, I really needed something to pick me up. I should have headed for a meeting, but it was too late. I thought I'd call you or somebody else. But then I thought I'm a big girl, I can handle these little things. Looks like I couldn't. After dithering on the pavement for a while, I decided to go to Sugarloaf and have a small drink. Just one. But I kept drinking and then a guy from the next table approached mine and asked if he could join me for a drink. He was very polite. And bought me a drink. Left after a while, but we danced together. By the time I decided to pack it up, it was after midnight, I think. I was pretty sloshed. Then this guy, he said his name was Soumitro, offered to give me a lift to a taxi. After that, my memories are jumbled. I think there were four other guys in the car. Two in the front passenger seat. At some point, I remember being raped. And being dumped in a taxi. This part is vague, Nilu. All I remember clearly is that I woke up in Minto Park, without a fucking clue about how I got there.'

Nilanjan nodded, a bit mindlessly. The full import of what Gloria had just told him hadn't quite sunk in. He kept nodding. Then he got up, on autopilot, and went to the kitchen to make some more tea. Shit, he was thinking, now what, in fuck's name? While the tea was making itself, Gloria's story was sinking into Nilanjan's subconscious and making its way into his conscious mind. And his conscious mind was telling him that the first thing they should do, right now, was go to the cops and register a complaint. Returning to the living room, he said, 'Glo, we need to go to the police and register a case. Then they need to do a rape test, I think, I'm not sure. Has to be done, Glo. I'll be with you all the way. We can get some others in as well, for moral support. But we have to do it.'

'I know,' she said. 'But I don't want anyone else in the picture. As long as you're with me.'

Gloria called the hotel and took the day off, pleading illness. Then she called her mother and told her she was busy and didn't know when she would be home. She spoke to the children—it was a school day—and told them she'd see them after she got off work, they shouldn't bother their grandma too much and they must leave in time for school. Everything sorted out, Gloria and Nilanjan sat down to craft strategy. First, there was the question of which police station they'd go to. Given the circumstances, they agreed, it would have to be the Park Street Police Station, bang opposite St. Xavier's College, where Nilanjan taught. Then, they had to get a fix on what Gloria's story would be. After some discussion, Gloria agreed that she should be absolutely truthful, no matter what. The story she'd tell the cops would be the same story she'd told Nilanjan. With all the fuzziness and the forgotten details. Before either of them could overthink it, they left for Park Street.

Nilanjan parked on the St. Xavier's College campus. As a member of the faculty, he could. Their hearts were pounding. Nilanjan was thinking he'd either have a cardiac arrest or some of his ribs would break. Gloria was too numb, too scared to think. They crossed the street and walked into the station, diffidently. Despite having been a heavy drinker for years, seguing into alcoholism, Gloria had never had a brush with the cops. This was, incredibly, her first visit to a police station. Nilanjan, older by several years and initiated into drinking at a much younger age, too, had never really had cop problems. It was only after he had been sober for years that he had been to police stations to extricate recovering alcoholics on a relapse or old drinking buddies in trouble. But those were minor misdemeanours. He'd never been to a cop house to file even a minor complaint. He squeezed Gloria's hand as they walked up to the enquiry desk and Nilanjan took over. 'We want to file a complaint,' he told the woman behind the window.

She yawned. 'Do you have pen and paper?' she asked, stifling another yawn.

'Yes,' Nilanjan said.

'Write down your complaint and give it to him,' she said, pointing at an officer sitting at a desk.

'Who's he?'

'Just do as I say,' she barked. Matter closed.

Nilanjan and Gloria walked up to the man. The tag on his pocket said, 'Abir Talukdar'. Nilanjan coughed mildly and asked, 'Are you the duty officer?'

Talukdar looked up at him. 'What do you want?' he asked, an affirmative reply and question rolled into one.

'We want to file a complaint,' Nilanjan said.

'First, you have to make a GD entry,' Talukdar said. 'General diary entry. Write down your complaint.' He pushed across a blank piece of paper. 'Theft, accident?'

'No. Abduction and rape,' Gloria said, suddenly finding a reserve of spirit within her, communicated by a hint of asperity in her tone. If she had intended to draw attention, she succeeded.

The ASI looked up, startled. 'What did you say?' he asked, his tone less assured.

'I was abducted and raped in a moving car and dumped in Minto Park, last night. Technically, this morning. I can't remember the exact time. Everything's hazy.'

Talukdar goggled. 'I think you'd better tell me the whole story.' All this was said in a much softer tone.

So, Gloria told him the whole story. Including the fact that she was a recovering alcoholic. Hadn't had a drink in five-odd years and had suddenly felt like having one, with various kinds of pressures piling up. ASI Talukdar listened with great attention, making what seemed to be minimal notes. When Gloria was done, he started asking questions. Where and with whom did she live? Could she provide an address? What exactly did she do at work, what were her duties? What were her normal work hours? Then Talukdar got to the business end of the questioning. 'Madam,' he asked, 'you were drinking all by yourself in Sugarloaf? Do you do that often?'

In an instant, Gloria felt the blood rush to her head. 'What kind of questions are these? I just told you that I haven't had a drink in five years. And is drinking alone in a respectable bar a crime punishable by rape?'

Talukdar was abashed. 'No, madam, please don't take offence. I'm just trying to recreate the scene in Sugarloaf in my mind. I'm trying to place you there.'

Nilanjan squeezed Gloria's hand. She calmed down. 'Sorry I snapped,' she said. 'I haven't been to a bar in five years. I don't drink anymore. And I've never been to Sugarloaf. Before.'

Talukdar nodded. 'I know that many people believe that rape victims are not victims. I'm not one of them. I'm a police officer and I'm on your side. I'll try my best to track down the men who did this. Please write down everything you've said and sign it. I'll make a GD entry on the basis of your written statement. That will be converted to a first-information report (FIR) when we establish prima facie evidence of a cognizable offence. Don't worry. It's just red tape.'

Gloria did as she was told. Talukdar disappeared for a while, to talk to the officer-in-charge (OC) of the police station. He was back in a few minutes. 'Please come with me,' he told Gloria, looking pointedly at her. She got the message and said, 'I want him to go with me.' Talukdar didn't seem too happy about this demand. 'Later,' he said, 'first, Sir and I would like to talk to you.' The just-knighted OC who turned out to be a benighted OC.

Gloria looked at Nilanjan. 'I'm right here, Glo,' he said. 'Go, don't worry. You're doing pretty well.' She looked at him for a long time, and then went with Talukdar.

From the moment she walked into the room, Gloria knew, not sensed, not intuited, not felt, but *knew*, that OC Gautam Biswas was not cut from the same cloth as ASI Talukdar. Hell, she thought, he wasn't even from the same fucking planet. Biswas was surly whereas Talukdar was personable, if not exactly friendly; Biswas's face was closed, his expression blank and eyes hooded; Talukdar was clean-cut and exuded an air of openness. That was the frickin' deal, Gloria thought silently as she accepted a seat, ungraciously offered. Then came the questioning, almost the third degree, as if she had committed a crime.

It was obvious that Biswas did not believe her story. He told her that to her face. 'You were drinking alone in a bar for four hours. You think that's normal? You got drunk and danced with a person you'd never met. You took a lift from him? You hardly remember what happened after 2300 hours?' 2300 hours. Now she knew exactly what she was up against. 'You expect us to take this complaint seriously?' he continued. 'Do you have any idea how short-staffed we are? Please leave. You're lucky I'm not arresting you.' All that was left for him to say was, 'You're a fucking whore. Get the hell out of here.'

Gloria's pale face was paler still. She stood up on shaky feet and said, 'How dare you say these things?' She was on the verge of breaking down, but somehow held herself up. 'How dare you say I'm lying, you fucking chimpanzee?' she shouted.

It was Biswas's turn to turn white. 'Get out,' he said, his voice barely under control.

Talukdar stood up and said, 'Madam, please come with me.' He was risking his boss's wrath. The two left the room. Outside, Gloria started crying, Talukdar standing helplessly by her side. Nilanjan came over. 'What's wrong?' he asked, with a pretty good idea about what was wrong.

And Talukdar said, 'He was not in a good mood.' Understatement. 'I'll talk to him. Try to open the investigation.'

Nilanjan taught Statistics in St. Xavier's College. But many of his friends, from school and college, had become journalists. First in newspapers and later in the electronic media. After Gloria recounted the encounter with the OC, Nilanjan was furious. 'Okay, we'll screw these motherfuckers. I'll personally stick a red-hot rod up his fucking ass,' he said. And started making calls. The seventh call was a long one. With Gloria's permission, Nilanjan provided an edited version of her story right up to OC Biswas's charm offensive. After what seemed like an age, he hung up. 'I was speaking to a friend who's a big noise in *Khabar Kolkata*,' he said. Gloria was not well acquainted with the television channel 'ecosystem'. Ecosystem. Optics. Atmospherics. Narrative. Multiple. The English language being mauled by a bunch of half-literate morons across the world.

Nilanjan explained, '*Khabar Kolkata* is one of the three biggest Bengali news channels. Maybe the second biggest. The channel's executive editor is Mainak Sinha. He has a major say in the programming on the channel and he personally anchors the prime-time slots: from 8 p.m. to 10 p.m.' Out of the blue, Gloria thought, 2000 hours to 2200 hours. Bastard OC. 'He's ready to discuss putting your story on the channel. That will shove a rocket up Motherfucker Biswas's ass,' Nilanjan continued. 'If you want that, of course. And if you feel up to it. I'll have to call him back with an answer soon. Then we need to go to his office to sort the details out. Your identity will be protected. That's a cardinal principle.'

Gloria nodded, thinking how lucky she was to have Nilu in her corner. 'Let's do it,' she said. 'We have several asses to nail to the door. Including Motherfucker OC Biswas's.' Anger at war with trauma.

Nilanjan called his friend, who asked them to meet him at 5 p.m. After they said no to tea and coffee, Mainak started the meeting. 'We'll do this on prime time tomorrow. I'll anchor the programme. It's too late to fit in today. My idea is that you tell your story first, with your face pixellated and voice doctored. Right up to your encounter with the OC. Then, I'll ask you some questions and you can add to your story or clarify some points. Just for dramatic impact. Sounds all right?' he asked Gloria.

She said, 'Yes. What time will the programme be aired?'

'At 9 p.m. You'll need to be here by 6. We have to make sure you and I get it all together and the team have their cues right. And you'll probably need to get some make-up done, even though your face will be pixellated. Okay?' Gloria said that sounded good. Nilanjan thanked Mainak, who said, 'How long have we known each other, Nilu? From kindergarten, that would be forty-plus years. You're most welcome ... And one other thing, Gloria. Please don't reveal personal details, including your name, to anyone in our office. Only Nilu and I know. That's enough.'

Nilanjan dropped Gloria home. She'd called a couple of times just to check in and make sure no one at home would worry. After returning from the cop shop, she'd showered, but kept her clothes in a plastic bag in case they were needed for tests. She'd bought new clothes and worn them. So, when she got home, no one could even begin to guess what she'd gone through. She spent some time with the kids and made sure dinner was ready at 8:30. The children went to bed at 9:30. Her mother, always curious, asked her what had happened. She kept it vague. 'Lots of work, Mom. So, I asked Nilu to pick me up from Park Street and spent the night at his place, instead of coming back here so late. Then, I had to go back to work early. So, I just went to the hotel straight from Nilu's.' The altruistic lie.

They were at the *Khabar Kolkata* office a little before 6 the next day after a normal, harrowing rush-hour drive. Gloria had left work early. Mainak and his team showed them the ropes. Then he left; he would be on air at 8. His team gave Gloria detailed instructions and a sort of a dry run, after the make-up guy had done his job. At 9, Gloria was on air. The impact of Gloria's revelations, made more dramatic by Mainak's Q&A, was instantaneous. In a few minutes, viewers were calling up friends and relations, telling them about the programme. Exactly how many people watched was not known, but busloads must have.

Commissioner Chanda left home to return to Lalbazar, anticipating trouble. He called DGP Roy to discuss the explosive revelations. The chief minister, who was in Nabanna, the new secretariat in the town of Howrah, Calcutta's poorer cousin across the Hooghly River, met some of her senior cabinet colleagues, a few of whom had to turn back after leaving for home. There was an air of crisis.

Chanda called Biswas for clarifications. Biswas told him that the story was thin and he didn't have the personnel to chase every wild goose that flew in through his window. Had it been absolutely necessary to misbehave with a member of the public? Did he have any reason to believe that she had made up the story? Couldn't he have been a little more sympathetic and diplomatic? Biswas snorted. 'Don't have time for that, sir,' he said, feeling dread settling in his stomach. He'd got the Park Street posting a couple of months ago. The post of Park Street OC was unofficially, not to mention illegally, auctioned, like most such lucrative posts. He hadn't yet recouped his investment. Shit, he thought, if I get transferred because of this fucking bitch, I'll kill her.

Chanda disconnected. He wasn't going to carry the can. So, it would have to be Biswas, if the need arose.

'Biswas is not particularly repentant. Says he doesn't have time to chase every wild goose. Or time for civility. But he's not half bad as an officer,' he told DGP Roy on the phone, damning Biswas with faint praise.

'He's got a point, of course,' Roy replied. 'If we had to investigate every complaint we got, we'd need, at least, our full, sanctioned strength of officers. And we're nearer two-thirds that. Still, Biswas needs to learn to behave better with members of the public who can create a stink. If I were you, I'd call him back and tell him that neither he nor anyone in Park Street should talk about this to whomsoever, especially the press. And that goes for everyone else, until you clear the matter up.'

As soon as he hung up, the phone rang. Chanda answered and said, 'Yes, sir,' a couple of times and left to meet the chief minister (CM). He'd been speaking to HS Datta. Touch and go, he thought. He made the trip to Nabanna in fifteen minutes.

Apart from the CM, there were three people in the room, when Chanda entered it. Datta and two senior members of the cabinet. The chief secretary was missing. He took a seat and the CM said, 'This is a conspiracy to malign my government. Park Street OC was right to turn her away. Did you see the interview?' Chanda hadn't really. By the time he'd heard about the 'interview', it had almost been over. He said so. 'We must issue a statement,' the CM said. Which meant, Chanda realized, that he would have to issue a statement, telling the press that the interview and the story about the rape were concocted with a view to maligning the police force, especially, and the administration, generally. But he tried a dodge. 'Shouldn't the DGP issue a statement, madam?'

'Hold a joint press conference. Roy will be there, but you'll have to address it. Do it tomorrow morning. First thing,' Datta said.

Having got the message, Chanda went back to HQ, hoping he wouldn't get a call before leaving for home, god only knew when. The phone rang as if in answer to his prayer. 'Commissioner Chanda here,' he said, in what he hoped was a suitably clipped tone. The voice at the other end said, 'I'm Raina Aqeel, sir. From *The Times of India*.' Chanda remained in clipped mode, though he was too much of a politician to be rude to a journalist from a national newspaper. 'Yes. What can I do for you?'

'Sir,' Raina said, 'I tried talking to officers at the Park Street police station about the *Khabar Kolkata* programme, but nobody's talking. They said any reaction would come from you.'

Damn them, Chanda thought. 'We're looking into the matter. There'll be a press conference here tomorrow at 9 a.m. Notifications will be sent out tonight.'

At the press conference the next morning, Chanda was terse. 'I've looked at the incident,' he said. 'And I don't think there is any truth to the story. The Park Street OC was right to dismiss it. This is a conspiracy,' he continued, the word sticking in his throat, 'to malign the police force and the administration.'

The journalists were too taken aback to ask questions.

'Sir, just to clarify,' Raina interjected, recovering the fastest. 'The woman who went on television told hundreds of thousands of people a fabricated story about being raped to discredit the government?'

Chanda winced, there was no getting away from it. 'Yes,' he said.

'Since she lodged a complaint at the Park Street *thana* a GD entry must have been made. And her identity must be known to the police. Are you thinking of taking action against her or going to court, sir?' Raina asked.

'Not at the moment,' Chanda said. 'I don't think we need to take any precipitate steps. That will be all.'

The story hit the front page of the papers the next morning—English, Bengali, Hindi, Tamil, Urdu and every other language in which newspapers were published in the city. Headlines splashed all the three parts of the story. First, the story of the rape—in fairly graphic detail. Speculation and imagination supplying details missing from the interview in the case of the more salacious tabloids. Second, the refusal of the Park Street officers to conduct preliminary investigations on the road to filing an FIR to probe the case. And, third, Commissioner Chanda's view that the story had been fabricated to tarnish the fair name of Kolkata Police and the government. One of the less sober papers ran the headline: 'Charges Fabricated, Rape of Truth: Commissioner'. Ouch, thought Chanda, when he saw that one, but it came with the territory.

That indefinable thing called public opinion started crystallizing as TV channels latched on to the controversy, sparing neither OC Biswas nor Commissioner Chanda. The commissioner's 'soundbite' was played through the day. The CM summoned Chanda, Roy, the home secretary, the chief secretary and some cabinet colleagues. There was a meeting, but no consultation. 'I'll have to address a press conference,' she said. 'And I'll say exactly what you said,' she said, looking at Chanda.

The press conference happened at Nabanna in the evening. The venue was packed. There was more than enough time to file reports. The CM read from a prepared script. She allowed questions, but did not answer a single one, sticking to her line: it's a frame-up to malign the government. Unfortunately for her, Chanda, the police and the administration, some of the papers and channels hadn't been sitting with their thumbs up their asses all day waiting for an official statement. They'd done their due diligence, going to all the late-licence bars on Park Street—Gloria had not mentioned the improbably named Sugarloaf for obvious reasons—trying to run down a lone woman drinking till after midnight (a known datum), from sometime in the late evening (assumption), who had left with more than one male, one of whom she'd danced with (again, a known datum). There aren't that many late-licence bars/nightclubs on Park Street. Most of the adventurous reporters located Sugarloaf by noon and got interviews of staff members, who confirmed Gloria's story in its essentials.

The channels, especially *Khabar Kolkata*, started running these stories from the evening. Right after the CM's presser. Two birds with one stone. The embarrassment to the government was becoming more and more acute. Late into the evening, after the prime-time telecasts, the CM called another meeting, with the same cast of characters.

No consultations again, but a climbdown. 'We'll have to order an investigation,' the CM said. 'Chanda, call the Park Street *thana* and get the process going. And issue a statement that we are reopening the case.' Meeting over, with Chanda left silently wondering: 'reopening'?

But the wheels started moving. Chanda called Biswas and told him to register an FIR in the rape case and begin investigations. Pronto. Then he prepared a statement saying the case was being reopened. He could visualize people doubling over with laughter or exchanging sly grins. A climbdown of monumental proportions, necessitated by sheer pig-headedness. Shit! And it was he, of course, who was having to eat humble pie. But he prepared the statement for immediate circulation to the press. And then he left for home.

The headlines were screaming again next morning. They practically woke Gloria up. She had never been much of a newspaper reader. Wasn't interested in politics. But now she was devouring the papers. After she'd said bye to the kids, she sat down with the papers. She knew the case was being reopened. Nilanjan, who generally kept his ears and eyes open (and mouth shut), had called to give her the news late last night. He'd got it from his friend Mainak. She read the news, feeling a river of satisfaction flow through her. The cops would get them now. She wondered what exactly would happen. And called Nilanjan. 'Nilu, what's going to happen now?' she asked. 'Will I have to go back to the police station? I was feeling better, now, I'm feeling scared again.'

Nilanjan reassured her. 'I'll be with you, don't worry

about anything. And that Talukdar guy was quite okay. We'll be fine.'

They weren't, however. Around noon, Talukdar called Gloria. 'Madam,' he began, 'can you please come to the police station? We will have to conduct medical and other forensic tests.' Gloria said yes and asked for a time. 'As soon as you can,' Talukdar said, 'but according to your convenience. I know you'll have to have lunch.' Gloria called Nilanjan and went over to his flat, telling her mother a story before leaving. She also called the hotel, saying she wouldn't be able to make it. Nilanjan was waiting, with lunch prepared. They ate hurriedly. 'I've got the clothes I was wearing that day. I haven't washed them or anything, as you said. Will that help?' Gloria asked. 'Should,' he said. 'It's probably not like the police procedurals I read. I don't think they'll magically find the bastards by DNA testing. But at least it could help prove that the rape happened.'

Talukdar, who had been made the investigating officer (IO), was waiting when they got to Park Street. 'You'll have to go through a medical examination. We'll take you to the hospital. He can't come with us,' he said, gesturing at Nilanjan. 'But he can follow.' Before leaving for the hospital, Gloria gave Talukdar a plastic bag. 'These are the clothes I was wearing that night. I haven't washed them. I thought they would help your investigations.' Talukdar accepted the bag and said, 'Wait. I'll have to record and store it.' He did the needful and Gloria, Talukdar and two constables left. At the hospital, the doctor who was going to conduct the examination called Talukdar aside. They had a brief conversation. Then the medical examination was conducted. And Gloria was free to go. 'When will I get the results?' she asked the doctor.

'We'll give the police the results the day after tomorrow. Then it's up to them,' she said. 'But if you give me your number, I'll call you and give you the results unofficially, after I've sent the report to the police, of course. You mustn't tell anyone though.'

Gloria mumbled her thanks and left the room to find Talukdar and Nilanjan waiting for her. 'You'll have to return to the *thana*, madam,' Talukdar said. 'We have to complete some formalities.' They headed back to the police station, where the 'formalities' were completed.

From there, Gloria and Nilanjan headed back to his place. Nilanjan brewed a fresh pot of tea. While they were drinking it, Nilanjan's phone rang. 'Good evening, sir,' a bright voice chirped. Nilanjan scowled. 'Am I speaking to Mr Chatterjee?' the caller asked.

'Dr,' Nilanjan countered, tersely.

'Sir, my name is Ritwika Sinha. I'm calling from *Khabar Kolkata*. Mainak sir asked me to speak to you about The Case.'

Nilanjan could hear the upper case in the last two words. 'Sure. But what would that be about, if you don't mind my asking?'

'Sir,' Ritwika continued, still a chirpy counterpoint to Nilanjan's gruff, tired tone, 'Mainak sir wants a story on the medical examination and today's developments. Where can I find madam?'

'I'll call you in just a bit,' Nilanjan said and disconnected. Filling Gloria in, he asked her whether she was up to it.

'He's done a lot for me, I can't say no. I'd feel bad about it,' she said.

Nilanjan called Ritwika and gave her his Southern Avenue home address. 'Don't be too late,' he cautioned her, 'I'll have to drop madam home after it's done.'

The crew was at Nilanjan's house in half an hour. 'Only madam, it's not a live telecast. We'll be on air at 9 p.m. So, you can relax,' Ritwika said. Gloria did actually feel a little less stressed.

Ritwika began. 'We have with us the very, very courageous rape survivor of the Park Street incident, which happened three days ago. She's going to tell us about the opening of the investigation.' She turned to Gloria. 'Do you feel vindicated, madam?'

Gloria mulled over the question briefly. 'I was raped, so, I wouldn't use the word vindicated. But yes, I'm glad that the police are going to investigate, so there's a chance of getting the culprits.'

Ritwika smiled, 'Absolutely. Did the Park Street police officers apologize for insinuating that you were lying?'

'Not in so many words. But they were very civil.'

'I believe you were taken for a medical test to National Medical College and Hospital? Did that go smoothly?'

'Yes,' Gloria said. 'The hospital staff was very kind.'

Ritwika smiled again. 'And you were accompanied by lady officers of the Park Street *thana*, of course.' Statement.

Gloria was thrown by the 'of course'. But she recovered her composure and said, 'No. I was accompanied by the IO, a male ASI, and two other male officers.'

Ritwika turned pale. Then she turned to the camera

and to Gloria. 'What!' she said, 'you were not escorted to the hospital by female officers? That's a horrible breach of established protocol.' She'd known all along and was milking it. During the rest of the interview, mercifully short for Gloria, she turned on her outrage several times.

The next day, the Park Street PS's procedural lapse was duly excoriated by the print media in the morning and by the electronic media through the day. Datta summoned Chanda before the CM could summon him. After Chanda was ensconced comfortably in a chair, having made the trip from police HQ, Datta barked, 'Why are your officers such complete idiots? How did this thug Biswas get the Park Street posting? If something goes wrong with the medical test, we'll be up shit creek. The media's baying for our blood. We have to do something. We could begin with transferring Biswas out somewhere safe. Out of the media gaze.'

Chanda nodded. He wasn't exactly the type to stand up for his subordinates. He knew that protecting juniors was good for morale, but not doing so hadn't exactly hurt his career. What the hell? 'Just give me the word,' he said, knowing that any action in this case would have to be cleared by the CM herself.

'Okay,' Datta said, 'wait for word from me, I have to make a few calls.' Dismissed.

Datta called the chief secretary. 'Lots of flak, sir,' he began.

Chief Secretary Pushkar Dasgupta cut in, unceremoniously. 'Angshuman,' he said, 'we have to do something. Divert attention. Any ideas?'

'Yes, Pushkar, we can begin with transferring OC Biswas out of Park Street. Out of Calcutta, as a matter of fact. He's too old school to deal with cases like this. And heaven knows when something like this will happen again.'

'Scapegoat, huh?' Dasgupta said.

'Yes and no,' came the reply. 'As you said, we need to do something and Biswas's conduct has been less than exemplary. We could wait till the results of the tests come out. But I wouldn't favour that. Even now, it will look like we've been pushed, but afterwards, it will look much worse.'

'Fine,' said his boss. 'Let me get that cleared by the CM. But I've already got something else cleared: transfer the case to DD. Direct supervision, if not investigation, by Tanya Samanta. Make an announcement to the press. Keep me in the loop. I'll get back about the Biswas transfer this afternoon if I can. Can't hustle the boss, you know.'

Tanya had been suffering from post-chase blues. Garcia and Nandi were untraceable and Singh's report had been shelved by Commissioner Chanda. There was no point in getting Delhi to send Dhaka on a fruitless chase. The job of dismantling the Garcia network had been progressing satisfactorily. As of now, Tanya's team was just winding up that operation. Alongside, the hooch case was also being quietly wound up. The Mollah brothers had disappeared. Kolkata Police wasn't, as promised, breaking their balls trying to locate them. The graph was flat and Tanya was feeling irritated. As, she presumed, was her entire team, the members of which were now working on sundry other cases.

She had just wound up her work, cleared her desk and was preparing to leave for home, when the internal phone rang. 'Samanta,' she barked, taking the call.

'Hello,' said the voice at the other end.

And she realized she was speaking to her boss. 'Hello, sir,' she said.

'Anything the matter?' Chanda asked, out of character.

'No, sir,' Tanya said. 'I was on the point of heading out of office.'

'I'm afraid,' Chanda said, 'that you'll have to postpone your departure. Please come to my office right away.'

Tanya sensed that something big was about to happen and hurried to the commissioner's room. Trying hard not to look or sound excited, she ventured a minimalist opening gambit, 'Sir.'

'At ease, Samanta,' Chanda said. 'I've got a gift for you and your department.' Tanya had never played poker, but she kept an impressively straight face.

'Following the Park Street case, aren't you?' Chanda continued. 'Park Street PS hasn't really covered itself in glory. The press and the public are all over us.'

'Yes, sir, Park Street PS could have handled things better, I suppose,' Tanya said.

'The case is being transferred to you as of this moment. Get in touch with Park Street PS, get the paperwork transferred. The IO will be on deputation to you. ASI Talukdar. Seems like he was the only one there who understood the gravity of the case. Everyone wants swift action. Tread on as many toes as you need to,' Chanda said. In a few minutes, she was on the line to Park Street; her usual self again. Brisk. Brusque, even. 'Tanya Samanta. From DD. I want to speak to ASI Talukdar, please.' Talukdar was on duty. Having already been advised both about the transfer and his deputation, he ran to the phone. He already knew it was best to keep on the right side of JCP Samanta, who was fair but tough. Didn't take a shine to sloth or stupidity.

'ASI Abir Talukdar, ma'am,' he said.

'I want you to put the file together tonight and report to headquarters by 9 tomorrow. Have the papers sent over tonight if possible or bring them with you. Bring *all* the papers. When is the medical report expected?'

'By evening tomorrow, ma'am,' Talukdar said. 'I don't know whether that will be the final report.'

'Who's the medical examiner?'

'Dr Mohsina Hamid, ma'am.'

'Report to my room.' Talukdar disconnected with a sense of relief. He hadn't yet been mangled and there was a chance the case would go somewhere, which he really wanted. He'd never suspected Gloria of lying. And he wanted the rapists to do serious time.

Talukdar put the file together. He had prepared them in the first place, so the possibility of making an error was on the low side. Not that there were many papers. Still... After he was done, he gave them and the evidence bag with Gloria's clothes to the duty officer to be despatched to Lalbazar, addressed to JCP (Crime) Tanya Samanta. Job done, he headed home.

Sharp at 9 the next day, he knocked on Tanya's door. He found her reading the file he'd sent. Just a couple of documents, since OC Biswas hadn't launched much of an investigation into the 'incident'. She motioned him to take a seat. After a couple of minutes, Tanya looked up. 'I'll introduce you to the team at the meeting, which will begin half an hour from now. Until then, locate the photocopier and make seven copies of the file.'

Talukdar said, 'Yes, ma'am. I'll report here in twenty minutes.'

Tanya gave him a long, even look and said, 'Wait.' She summoned Ishita. 'Please help Talukdar locate the photocopier. And help him make seven copies of these papers,' she instructed. The photocopier was somewhat temperamental. Dismissed.

Half an hour later, six people had assembled in the designated meeting room, five of them leafing through three sheets in the files. One seat was unoccupied, with a file on the table in front of it. A little later, Tanya entered the room. 'Hope you've had the time to go through these papers,' she began, even before she was properly seated. Ever so often, Tanya could sound sarcastic, without apparent cause. Ever so often, she wasn't being sarcastic. It was tough for many, including her superiors, to make out whether she was being sarcastic or just making a plain statement or asking a simple question. It didn't endear her to fellow officers, especially seniors.

She had read the papers. So had Talukdar, obviously. And her team members, well acquainted with their boss, had made speed reading part of their skill set. They all nodded, without having figured out whether Tanya had intended to be sarcastic or not. Tanya, at the head of the table, made the introductions, anti-clockwise. 'Inspector Jadunath Majumdar, Inspector Gopal Barui, Sub-inspector (SI) Ramadhar Tiwari, ASI Mrinal Mallik, Constable Ishita Pal,' she said, not bothering to gesture. 'ASI Abir Talukdar. Since you've all gone through the papers, we'll cut to the chase. The medical report, either preliminary or final, will be available today. Afternoon, early evening?' She looked at Talukdar.

'Early evening, ma'am,' he said.

'It's your job to keep track. Bring it here as soon as it is available and inform me. Jadunath and Mrinal will go to Sugarloaf and get CCTV footage of that evening, from 6 p.m. to closing time. Tread on as many toes as necessary to get it. We've got the commissioner's clearance in the toe-treading department. If they are hesitant about playing ball, don't think twice about threatening to close them down. Actually, you can also threaten to arrest the manager for obstructing justice. Gopal and Ishita will make an appointment with the survivor and visit her as soon as possible. Explain that the case has been reopened and DD is investigating it and you'd like to talk to her. Ramadhar will talk to this Nilanjan Chatterjee fellow.'

She looked at Ramadhar, a mean, maverick, but an especially honest and competent cop, who could be a really tough interrogator. 'Try to find out why he's so involved in this case. Some of it seems obvious, but…' Ramadhar nodded. 'Ramadhar, kid gloves needed. Please remember that he's not a suspect. He's a respectable professor at

St. Xavier's College. A friend of the victim's.' Ramadhar smiled but didn't say anything.

Meeting over, everyone dispersed. Jadunath and Mrinal left for Park Street, expecting to tread on toes. Ishita went to the room she shared with Mrinal and others (including, for the duration of the case, the Park Street PS loanee) to call Gloria. Ramadhar went off to polish his kid-gloves technique. Gopal went to the room he shared with Jadunath and others to wait for the outcome of Ishita's call. And Talukdar settled down at his desk, to organize his meagre possessions, including the Park Street Rape file, before beginning to chase Dr Hamid for the medical report. Tanya went to her room to strategize. Plans A, B, C and whatever else it took.

Jadunath and Mrinal had copped the most important assignment of the morning. Almost a week had passed since Gloria, to the public the unnamed victim/survivor, had walked into Sugarloaf for a drink. Jadunath was keenly aware that even if the Sugarloaf cameras had caught anything significant, the tapes could have been recorded over. Private establishments did not have to maintain CCTV surveillance. When they did so, it was up to them to decide how long they'd archive their footage. 'If they have the footage, they'll have to give it up,' Jadunath told Mrinal, who nodded. Mrinal knew that the big and greying inspector, sometimes affable to a fault, could explode at practically no provocation. He could really unsettle people, which made him a pretty decent cop. 'They may not have any footage for the evening,' Mrinal said, dampening down expectations. Jadunath didn't answer. The rest of the trip passed in silence since both knew exactly what they had to do. They'd worked together earlier.

They reached Sugarloaf around half an hour after leaving HQ. Traffic was a bitch, as always. Road space in Calcutta was about 4 per cent, with little room for expansion and the number of vehicles increasing by the day. By the time they stepped out of the car, their mood was pretty grim. Not good for people in the way. The establishment was closed. They'd known it would be; it didn't open till afternoon. They also knew, however, that the office opened in the morning and someone would be around. After they'd leant on the bell and hammered on the door loud enough to wake up the whole city, it opened. Jadunath flashed his ID. 'Police,' he said. 'DD. We need to talk to whoever's in charge.'

The young man who opened the door was really just a boy. He hastily ushered them in. 'Please sit,' he said, gesturing at some chairs. 'I'll be right back.' He wasn't, but a corpulent man of indeterminate age (Jadunath and Mrinal both made him out to be in his late forties) waddled over to them. 'Hello,' he said, beaming. 'What can I do for you?'

'You can begin by answering a few questions,' Jadunath said. 'In your office. You have one ... ?'

'Of course, sir, do follow me,' he said, in an unctuous tone.

'I'm Inspector Jadunath Majumdar and this is ASI Mrinal Mallik.' Jadunath reached into his pocket.

'That's fine,' the manager said. 'You don't need to show your ID. I'm Probir Guha. Assistant manager. What can I do for you?' At the moment, it appeared, he was anxious to cooperate.

'How long do you keep your CCTV footage?' Jadunath asked, without any pussyfooting.

Guha's face fell. 'I'm not sure, exactly. Could you tell me what this is about?' he asked, obviously stalling.

'Not right now,' Jadunath said, tumbling to Guha's tactic. 'Please find out. We can wait outside if you want.'

'No, no. That's fine,' Guha said. He made a call. 'We keep footage for a fortnight, then we record over them,' he said, replacing the receiver. 'Could you tell me what this is about?'

'This is about an investigation by Kolkata Police's Detective Department into a crime,' Jadunath said. 'We need the tapes from the evening a week ago. From 6 p.m. to closing time. Now.'

Guha squirmed in his seat. It wasn't a pleasant sight. 'I'm sorry, Inspector,' he said. 'I don't have the authority to release the tapes.'

'Call whoever has the authority. Ask him to authorize you or to come over. Now. If you want us to get a warrant, we will. But that will cause unnecessary delay and we'll get a little pissed off. I know you guys wouldn't want that. After all, we're investigating a serious crime. We're not crawling up your ass just because we've nothing better to do.'

Guha was intimidated, as per plan. Mrinal remained silent. Guha made another call. 'Hello, this is Probir here,' he began. 'Two policemen are here from the Detective Department. They want CCTV footage for the evening a week ago. Right now. What should I do?' He nodded for a while and said, 'No. They haven't told me.' He nodded some more, looking happier. 'I think that'd be better,' he said. Turning to the detectives, he said, 'The manager will be here soon.'

The manager was a completely different customer. Athletic and tall, he breezed into Guha's office. His gait and demeanour matched his confidence. No pushover, both the cops thought. 'Please come to my office. Would you like a cup of tea or coffee?' he asked.

Jadunath answered for both. 'Tea. My name is Jadunath Majumdar, I'm an inspector with the Detective Department. This is ASI Mrinal Mallik.' They followed the manager to his office. On the way, the manager said, 'I'm Rajat Bansal, pleased to be at your service.' Once they'd settled down, he said, 'I believe you want some CCTV footage from the nightclub.' Neither detective could make out whether that was a statement or a question. So, both kept silent, letting the manager proceed. 'There are privacy issues,' he continued, but Jadunath cut him short. He wasn't a pushover either.

'We are investigating a serious crime. We need, want, the footage. I'm sure you've been reading the papers the past week or so since your establishment has been mentioned quite frequently,' he said.

Bansal nodded. 'Yes. But you will appreciate that there are privacy issues.'

Jadunath was losing patience. 'I don't have time for this bullshit. If you think privacy issues are more important than the investigation of a serious crime, my colleague will go and get a warrant, while I sit here to make sure the footage is not tampered with. After that, my boss will make sure your establishment, which is part of the scene of a crime, will be sealed until we are through with our investigation. Take your pick.'

Bansal leaned back in his chair, eyes closed, head turned towards the ceiling, as if seeking divine inspiration. 'What gave you the impression that we'd even think of tampering with records connected to a crime?' he finally asked.

Jadunath and Mrinal remained silent, the senior partner trying to figure out whether it would be better to treat the question as rhetorical and ignore it, or take it seriously and answer it. 'Your reluctance to comply with a simple request, which is of critical importance to an important enquiry. Your accent on privacy issues,' Jadunath said. Bansal remained silent. 'We don't have all day. I'll give you five minutes and then my colleague will go to Lalbazar to get a warrant and take instructions from the bosses. I'm telling you free of charge, they won't be happy,' Jadunath said, and turned to Mrinal, who, in turn, started stirring. 'Wait,' said Bansal, blinking first. 'I'll get you the tapes, but you'll have to sign for them. No chance of getting them back, I suppose.'

'If we can't crack the case and close it soon, you may get them back. If we can make a case and take it to court, you won't, because they'll be evidence,' Jadunath replied, itching to be on his way. People like Bansal and Guha had a bad effect on him. Something like an allergic condition.

In fifteen minutes, however, the CCTV tapes arrived in two boxes tagged 'Tuesday Evening-I & II' and 'Tuesday Evening-III & IV'. Jadunath signed for the boxes and they were on their way. He called Tanya from the car. 'Got the tapes, ma'am,' he said.

'Trouble?' his boss asked.

'Not really,' was the laconic reply.

Back at office, Jadunath and Mrinal discovered that arrangements for viewing the tapes had already been made. Talukdar, Ishita and Gopal were out. The tapes would first be seen by Tanya, Jadunath, Mrinal and Ramadhar, back from a kid-gloved chat with Nilanjan, which had yielded little of interest. Mrinal took charge of the projector and started from the beginning. They watched for a while to get a sense of the place, the rhythms of the patrons and the staff, and then Tanya asked Mrinal to speed it up. After a few tries, they spotted Gloria entering the bar/nightclub/discotheque. She entered quietly and occupied a table at 20:41 hours, according to the tape. A waiter came up and she ordered. She was served a colourless drink. Could have been gin, vodka or white rum. Wasn't water by the looks of it. By 23:00, Gloria had just had three drinks. Large, small? They couldn't make out.

Then her pace picked up. Before the witching hour, she had almost finished her fifth. Which was when a clean-cut young man walked up and joined her. He ordered two drinks. Gloria's sixth. His, who knows? After about fifteen minutes, they danced for a bit. Then they went back to their respective tables. Gloria was obviously a little the worse for wear. Six drinks after five years of abstinence. Six drinks after anything, most people would be legless. But Gloria paid her bill and got back on her feet. On her feet, but looking like she was on autopilot. When she passed her new acquaintances' table, they exchanged a few words. Drowned out by the din. She sat with them while the bill was paid. Then, all of them: Gloria, her 'friend' and four of his friends, left. Cut. There was no CCTV footage after they'd left Sugarloaf. Good job, though, Tanya thought. 'Congratulations!' she said, turning to Jadunath and Mrinal. 'We'll get these guys. But first we have to see this tape with Gloria. Ask her a few more questions. Disperse, think. Ramadhar, track Talukdar. See how far he's got. I'll speak to Gopal.'

Tanya got through to Gopal. He was at Gloria's place. 'We're talking to her,' he said.

'I want to speak to her,' Tanya cut in.

Gopal handed Gloria the phone, 'The boss wants to speak to you.'

'Ms Stevens, we've got the CCTV footage from Sugarloaf. It would be really helpful for us if you could accompany the officers at your place and see the tapes with us. As soon as we have positive identification and you've clarified a few points, we can move. If it isn't inconvenient.' Tanya was being more diplomatic than usual.

'No, it's all right,' Gloria said. 'It's just that I've told my story so many times. I was just repeating it to your officers.'

'Once we've seen the tapes together, a few clarifications may be necessary,' Tanya said. 'I promise not to grill you.' Tanya knew, while Gloria didn't, that the more versions you had of an incident, however different, the more it helped to straighten a story out rather than complicate it. 'It won't take long,' Tanya said, soothingly. Gloria agreed to make the trip, right then. 'I'd like to bring my friend along. I'd feel more comfortable,' she said.

'He can join in later,' Tanya replied. '*You* have to do it, Ms Stevens. Your friend wasn't there. You'll have to trust your impressions. That's critical.'

Gloria sighed. 'Okay,' she said, and started getting her stuff together.

In an hour, seven people were seated in the room with the projector. Talukdar was still chasing Dr Hamid for the medical report. They watched in complete silence, until the guy came into the frame. Gloria almost jumped up. 'That's him.' There were really no questions about it. The CCTV footage bore out Gloria's story without a misstep. The point, however, was about what had happened after they had left Sugarloaf. The part for which there was no CCTV footage. The lights came on. Tanya asked Gloria, Ramadhar, Ishita, Jadunath and Gopal to get to her room. Mrinal was tasked with getting hold of the absent Talukdar, himself on the trail of the hard-to-get-hold-of medical examiner.

Tanya read Ishita's notes of the conversation recently conducted with Gloria and found nothing new. So, she began her own examination, which wasn't just about verbalized questions and spoken answers. 'Up until the time you left Sugarloaf with Soumitro, the sequence of events is quite clear,' Tanya began. 'So, what happened afterwards? Do you remember better now? When you're traumatized, events often seem jumbled. As you recover, things become clearer.'

Gloria shook her head. 'No,' she said. 'I still have no

clear recollection of what happened between the time I left Sugarloaf and the time I woke up in the park. I remember being manhandled and raped though.'

Tanya knew there was no point in pushing it. 'The others at the table? Did you talk to them?' she asked.

'Not in Sugarloaf.' She shook her head.

'Fine. We'll drop you home,' Tanya said, asking Jadunath and Gopal to remain seated. 'Okay. We'll have to identify these jokers. Go back to Sugarloaf. Find out whether they are regulars. Get receipts. Get printouts of the jokers and have them cleaned up. Talk to other patrons when Sugarloaf opens. You know the drill. If the waiters who were on duty at that time have to be summoned, do it. You can go as far with Mr Bansal as you have to.' Jadunath smiled; Gopal remained impassive. They left to break heads.

Tanya called Chanda. 'Sir,' she said, 'plenty of new developments on the Park Street case.'

'I'll call you back,' he replied.

Must've disturbed his siesta, Tanya thought. Wasn't the case, however. He called back in minutes. 'Meet me right now.'

She filled him in on what had happened and what was supposed to be happening. Just then her phone beeped: Mrinal. 'Ma'am,' he started, excited. 'I just spoke to Talukdar. He's got the report.'

'Has he talked to the doctor or seen the report?' Tanya asked.

'No, ma'am,' Mrinal said. 'He's on his way back with the report. He hasn't opened the cover. But the doctor confirmed to him that there is evidence of rape.'

Tanya gave Chanda the news.

'Move fast,' Chanda said. When the arrest happened, or if it did, he'd make the announcement to the press. That was enough for him, especially since he had had to tell the media that the story had been fabricated to malign the government. He liked coming out of situations smelling good, especially after having had nothing significant to do to influence the outcome. Nothing ventured, everything gained!

At roughly the same time, Dr Hamid called Gloria and told her, as promised, what her findings had been. Gloria thanked her and called Nilanjan to update him about all that had happened. Nilanjan was in college. In the shared staff room. He couldn't express his elation, so he just said, 'That's great news. Why don't you come over to my place, say at 8?' Gloria said she would. Feeling, for the first time in days, that her life had started to be pieced together.

Tanya went back to her room to find Mrinal and Talukdar waiting outside. Talukdar handed her the sealed cover. There wasn't much scope for detail. Gloria had been examined approximately a hundred hours after the rape. What the report boiled down to was that there was physical evidence of genital bruising, beginning to heal, and bruising on the thighs. There was no recoverable residue of semen, which could be the result of the delay in examining the survivor or because the rapist/s used condoms, or both. The conclusion was that either rape or very rough consensual sex had happened. The evidence, in the shape of other bruises, pointed to the former. Gloria's story was now difficult to discount. Tanya informed Chanda, who received the news with no comment. It would be a long evening. Just how long would depend on what Jadunath and Gopal turned up at Sugarloaf, from the reluctant manager and his smarmy assistant. Or, for that matter, the yet-to-be-examined waiters, who were likely to know a little more than the suits, such as they were.

Jadunath called in at around 6 p.m. 'Manager and assistant remember their faces vaguely. Their testimony is useless. We've asked for all the waiters on duty that day to be summoned. Most are already here. Opening time's almost upon us. The others should start trickling in soon. Guha, the fat assistant, is looking for the receipt signed by Soumitro. I'll call you as soon as we have something solid,' he told Tanya. That turned out to be sooner than he'd reckoned for. Jadunath and Gopal began questioning the waiters separately, to get through the job quicker. They'd decided to shortlist the 'probables' and grill them again, if the need arose. Jadunath had gone through three, one of whom admitted to recognizing Soumitro and the four other patrons. The other two were willing but vague.

Gopal had gone through three as well. Of whom two admitted to having served the four men but couldn't remember dates. They were regulars and, it appeared, sat together. Another thought that he'd seen the faces, but wasn't sure. At that point, Guha came up to Jadunath with the receipt for the debit card transaction and a copy of the bill. The receipt would have to be used the next morning to get a fuller picture of the man who had used the card. It would be tough; banks and card companies didn't part with information easily. Just when Gopal was about to call Tanya, Guha came up to them again. 'The man who was at the door has arrived. If anybody knows anything useful it will be him,' he said.

'Bring him here,' Jadunath said. 'Thanks.'

Kamal Yadav, a burly man with a luxuriant moustache, often worn by doormen/bouncers at Park Street establishments to suggest a colonial-era ambience, came in and sat down with the inspectors. Gopal showed him the photos of the four men. 'Do you recognize them?' he asked.

'Yes, sahib,' was the unhesitating answer.

'They come in often?'

'Yes, sahib,' he said. 'A couple of times a week.'

'Since when?'

'A few years, I think.'

'At what time do they usually come?' asked Jadunath.

'Around 8:30 to 9 in the evening, sahib. Rarely before that, sometimes a little later. But by 9:30. Not always together.'

'How do they get here, usually?'

'Soumitro sahib comes in a car. The others in taxis. Dipak*ji* sometimes on a bike. Usually, they leave together in Soumitro sahib's car.'

There was silence for a while. Then Gopal asked, spacing out the words, enunciating them extra carefully, 'You've seen this car?'

Yadav guffawed. 'Of course, sahib. Most days, Soumitro sahib just leaves the car in front. I get someone to park it and keep the keys. He takes the keys from me when he leaves. Finding a parking slot takes time at that hour.'

Jadunath and Gopal exchanged hopeful looks. Gopal asked, 'So, you know the make and colour?'

'Mercedes. Steel grey.'

'And the number?' asked Jadunath, hoping he wasn't pushing his luck.

'6269,' Yadav said, before reciting the full registration details. Jadunath had it down on his mobile in a flash. Gopal asked him for his address, phone number and duty hours. 'Which address, sahib?' Yadav asked. 'Bihar or Kalkatta?'

'Both,' Gopal said, as he wrote down the information about Yadav. 'These details are also with the manager, I hope?' he asked.

'Yes, sahib.'

'Don't leave the city without informing the police,' Gopal said, before giving Yadav both their names and numbers. Then Gopal called Tanya. 'Ma'am, we've made good progress. We've got the receipt for the transaction. The card was used by one Soumitro. At the moment, he doesn't have a surname, but he will by tomorrow. The doorman knows him well, by name and face. And his four cronies. Soumitro drives to the bar. The doorman gave us the make, colour and licence-plate details of his car. Do you want the number now?'

'No,' Tanya said. 'Get back fast.'

After Gopal and Jadunath gave Tanya a verbal report, she told them to go home. 'Aim to be in by 8. One of you type the report, the other locate the owner of the vehicle. We'll have a meeting at 9:30.' They broke up, weary but charged up. The case would break tomorrow. Soumitro, whoever-you-are, you'll be here in Lalbazar before noon, thought Tanya as she headed out.

Jadunath returned home to find his son and heir had been packed off to bed. His wife was waiting for him. He showered and they ate. Bone-weary, with the adrenaline rush winding down, all he wanted was to go to sleep and make an early start after dropping his son off to school. Gopal was a bachelor. He went home, showered, dined and read for half an hour, before turning off the lights.

Tanya reached home at around 9:30. Moni*di*, had tried to send Shaman to bed. But as always, he'd resisted. He was loath to go to bed before his mother returned. He would do that only if she called and said she'd be late. Shaman said hi to her as Tanya entered the flat. She desisted from asking him why he wasn't in bed.

'What did you have for dinner?' she asked.

'Oh! Just food, I guess,' he said.

'Played games on your computer all evening or did some schoolwork as well?'

'I played in Central Park, came home and did my homework first. Then I played on the computer,' he said, guilelessly.

'Good. Let me take a shower and you go to bed young man,' Tanya said, and headed for the bedroom. Satisfied, Shaman did the same.

Jadunath and Gopal were in Lalbazar a little after 8. Of the two, Gopal resented paperwork a mite less than his partner; his linguistic proficiency was also marginally better. So, he elected himself for the job of writing the report on the past day's work. Jadunath, always happy to be doing something he saw as moving ahead, tackled the task of running Soumitro-Whoever down to ground. It wasn't the most onerous of tasks. The cops had a database for vehicle owners. All Jadunath had to do was feed the relevant details into it. The only problem could be that Soumitro X had sold his car somewhere outside the state of West Bengal without registering the transaction, thus rendering the information in the database irrelevant. Happened, though not so often with the higher-end wheels like Mercs. And, indeed, Jadunath seemed to have got out of the right side of the bed in every way. The computer screen lit up the inspector's face: Soumitro Saha. The residential address was recorded as well. An upscale Elgin Road address as befitting the owner of a Merc. A couple of calls got him Mr Saha's mobile number and office address, without having to resort to any early-morning arm-twisting. The benefit of having friends in unlikely places.

Job done, Jadunath went up to Gopal to see whether he needed help. Between them (it wasn't clear whether Jadunath's help speeded up the task or delayed it), the report was done by 9:15, by which time, they reckoned, their boss would be safely in office. Tanya received the news and the report, and called Ramadhar and Mrinal immediately. 'This is the office address of our prospective accused,' she said, handing Ramadhar a piece of paper and a copy of Soumitro's photograph. 'Get there as fast as you can. It'll obviously be a block of flats. Take Ishita and Talukdar along. Make sure he doesn't bolt. His car is a silver-grey Mercedes, I've written down the registration number.'

Tanya gave Ramadhar and his team time to get to Soumitro's office and mount surveillance, then she called Soumitro Saha's number. The palaver was brief.

'Hello, this is Tanya Samanta on the line. I'm with Kolkata Police and I would like to have a few words with you urgently, Mr Saha.'

Crackle and a distant voice.

'Urgently means as soon as possible. In the next hour or so. Can you give me your office address? I'm guessing you aren't home at this hour. Alternatively, you could come over to Lalbazar.'

'About? It's about an incident that took place around a week ago and on which you may be able to shed some light, Mr Saha. May I ask what you do at Sreeguru Enterprises?'

'In an hour? Fine. The name's Tanya Samanta—T-A-N-Y-A S-A-M-A-N-T-A. Joint commissioner, Detective Department. I'll be waiting.'

Though they were listening to one side of the conversation, what had transpired couldn't be plainer. 'He owns a company called Sreeguru Enterprises. Said he'd be here after taking care of some work. Didn't seem rattled. What do you think?' Tanya asked her inspectors.

'Could be he's completely innocent. Hasn't connected the news coverage with the woman he met a week ago. Could be he doesn't read the papers or watch television,' Jadunath said. 'Doesn't seem very likely, though, does it?'

'Or could be he's guilty as hell, but figures he can brazen it out. Many people think that the coppers are easy to hoodwink. Maybe he's one of them. If that's true, he's in for a surprise,' Gopal said.

'Jadunath, Gopal. You'll be there when I interrogate him,' Tanya said. Now, all they could do was wait for Soumitro Saha to turn up. And he did. Making it to Police HQ not in his silver-grey Merc but on foot, perhaps because he didn't want the parking hassles. The detectives who had staked out the building inside which his office was located, alongside hundreds of other cubbyholes, spotted him as soon as he'd exited the building and didn't have any problem trailing him back to their office. Soumitro didn't seem worried or hurried; he walked at a normal, even pace and betrayed no obvious sense of nervousness. That could mean he was innocent, a fine actor or a complete cretin, his followers concluded. Once he'd made it to the enquiry desk, they dispersed to make their way to their offices.

Soumitro was soon knocking on a door with a nameplate that said Tanya Samanta, Joint Commissioner of Police (Crime). And he heard a voice say, 'Come in'. He'd never dealt with a female cop, though, as a fairly successful businessman, he had had to deal with many male officers. He entered to find a presentable woman behind the desk, though her extremely severe expression left no doubt in his mind that she wasn't there just to make up the numbers. Two other men, one burly and a touch surly, the other gangly, with a somewhat more pleasant expression, were seated on the opposite side of the desk. They stood up as soon as he entered. Without a hint of a greeting, the gangly one said, 'Mr Saha.'

Soumitro said, 'Yes.'

'Please, come with us,' the gangly officer said. Slightly dazed, Soumitro complied. He was taken to a middling-sized room and asked to sit, which he did. His companions did likewise. Nobody spoke. Finally, Soumitro broke the silence. 'Could you tell me what this is all about? I have to get back to work. I have a busy day ahead of me.'

The man who had addressed him, said, 'We're waiting for ma'am. As soon as she arrives, things will start moving.' Soumitro shut up, feeling slightly anxious for the first time that morning. The cops wouldn't summon him for anything related to his business. He ran a more or less clean shop, he thought. Jadunath's initial surmise hadn't been too far off the mark. Soumitro didn't spend a lot of time following the news. He read the pinks for news about the economy. Stuff that affected his business and, therefore, affected him. When he watched television, it was usually the business channels. He got the political news he needed to run his business by word of mouth. He'd seen some reports about a rape, but hadn't paid attention. Stuff like that was happening all the time, all over the place, he reckoned. The longer Tanya took to come to the room to begin the interrogation, the more worried he was getting. That was why Tanya was delaying her appearance. And that was also why Jadunath and Gopal were crowding Soumitro just by sitting in the same room, silent and impassive.

By the time Tanya made it to the room, Soumitro was sweating. And it wasn't because it was hot or humid. Tanya sat down. 'This interview will be taped, Mr Saha,' she began. Telling him, not asking for permission. She nodded and Jadunath switched on the video-recorder. 'JCP Tanya Samanta interviewing Mr Soumitro Saha in Room 312 in Lalbazar. Also present Inspector Gopal Barui and Inspector Jadunath Majumdar.' Tanya paused. 'You are the owner of Sreeguru Enterprises. What is your firm engaged in?'

'Actually, I'm a partner. I hold a 50 per cent stake. The rest is divided equally between my elder brother and father. But I run the firm. We make and export leather products to East Asia and East Europe. We have a factory producing stainless-steel utensils, which we sell in India. Apart from that, we export products we don't make.'

'You live in Elgin Road with whom?'

'My wife and daughter. She is fifteen years old. Class IX. My parents live in our ancestral house in Beliaghata, with my brother and his family. He has his own businesses. I have a sister who lives in Pittsburgh.' A mine of information.

Soumitro seemed open and frank. A little worried, which seemed to be in his favour. An innocent person summoned to Lalbazar and grilled would feel worried and likely show it. A guilty person as well, though.

'You frequent Sugarloaf, don't you? A couple of times a week.'

'I do. I like the place. A couple of times might be an exaggeration. I'm often held up by work.'

'You go there with four friends. Who are they?'

Soumitro looked distinctly more anxious. 'Old friends of mine. Same school, same neighbourhood. We grew up in Beliaghata.'

'We'll need names, addresses and occupations. Please don't try to get in touch with them until we say you can.'

'Robi Saha, he's a cousin; runs a gym in Beliaghata. Dipak Karmakar; manages the Central Hotel in Central

Avenue. Atanu Lahiri; runs a repair shop in Beliaghata. And Pabitra Kumar; teaches at Jadavpur University.'

'You were in Sugarloaf a week ago. When did you reach the bar and when did you leave?'

Soumitro was sweating profusely now. Could be he was just worried, could be he knew he had been nailed. 'I reached at around 8:30. The others reached by 9. Pabitra arrived first, minutes after me. We all left at around 12:30.' Borne out by the CCTV time-stamp.

'Just the five of you?'

Soumitro's eyes widened, his mouth opened soundlessly. 'There was a woman with us. I met her at Sugarloaf. We had a drink together and danced for a few minutes. I thought she'd find it a little difficult to get a cab, so, we helped her get one. Near Jeevan Deep. She was going to Behala. I don't remember her name.'

'You just said you live with your wife and fifteen-year-old daughter. You make a habit of befriending single women in bars, and drinking and dancing with them?'

Soumitro flushed. 'What makes my private life any of your business? You dragged me in here without a word of explanation. I've obliged you by showing up in the middle of a working day and answered questions about my private life. Who the hell are you to judge me?' The eager-to-please businessman was gone.

'Let me tell you something that won't be news to you, pal,' Tanya set off. 'The woman with whom you drank and danced, whose name you don't remember, woke up around four hours after she left with you, inside Minto Park, aching all over. When she managed to put her thoughts together, she realized she'd been raped. So how about accounting for your time between midnight and 0500 hours the next day? Before that, I want phone numbers and addresses, residential and workplace, for your friends. Now.'

Soumitro's brief flare of bravado had disappeared. He recited the names, numbers and addresses in a daze.

'Gopal, arrange for all of them to be picked up and brought here right now. Call them only if you can't find them.' Gopal left.

Soumitro stared at the floor. 'Ma'am,' he said, 'the four of us helped her find a cab. She'll tell you. I'll account for my movements. I dropped my friends at Beliaghata, all of them still live there. Then I went home. I didn't check the time, because I was too tired. It must have been past two in the morning. I went straight to sleep. My wife and daughter are at my in-laws' place in Shillong. Otherwise, I wouldn't have been out that late. I woke up at around nine in the morning. I reached office at around 11:30. That rarely happens unless I've got work elsewhere.'

Tanya looked at their prime suspect. They had no smoking gun, but he had no alibi. She glared at him. Then she said, 'You implied the woman was not in a condition to get a cab on her own. So, who negotiated the fare with the cabbie?'

'I did,' Soumitro said. 'He agreed to take her to Behala for Rs 200. I asked her if she had that much in cash. She scrabbled around in her bag. In the end, I just paid the cabbie. Ma'am, I go out drinking when I find the time. With old friends. To have a good time. We are all decent folk. We would never take advantage of a woman who was incapable of looking after herself. Believe me, please.' There was desperation in his plea and, Tanya thought, despite herself (because Soumitro and company had already been nominated for the rapists' role) that there was some sincerity as well. It could be fake, but it was there.

'Well, well,' said Tanya. 'You were concerned about your new acquaintance. Yet, you dumped her in a cab and left her to fend for herself. You could have dropped her home, since you were traipsing half-way around the city anyway. But that isn't a crime. Did you note the number of the cab? You were driving. After how many drinks? You were at the bar for four hours.'

'I never ever have more than three large ones. And you are right. We should have dropped her home. I'd have got home an hour later, maximum. It was an error of judgement. But we keep thinking that Calcutta is safe for women, however late the hour. We forget it's changed. I should have thought about that. Shit!'

His contrition seemed genuine. But Tanya was a cynic because she'd seen people as guilty as they could possibly get act even better than Soumitro. If he was acting. 'I'm afraid, Mr Saha, you'll have to be our guest until we can sort this matter out. Would you like some water, a cup of tea? You're entitled to consult a lawyer at any point of time.'

Soumitro let out a huge sigh. 'Both water and tea. I'll waive the lawyer.'

Tanya and Jadunath left. Gopal stayed, but remained completely silent, ignoring Soumitro, but looking at him furtively. Though Soumitro had no way of knowing it, this was just a part of the softening-up process. Stick and carrot. He'd remain in the room till all his companions had been brought in and questioned, separately. Till all the five versions had been compared. The cops had twenty-four hours. Almost. That was a lot of time.

It took a couple of hours for three cops to round up the four friends, Pabitra being the toughest to run to ground. They were all interviewed at Lalbazar, Robi proving to be the stroppiest of the lot. Stroppy or not, Tanya had his measure. The realization that they weren't going anywhere until all questions had been answered, and transcripts prepared and signed, cooled even Robi down. When he threatened to leave—'let's see who stops me'—Tanya had him put into a lock-up. Fifteen minutes behind bars worked magic. But neither Robi nor his friends, including Soumitro, the most obliging among the generally cooperative men, could leave before the statements were tallied and further rounds of interrogation conducted if necessary. In fact, none of them could leave until the police, specifically JCP Tanya Samanta, were satisfied that they could be provisionally considered witnesses rather than suspects. Even if the police released them, they would be produced in court the next day for bail to be posted.

Luckily for them, their versions matched, but not suspiciously so. They had been having a good time. Not all of them had been as cautious as Soumitro, because they drank more in any case and none of them had to drive. Childhood friend or no, Soumitro would never let anyone drive his beloved Merc. If the dissonances in their accounts had been choreographed, Tanya told members of her extended team as they compared the five versions of what had happened that evening, night and next morning, they were either natural-born criminals or had extensive criminal experience. The former did not seem to be the case and the latter could be discounted since a sweep of their backgrounds had revealed that none of them had any criminal record whatsoever.

During the fresh round of questioning, Tanya asked Soumitro a crucial question: 'What do you remember of the cabbie?'

'He was tall and kind of gaunt. I think he had a slight stoop.'

'How could you tell while he was sitting in his cab?'

'Ma'am, he got out of the cab. He was on the fair side. His head was shaven. I remember the man not so much for his looks, but because he spoke like an educated man. Maybe that lulled me into a sense of security.'

'When you were talking to the cabbie was anyone else around? Other cabbies. People waiting to hail cabs. Anyone who could have noticed the licence-plate details?'

'There was no one anywhere near. Even if people had noticed, I doubt they would have noted it.' Everyone's becoming an expert, thought Tanya. The problem was that most people did not understand that cases were usually broken by routine work and attention to detail. Not virtuoso feats of logical reconstruction, because criminals were rarely logicians and clairvoyants rarely joined the police force.

With minor changes (or embellishments) the other men's description of the cabbie matched Soumitro's. They had only seen him from inside the car and had vague impressions, plus they hadn't heard him speak. Which made Soumitro's impressions critical. In any event, not much remained to be done. The five men were set free; the team was dismissed for the day; the officers left, with a collective exhalation of relief.

The next morning, Tanya went through the case notes and interview transcripts with a fresh eye, absorbing them with a refreshed mind. Tanya felt let down, partly because she felt she had let Gloria down in the first place. But a lot of things pointed to the innocence of the men picked up; she had no grounds to hold them. She could have issued an appeal for information on cab drivers who had taken a somewhat inebriated passenger from Jeevan Deep to Behala, but considering the fact that if Soumitro and his friends were telling the truth, it was very likely that it was the cab driver himself who was the rapist, she didn't think there was any point.

Tanya called Jadunath and Gopal for some brainstorming. Sitting in her office waiting for something to happen would bug her no end. 'What do you think? Are these guys telling the truth? Are you getting any sense of the case?' she asked. If they had to get anywhere anytime soon, they'd have to glean some kind of insight. Spot something that was missing, fast, because the case was more than a week old. Trails have a tendency of petering out within forty-eight hours. In a week, they practically became archaeological dig sites. But Jadunath and Gopal's night of rest had not provided them with fresh angles, even though they too had combed through the files in the morning.

Something was tugging at Tanya's mind, though. She picked up the file and riffled through it. Musing aloud, she said, 'Does the description of the cab driver ring any bells?' She lifted the transcript of Soumitro's second interview and read aloud: 'I remember he was tall, gaunt, stooped and on the fair side. His head was shaven. Age, fifty or so. Certainly middle-aged. I remember the man not because of his looks, but because he spoke like an educated man.' She looked up, 'Soumitro's no fool and he wasn't plastered. So, we have to take his description seriously. If a cabbie speaks like an educated man, he must *be* one.'

'Depends, doesn't it?' said Gopal. 'What sounds educated to most people would not necessarily sound educated to Soumitro. He must have gone to a fairly good school and college. His diction is quite polished. So, the cabbie had to be speaking in a pretty educated way.'

'You're right,' Tanya said. 'We have to locate a taxi driver who's well educated and whose speech betrays his background. Any takers?' They laughed. The community of taxi drivers in Calcutta was fluid. Not only did cabbies move from one profession to another depending on opportunity and profitability, but they also moved frequently between the city and the village they came from, usually in Bihar. When one left for home, his place would be taken by another because few drivers owned their cars.

When a guy returned from his village sojourn, he would normally either drive the taxi he used to drive or find another one, failing which he could start driving a three-wheeler, a bus or a goods vehicle. He could even change professions totally. In the event of finding nothing adequately remunerative, he could go back to his village or relocate to another city. Mumbai and Delhi were always there to beckon job-seekers. He could return to the city, say, five years later. In other words, the community of taxi drivers was very mobile. It was also a closed one.

Going around asking questions or trying to locate an individual usually had the effect of shutting people up. And if there was the merest suspicion that it was the fuzz that was asking the questions, a stone wall would suddenly be erected. Taxi drivers had a siege mentality because their relations with the taxi-riding public was less than cordial. Moreover, union records were sketchy. They had to be because of the character of the trade. So, looking for an educated taxi driver with a polished diction was a bit of a joke. There was also the chance that the mystery man was a college student or an unemployed man driving a taxi one evening just for a lark. Nevertheless, it was a lead to be chased down.

Tanya decided that Talukdar was ideal for the job, because he had been working out of the Park Street *thana* for a number of years, knew the area well and should have access to a network of informants. Talukdar was duly summoned and Tanya explained what she had in mind. After that came a chapter of reversions. Ishita and Ramadhar reverted to a city-wide string of burglaries, aggravated frequently by apparently needless violence, they had been working on. Gopal and Mrinal reverted to a case linking the lynching of two people—a man and a woman—suspected to be 'child-lifters', as the English-language media insisted on calling kidnappers.

Jadunath reverted to a murder in a posh south Calcutta neighbourhood. Talukdar had nothing to revert to, except Park Street PS, which was why he stayed with the case.

That suited Talukdar, because he did not want to revert to Park Street PS, even though his former and particularly unloved boss had been transferred to the boondocks of Egra, a town in East Medinipur district in south-western Bengal, 115 kilometres from Calcutta as the crow flies. He wanted to nail the taxi driver who had raped Gloria. Talukdar was by and large a mild-mannered man and a law-abiding cop. But some things pressed the wrong buttons for him. One day, he heard from an informant about a graduate who drove a cab. He tracked him down to his home and went there with Ramadhar who happened to be at a loose end. Talukdar took the man to Lalbazar. He who looked like he was in his late twenties or early thirties, was tall and gaunt, but was neither stooped, nor particularly fair. He had very short hair that could in some circumstances give the appearance of a shaven head. He spoke like an educated man, because he was. His name was Ananta Haldar and he had a Master's degree in Philosophy from the University of Calcutta.

'Where were you around midnight, eleven days ago?' Talukdar asked.

'Midnight? In bed, asleep. I go to sleep at eleven every night.'

'Do you live alone?'

'Yes,' Haldar said.

'Can anyone confirm you were at home?'

Haldar thought for a moment and said, 'No.'

'What if I said you picked up a passenger near Jeevan Deep?'

'Jeevan Deep?' The man seemed genuinely taken aback. 'No, I haven't been there in a long time.'

Suddenly, the easy-going Talukdar exploded. He shouted at the man, 'You fucking piece of shit, you're fucking lying. You want me to beat the shit and the truth out of you?' He took a couple of paces forward and, uncharacteristically, Ramadhar had to cool things down. Usually, it was Ramadhar who went ballistic. He placed a restraining hand on Talukdar's shoulder. Talukdar backed off, realizing that Soumitro's description didn't fit the man. 'Go,' he said.

'Take it easy, brother,' Ramadhar said. 'Want to tell me what all that was about?'

Talukdar agreed and they headed to a nearby roadside tea shack. Talukdar said, 'Rape really sets me off.' He remained silent for a while. 'I had a sister,' he continued. 'Two years younger than me. We were very close, especially after we lost our mother. I was just thirteen. She later got married to a man we used to know from childhood; lived in our neighbourhood. He got a job in Jaipur and three months after they moved there, two men barged into their house in broad daylight and raped her. The police did nothing. Nothing, literally. Like my cock-sucking OC in Park Street. I'd like to kill him as well. My sister committed suicide about a month after that. I went to Jaipur and tried to persuade the cops to investigate. After all, I was also a cop. I realized the rapists must have had political protection. My life's ambition was to kill rapists with my bare hands. I've cooled down now, but every now and then, I feel like that. I want to kill Gloria's rapist.'

Ramadhar stayed silent and they went back to work.

Tanya, too, remained with the case, at the very least in spirit. Having redeployed her troops, she was really pissed off. One case had already been burning a hole in her unsolved tray, another was threatening to do so. In her book, the Clayton Garcia case had to be closed out—with his arrest and long-term incarceration and Gloria deserved to see her tormentor brought to book. Tanya knew that she didn't have all the time in the world to do these and suspected they wouldn't get done unless they got done pretty damn soon. But the outside was a couple of years, because after that she would be moved out of the post of joint commissioner, DD, in accordance with the force's long-established transfer (and promotion) policy.

The harsh ring of the phone interrupted Tanya's musings. It was her boss. 'Samanta, please come to my office immediately,' was his terse command. Tanya jumped to it. 'Problems, Samanta,' Chanda said. 'We've got another rape victim dumped near another lake in the small hours. Today. In Santoshpur. Luckily, the Jadavpur *thana* OC has more sense than Biswas. You'll need to take a team to Jadavpur first. Speak to the cops there. The OC is a man called Ronojoy Mishra. Scene of crime, scene where she was dumped. And, of course, as many interviews as you need to do.

'The victim's name is Aparna Das. She's middle-aged. Divorced and lives in Santoshpur's Survey Park area with a nineteen-year-old daughter and an eighteen-year-old son.

Was returning from a relative's place in Belghoria. Long trek. Boarded a train late evening, which stalled at Park Circus because of some kind of power failure, I think. Took a bus from Park Circus to Jadavpur *thana*, by which time it was getting seriously late. Called her daughter just before 11 and told her she was taking a cab. After that, she went off air. Her children tried to call her, but her phone seemed to have been switched off. They debated going to the police, but since it was already midnight, they thought they'd wait till morning. Woman woke up near the big lake in the Survey Park area at around 5 a.m. Couldn't remember anything at first, just like the Stevens girl, though she was stone-cold sober. Then, remembered being assaulted by the cabbie. From her account, he had hit her on the head and stunned her. Then raped her in the cab. Afterwards, he took her into the shrubbery, knocked her out and left.'

'Serial,' Tanya whispered. 'I'm on my way.' In minutes, she'd pulled the Gloria team back, brought the others up to speed and left for Jadavpur with Gopal, Jadunath and Ishita.

Part Three

Santoshpur, Calcutta, June

~

Tanya and her team made it to Jadavpur *thana* in good time, shaking hands, so to speak, with OC Mishra in under an hour. The IO, ASI Sukalyan Giri, filled them in. They learned that Mrs Das was in shock. The events of the night before and the early hours of the day had been 'pieced together' from her disconnected narrative. 'Creatively?' Tanya asked.

Giri nodded. 'She's in no state to make a coherent statement. She has been escorted by two officers from the police station to the hospital where she will be examined. Both are female officers, an ASI and a constable. After she's tested, she will stay in hospital till she recovers. We can't talk to her till the doctors give the go-ahead.'

'No way,' Tanya expostulated. 'We lost almost a week when this started. You know the trail grows colder with every passing minute.' Nerves frayed, temper on hair trigger.

Giri said, 'Ma'am, I tried, but she can barely speak.' What he did not tell his senior officer was, let's not waste our time; let's allow her to recover. He continued, 'We haven't spoken to the children. Would you like to see the crime scene, ma'am?'

Tanya cooled down. Fast. 'Okay. Let her recover. She'll

probably be able to reconstruct the evening faster if we let her be.' Businesslike. 'I want to speak to the children. And, yes, we'll go the crime scene first. Of course, it may not be the crime scene at all. After that,' she gestured at the team first and then at Giri, 'you will speak to neighbours to find out about the family. How they fitted in; their routines.' She turned to Giri. 'We'll need more officers when you canvass the area.'

Giri nodded. 'Yes, ma'am.'

They left for the small lake—or pretty big pond—by which Aparna had woken in the early hours; the four officers from Lalbazar and two from Jadavpur, including Giri, in his capacity, soon to be relinquished, as IO. Two-thirds of the lake was surrounded by thick underbrush and some isolated trees. About a third was an open grass verge that allowed access to the lake. This didn't face the road. A picket consisting of two very bored constables was guarding the spot where Aparna had woken up, just deep enough into the underbrush to prevent it from being spotted from the road.

Giri and Jadunath went gingerly into the area and had a look around. They'd have to get crack forensic teams from the US to find anything. Kolkata Police budgets didn't run to crack Crime Scene Investigation (CSI) teams. With their naked eyes, however, they made out a relatively clean line of disturbance connecting the road with the spot where the victim had been dumped, marked by a human body-shaped indentation, and a relatively erratic line of disturbance connecting it to the road. It didn't take CSI teams to figure out that the cleaner line was the one taken by the rapist when he went in to dump the victim and the other was the route taken by Mrs Das when she desperately scrambled her way out of it. Tanya went over to join the men. 'It's obvious,' she said. 'Keep the place out of bounds, just in case.'

Tanya then went back to Jadavpur PS with the others, taking possession of the crime file. Giri had been thorough about making a list of immediate neighbours and providing addresses and phone numbers. Once these formalities had been completed, Tanya asked Giri to accompany her and Gopal to the Das home, which was, they discovered, pretty close to the place Aparna had found herself, which led Giri to speculate about a connection. This line of speculation was scotched abruptly by Tanya. 'She'd taken a cab. Must have given the cabbie the general area where she wanted to go. Like, near the big pond in Survey Park,' she said. Giri shut up, suitably abashed.

At the flat where the family lived, the son and daughter were being looked after by a cousin of their mother's. If they had been in shock, they had recovered somewhat. Police protection had been offered and refused, but a police van was, nevertheless, parked outside the building. Having introduced all three of them, she asked the two children, Darshan and Debjani, what they did. Debjani was studying Mathematics at Jadavpur University, still in her first year; Darshan was in the final year of school. 'And what did your mother do?' asked Tanya.

'She worked as an insurance agent,' Debjani answered. 'She had been working in the same office for the past fifteen years.' Past tense, Tanya noted with surprise. Usually, friends and relatives of even murder victims kept using the present tense until the truth finally sank in.

'What were her normal hours?'

'Her hours are not fixed. Some days she doesn't have to go out at all. Does her work over the telephone.' Darshan this time.

'And what are your hours, Darshan?'

'I get back from school at about 3:30. After that, I have to go for private tuitions almost every day. Usually, I leave at around 5 and return at 8:30-9. I don't go out after that, unless I have to go to the shops or something. On weekends, I go out with friends for a few hours in the evenings. Have my board exams next year, so I can't fool around much.' That inestimable rite of passage: the board examinations, your ticket out of school and into college. In most cases, the passage from childhood to adulthood.

'And you?' Tanya asked, turning to Debjani.

'I leave for university around 9:30 and I'm home by 5:30. After that, I don't go out much, unless I'm going to watch a film or something. Sometimes I go somewhere else from the university and get back a little late. Rarely later than 8 though.'

'I'm sure both of you help your mother to run the house?'

'Darshan does most of the shopping and goes to the market every other morning and I help around the house. We have a cook. And a woman who does the cleaning. So, there isn't that much to do.'

'You have friends in the neighbourhood? Do you socialize?'

'Not really. We know a few people and we say hi and hello, but we don't have close friends. We don't hang out here,' said Darshan.

'Your mother?'

'Same with her. She knew many people, but didn't have close friends. Mostly of the hi-and-hello variety,' Debjani said.

They'd have to canvass the area, Tanya thought. Was it natural to have only a few friends in the neighbourhood? Then she thought of herself: divorcee with a kid, living in a building with eight flats in it. How many of her immediate neighbours had she had over to her flat? Not one. How many kids in the building did her son play with? None. Mainly because there were no kids in the building close to his age. Maybe the Das family was not so unusual. She gave Debjani her card. 'If you need anything, you can get in touch with me. Or, you can talk to officers in Jadavpur. For the next few days, a police car will be parked in front of your house twenty-four hours. I know you've said you don't want protection, but you'll get it in any case.' She smiled at the boy and the girl.

Outside, Tanya got the neighbourhood canvass organized. Giri, being a local, was elected point man. Members of the DD team and officers from Jadavpur PS would participate.

'I'm not getting a sense of what's going on,' Tanya said on the way back to HQ. 'Seems like a normal middle-class family doing completely normal things.'

'Ma'am, I think it's a crime of opportunity. We should look at the other end. Canvass the area around Jadavpur *thana* and try to locate the cabbie and the cab. The Jadavpur PS people can do that. You know how cabbies work, ma'am. They usually pick up fares from their area to begin with, then, of course, they have to move around. The good news is that it was 11 p.m. or later when Mrs Das hailed the cab and the cabbie agreed to take her. That has to mean that the cabbie's garage is in the Jadavpur or Santoshpur area. That late, no Calcutta cabbie would be ferrying passengers outside his patch unless he was going to one of the big railway stations or the airport,' Gopal said.

'You could be right, Gopal. Get on the case tomorrow.'

Giri supervised the canvass of the neighbourhood over the next four days. They weren't looking for sightings of the cab or the cabbie. Not really. They were just trying to establish mobility patterns and, especially, in the light of what the kids had said about not really having friends on the block, about what the people in the area thought of the Das family.

In all, a team of eight greatly overworked cops, sometimes working solo, sometimes in pairs, interviewed close to 600 people from 162 families over four days. Precautions had been taken for a number of reasons to prevent the circumstances of Aparna's hospitalization from being publicized. The police just said she had had been attacked, which come to think of it was the truth, and was temporarily incapable of remembering precisely what had happened. Even her family had been told she had been assaulted, not raped. It would be Aparna's call, when she recovered, to disclose whatever details to whomsoever she chose.

When the reports of the interviews were read, summarized and reduced to a report in bullet points by analysts, what they amounted to was just about a row of beans. Most of the people didn't know the family too well and didn't have an opinion beyond obvious ones. They'd seen the family and smiled or said polite, meaningless words in passing. That was the first category. Some people knew them a little better. Like some women of Aparna's generation who didn't really visit each other or have each other's mobile numbers, but who would stop and exchange pleasantries in the market or on the street if they weren't stretched for time. They found her a pleasant, well-spoken woman. Take Nilanjana Karmakar, 51, housewife. She would occasionally stop to talk to Aparna on the streets, exchange pleasantries on the state of the weather, swap recipes and talk about the difficulties of bringing up teenage children. 'Very nice woman. Very responsible. It's not easy to earn a living, run a household and take care of two children you know, but she managed quite well and very quietly. Not showy at all,' she told the police. Some of the younger lot knew Darshan or Debjani or both a little better and seemed to have generally positive views about them. Studious, sober, but pleasant and polite. That was the second category.

In the third, microscopic category, were those who qualified as friends. They numbered thirteen. Four women who knew Aparna quite well, four who were similarly friendly with Debjani and five friends of Darshan's. The youngsters were friends of the hang-out-together-in-the-neighbourhood variety, rather than of the visit-each-other-at-home variety. Darshan's friends included three who went to the same school and they bonded mostly by playing various sports together. Mainly cricket, of course, in a city that had turned its back on its football heritage. Debjani's friends were girls who'd occasionally go for a film together, otherwise hang around in the area. Two of them went to Jadavpur University, but studied different subjects. Being friends, they had no mean things to say about the two.

Aparna's friends weren't friends of the same sort. They were all working women who also managed the house and brought up children. One of them, a widow, was a single mother. This is what tied them together. They had each other's numbers and would chat on the phone when they found the time. Sometimes they'd go shopping together or, rarely, for a show. Not necessarily all of them together, of course. They weren't a group in any sense. They had much the same to say about her. Industrious, responsible and pleasant. Not given much to gossip. In short, thought Tanya, anodyne, useless.

Why couldn't people be more honest in their opinions? She knew why, obviously. Because people did not want to speak to the cops in the first place and, when they didn't have the option, would rather say something inoffensive and stay off the radar screen. Tanya knew that some people must have disapproved of Aparna because she was a divorcee, assuming there was something wrong with her, 'loose morals' perhaps. But under the circumstances, they would hardly express such opinions to the uniforms.

The attempt to locate the cabbie had been a complete waste of time. Giri said he must have been from out of the area and was maybe a night-shift driver. There were a few of those. They'd do something else in the day and work late evenings to the very early hours, when they could earn serious premiums.

Which meant that all Tanya and her team could do was wait for the green light from the doctors before talking to the person who could best shine a light on the incident.

Enquiries were instituted at the hospital. The doctor in charge of Aparna's treatment told Ishita, who had been given the task of urging the doctors to allow the police access, that though the patient was physically much better and could even be released in a few days, she was still in shock. Understandably. And she was not in a position to talk to the police. The trail gets colder with every passing day, Ishita had tried to explain. 'We understand that,' the doctor had replied, 'but my patient and her health come first.' There had been more back and forth along these lines before Ishita had given up. When she reported to Tanya, she was livid, but there was nothing she could do. She conceded that a few more days of waiting would perhaps be for the best.

So, what could be a double rape was stuck in a quagmire. Even if it wasn't a double rape, the JCP

(Crime) was stuck with two rapes. In one, a taxi driver had presumptively raped a woman, dumped her in Minto Park and disappeared. In that case, they had some kind of description of the man but a weaker case against the cabbie. In the other, a taxi driver had raped a woman and disappeared. They hadn't the faintest clue about that one, apart from the presumption that the same man had committed both the crimes. All Tanya and her team could do was wait. And since other cases demanded attention, Tanya once again found herself drifting away from the case, getting caught up in administrative and supervisory matters that were really her territory.

Ishita had, however, been kept on hospital lookout. Three days later, she arrived at Tanya's office, bright and early, and told her somewhat breathlessly, 'Ma'am, Mrs Das has told the doctors she wants to talk to us. We can go see her in the hospital today, anytime. She's going to be discharged tomorrow.'

Tanya sprang up. 'Let's go,' she said.

In about an hour, they were talking to the doctor. 'I must insist that you don't upset her, Mrs Samanta,' she began.

'Ms,' Tanya said.

The doctor ignored her interjection. 'She has undergone unbelievable mental trauma. Reliving it will not be good for her. I'm sure you will understand, as a senior officer, that the most important thing is that she should be helped to rebuild her life. She is pressured by being the only breadwinner of the family with two children to look after. Let her tell her story as she wants to. Do not push her.'

As a senior officer? What's seniority got to do with empathy? Tanya thought. But she was diplomatic. 'Don't worry,' she said. 'We won't upset her.'

The woman in the hospital bed looked every bit her age. Physically, she seemed to have recovered. The bruises that must have been there had healed. And she looked well nourished. But she was also pale, with a haunted look in her eyes, which made her seem not so well after all. 'Sit,' she said, gesturing at two chairs beside her bed. 'How are you feeling, Mrs Das?' Tanya asked, aware of the vacuity of her question.

'Getting better,' Aparna said, without bitterness. Her response had the ring of sincerity. She's not a victim, Tanya thought, just like Gloria. She did the introductions. 'I'm Tanya Samanta, joint commissioner in charge of the Detective Department. I'm heading the investigation personally, Mrs Das. And this is my colleague, Constable Ishita Pal.' Aparna nodded and sat up straight. 'Would you like to tell us what you remember?' Tanya asked softly.

Aparna remained silent for a while. 'I can't remember all the details after a point,' she said, and relapsed into silence. Tanya and Ishita, too, remained silent. Aparna resumed her story after a while. She seemed to be looking at something far away and her voice seemed to be coming from somewhere far away as well. 'I had gone to Belghoria to visit a cousin. She's hasn't been keeping well. I reached her house around 6:30 in the evening. I'd thought I'd spend an hour or so with her and get home in time for dinner. But she insisted we have an early dinner. I couldn't refuse, especially because I knew I wouldn't be visiting anytime soon, given the distance and the transport difficulties.' She paused. 'Some water?' Tanya asked. Aparna reached out for her glass and had a few sips.

'By the time we sat down to eat it was already 8:30. I'd called the children and told them I'd be late. By the time I left my cousin's place it was almost 9:30. I took a train to Bidhannagar station and went to Ultadanga to get a bus. The bus broke down in Park Circus and it took time to get another one. By the time I got to Jadavpur *thana,* it was getting seriously late—past 11—and I spotted a taxi from the bus. So, I got down and took the risk of persuading him to go to Survey Park. I was surprised that he readily agreed. I remember the taxi passing the Santoshpur Lake. After that, he stopped and hit me on the head and raped me. I was semi-conscious. Then the taxi began to move again and stopped after a while. He hit me on the head and I became unconscious. Then I woke up next to the pond.' She seemed to be on the verge of tears, but managed to control herself.

There was silence in the room. That was a very clear statement, considering everything, Tanya thought. With trepidation, Tanya asked, 'Did you note the number of the taxi, Mrs Das?' Aparna shook her head. 'I know I should have, but it was getting late. I was flustered. And then I was so relieved that he agreed that I just got in.'

'That was quite natural,' Tanya said. 'Can you remember what he looked like? Tall, short? Fat or thin? Complexion? Any distinguishing features?' She felt foolish. Who the hell gave a cab driver anything but the most cursory of looks? But Aparna nodded. 'I remember. Since he was sitting, I can't tell you whether he was tall or short. Medium height, I suppose. But he was fair and lean. His cheeks were sunken and his head was shaven.'

Tanya and Ishita felt a jolt of electricity run through them, but remained impassive. 'Mrs Das, thank you for talking to us. You've been very helpful. If you need anything, don't hesitate to get in touch. Your children have my personal number and the office numbers. Please rest. I'll drop by to see you some time.' Aparna eased down, feeling a little reassured. Sometimes JCP Tanya Samanta had that effect on people.

Neither woman spoke before they'd left the hospital. Once they were in the car on the way back to headquarters, Ishita said in an awestruck voice, 'It's him, ma'am.' Tanya kept silent for a while. Then said, 'We'll get him.' To herself she said, 'We're going to get you, you bastard.'

~

Back at headquarters, Tanya summoned a post-lunch meeting of the entire team, including ASI Giri from Jadavpur PS. 'First, we need a sketch of this taxi driver from Soumitro. He wasn't flustered and he was sober. Get him in with an artist and do a sketch. Later, we'll take it to Mrs Das and see how it matches her memory. Ramadhar it's your responsibility to get this organized, today.' Ramadhar smiled broadly. He relished these situations. They gave him the opportunity to kick ass. Tanya continued, 'Any ideas about what we can do with this sketch?'

Jadunath cleared his throat, as he always did before

saying something he considered important. 'There are a few circuits through which the sketch must be taken, I think. First, we can show it to random cabbies in the Park Street-Theatre Road-Russell Street area because that was where he was engaged. That's a long shot. Second,' he continued professorially, 'all the police stations in that area must be given large numbers of copies to be circulated among its personnel with a red-alert level warning that this man is dangerous and anyone spotting him must act immediately. Third, we have to take the sketch to the associations of taxi owners and taxi-drivers' unions. Obviously, their office staff will not be able to recognize it, but it has to be done. More important, we have to get a list of taxi owners and go around to them individually to see whether one of them has rented out his vehicle out to this man.' Jadunath's statement was comprehensive.

Tanya asked for more opinions. Giri said, 'I suppose the sketch has to go to Jadavpur PS as well, along with Gariahat and Lake PS. Maybe, it should be circulated to all *thana*s in the Esplanade-Dalhousie area, perhaps all of central Calcutta.'

That would be a hell of a lot of *thana*s, thought Tanya. 'Both of you are right. We should go for maximum coverage and all *thana*s have to be warned that maximal attention must be paid.'

Gopal could be professorial as well. 'We should look at the profiles of the victims and the situations, ma'am.'

'Go on,' Tanya said.

'Gloria was returning from a bar and she may have been drunk. The problem is that she didn't find the taxi near the bar. Soumitro found it almost a kilometre away where there are no bars. A taxi driver who is inclined to sexually assaulting women wouldn't wait for these kinds of random chances. It would make sense to park near the bars and wait for vulnerable targets.' He stopped. Tanya nodded him on. 'The second case is purely opportunistic as well. He could not possibly have known that he would get the kind of fare he did. It could have been anyone. I'm trying to say that if this man is a predator, which he obviously is, and he is psychopathic, as I understand the word, he is not ungoverned. He will prey, but only when he can escape undetected. Nevertheless, I think we should pull CCTV footage in the Park Street and Theatre Road area to scan the roads around the bars.'

'I think you're right Gopal, unfortunately. We've got a kind of psychopathic sexual predator, but one who doesn't feel compelled to indulge himself at a given point of time. He can wait until he finds the perfect opportunity. I have another problem with this situation. We have a sexual predator who drives a taxi. So, either he's just come to the city or he's preyed before. If he's preyed before, why don't we know about it? How many rapes are reported in Calcutta every year?'

Piya Kanungo, an SI with a penchant for statistics, spoke up. 'Over the past five years, the total would be 70-80, ma'am, I think. Given that most rapes, as much as 90 per cent perhaps, are committed by people known to the victim, I would say that not more than in an average of four cases annually have we failed to identify the rapist. That's about twenty cases or less.'

'Excellent,' the JCP (Crime) said. 'So now we know what we have to do going ahead. Ramadhar's handling Soumitro and the artist.' Ramadhar, who wasn't overly fond of attending meetings had, in fact, already left to carry out his assigned task. Tanya looked around. Didn't find him as she had expected. 'Jadunath, coordinate with Ramadhar. Assemble the team that is going to take it to the taxi people and the drivers' union, get the lists and all of that. As soon as the sketch is ready, start running.' Jadunath, another meeting sceptic, was already on his feet.

Tanya continued. 'Piya, pull the records for every rape case in the last five years in which the rapist wasn't identified. After that, work with Gopal to eliminate cases in which a taxi driver could not have been involved. If Gopal's busy, come to me.' Piya, drafted into the team after the second rape, remained seated, obviously not sharing Ramadhar and Jadunath's antipathy to meetings. 'Gopal, you and Mrinal pull CCTV tapes. Begin at Sugarloaf. Also, pull our CCTV tapes. Ishita whichever team you're with, I'll need you to go with the artist to Mrs Das for her version of the man.'

~

Ramadhar might not have been the most communicative of men, but whatever job was on hand he got done on a priority basis. Without fanfare. As soon as he'd been given his assignment, he left the meeting and got in touch with the police artist. 'Ramadhar from DD. Got a job for you,' he growled over the phone.

'Well, I'm busy,' Shashanka, the artist, told him.

'Doing what, sitting around with your thumb up your ass. Get it out and be ready. I'm bringing a guy in to get a sketch done. Hopefully, in an hour or so.' He didn't wait for a reply. In twenty minutes, he was in Soumitro Saha's office. A middle-aged lady was at the reception.

'Want to meet Mr Saha,' Ramadhar said.

'May I know your name, sir?'

'Ramadhar Tiwari from Kolkata Police.'

The receptionist blanched. And quickly called Soumitro. 'You can go in, sir. That door.' She gestured.

Ramadhar knocked once and strode into Soumitro's chamber. 'Mr Saha,' he said, taking a chair. 'We have an emergency. You have to accompany me to the headquarters—now.'

Soumitro looked as if he'd been hit with something blunt. 'What's the matter? I've told you all I know.'

'You won't be interrogated. We need your help. You should be back in a few hours.'

'Hours,' Soumitro said. It was true that Ramadhar had said 'a few hours' as if he had been suggesting a quick smoke or cup of tea, fifteen minutes max. 'I have lots of work, which I can't postpone. If you'd given me notice ...'

'If I could have given you notice, Mr Saha, I would have been in a different profession.'

'Look, if this has anything to do with what happened that night, I want to help. I want that cabbie nailed as badly as any of you. But I've got important work. Can't we do this tomorrow?'

'When will you be free today?'

Soumitro looked at his desk diary and said, '7 p.m.'

'Fine. Ask for me. I'm SI Ramadhar Tiwari. They'll point you in the right direction.' He made a call. 'Shashanka,' he began, without preliminaries. 'We'll start at 7:30.' That's it. He disconnected and said, 'Be there by 7:30, Mr Saha. It's important.' With that, he left, leaving Soumitro shell-shocked.

Back in Lalbazar, Jadunath was assembling his team. It consisted initially, apart from him, of Ishita and Talukdar. He'd rope in Ramadhar, who'd be free after the sketch was done. But he needed more manpower. For the moment, he refrained from bothering his boss.

Piya went to central records and despite the difficulties, managed to get into the system and after diligent trawling well into the evening succeeded in getting her job done. She had a list of fourteen cases spread over twelve police station jurisdictions, along with all the reference numbers and whatever details central records had of the cases.

Mrinal's return to Sugarloaf, this time with Gopal, didn't quite make Probir Guha's day, but he was willing to cooperate in his own oily way. When they asked him to pull the rest of the footage from the night of the rape, however, his face registered dismay. 'If I may ask, officers, is there anything specific you want to see?'

Both the cops remained silent for a while. After figuring out that being specific would also help them save time, Gopal said, 'We want to see the images of the street in front of your establishment.'

'But our cameras don't cover the street. They focus on the doorway going in and the other cameras are inside.

You won't find anything. In any case, we gave you all the tapes.' The two officers left. After visiting at least twenty establishments over four hours and being given the same story, they returned to Lalbazar to find that everyone had gone home other than the indefatigable Ramadhar, who, they were informed, was with Shashanka and someone else doing something or the other. With this underwhelming bit of information ringing in their ears, they, too, went home.

Ramadhar had waited patiently, finishing tasks related to other cases in progress. Soumitro, true to his word, had walked into headquarters at around 7:10. By 7:30, he had been ensconced with Ramadhar and Shashanka to help make a sketch of the man into whose cab he had delivered Gloria. The work proceeded quickly, because Soumitro had both a good memory and a thing about faces. It took a couple of hours to get the sketch done to Soumitro's satisfaction. The problem was that when it was completed and Ramadhar, as master of ceremonies, was handed it for inspection, he almost had a heart attack, but recovered fast. 'Are you sure this was the man?' he asked Soumitro.

Surprised, Soumitro said, 'Pretty sure.'

'Not mistaking him for someone else?'

'No.'

Ramadhar nodded, face still pale, but otherwise composed.

Soumitro offered to drop them somewhere convenient. Shashanka was going in the opposite direction. Ramadhar, too. In any case, he had a bike. A 500 cc Bullet, which he cherished as much as Soumitro cherished his Merc. Ramadhar lived nearby, in a neighbourhood called Taltala, close to Sealdah station. It was a ten-minute ride. Ramadhar was a tough guy, but he was also a kind of home bird. Though he was born and bred in Calcutta, he had married a girl from his native Bihar, chosen by his family. His wife didn't like Calcutta and escaped to Samastipur, her home, whenever she had the chance. And sometimes when she didn't. When they'd had their child, a daughter, she'd mooted the idea of relocating to Bihar. Ramadhar had shot down that idea without ceremony. That had been sixteen years ago. His wife had responded by making long trips to Patna with their daughter, Aakriti. Ramadhar had not protested because he had to spend long hours, including days off, at work.

After Aakriti started going to school, Ramadhar had to look after his daughter and run the household for over half the year. He didn't protest, because he didn't like hassle in his personal life, he got enough at work, which he didn't mind. He just got on with what had to be done. His daughter would return to school by herself, now that she was old enough. On this day, he got home at around 9:30. Aakriti had finished dinner and was waiting for him. Reading a book. It seemed to Ramadhar that she was always reading. He liked it. Ramadhar went off to shower. By the time he was done, Aakriti had heated dinner and set it on the table.

'I would have done it, pet,' he said.

'Why?' Aakriti responded. 'You must be tired. Have dinner and go to sleep.' Ramadhar ate, while his daughter sat with him. They chatted until a while after dinner, though both had an early start the next day.

~

It started with a meeting at which, first off, Ramadhar produced the sketch that stretched the already thin atmosphere in the room. He gave it to Tanya who was standing next to her chair. The sketch produced in her a reaction not unlike the one that Ramadhar had exhibited some hours ago. She went pale, her eyes narrowed and she abruptly sat down on her chair. For a long minute or so, she remained silent as did everyone else in the room. Then she seemed to recover.

Ramadhar had had the sketch scanned into a laptop. It was projected on to a screen so that everyone could see it without the hard copy, now pressed into a plastic sleeve, having to be passed around. Tanya sat down and asked Mrinal, the 'tech expert', to do the projection. As soon as the picture appeared on the screen, there was a collective gasp from all except Talukdar. And then moments of pure silence. For, the fact of the matter was that the face on the screen had an uncanny likeness, albeit in a somewhat gaunt fashion, to a certain Clayton Garcia, lately DD inspector, now mobster on the run with his MLA moll, presumed to be alive and well in Bangladesh or elsewhere. Not in Calcutta, and not driving a taxi. And not embarking on a career of serial rapist.

It was Gopal, who had been close to Garcia without ever having suspected the truth, who broke the silence.

'Good god,' he said. 'It can't be him. It just can't.' Jadunath, too, had worked with Garcia, though he had never been particularly close to him. 'It just can't,' he said softly, echoing Gopal. Then Tanya stepped in. 'It looks like Garcia,' she began, 'but let us not forget that it is not a photograph. It's a sketch, an artist's impression of what someone remembers from days ago. Also, it looks like Garcia in a generic sense. A lot of people look like that. You take a gaunt face and shave the hair off the head. Well, my experience is that when people shave their heads, they seem to look similar if their faces are roughly of the same shape. So, yes, we've had a shock. But we're not assuming anything. Actually, we are making an assumption. That is a random taxi driver, not Clayton Garcia. We'll get both in good time. Let's begin the meeting with the reports. We know what Ramadhar's been up to. Jadunath has just been putting together a team, which will now go into action. Ramadhar they're short, join them. So, Gopal?'

'Ma'am, we went to over twenty bars. Some have CCTV cameras, some don't. But none of the bars have cameras turned towards the streets. So, none of them have anything for us. Today, Mrinal and I will coordinate with the traffic police to see whether we can get something from our own footage.' His tone suggested that it wasn't very likely.

Tanya, too, thought it was unlikely, but they'd have to try. 'I'll talk to the commissioner after the meeting to see whether the traffic people can provide you some bodies,' she said. 'Piya?'

'Ma'am, I've made a list of the cases where the rapists didn't get caught over the last five years. Leaving our own two cases aside, there are fourteen spread across *thanas*. I can pull those files, but I'll probably have to visit each PS—Amherst Street, Muchipara, Shyampukur, Phoolbagan, Sinthi, Chitpur, Entally, Garden Reach, Watgunge, Lake, Garfa and Haridevpur.' North, east, west and south. Covered.

'Fine. You'll have the authorization in an hour. Stick around, I'll call you. Gopal will be too busy. So, once you've got all the files bring them to me.' Tanya's brisk tone had dispelled the nameless apprehension that had paralysed the team. There was a rapist out in the city. He was a cabbie. He had to be caught. In pursuance of which specific tasks had to be performed. For the present, end of story.

In her boss's office, Tanya told him, 'I'd like to show you something, sir.' She gave him the sketch. Chanda inspected it carefully. 'What's it? Face looks familiar.'

'Sir, it's a sketch made of the taxi driver who most likely committed the Park Street rape. It's been made with the help of Soumitro Saha, the man who assisted Gloria Stevens. And the man in the sketch bears an uncanny resemblance to Clayton Garcia.'

Chanda inspected the sketch all over again. 'Good god, you're right.'

'Sir, we need a few things. We've gone through the records of the past five years for rape cases in which the rapists have not been identified, forget apprehended. They are spread over twelve PS jurisdictions. I need copies of all those files to be delivered here. Otherwise, I'll have to depute someone to run all over the city collecting papers. It could take days. Second, we're planning to inspect footage from our CCTVs in the Park Street and CBD areas to see if we can spot this cabbie and his cab. We'd be obliged if the traffic wing assigns some bodies to help scan the footage. It's a little like looking for a specific blade of grass in the Maidan.'

Chanda flashed a brief and rare smile. 'Call me in half an hour.'

'Another thing, sir. The canvassing with copies of the sketch will take time. Can we have a few bodies temporarily?'

'Half an hour,' Chanda said. Dismissed.

Dismissed but quite satisfied, Tanya headed to her office and asked Jadunath to join her. 'We need to plan your campaign,' she told him after he'd taken a seat.

'The first part is easy, ma'am. We approach the owners' associations and drivers' unions and give them the sketch and ask for help. There are three main associations and two unions. We'll tell them it's very important and give them some sort of song and dance. They'll cooperate, ma'am, but it's unlikely they'll be able to help. But canvassing owners and drivers,' Jadunath paused, 'that's going to be a huge task. We'll just have to take the list randomly.'

'Fine. Just start. I'll see what I can do to help.'

In exactly half an hour, Tanya went to the commissioner's room, not quite knowing what to expect. Chanda gestured at her to take a seat. 'One,' he said, counting off one finger, 'start calling the OCs of the relevant stations. Deputy Commissioners (DCs) have been told to pass instructions along. Give it till after lunch, though. Two, speak to JCP (Traffic) to work out the CCTV modalities. Three, send me a mail and let me know how many bodies you need for the taxi canvasses.' Dismissed.

'Thank you, sir,' said Tanya, smartly, feeling a grudging respect for the man. She'd placed a tallish order; he'd delivered it in thirty minutes.

Tanya called Piya, Gopal and Jadunath to her room. 'Piya, wait till after lunch and start calling the relevant *thana*s. You should have the files by the end of the working day tomorrow. Till then, assist Jadunath. Gopal, wait till after the others have gone, I'll call JCP (Traffic) and sort out your problems. Jadunath, how many do you have in your team?'

'Apart from me, Ramadhar, Ishita and Talukdar, ma'am.'

'How many people will you need to wrap up in a week?'

Jadunath had done some back-of-the-envelope calculations. 'Three or four more people, ma'am.'

'All right. Wrap up the associations and unions and report to me.'

Once the others had left, Tanya called JCP (Traffic) Anand Malhotra. They knew each other from their Academy days. Tanya said, 'Anand, has the commissioner spoken to you?'

'Yes, Tanya. What can I do for you?'

'My people want to examine CCTV footage in the CBD-Park Street area to try and locate the cabbie involved in the two rapes. They need help and extra eyes.' Reacting to something from the other end, she added, 'Yeah, as soon as both of us can spare the same evening.'

'Okay, send your boys to me. I'll fix them up.'

'Thanks,' Tanya said, hanging up with the feeling once again that things were on the move. She told Gopal and Mrinal to talk to the JCP (Traffic) and leaned back in her chair to think. The subject of her thoughts was inevitably Clayton Garcia. She'd made a reasonable pitch at the meeting to calm her team's nerves. But something in the deep cavernous spaces of her mind was twitching. Could the resemblance be accidental? It could. She had been right; the look was kind of generic. Could the face itself be distorted by the fact that it had been drawn several days after Soumitro had seen it briefly in the light of artificial, orange halogens after he'd had a few? It could. Did she believe the above to be true? She desperately wanted to, because she knew that if the man they were looking for was Garcia he'd lead them a merry dance while the damages piled up. But she wasn't as sure as she'd like to be.

Later, Tanya called Aparna. 'Mrs Das, are you back home?' she began. Having received confirmation that she had indeed returned, she asked, 'Can I send an officer to you with a sketch? She'll be accompanied by a police artist. Another version would help.' Aparna agreed and Tanya sent Ishita to her with Shashanka in tow. If Aparna had looked fragile on her hospital bed, she looked much more robust now, Ishita thought. 'How are you feeling, ma'am?' she asked.

'Much better, thank you,' Aparna said. 'I've started working again. Work has a therapeutic quality.'

'And how are the children?' Ishita asked.

'They've adjusted and they don't know the details. In

any case, they have school and college and studies that keep them busy.' Ishita admired the steel in the woman.

The new sketch looked very much like the first one, only as if seen from a slightly different angle and, therefore, with certain features seemingly proportioned in a different way. As generic as the last one. The two sketches would now be doing the rounds.

~

The routine of police work inched ahead over the next few days. Piya's assignment was the first to get cleared. By lunch the next day, after twelve telephone calls had been made, fourteen files had piled up on Piya's desk. She discarded the ones that were obviously unrelated and took four files to Tanya's office: one each from Phoolbagan, Sinthee, Entally and Garfa. They took two each to go through with a fine-toothed comb.

The Garfa case had a vague connection. 'Doesn't really fit,' Tanya said, 'though it's geographically close to Santoshpur and separated only by twenty months or so. The police suspected the brother-in-law but couldn't make anything stick. I've got an idea, though, which might help open this case again. Collateral gain.'

'But blind alley, ma'am?' Piya said, hesitantly.

'Yes. You better join Jadunath's team again.' Once Piya had left, Tanya leaned back in her chair once more. Looking up at the ceiling. Letting a bad feeling wash over her. Another possible line of investigation dead. Now they'd have to hope that the canvassing turned something up.

She shook off her feeling of fatalism and lassitude. There were other cases and lots of work to be done. To which she turned her energies.

At the meeting next morning, no one had anything really to report. Gopal and Mrinal had been going blind looking at CCTV footage but nothing had emerged. Tanya could tell that Gopal wanted to say, 'and nothing will'. But the bases had to be covered. Suddenly, something would break. Criminals committed crimes and made mistakes. The cops plugged away and usually caught them. Especially when murder, rape and assorted mayhem were perpetrated. Jadunath's team had left copies of the sketch with the offices of the associations and unions. The guys there had promised to get back the moment they spotted anyone remotely resembling the sketch. Bullshit, Tanya thought, they probably screwed the sketch into a tight ball and chucked it into a corner of the room the moment the cops left. But, hey, it had to be done. Jadunath's voice cut into her reverie. '... and we've photocopied the list of owners, we'll start canvassing today.'

'Piya's joining you. I've spoken to JCP (Headquarters). Go meet him after the meeting. He'll have three people join you,' Tanya said. 'How long do you think this will take?'

'Anything from three to five days, ma'am. If we don't turn up anything by then, we can safely conclude there's nothing to be turned up.'

'All right. Meeting over. I'll be here all day, if you need me. Otherwise, we're meeting same time tomorrow.' All of them knew deep down, or not so deep down as a matter of fact, that the canvass wouldn't yield anything. But what the hell, it had to be done.

The next couple of days, Tanya held the meetings just to get the sense that things were moving and, thus, under control. But all that happened at the meetings were pointless reports. Gopal and Mrinal going blind, with some seconded colleagues from traffic, looking at CCTV footage. And Jadunath and his team tramping all about the city, producing the sketch for taxi owners to look at and nod sadly. Ditto taxi drivers. Jadunath and the members of his team were realizing afresh how generic faces could be. It could have been a photograph instead of a sketch, it wouldn't have helped. Nor, in fact, did it help that all taxi drivers in the city had to wear the blue uniform. Put someone in a uniform, you make him so anonymous that people think twice before committing themselves.

After the second meeting, Chanda called Tanya to his office. 'Any progress?' he asked, without preliminaries.

'I'm afraid not, sir. We're plugging away, but locating one particular taxi driver in a city as big as Calcutta… there are close to 20,000 taxis. God knows how many taxi drivers there are.'

'I know. Keep plugging away. No silver bullets, right?'

'Thank you, sir,' said Tanya, as she prepared to leave. Surprised and trying not to show it.

The next day, a cross-eyed Gopal reported that he and Mrinal had found nothing of significance. Another line of investigation closed. Tanya told them to join the canvassing team and she called JCP (Headquarters) Arup Rath, thanked him and told him the services of the loaned personnel were no longer required. The entire team set off to traipse around the city and Tanya, thoroughly dispirited, went to her room to catch up with other stuff. At least, she thought, I have a department to run. One of the most important ones in the city. She made up her mind at that point that she'd call the canvassing off after the next—fourth—day.

Just after lunch break the commissioner called her. She went to his room to find DGP Roy lolling in the only comfortable chair in the room. Chanda motioned her to take a seat. Once she was seated, the DGP, who'd come to Lalbazar on some other work and stopped by the Commissioner's office, said, 'Ajoy tells me that your case has come to a standstill?'

'Yes, sir. Looks that way.'

'So, where exactly are you now?'

'Sir, we thought we'd look at some unsolved cases to see if our perpetrator has a history. It doesn't look like it. So, we're assuming he's blown into town recently. We've checked all available CCTV footage in the Park Street-CBD area. Nothing. Now, my team is out canvassing taxi owners and drivers with two sketches we've prepared with the help of Soumitro Saha and Mrs Das. I think I'll call it off after tomorrow, sir. Oh, yes. The man in the sketch has a resemblance to Clayton Garcia in a generic sort of way.'

'Pull out of the canvass and do what?'

'We'll have to think of something, sir. But wasting time and resources indefinitely is not an option. Other cases have to be investigated, sir.'

Roy looked at her evenly, nodded, but didn't say anything.

But she didn't have to wait for the morning meeting

on the fourth day for the case to blow itself open all over again. She'd returned to her room after her chat with her bosses, when an envelope was sent up to her from reception. It was a plain brown envelope of standard dimensions, with her name on it—typed on a typewriter, not a computer. It said:

Tanya Samanta

Private and confidential

To be hand delivered

Inside the envelope was a white sheet of paper with the words:

You think you're smart, bitch. Find me before I get number three.

Tanya felt an electric current shoot through her. 'Hell!' she exclaimed aloud. And immediately went to the commissioner's room. There wasn't any point in trying to protect the exhibit for fingerprinting. A million people must have handled it already. Still, she thought, holding it with a handkerchief as she took it to Chanda's room. She lay the envelope down on the commissioner's table like it was a live king cobra and said, 'Look at this, sir. Reception sent it up right now. While you're looking, I'll call reception and try to find out who dropped it by.'

Reception, as it turned out, had no idea. Thousands of people were processed. Somebody dropping a letter by? Hey! Tanya persisted. And the somebody she'd been speaking to promised to institute enquiries. By the time she'd finished, Chanda had finished examining the letter. 'They have no idea who dropped the letter off at reception,' Tanya said.

'We need to give you more security, immediately,' Chanda said.

'I don't need security, but there are millions of women in the city who do,' Tanya said. 'Whoever raped Gloria and Aparna is making this personal. Between us. Me and him. And there is only one person who could be doing that. It's Clayton Garcia, sir. Now he knows we know. And he thinks we can't get him. Which is why he's sent the letter.' Chanda remained silent, acknowledging her point. 'I need to have a meeting tomorrow morning. We must come up with a new strategy to get him.'

'Keep your mind open. Keep your options open. There's a chance it's someone else. But we'll have to do something about enhancing your security,' Chanda said, as there was a knock on the door. 'Come in,' Chanda bellowed. And a young woman came in. 'From reception, sir,' she said.

Tanya took charge. 'Yes.'

'Ma'am, I took delivery of the letter. It was delivered by a boy. Teenager. Dropped it off and split. Nothing remarkable about him, ma'am.'

'Fine. It's all right.'

With no joy in sight, they broke it up, deciding that forensic tests on the message and envelope would be a waste of time and resources. Back in her room, Tanya had regained her composure. She called Jadunath. 'The canvassing is over for now. All of you get back soon. We need to have a meeting urgently. In an hour.'

Tanya was in the meeting room in an hour. Everybody had been able to make it back with the exception of Ramadhar, who, as usual, had been flying solo and incommunicado. Tanya passed the letter along. There were ashen faces in the room. 'It's pretty clear now that the rapist is someone with a grudge against me and the department. None of us are psychoanalysts, but it seems to be clear that the man is committing his crimes to draw our attention. Specifically, mine. And he seems to be casting this as a duel between the two of us. Which means it's someone who has a recent grudge. And the man who answers to that description is Garcia. The sketch wasn't lying.'

'He seems to think he's invulnerable. Either he has a hideout or he has accomplices who will shield him,' said Piya.

'Garcia is not the kind of man who would trust accomplices. He's your classic lone wolf. But we must not make the mistake of assuming it *has* to be Garcia. We must keep our eyes and ears open. It could be someone else.'

Though the letter to Tanya seemed to indicate that the man they were looking for was Garcia, working on that premise would be methodologically erroneous as DGP Roy had pointed out to Tanya and Chanda. 'What have we really got here? A sketch made under the direction of people who were a little stressed, a little high, in bad light. The sketched face somewhat resembles Garcia, but that's it. On top of that is the letter. Tanya you've been in business long enough. You've busted more people than anyone of comparable seniority. Many of them have spent a considerable number of years in jail, including for rape. You should get one of your young colleagues and review all the rapists you've sent to jail and what their status is.'

Roy had had a point, Tanya conceded. Not many of the

rapists she had helped convict were literate in English, but some were. Rape was hardly a monopoly of the poor and semi-literate. Tanya got hold of Piya and explained Roy's hypothesis to her. 'Look Piya, if it's Garcia, there's not much we can do other than mount extensive surveillance in some areas. Garcia's been there, seen that. This looks like a possibility.'

Tanya had served all over the state. It wasn't possible to make the whole state the ambit of her search. First, Piya interviewed Tanya herself. Luckily, it turned out that Tanya had kept a professional diary from her first day at work. So, Piya began with the diary. Tanya had begun, like all other officers, by serving in the districts. She'd served in the city for six years, including the current assignment. The diary showed that Tanya had investigated twelve rape cases in all these years. The diary didn't record the outcome of the investigations. But Piya had dates. No names. Frustratingly, no *thana*s. Piya used her contacts. With help from Mrinal and Talukdar, she tapped the grapevine and the newspaper archives at the National Library. It may not have been textbook, but it got them all the details in five days. Didn't sound fast. But it was, given the magnitude of the demand.

Once they had put everything together, they had a meeting with the JCP. Piya was the spokesperson. 'Ma'am,' 'she begun, we've got some good news and some bad news, which do you want first?'

'The good news, I guess,' Tanya said, laughing.

'The good news is that of the twelve cases you investigated, nine resulted in convictions. That's actually both good news and bad news because, on the one hand, it indicates a high conviction rate which we all want, but bad news because we have nine potential rapists to chase down. Of the other three, one is dead and two have moved out of Bengal.'

Piya stopped, drank some water and continued. 'Of the other nine, three are still in jail—Liaqat, a plumber, Tarun, a peon in a bank, and Sudipto, some kind of actor. So, we're left with six people who have spent time in jail for rape because of your tender mercies and are now free.'

Mrinal pulled out a slim file. 'One, Rabin Yadav, garage mechanic, out for a year or so. Works at a garage in Garcha, sleeps there; two, Ashu Khan, corporation sweeper, lost his job after going to jail, does odd jobs, lives in the Keyatala slums with family; three, Shayan Dhar, graphic artist, released a year ago, lost a very senior position in an advertising agency. He'd raped a colleague after a party. Seems now to be the official pariah of the ad agency world, lives on Southern Avenue; four, Kalua, seems to be his only name, gangster in Lyangda's outfit, out two months ago; five, Abhinav Morarka, son of an industrialist, got out two years ago. Family has rehabilitated him in the business; and, six, Sukhomoy, worked in an NGO. Out four months ago.' He stopped.

Talukdar had another file. Good choreography, Tanya was impressed. 'All of them currently between the ages of 28 and 42. When the crimes were committed, they were all between the ages of 22 and 38. As we've seen no obvious connections between them. None of them shared time in the same jail,' he added.

'Right,' Tanya said, 'I'll make a plan. Be back in an hour.' She knew no one was doing anything that couldn't wait a few days or be done by someone else. An hour later, Tanya was giving out the assignments. 'Team One, Jadunath and Ishita; Team Two, Gopal and Piya; Team Three, Talukdar and Mrinal; Team Four, Ramadhar; and I'll be Team Five. 'Team Two, take the designer fellow; Ramadhar, take Kalua; Team One will take on Rabin Yadav and later the NGO fellow; Team Three will take on Ashu Khan; and I'll go and meet Morarka. Get cracking.'

Tanya went off to meet Morarka at his office. Junior Morarka wasn't in she was told. I'm a cop she told the receptionist. 'Would you like to see *Mr* Morarka?' the receptionist asked.

'Yes, I would,' Tanya said. After parleys with a smooth operator, Tanya got to meet The Man. 'My name is Tanya Samanta, joint commissioner of police heading the detective department. We need to speak to your son,' she said.

Morarka smiled, not wholly agreeably, and said politely, 'Won't you take a seat, ma'am. Would you like an orange juice?'

Tanya said, 'I don't really want anything. I just want to have a chat with him.'

'That won't be possible, ma'am. Abhinav is in Australia, studying management.'

'Since when?'

'February.'

'Hasn't been back since.'

'No, ma'am.'

Tanya looked at him evenly. 'Fine, I'll leave you to your work.' Outside, she called Mrinal and told him to check Morarka's story with immigration control. But she knew it was the truth.

The team met the next morning. Tanya made her report. Mrinal added that he had checked with immigration and Abhinav had not returned to the country. In any case, he was a rich kid who felt he had the right to grope girls at parties. One such incident had resulted in rape. He wasn't the type to drive taxis and look for victims.

Team One took over, Jadunath doing the reporting. 'Rabin Yadav's not a likely candidate,' he said. 'After coming out of jail, he started working in a garage. Was a good mechanic. One day while he was working under a car, a jack or something broke and the car crushed his legs. Couldn't drive a car for sure. We'll catch up with this NGO fellow later, ma'am.' Two down, three to go.

Team Two went next, Piya leading. 'Shayan Dhar,' she began. 'Didn't like the look of him and his behaviour was certainly suspicious.' She really hadn't needed to meet him to find this out. Practically everyone he knew said he was a sleazeball. 'First, he practically threw us out when we went to his posh Southern Avenue flat. Then Jadunath*da* got tough. He gave him a choice: answer questions there or at Lalbazar. He says he does freelance designing; works from home. Doesn't have much of a social life. Stays home in the evenings. Drinks a bit. A bit? Ma'am, we met him at 3 p.m. and he was stinking. He was quite nasty throughout the interview, very guarded.'

Jadunath cut in, 'Nasty type. Wouldn't say he wouldn't

do it again if he got a chance at a party or something. But this driving around in a taxi thing, neither has the energy nor the bottle, ma'am. Looks a little like the sketch, though. But we chatted with the gatekeeper. He said Dhar hardly ever left the building. Even his shopping is done by his domestic.'

Strike three, thought Tanya. Ramadhar had found Kalua pretty easily. He wasn't bright, even by criminal standards, and had thought hiding in plain sight some kind of a genius-level strategy. The big man had come out of jail in the midst of Tanya's crackdown on Garcia's criminal network. By the time he had been freed, around 70 per cent of the network had been taken out. With raids continuing apace, soon all that was left was a vestige of the network. Everybody, including Tanya, knew that the underworld abhors a vacuum and that bit by bit, other players would move in with drugs, whores, extortion and petty crime. But for some time, the general citizenry could breathe a little easily. But for Kalua this was a problem. His only talent ran in the direction of crime. There wasn't anything else he was cut out for, unlike the Mollah brothers. So, he managed to locate Lyangda Jayanta of Sonarpur and teamed up with him. The bigger things were not possible: women, trafficking, drugs, abduction, liquor and big-time extortion. So, the two new comrades set off with small-time extortion in small local markets. It wasn't much of a living. When Ramadhar caught up with Kalua, he was a shadow of his ferocious self.

Ramadhar accosted him. 'Hey, Kalu,' he said, 'looks like you haven't slept for a month. At least you haven't bathed or shaven since you've been out of the jail. How's it going?' Kalua growled and looked up to see Ramadhar. They were well acquainted. Ramadhar had been in the team that had nabbed Kalua, before the Garcia case had broken. Ramadhar continued to taunt the once big, now shrunken, man. 'Any idea where friend Clayton*da* is?' Kalua kept looking at Ramadhar, saying nothing. 'You'll need to answer some questions. You'll have to come to Lalbazar with us,' he said.

'What is it that I am supposed to have done?' Kalua growled.

'Extortion, consorting with known criminals and covering up for major crimes,' Ramadhar said, making it up as he went along. 'Lyangda is already in jail. If you come in, you can give us your side of the story. Or you get caught and Lyangda walks.'

Kalua looked at Ramadhar. 'Spoke to Jayanta last night. He was at home. Don't try to bullshit me.'

But they'd really taken Lyangda in and banged him up, just to get Kalua. 'Try his mobiles again,' Ramadhar said. 'All his three phones are with us. Try a number.'

Kalua tried a number and the phone rang in the big cop's pocket. For a minute, Kalua looked panicked. Then he lumbered up. 'I'm going home.'

'You're going to jail Kalua. Better for you if you come peaceably,' Ramadhar said.

'That was how I got Kalua,' Ramadhar said. 'I'm sure he knows something. We'll just have to work on him.'

That was the climactic moment in the meeting, but the last team had to make its presentation. Mrinal and

Talukdar had gone to talk to Ashu Khan in the Keyatala slum. Within minutes, they knew this could not be the man. According to the records, Ashu was forty-six years old. The man they spoke to looked more like a broken-down sixty-five. His back was bent, he walked with a shuffle and one of his arms appeared to be permanently stiff. As soon as Mrinal and Talukdar had introduced themselves, he said, 'So, where's my compensation then?'

'What compensation, old man'? Mrinal asked.

The man went dark with rage. 'When I went to jail, I was forty-one. I was a fit young man. When I left five years later, jail made me like this. An old, crippled man. Who's responsible? I can't do any work. Who'll compensate me for my losses?'

Mrinal and Talukdar beat a hasty retreat, advising him to take up the matter with the prison authorities.

All potential suspects had been eliminated other than Kalua and Sukhomoy, who was incommunicado. So, Kalua would have to be grilled. Tanya elected Ramadhar for the job. He had that undercurrent of brutality that men like Kalua understood, respected and feared. Kalua had been put into the most cramped interview cell and left to stew all night and well into the morning before Ramadhar, Jadunath and Gopal went into the room at around 10 in the morning. Before that Ramadhar had told Tanya and the others that it was unlikely Kalua was their man. 'Ma'am, I really can't see Kalua doing all that planning. Or getting hold of a taxi in the first place. He's not a genius, ma'am. We all know geniuses don't take to crime to make a livelihood. But he's particularly thick. We can use him to trace Garcia, though.'

Tanya had agreed. Once in the room, they started chatting amongst themselves about mostly irrelevant things. They knew that Kalua knew the technique, having been interrogated many times during his undistinguished criminal career. They figured it would work. And it did. After about half an hour of cop talk, Kalua growled, 'Why've you brought me in here? Haven't done anything illegal since I came out.'

'Really?' said Ramadhar.

'You have anything on me?' Kalua growled again.

Ramadhar swung his feet and got off the table on which he was perched. And walked close up to Kalua. Violating personal space. 'Builder from Santoshpur said someone extorted Rs 1,00,000 from him. By the way, heard anything about that rape near Survey Park?'

Kalua remained silent. Ramadhar remained silent. So did Jadunath and Gopal. The silence lasted for almost ten minutes. Then, Kalua said, 'Some lousy builder gets extorted in fucking Santoshpur and you pick me up. I live in Sonarpur. Know the difference?'

Ramadhar smiled. 'Yeah, Kalu boy, I know the difference. I also know you get around a lot on the bike Garcia used to drive before he did a runner. Heard from Clay?'

Kalua wasn't a genius, but there was nothing wrong with his instincts. He kept shut. But a brief flicker of surprise had given him away.

'So,' Ramadhar said, 'the builder who was extorted in fucking Santoshpur told us that he could positively identify the guy he paid the money to. The description he gave of the extortionist made him sound a lot like you. We'll put you inside and organize a test identification parade. We have to. Rs 1,00,000 is a lot of money.'

Kalua looked at the three of them. 'I'll return it,' he said.

Ramadhar hooted. 'You've been around, Kalu boy. It doesn't work that way and you fucking know it. You return the money and you get a reduced sentence. But you go to jail just the same. Unless, we use our good offices to make the fucking Santoshpur builder withdraw his complaint. But why would we do that? You're not some kind of drinking buddy.'

'What do you want?' Kalua growled.

'Information,' said Ramadhar. 'And you know about what and whom.'

'Haven't seen him since coming out of jail. He's in Bangladesh, they say.'

'Who are "they", Kalu?'

'The lads.'

'So, you know nothing. You pay our builder back his money and get a reduced sentence, but you still go to jail.'

'There's a boy called Suleiman,' Kalua said. 'He runs a tea stall not very far from Lalbazar. Sleeps there. He wanders around, goes everywhere and knows everything that's going down. He was Garcia's gofer. Garcia set up the tea stall for him. If anyone knows anything about Garcia, it will be him. Just walk a hundred metres left after you leave your HQ and ask for Suleiman. Someone will show you his stall. But he's got a good antenna. Gets spooked easily. If he does, he'll just disappear.'

'Thanks for the advice, Kalu,' Ramadhar said, dripping

sarcasm. 'I'm sure you'd make a great cop. But until we find Suleiman, we'll keep tabs on you. And, anyway, where were you on the 14th of May, midnight to morning?'

'In jail,' Kalua said, as he was taken to a cell, uncomplainingly. He'd been around the crime scene since his early teens and knew what to expect. But the important thing was that he'd come clean. And if they got Suleiman, and Suleiman gave them some dope, he'd be free after the small matter of refunding Rs 1,00,000, which, luckily, he hadn't spent.

Ramadhar, Gopal and Jadunath trooped off to Tanya's office. But she wanted to hear the story with the rest of the team. She had some weird notions about leadership which most of her subordinates didn't really cotton on to, but which somehow made them feel good. So, the team was summoned and Ramadhar told them the entire story. Talukdar would type it up later.

Now, it was tactics time. How should Suleiman be snared? Everyone had a view. 'Cops drink tea, right?' she asked. Heads nodded. 'Cops drink tea at roadside shacks, don't they?' Heads nodded. 'In that case, it's pretty simple. Find out which shack Suleiman runs. Shouldn't be that hard for DD, huh?' Heads nodded, sheepishly. 'Once you've found out, Ramadhar, Jadunath, Gopal and Talukdar can just stroll over, have a cup of tea, pick him up and bring him here. Not advanced astrophysics, is it?' Some more sheepish nods later, they left. Gopal discovered the identity of the shack Suleiman ran and the quartet went for an afternoon cuppa. And lo and behold! There was this fresh-faced young man, just a boy really, serving tea and biscuits, hardly a hundred metres from HQ. They ordered four cups of tea, which were served with a gravely pleasant demeanour. The cops were not feeling good about what they were about to do. They finished their tea, paid for it, and Ramadhar, the least sentimental of beings, said, 'Pack up for the day, boy. Shut shop.'

Suleiman looked genuinely confused. 'Why? Is something wrong, uncle?'

Gopal cut in. 'Don't worry, boy, it's just for a few hours. You'll have to come with us to the headquarters there.' He pointed at the imposing red edifice. 'And answer a few questions. Police business. You'll be free in a couple of hours and back in business.'

Suleiman seemed to quail at first. But then he stiffened, shut his shop and prepared to go with them to HQ. At Lalbazar, he was kept in the same dank cell Kalua had previously occupied. For an hour. Kalua was a hardened criminal; this kind of treatment didn't mean much to him. But Suleiman was scarcely more than a boy. A free bird who sold tea and wandered the lanes and by-lanes of central Calcutta. In the course of his wanderings, he met all kinds of people. Some of them were criminals, he wasn't.

Tanya decided that the gentler touch would be more useful with Suleiman. So, the interrogators who entered the dank cell to question Suleiman were Gopal, Mrinal and Piya. 'Need anything?' asked Gopal, though Piya had been designated lead interrogator. 'Water, uncle,' Suleiman said. He was given water, which he guzzled. Then Piya stepped in, 'How many years have you been running your tea shop?'

'Two years, auntie.'

'And before that?'

Suleiman thought for a moment. 'I am nineteen now. I came to Calcutta six years back when my parents died. Somehow, I landed up in this *mohalla* (neighbourhood). For four years, I just used to just wander around. I made friends who'd give me odd jobs and food and money. I also met many shady types. You know.' Suleiman paused. Piya remained silent. 'Drug dealers, pimps, musclemen, extortionwallahs, men who run gambling rackets. I was friendly with them as well. Sometimes, they'd give me a meal. But whatever happened, I never did any work for them. Never ran errands for that crowd. Allah made me strong.' Suleiman stopped and drank some water. 'Three years after I came here, I met Kali*da*. And I started working for him. I'd clean his house, sometimes cook for him, and run errands like going to the bazaar. And Kali*da* looked after my needs. A year after that, he gave me money to start the shop. It's quite profitable. Then those raids happened. I knew that Kali*da* was a policeman. Suddenly, I began to hear he was in charge of all the bad things that used to happen. I thought I'd sell the shop, give away the *churir paisha* (proceeds of crime) and go somewhere else. But the people here said stay, you haven't done anything wrong. And I thought, well, I'd earned it. So, I stayed back.' He stopped abruptly, eyes glistening.

Piya let the silence ride for a while. Then said, abruptly, 'Suleiman, I'm going to ask you a question. You must answer with complete honesty.'

Suleiman looked at her with a puzzled expression. 'Honesty? Of course. I'm always honest.'

'Have you seen Kali*da* in Calcutta recently?'

'Yes, I think so.' Suleiman said. 'I saw a man who looked like him in Chitpur, near the Nakhuda Masjid. I was coming out after prayers. He was in a taxi. I mean, he was the driver. I wanted to go and meet him and then I thought I shouldn't. The police were looking for him. He wasn't a good man. So, I went off in the opposite direction. He didn't see me. He was wearing a skull cap, like a Mussalman.'

'When was this, Suleiman?'

'About two months ago.'

'Why didn't you tell the police?'

'Auntie, what would I have told the police? That I saw a man who looked like Kali*da*? I wasn't sure because I ran away fast.' There was nothing disingenuous about the boy, so they let him go.

'Be careful, next time you see Kali*da,* note down the number of his taxi and let me know here at the station,' Piya said.

Ramadhar was waiting outside HQ, on the pavement. He called out to Suleiman as he left and gave him a Rs 50 note. 'Compensation,' he said. 'For lost earnings. Now, scoot.'

They trooped into Tanya's office. Everyone except lone wolf Ramadhar. While Piya was recounting Suleiman's story, Tanya's phone rang. Commissioner Chanda. 'Come to my room immediately,' he said.

Tanya asked everyone to stay put and hurried to Chanda's office. 'Your third case has happened,' Chanda said. 'Woman was from out of town. Last night, or should

I say early this morning. PhD student from Delhi, Chitra Srivastava. Had been staying at the Ramakrishna Mission hostel at Gol Park. Befriended a man at National Library who invited her home for dinner. He's kosher apparently, a private tutor. Lives near Deshapriya Park. She got a cab right in front of Deshapriya Park on Rashbihari Avenue. Driver agreed to go the short distance. Dumped her at the Southern Avenue-Southend Park intersection inside the Dhakuria Lake enclosure. Case is with Lake police. You need to go there right away.'

'Shit,' said Tanya, as she started to move, not even bothering to update her boss about developments. In ten minutes, she was on her way to Lake PS with Gopal, Jadunath and Ishita in tow; the others in a state of readiness.

Part Four

Dhakuria Lake, Calcutta, June

The morning traffic from Lalbazar to the Dhakuria Lake would normally have been murderous. It was, until they cleared the CBD, but it was past 1 p.m. and they had the one-way movements in their favour. Tanya made it in forty-five minutes. The spot where the body had been dumped had a security ring. Not that a hell of a lot of forensic evidence would be found in a place as public and trampled-over as the Dhakuria Lake precincts. Tanya jumped out of the car, looking for whoever was in charge. It turned out to be one SI Sushila De. 'So, what do we know?' she asked, cutting to the chase.

'Ma'am, a guard found her a little before noon. She had been dumped in that corner of the Lake premises and some burlap and cloth were thrown on top of her. A man who was walking down Southend Park saw the suspicious bundle on the grass with what looked like a foot sticking out. He immediately alerted the guards, who found the woman. They called the police right away. We got here at around 12:15 p.m. Ma'am, she's been badly beaten. We immediately called an ambulance and sent her to the AMRI hospital, which is practically next door. And we secured the area. Then we called Lalbazar and did some preliminary examination of the area.'

'Badly beaten?' Tanya asked. 'How's she doing?'

'Don't know, ma'am. I've been staking this place out. There are officers at the hospital. But before the ambulance arrived, I poured some water on her face, to wash away the blood. She recovered briefly and said, "Palash. Tutor". At least I thought she said "tutor". Later, at the hospital she recovered enough to say she'd been raped and beaten by a taxi driver, along with a basic timeline for the evening. She's been sedated at the hospital, I was told.' Sushila repeated the story Tanya had already heard.

'One person goes to the hospital to monitor her condition. Ishita, that's your job. Someone has to get the survivor's details.' She turned to Sushila. 'How did you get her name?'

'Ma'am, she had a DU identity card which gave her name and a hostel address. She also had papers showing she was living right across the street in the Ramakrishna Mission scholars' hostel.'

'What else did she have in her bag?'

'Some money, ma'am. Debit card, mobile phone, university ID card, Aadhaar and voter cards. And knickknacks.'

'Gopal, go across to the hostel and see what details they have. We'll have to inform her parents.' Gopal was the urbane one. Jadunath, her best physical investigator. He'd spotted things others didn't. But in this public place, what the hell was he supposed to spot? Still, he went over to the spot where Chitra had been dumped. All he could see were indentations in the grass and traces of blood.

He sniffed around and returned. 'Ma'am, nothing to see. He picks his spot well. But how the hell did he dump a body in broad daylight in a busy place like this? Anyone else would have headed for the other side of the Lake. Or somewhere else entirely. Has Garcia gone mad?'

Tanya turned to Sushila and Jadunath and said, 'We must locate Palash, this private tutor chap, and speak to him. We know that Garcia's in disguise and he's good at changing his appearance. Even Suleiman hadn't been sure if the cabbie was him. We need as many descriptions of him as we can get.'

Sushila, who would have been the IO had DD not horned in, was given the task of locating Palash. 'We'll go to HQ. I'll sort out the deputation issue.'

While these confabulations were on, Gopal loped back from the hostel. 'Her name is Chitra Srivastava. She's doing a Ph.D. at DU, but she's actually from Patna. I've got her home address and a residential landline number. She's been in Calcutta for a couple of weeks, planned to stay for about a month more. Was working mostly at the National Library and the state archives in Bhabani Datta Lane, off College Street. Seems the quiet type. Gets back early, eats and goes to bed.'

Tanya looked thoughtful. Then, she called Ishita to enquire after Chitra Srivastava. 'Ma'am,' the young officer said, 'Apparently, she's broken a few ribs and her face is a mess. And the rape itself was quite savage. She's under sedation.'

'Stay there,' Tanya instructed her. 'I'll want updates.'

Everyone headed back to headquarters. Tanya had not

really needed Sushila's services, but as with Piya, she'd got the instant sense that she would be a good, thorough and reliable investigator. And she was right. If any one word defined Sushila, it was 'conscientious'.

Back in Lalbazar, Tanya mulled her options. Now that they were almost sure that the man they were looking for was Garcia, their tactics had to change. Within the team, Jadunath, Gopal and Ramadhar knew Garcia best. Tanya knew him as a subordinate, a useful subordinate, but the others knew him more collegially. So, the main thrust of the manhunt would be directed by these three. Ishita, Piya and Sushila would, Tanya decided, be kept tied to operations least likely to bring them in contact with Garcia. She thought, perhaps correctly, that they would be unable to deal with him. Of herself, she was pretty sure. She trained a few days every week at the police gym. Went for her martial arts classes as often as she could; she was a crack shot, practising as often as possible, and she was handy in general combat. Not many IPS officers bothered about these skills. They were the twice-born elite, unlikely ever to need them in rough-and-tumble situations. But Tanya enjoyed the workouts and was certain she could deal with Garcia.

After Tanya's brief respite for some cogitation, the expanded team had a meeting. There were eight of them: Ishita, Piya, Sushila, Talukdar, Mrinal, Jadunath, Gopal and Ramadhar. 'We know quite a lot now,' Tanya began. 'First, we are almost certain that Garcia is our man. Second, we know he is following some of the typical patterns of a serial rapist. His attacks are becoming more frequent and more violent. With Gloria it was an opportunistic rape. He didn't beat her. With Aparna there was an escalation: the whacks on the head and the rough way in which she was dragged into the underbrush. In Chitra's case, it's maniacal. My big fear is that we'll have a rape and murder on our hands soon. Any thoughts?' Tanya stopped. No one spoke.

She continued. 'He's getting bolder or more careless. Seems to be taunting us. Gloria's rape was opportunistic but under the radar. He had the chance, drove her to a quiet spot, then dumped her in Minto Park when no one was around. With Aparna, it was late and she was alone. He whacked her on the head. Took her to a quiet spot, raped her, but took a chance dragging her to that place in a busy neighbourhood, where people stay up late and are out on the streets. He could have been spotted. But with Chitra, it's madness. In the middle of the day, inside the Lake compound, metres from a watchman. Sheer exhibitionism. And he didn't touch her bag. No money taken, cards untouched. ID cards still there, so we could figure out who she is.'

This tirade was met with silence. The anger in the room was palpable.

'Sushila, you lead the search for Palash. Talukdar, Ishita and Piya will help.' Tanya knew that if there was anyone on the team who could corner Garcia, it was Ramadhar. He had the same ruthless streak. And under his sleepy manner, he thought fast and moved faster, despite his bulk. 'The rest of you will comb the city for Clayton Garcia. Mrinal and Jadunath, you're a team. And, Gopal and Ramadhar. Jadunath, close out the hunt for the NGO guy. Sukhomoy, is it?'

'Yes, ma'am,' Jadunath said.

~

While Ishita and Sushila headed out to the National Library to trace Palash, Talukdar headed to the state archives. Chitra had had no visitors at the hostel. While the hunt for the 'tutor' picked up, a bearded taxi driver snoozed in his cab in front of the University of Calcutta campus, spitting distance from the National Library.

Garcia had had an unusually hard time. He'd taken passengers in divergent directions two days back, leaving his home in an Entally *bustee* (slum), where he was known as Murtaza, around 3 p.m. and driving practically without a break till 2 a.m. His garage was in Janbazar, near Dharamtala-Esplanade, which was a longish walk to Entally. He'd gone to sleep after 3 a.m. and woken up by 9 in the morning. He's set out again after, ablutions, newspapers, errands and lunch at around 2 p.m. He'd been hoping the night would bring him something.

Garcia was at this point one hell of a frustrated dude. His hope of building an idyllic life with Shila had gone down the tube; she wasn't around anymore. His business dealings, as he thought of his criminal activities, had been rolled over. Bangladesh had frozen his accounts. He'd just managed to sneak back across the border, with pretty much what he was carrying on his back and in his trouser pockets, though he still had access to two accounts in Nepal. On the flip side, he was healthy and had another false identity. Which meant he could stay in his city and prey, until he finally got Tanya Samanta where he wanted her. She'd suffer, he'd promised himself.

Garcia had got whatever he'd wanted after joining the police: power, women and the opportunity to set up a criminal network that earned him a lot of money. Paradoxically, he'd been an austere man, with no heirs. His criminal enterprises were partly for their own sake. Which is why he'd lived in a pokey flat in Bowbazar, which he cleaned himself until Suleiman became his gofer, cooked his meals, washed his own clothes and tried to be self-sufficient. Garcia also had a hygiene mania. He'd wash his hands about a hundred times a day with soap he'd carry all the time. He'd bathe as often as he could—especially when it got unbearably hot and humid. And his flat always smelled of disinfectant.

All that was shot to bits. In the Entally slum, he had a ten-by-ten-feet room. He lived, slept and cooked there, when he had to; shared a toilet with twenty others; and bathed in the open from a tube well. His hygiene had gone to hell in a handcart and his privacy had gone with it. On top of everything, Garcia's earnings were now definitely in the chicken-shit bracket. Even in his austere days, Garcia had to have a certain amount of money to live privately and hygienically and eat well. What he earned driving his taxi didn't cut it. No, sir, not by a long shot. In any case, Garcia's days of spartan living had also been substantially revised ever by Shila. Garcia had had women before: regular girlfriends, one-night stands and whores from the Bowbazar area. As a cop, he never had to pay. He just had to be careful of the clap and AIDS, which he was. But Shila had been different; in her own patient way, she had changed Garcia's lifestyle. Until it wasn't so austere. So, Garcia was chafing. And the concentrated, singular focus of his anger was JCP Tanya Samanta. And he'd decided that on the way to getting her, he'd cut a wide swathe through his city.

The first one had been an opportunistic rape, he reminisced. The cunt was drunk. The second one had just fallen into his lap and the third one as well. Stupid bitch, he'd thought. She'd have been safe if she'd walked to Gol Park with that wimp. He'd taken her to the Menoka Cinema side of the Lake, into a side lane, feeling angry, dirty, frustrated, and beaten the crap out of her. And then he had a brain wave. Why not drop this silly fucking bitch where she'd wanted to go in the first place? He knew his plan was fraught with danger, but wasn't that the point? Taunting the bumbling, fucking cops. Especially, Tanya, the chief whore at DD. He'd done it in daylight and got away unscathed.

As he dozed and mused, Garcia felt sexually aroused. But no, he thought. It's too early. Ultimately, I'll probably get caught. But not before I get JCP Samanta, at my feet, pleading for mercy. He'd have to wait, though. Not too long. He'd take a risk, if necessary.

~

While Garcia was thus dozing and musing on his activities over the past few months, he had no idea that two cops, dedicated to locating him, but with strict orders not to engage, were less than half a kilometre away at the National Library making enquiries. Neither Sushila nor Ishita had ever been there. They had no clue whatsoever about where they could start. So, they asked the guards at the main gate and were directed to Bhasha Bhaban, the main building. There they met an assistant librarian called Biplab Guha. Unfortunately, they just had a name, no photograph. Fortunately, Guha knew the name. Chitra had sought his help on a number of occasions. And because she was an out-of-towner, he placed her pretty easily.

After introducing themselves as two of the city's finest, Sushila began the questioning. 'Sir, a girl from Delhi, Chitra Srivastava, frequents this library. Do you know her? We don't have a photograph.'

'Yes, I know her. What's the matter?'

'She was in an accident and is badly hurt. Could you clear some things up for us, sir?'

Guha was obviously not a librarian with his head stuck in his bookshelves. He said, 'If she's had an accident, what can I clear up? I know she's working on the Quit India movement and she's a Ph.D. student from DU. I think she stays in the Ramakrishna Mission hostel.'

Sushila was in a quandary. She'd have to give something to get something. But how much would her seniors approve? She said, 'Sir, Chitra was assaulted last night. She mentioned a name. Palash. And said, "tutor". She was apparently with him last evening. We've gathered that she spent some time at the Library. We were hoping to get a lead here.'

Guha looked at Sushila first and then at Ishita. There was a glint in his eyes. 'Is this yet another attack by the madman in the city?' he asked. Sushila remained poker-faced. 'I know the man you're looking for, Palash. I don't know his surname. Yes, he's a private tutor. And he also assists researchers. He's been around here for some years. I don't know him personally, but I think it highly unlikely he would do something like that.' Avoiding the 'r' word.

'Have you seen him today? He's not a suspect, but we need to speak to him.'

'Please wait outside the reading room. On the terrace, preferably. I'll bring him to you.'

In five minutes, Palash was with them. Late twenties or early thirties, clean-cut, pleasant demeanour. Guha clearly hadn't told him whom he was going to meet, far less why. So, he came up to the ladies, one young, another approaching middle age, with an uncertain smile on his face. After the introductions, which left Palash even more mystified, Ishita asked, 'May we have your full name, profession and address?'

'Palash Banerjee. I am a private tutor and research assistant. My address is 17J, Manoharpukur Road. Can you tell me what this is all about?'

'Do you live alone?'

'Yes. My parents are dead.'

'Did you know a woman called Chitra Srivastava?'

Palash was getting agitated. 'Yes,' he said, 'she's a friend. Please, what is this all about?'

'We need to know where she was last evening. Did you see her yesterday?'

Palash cleared his throat. 'Yes. We were both here, at the Library. I invited her to dinner. She's from Delhi and doesn't know many people in Calcutta. We finished work at around 6. We reached my place around 7. We had a couple of drinks each. By the time we finished it was around 9:30.' Palash stopped, an embarrassed look on his face. Ishita prompted him with a 'Yes'.

Palash continued, 'At around 10, we had dinner and had a small drink each, for the road. Then we went looking for a taxi and found one near Deshapriya Park. I was surprised that he agreed to go such a short distance past midnight. I thought maybe his garage was there. Some taxi drivers live in the Panchanantala slums. Chitra left and I walked back home. We are supposed to meet here, but she hasn't arrived yet.'

'Did you notice the cabbie?' Ishita asked.

Palash nodded. 'He was leaning against the bonnet of the car, so I had a good look at him. Fair and lean. Muslim. Had a skull cap and a beard.'

'Did you note the number of his taxi?'

Palash looked crestfallen and anxious. 'No. Why? What's the matter?'

Ishita told him as gently as one can break such news. 'He assaulted Chitra. She's in the hospital.'

Palash's face crumpled. He stumbled to the terrace wall, leaned over it and retched. After a while, he calmed down. 'Where is she? I want to see her. Shit, I should have walked her to the hostel myself. Shit.'

Ishita tried to be compassionate. 'It's not a good idea for you to go to the hospital now. But, in the meanwhile, could you come to Lalbazar with us to help our artist make a sketch of the driver's face?' Palash smiled a grim, fleeting smile. 'With pleasure. I'd like to tear him apart.'

Sushila cut in. 'Mr Banerjee, if you happen to see him anywhere, you'll call us. We'll give you some numbers. He's very dangerous. The best way you can help is by helping our artist make a sketch.' Her tone brooked no argument.

Palash collected his stuff and they went back to headquarters, reaching just when Talukdar was returning empty-handed. Palash, Sushila and Shashanka spent the best part of three hours putting the sketch together. The result was quite uncanny. In the first two sketches, the taxi driver looked remarkably like Garcia. Seen from different angles to be sure, but like Garcia nonetheless. In the third sketch, bearded and with a skullcap on his head, Garcia was a vastly different proposition. They took the sketch to Tanya who immediately set in motion the process of circulating the sketch to police stations, taxi drivers' unions and taxi owners' associations, pretty sure that nothing would come of it. At least, she thought, there's going to be some activity for the next few days.

The team members were going nuts working on other cases and waiting for the next attack. They wanted 'closure', which, translated into English, meant they either wanted to put the rapist behind bars or in hospital, preparatory to that, or kill him. Running pointless routines helped. They had to do something. 'Start first thing tomorrow morning,' she told the team. 'And be thankful that the press hasn't figured out that there could be an ex-cop serial rapist on the loose who drives a taxi.' She stopped almost in midstride, and called on the commissioner. 'Sir, I think we need to notify the press and the public about the situation.'

Chanda almost fell off his chair. 'What? What are you talking about? They'll crucify us. You want to be posted to "Training"?'

'Sir, there's every possibility that the press will figure out what is happening. If that happens, they'll burn us at the stake for not warning single women against taking taxis at night until this man is caught. We don't have to tell them that we suspect that the rapist cabbie is ex-cop Clayton Garcia. Moreover, sir, it's an ethical question. Can we allow women to put themselves at the risk of being raped, beaten, perhaps killed, just to prevent the public from knowing an ex-cop serial rapist is on the loose and we have no idea how he operates?'

'Point. I'll talk to the home secretary. If things work out, I'll ask JCP (HQ) to hold a press conference. There'll be a clear advisory for single women: do not take a taxi all by yourself after dark.'

That evening, JCP (HQ) Arup Rath held a press conference organized in haste. Not too many reporters were present. The indefatigable Raina Aqeel was there. The English and Bengali media, both print and electronic, were represented. Enough to send out the desired message: *'There's a serial rapist on the loose. He's a taxi driver. He claimed his third victim last night. We weren't sure until now that the assaults were related, but now we strongly suspect they are. Single women are strongly advised against taking taxis after dark. Or even during the day if they are headed towards sparsely inhabited destinations, or if they plan on passing through deserted stretches. TAKE CARE.'* Rath did not field any questions.

~

Jadunath and Mrinal set off to locate the elusive Sukhomoy, who shared a flat with a friend in Keshtopur, on the way to Dum Dum airport, which was about ten kilometres further north. They had visited once and found the flat locked; talked to neighbours, who hadn't been forthcoming. Maybe they had no information to share. This time, the door was opened by a man in shorts, bare-bodied, hair tousled. He appeared to have been sleeping. At 3 in the afternoon. Jadunath said, 'We are looking for Sukhomoy Bhar. Is he around?'

'Who are you?' the man asked.

'Acquaintances. We need his help for a job.' Jadunath had no idea what this man actually did. All his record said was that he had a BA degree and used to work for an NGO that provided education to street kids. He could have been a teacher, an administrator or a dogsbody.

It didn't matter, however. The man didn't ask any questions. 'He went out some time ago. I've no idea when he'll be back.'

'Can we come in and wait?' Jadunath asked. 'And I'd like a glass of water.'

The man let them in. He got them two glasses of water. And then they smelt the booze. He'd been sleeping that off, obviously.

Jadunath stood up. 'We'll come some other time,' he

said. Mrinal and he left, and drank tea at a roadside stall. The file on Sukhomoy had had a photograph, but it was a little out of focus and faded. Like one of the 'missing' photographs they print in the newspapers: you'd have to be way beyond fortunate to identify anyone from them. About an hour later, a man who looked like he was in his late twenties or early thirties, entered the building. They knew Sukhomoy was thirty-one. So, they followed him up the stairs, having already seen his flatmate leave the building some time ago.

They gave the man a start and proceeded slowly up the stairs. They reached the door; no padlock. When they rang the bell, the man they'd followed opened the door. His head was shaven, and he was tall, wiry and fair. He didn't look like the face in the first two sketches, but you couldn't rule anything out. As Tanya had said, the sketches were generic, especially with the shaven head. 'We're looking for Sukhomoy Bhar,' Jadunath said.

'I'm Sukhomoy Bhar.' He spoke like an educated man, but as far as they knew, he wasn't a cabbie.

'We're from the police,' Jadunath continued. 'We need to speak to you. May we come in?'

'Why?' Sukhomoy responded, alarm flaring in his eyes.

'Need to ask a few questions.'

'Okay,' Sukhomoy said.

Once inside, Jadunath asked, 'Can you account for your movements between 11:30 p.m. yesterday and 12:30 p.m. today?' He did not just say, 'Where were you between blah, blah, blah?' Such are the ways of the cops.

'Account for my movements? I don't understand.'

Mrinal translated. 'Where were you between 11:30 p.m. yesterday and 12:30 p.m. today?'

The man shrank in his chair. He was looking blank.

'Yes,' Mrinal prompted.

'Oh!' the man exclaimed, as if rudely awakened. 'Let me see. I went to sleep at around 1 a.m. My flatmate and I'd been drinking all evening. I must have woken up at around 9 o'clock in the morning. I was at home till noon, then I went out to meet a friend.'

'Can you call your flatmate? We want to talk to him,' Jadunath said.

Sukhomoy called. 'Irfan. The police are here. They want to talk to you. Where are you?'

He waited for a few seconds and said, 'Please come back, right away.'

Irfan returned in fifteen minutes. As soon as he was in through the door, Sukhomoy was asked to go into his room and stay put. 'What's this? Who are you? What do you want?' Irfan began.

'We're police officers,' Jadunath said. 'We need to ask you a few questions. To start with, what's your full name and permanent address?'

'Irfan Momin,' he said. And gave the two cops the name of a village in the neighbouring Hooghly district.

'Can you account for your movements from afternoon yesterday till this morning?'

Irfan looked nonplussed. Mrinal translated again.

'I was at my office till 6 in the evening. I reached home around 8. A little later, Sukho came home. Then we went out to get two bottles of whisky. We started drinking at around 9. A little after 11, Sukho said we should eat, but I was high. So, I went to sleep. I woke up later at night feeling hungry and I had dinner. Must have been around 3 a.m. I had a couple of drinks and went back to sleep. I woke up at around 11 in the morning.'

'Where do you work and what do you do?' Mrinal asked.

'I work for a courier company, Fast Delivery. I'm one of the office guys. I take parcels, enter them into the system, make sure everything's fine with them and take the payment. There are two of us.'

'How many people were in office when you left? What proof do we have that you came straight home? And what time exactly did Sukhomoy get back?' Jadunath asked.

'There were four people in office when I left. Our office is in Bhabanipur, near the police station. I left with a colleague and took the Metro to Esplanade. With him. Then I took a bus. Got back at around 8 o'clock. My friend saw me boarding the bus. What's this about, sir?' he asked.

'Never mind. Just tell us.'

'I met a neighbour, she lives on the second floor, as I was getting in.' He stopped and thought for a while. 'Sukho must have come in before 8:30, because we started drinking at 9. I checked.'

'Where was Sukhomoy when you were eating at…3 a.m.?' Mrinal asked.

'Must have been sleeping. I tried to be quiet, so he wouldn't wake up. His bedroom door was closed.'

In effect, both officers thought, Sukhomoy had no alibi after 11 p.m. If he had had access to a taxi, getting to Deshapriya Park by midnight wouldn't be a problem. He could be the guy in the sketch. He wasn't middle-aged, but he could look it if he was tired or had a bad hangover.

'Go to your room,' Jadunath told Irfan, who seemed to be glad to. They were sure his story would check out. They'd have to check with his office and his neighbour, of course. They summoned Sukhomoy again.

Jadunath was on the front foot now; brusque to the point of being menacing. 'What do you do exactly, Sukhomoy?' he asked.

'I'm not in regular employment. Sometimes I get called in to help out on various projects. I'm starting work in a few days as an assistant on a film shoot. It'll be in the Sunderbans.'

'What's the name of the friend you were with, this morning?'

Sukho shrank again. 'Renu. She's my girlfriend. Please leave her out of this, sir, please. I promised her I'll never get into trouble again. She'll leave me if she knows you're here.'

'Why? Have you done anything?'

'Sir,' he said, addressing Jadunath, 'you're the cops, you know how it works. I made a mistake, while I was drunk. It was bad. But it was a mistake. I didn't actually rape her, sir. But I did grope her. There was no excuse, so I didn't offer one. I admitted my guilt. Didn't even get a lawyer. Went to jail. I've been out for four months, I'm sure you know that. I work when I get work. I'm lucky my girlfriend forgave me. But I tell myself as many times as I can every day that I'm never going to do something like that. I know why you're here, sir. It wasn't me.'

Sob story to deflect attention or the truth? Jadunath knew, however, that the world could be very unforgiving to men in Sukhomoy's position. The crap about having paid one's dues was just that: a load of crap. Maybe, one in a hundred got back their self-respect. This wasn't the guy, Jadunath thought. But he pushed on, brutally. That was his job. 'Where were you on the 14th and 15th of May?'

'Middle of last month, sir?' He thought for just a moment, brows creased in puzzlement. 'I was in Darjeeling, sir.'

'What for? Whom did you go with?'

'Sir, for about two months. I'm from Siliguri. I'd been meaning to visit my parents, but I didn't have the guts to face them, sir. Renu kept telling me they'd forgive me, but I couldn't go. Renu is a make-up artist, sir, in the film industry. She was going on a shoot to Darjeeling and got me an assistant's job, sir. So, I went with the team. Can I go to my room for a second?'

Jadunath nodded. He was back in maybe thirty seconds, with a diary in his hands. 'Sir,' he said, 'Ever since coming out of jail, I've been keeping a diary.' He flipped through the pages. 'Yes,' he began, 'Sir, we left together on the 14th of May. The shoot wound up on the 19th. Then I finally went to meet my family. I spent almost a month with them. I returned to Calcutta on the 9th of June, sir.'

Ruled out for Gloria, ruled out for Aparna as well, Jadunath thought, with some relief. 'Your family forgave you, then?' he asked.

'Yes, sir. They wanted me to live at home, work in Siliguri. But there's nothing to do there. I'll stick to the film line.'

Jadunath gave him a card. 'Call me if you have work out of town.'

'I'm glad it wasn't him. He's learned his lesson it seems,' Mrinal said.

Jadunath kept silent.

~

Tanya was feeling seriously pissed off when the phone rang. It was a call from Bhabanipur PS. 'Ma'am,' said a voice, 'I'm Rajib Dhar, OC Bhabanipur. A man called Tapan Talapatra, a businessman, was shot near Ganja Park at around 7 today, while on a morning walk. He lives near Jadubabu's Bazar. The shooters were on a bike. He was hit by two bullets in the right shoulder and the right arm. Luckily, people raised a commotion and the assailants ran. Our officers reached the spot after calling an ambulance in ten minutes. He's at Shambhunath Pandit Hospital and insists on speaking to you, ma'am.'

'Okay. Do you have security at the hospital?'

'No, ma'am.'

'Post two policemen outside his door. No one but staff should have access, until I get there.'

The mystified OC despatched two officers to the hospital. Tanya and Ramadhar were in Tapan's room in an hour. 'Do you have any idea how this happened? Have you received any threats?'

'No, ma'am. Nothing. I've even spoken to some of the people still out of jail about reviving the network. I got no hint that someone knew.'

'Must be Garcia. I'll provide security for you and your family as discreetly as possible. Watch your back.' She'd need him, if Garcia was caught and the case went to court.

On the way back, Ramadhar said, 'Someone must have seen him either entering or going out of Lalbazar and identified him, ma'am. I think it's a cop. I'm sure it's not someone from the team.'

'I agree, it must be a policeman in HQ. And I don't think it's anyone from our team. Make very discreet enquiries.'

The reports that the newspapers carried the next day were 'briefs'. Small, single-column reports with headlines like, 'Morning walker shot at'. Tanya saw the heading and report and immediately thought, 'shot', Mr Sub-editor, not 'shot at'. At Lalbazar, Tanya called a meeting and informed her team about the development. Not a word was to be breathed of the morning walker's connection with the police. She'd personally make whatever enquiries were necessary and handle the fallout.

~

On the same day the shooting happened and the police briefed the press making 'sensational disclosures' about the rapes and issuing an advisory, something even more sensational happened. A twenty-one-year-old called Ghazala Alam caused it. Ghazala was a student of Economics at Calcutta's Presidency University. At the age of fourteen, she had been molested by three boys in her neighbourhood and raised an alarm; luckily, passers-by had come to her aid. Tempers ran high and the spectacle of the unrepentant boys, led by the son of a wealthy local businessman, so enraged the folks who had caught them that they gave them a proper hiding before calling the police. The boys spent a considerable time in hospital and the ringleader left the hospital with a permanent limp. This did not endear either Ghazala or her family to the local plutocrat, who had delusions of grandeur and unfulfilled political ambitions. The fact that Ghazala was a Muslim in a predominantly Hindu neighbourhood meant that a lot of anger was directed at the Alam family even though Ghazala was the injured party and the boys had been beaten by strangers who had nothing to do with the Alams.

The often crudely expressed hostility directed at the family made Ghazala's father, an executive in a multinational, think of moving elsewhere. Ghazala refused to be browbeaten and persuaded her father to remain in the neighbourhood. But Ghazala was neither dumb nor impractical. She realized that she could not let herself be at the mercy of anyone who fancied trying to molest her again. So, she started learning martial arts. Which, independent of her original motives, became an obsession. At seventeen, after three years of training, she won both the state judo and karate championships in her weight category. Subsequently, she also won the senior nationals in her weight category thrice in a row.

But winning the first title fuelled dissatisfaction more than pride. She went to meet her only uncle on her father's side, his elder brother, who was by then a senior officer in a central government paramilitary force. Ghazala told her uncle that while she was committed to continuing with her judo and karate training, she also wanted to learn proper unarmed combat, full contact. The half-assed, half-contact tournament stuff was fine, but not enough. Her uncle agreed to provide her the kind of training she desired, clandestinely. That is, without her parents' knowledge. Anybody's knowledge, in fact, other than those directly involved. After two years of training with personnel under her uncle's command, Ghazala became a formidable fighting machine, not least because she had the aptitude and a kind of unbuttoned aggression.

Even that did not satisfy Ghazala. She went to meet her uncle, by then retired from the force. 'Jyatha (father's older brother),' she said. 'Economics is an interesting subject and I might do a Master's degree as well. But I want to get into the armed forces. Baba (father) and Ma (mother) won't be happy, but I'll convince them. In the meantime, there's something else that I want to learn.' Her uncle arched his eyebrows, preparing himself for some outrageous request. 'I want to learn how to fight with a knife at close quarters.' Her uncle told her that he had retired and couldn't pull strings anymore, and second, the force to which he had belonged did not do that kind of training.

Ghazala pointed out quite calmly that he was a popular man with a distinguished record and she was sure he could persuade someone to pull some strings. Strings were pulled discreetly and Ghazala Alam learned, illegally, how to fight with knives at close quarters, becoming an even more formidable fighting machine. She didn't pick fights, but somewhere along the way, the need for self-defence had been transformed into a desire to learn how to fight. It was only when she tried to inveigle her uncle into arranging training in firearms that he put his foot down. Ghazala accepted his refusal with fortitude.

When JCP (HQ) Rath was holding his press briefing, which began at 7:30 p.m. and ended at 7:40 p.m., Ghazala was in a judo/karate session after classes in a large hall in a private residence, converted into a gymnasium, where martial arts contests were held, and training imparted in a number of martial arts. It was called the Mirzapur Martial Arts Club because, one presumes, it was on the corner of Mirzapur Street and Amherst Street, a short walk from the fabled College Street, where Presidency University was located. Ghazala trained for some time. Participated in two matches, both of which she won easily. By the time she was through, it was past 8 p.m. Ghazala knew that at that time of day, it would take her an hour by bus to get to her south Calcutta home on Ironside Road. But she was sweaty and needed freshening up. So, she decided to drop by at a friend's place on Amherst Street, just down the road from the club. She showered, borrowed an outfit from Pritha, her friend, and prepared to head home. But neither Pritha nor her mother would hear of it. Pritha's mother chided Ghazala, 'I don't know why you have to do all this judo-karate and fighting business. Girls are not meant to do these things.'

Ghazala cut short a lecture she'd heard hundreds of times. 'It's for self-defence, Mashima (aunt),' Ghazala said. 'It also improves concentration, confidence and inculcates a sense of self-reliance and self-worth. Just look at Pritha.'

This clinched the argument. When Ghazala and Pritha had become friends at school, the latter had been overweight, timid and good only at Mathematics and natural sciences. At Ghazala's instigation, much to the chagrin of her parents, she joined a judo class, lost weight, and became fitter and healthier. In a year, she was a changed girl. Confident, she improved in her studies all round and acquired extra-curricular interests. And ultimately joined Ghazala at the Economics department of Presidency University. Pritha's mother changed tack. 'You must be very hungry and it'll take you an hour to go home at this time. Have something to eat before you go.' Ghazala said yes; Pritha's mother was an exceptionally good cook.

Ghazala left Pritha's home at around 11 p.m. There wasn't a taxi in sight and she knew she wouldn't find a bus going her way at that time of the night. Having walked for around ten minutes in the direction of Sealdah station, a centre-of the-city landmark that serviced both suburban and long-distance trains, she found a cab. The cabbie was leaning against the side of the car. He was bearded, wore a skullcap and looked mean. Ghazala, the combat expert, could see that his lean frame was sinewy and tough. A fighter, she automatically thought. Ghazala never watched television, except for judo and karate championships. Or Sumo wrestling, which fascinated her. As for the papers, she'd read page one, and scan the rest quickly, lingering for a while on the business page. Consequently, she wasn't much aware of what went on in the city. Mostly what she picked up from her friends. When JCP Rath had been giving his presser, she'd been at the gym. Unfortunately,

Pritha and her mother had gone out shopping and missed the presser as well.

As a result, Ghazala, who was a pretty confident young woman, had no hesitation about approaching the cabbie. 'I want to go to Ironside Road,' she started off. 'You know where that is?'

'Near Birla Mandir, *behen* (sister),' the man said.

'Correct. Will you go there?'

'Yes, *behen*,' the man said.

'I'll pay you what's on the meter. Not one extra rupee,' Ghazala said.

'That's all right, *behen*,' the cabbie replied.

Ghazala sat down on the backseat. 'Okay, let's go,' she said, pleasantly surprised.

The taxi cruised past Sealdah on the empty road and reached the Moulali intersection, turning left into CIT Road. No cause for alarm, thought Ghazala, he knows I know the route, he won't try to give me a grand tour. Unfortunately, CIT Road was almost deserted at 11:30 p.m. Traffic was thin. CIT Road takes a right angle turn about half a kilometre from the Moulali crossing. The taxi took the turn, travelled a short distance and suddenly slowed down to turn into a badly-lit lane. Ghazala had trained one way or another for exactly this kind of an eventuality for over six years. Before the taxi turned, slowed further and stopped in front of a vacant plot, she drew the knife with a six-inch blade, finely honed, from the sheath she wore at the small of her back. It was practised, smooth.

The man stopped the car and turned, which straightaway put him at a disadvantage. Then he said in good English, dropping the *behen* shit. 'You should have walked, bitch. Didn't you read about what happened to that other fuckwit bitch in the Lake?' he said, grinning wolfishly. Ghazala chose that moment to strike with her right hand, the knife was in her left. She didn't punch. The balled fist is not the most efficient of weapons. She used the side of her hand to deliver a karate chop on the left side of his neck he had exposed when he had turned. Garcia almost passed out. He didn't because Ghazala couldn't generate enough force in the confined space. But it was good enough. She opened the door on the side away from the driver, where she'd been sitting, and stepped out coolly, knife in her left hand. No scrambling, no panic.

Garcia was still stunned. Ghazala went around the bonnet, went up to Garcia and punched him in the face, through the window. Then she opened the door and pulled him out and beat him mercilessly, bones broken, nose and a patella smashed. The first by a well-aimed elbow and the second by a foot encased in heavy military boots stomping repeatedly on it. Finally, she slashed him across the face with her knife as she belatedly remembered hearing something at the university about a rape near Dhakuria Lake.

She cleaned her knife on Garcia's shirt thoroughly using some water she found in the car. Dried and sheathed the knife, kicked him in the face again, one for the road, and took off. She walked all the way to Park Circus, which took her under half an hour, texting home to say she'd be late. She finally found another cabbie in Park Circus, who agreed to take her to her Ballygunge home for a premium. Normal. She reached home at around 2 in the morning.

All city papers led with the press conference next morning. With reports recounting in graphic detail the three rapes that had occurred. It was sensationalized stuff, obviously. The only thing they didn't have were 'quotes' from the victims or relations and friends of the victims. Or even neighbours, or the local grocer, because protected by the law, the police had been assiduous in concealing the identities of the victims/survivors. Tanya had once again issued the warning that if there was any leak whatsoever, she'd find the culprit and flay him or her.

Ghazala woke up late by her standards: at 7 rather than at 4. She didn't have time for her 3 km-run to the gym and back, sandwiching an adequate workout. An off day once in a while, an instructor had once told her, helps keep you physically and psychologically sharp. Was necessary, in fact. So, Ghazala made this one of her periodic and random off days from physical training. Instead, after some stretching exercises, she drank a cup of coffee and read the papers, only to be greeted by the report about the cabbie who was a serial rapist, the appeal by JCP Rath and the sketch of a face that suspiciously resembled one she had encountered some six or seven hours previously. She'd had to alter the topography quite a bit, of course.

After scanning all the reports about the rapes, she pillaged the papers for a report about a badly wounded cabbie found lying beside his vehicle in a dark lane off CIT Road, near the Ananda Palit bus stop. Zilch. She came up with nothing and realized that she'd have to get in touch with the police. She didn't think they'd hold her for assault. But, while wondering why the news hadn't even made it to the inside pages despite the ferocity of the beating she had administered, she thought she needed moral support. Her parents would probably have to be taken to the hospital if she told them what had happened. Pritha as well. Thus was it that her mentor, her truly beloved, self-effacing, bachelor uncle was nominated for the job of providing moral support.

Ghazala visited her uncle and gave him a blow-by-blow account, literally, of what had happened the previous night. 'Why wasn't it reported?' she asked. 'Someone must have found him and taken him to hospital. The police would have found out. If I'd known what he'd been doing, I'd have dragged him to the nearest police station.'

Aftab Alam was not a man given to displaying emotion, though he sometimes made an exception when it came to his only and beloved niece. 'Ghazala,' he said, 'why do you think the beating was not reported?'

'He must have somehow recovered and taken off. But now it'll be easy to catch him.'

'I'll find out who's handling the case. We'll report it straightaway. The more time we lose, the more time he gets to make an escape.'

Aftab made a call. To DGP Roy as it happened. Though they weren't exactly friends, they knew each other and had the occasional drink together at the club of which both were members. 'Chandan,' he began, without formalities. 'My niece has some important information about this rapist cabbie. Who's handling the case?' He nodded, seemingly with satisfaction, at the reply. And said, 'So we can just turn up at Lalbazar and meet Tanya, I suppose. Can you give her a heads-up, please?' He nodded again. 'Tell her we'll be there in an hour.'

It turned out that Aftab knew JCP Tanya Samanta, he didn't say how. They went to Lalbazar, where Tanya was waiting, impatiently. Aftab greeted her and introduced his niece to Tanya. 'My niece, Ghazala. She's been up to things last night.'

Ghazala was rarely overawed by any occasion or person. But now the enormity of the situation got to her. She gulped, greeted Tanya and narrated her story in excruciating detail. 'I don't watch television. And I was training, anyway. I had no idea of what had been going on. Otherwise, I'd have beaten him some more and dragged him to the nearest station.'

'You did well, Ghazala,' Tanya said. 'The taxi driver you beat is a trained, tough man himself. Not many people would have been able to do what you did. I'll let you in on a secret we haven't shared with the media or the public, since Aftab is the soul of discretion and you're his niece.' She turned to Aftab. 'Remember the case of the rogue cop and the Jadavpur MLA?'

Aftab had a naturally good memory, rendered sharper by training. 'Inspector Clayton Garcia and Jadavpur MLA Shila Nandi, widow of Chhoton Nandi.'

Tanya nodded. 'Garcia is the taxi driver.' She opened a drawer and pulled out a copy each of the three sketches and pushed them towards Ghazala. 'It's him. The one with the cap is exact, but even the others are him,' Ghazala said, disregarding grammar.

'Okay, thanks Aftab. Thanks for coming in Ghazala. We'll get him. After what you did to him, he'll have to get treatment. We're keeping this off the record for now.'

Aftab and Ghazala left. On the way back, Aftab told his niece, 'Wasn't too bad, was it? First time I've seen you fazed. But from now on, always carry your knife. It's not legal, but I'll get hold of some pepper spray for you. Good thing he's a lone wolf. But be very, very careful. Call me whenever something unusual happens. Bravado isn't smart, but don't worry too much, Tanya is a very good cop.'

The reason why neither the cops nor the media knew about the savage beating Garcia had been administered was that after being semi-conscious for about an hour, he had somehow surfaced, albeit with a broken nose that was making it difficult to breathe, a smashed patella, a couple of broken ribs and a slash across his face that had stopped bleeding, because the blood had coagulated. He had staggered into his taxi and, against the odds, driven to a doctor who his criminal associates used to go to when they did not want serious injuries reported to the police. But by then it was well past midnight and the quack was asleep. Garcia had managed to wake him up by leaning on his doorbell and passed out again. The doctor stitched his face, fixed his broken nose after a fashion, taped his ribs and plastered his knee after administering painkillers and a sedative.

Garcia came to well into the morning in the spare room

the doctor kept precisely for emergencies such as this. He had quenched a raging thirst with the bottle of water the doctor had thoughtfully kept beside his bed. The doctor had himself left for the legitimate side of his practice, leaving a note for Garcia in which he had specified what medicine to take at what time and warned him against leaving his bed other than to go to the bathroom. The warning had not really been necessary. The smashed and plastered knee-cap made mobility extremely difficult, while the broken ribs made movement very painful.

Garcia's face stung and his nose, roughly reset, still hurt like the blazes. The Crooked Samaritan had thoughtfully left a couple of boiled eggs, some slices of bread and a glass of milk by the bed. The note had instructed him to eat the food before taking his medicines. Garcia complied. And since the medication was mostly painkillers and sedatives, he passed out again. When he woke up, it was early evening. He drank a lot of water and hobbled to the bathroom and back.

He lay down again and started planning. The Crooked Samaritan wasn't doing him any favours. He would have to pay a goodish bit for the services and sanctuary he was being given. Garcia had some money stashed away for emergencies, but didn't want to draw on that. Even though if ever there had been an emergency in his life, this was it. He decided he'd have to call in some favours. Luckily his mobile phone was still intact, he thought. And the taxi was his own, registered in the name of Murtaza Baig. If he'd been driving someone else's on hire, the owner would by now have been raising hell. And would have increased the possibility of him being identified during the police canvasses.

The doctor returned while Garcia was planning his next few days. Thankfully, Garcia thought, he didn't ask how he was feeling. He changed the dressing on his slashed face and said, 'You'll have to get bed rest for at least a couple of weeks. If you want you can stay here. Or you could move to your own place. Here, you'll be on your own for most of the day. I can arrange an attendant, if you want, though.'

Garcia remained quiet for a while. 'I'll stay here. And I don't need an attendant. What's all this going to cost me?' he asked.

'I can't put a figure on it yet. Your knee will have to remain in plaster for around six weeks. But I'll tell you when I'm sure how long you'll have to be here, what the medicines will cost and the rest of it. All I can tell you at the moment is that it won't be cheap. Anyway, you should rest now, I'll have dinner sent up soon and the medicines you'll have to take. Don't fret, it won't help.'

Dinner was sent up to the garret-like room Garcia had been put up in. After dining and having his medication, Garcia lay awake for some time, despite the sedatives and painkillers. As he thought of his situation, rage welled up in him. Fucking bitch, he told himself, I'm going to get her, if it's the last thing I do. Fucking slip of a cunt, she sucker punched me once. Won't do it again. Even as he ranted silently, he realized he was just kidding himself. He had not been sucker punched. He'd been beaten up and brought to his knees by a girl who couldn't have been more than five feet six inches tall and fifty-odd kilos. She was a pro. He'd picked the wrong girl this time. But he'd get her, he promised himself, as soon as he could start moving around. About a week later, his nose had healed. The doctor told him, however, that the stitches on his face would leave a scar that could only be removed by expensive cosmetic surgery. 'You know, Garcia,' the doctor told him, 'If I'd been able to do the job in a hospital, it's possible that I could have avoided leaving a scar. But here ...' He'd shrugged. Garcia couldn't give a flying fuck about the scar, which he told the doctor in so many words. 'It doesn't matter doc. In fact, it might be a blessing in disguise, if it changes my appearance enough,' he'd added.

Clearly, Garcia had become completely out of touch with police work. The work that he'd done for over three decades. Equally, he seemed to have forgotten how his former boss operated. Days after Ghazala had visited her, Tanya had called her to the office and with her help, simulated a scar running across all the three faces they had sketched with the help of a computer. The cops had a pretty good idea of what Garcia would look like with a scar.

If that was bad news Garcia didn't know, the doctor gave him some straight up. 'Garcia,' the doctor said, 'there's something you should prepare yourself for. The people who hit you, practically pulverized your patella. It was broken into so many pieces that there is no chance it will knit together properly. With the equipment I have here, all I could do was plaster the knee and hope for the best. Ideally, I would have removed the broken pieces and replaced the kneecap with an artificial one. In that case, you would have been able to move around more or less freely. At your age, you wouldn't be able to continue with your jogging routine, but you'd be walking almost normally. Now, however, it's a completely different story. You'll walk with a pronounced limp, probably with the help of a walking stick unless I have the opportunity to take you to a hospital and have someone operate properly.'

Garcia stared at him. 'Fucking bastard,' he said, softly, 'I'll get you.' The doctor kept a straight, noncommittal face. Garcia hadn't told him that he'd been hammered by a girl he'd lined up for rape and a beating. In fact, the doctor had no idea that the sensational rapes had been perpetrated by Garcia. Had he known, he would have given him up to the cops, in a beat. He had known Garcia for some time, but as a cop who was also a crime lord. He had no idea that Garcia was, or had become, a psycho.

Tanya had known Garcia for a far shorter period of time. She'd thought of him as an exceptionally capable police officer, an asset to her department. Now, however, she knew he was a damaged man. She wasn't a psychiatrist or psychoanalyst, so she couldn't say for sure that he was a psychopath. But definitions didn't matter. She had to get him before his next rape, or maybe murder. While Garcia was flat on his back, Tanya had no idea that his right knee was completely shattered. Had she known, it would have cheered her up a whole lot.

What Tanya realized when no trace could be picked up of a man by all accounts badly wounded, she figured out straightaway that he'd gone to one of the many quacks frequented by criminals who couldn't afford to go to a hospital, nursing home or legit doctor. In fact, all the members of the team had kind of figured that out. On the third day after Ghazala's revelations, Tanya told the team that he must be in one of the shady clinics in town. 'Ma'am, we need to round up all the shady doctors we know about. If they haven't seen Garcia, we can sweat them to reveal the names of other doctors like them. That way, we'll locate Garcia soon enough,' said Jadunath, always eager for action. Thus began 'Operation Quack' as the search for Garcia's doctor came to be known.

The team broke up into pairs and hunted down the quacks criminals went to. From them, they got other names as well. Most of the doctors injured criminals went to operated out in the suburbs, because they didn't want to risk operating in the city, where the chances of being raided were much higher. So, the team members had to travel to semi-urban destinations like Sonarpur, Baruipur, Diamond Harbour and Canning to the south of the city proper; and Barasat, Barrackpore, Madhyamgram, Dum Dum and Teghoria to the north. They even went outside the metropolitan area to Ranaghat, Arambagh and Howrah, in nearby districts, in search of criminal quacks. But even after ten days, they were no closer to running Clayton Garcia down to earth.

Unsurprisingly, Garcia's Samaritan, a man called Dr Shivshankar Varma, whose brother ran a gang in a small town called Chhapra in Bihar, came to know that the police were making assiduous enquiries about the doctor who was treating or had treated Garcia. He also realized that if the police kept at it, they would locate him sooner rather than later. On the tenth day of 'Operation Quack', a couple of days after he'd come to know that the cops were sniffing around, he told Garcia that he'd have to pay up and leave, in the interests of both of them. He'd taken off the stitches on the face and the nose though slightly puffy had healed. The scar was livid and needed daily application of ointments. But the main problem was the knee, which was still in a cast.

Garcia was aghast. 'What do you mean by pay up and leave? I can barely make it to the bathroom. Where the fuck am I supposed to go?'

'The problem, Garcia, is that the cops are looking for you and they've figured out that you are holed up in a place like this. The person who assaulted you must have informed the police about the extent of your injuries. So, they have been looking for doctors who treat people in the kind of position you're in. And they'll soon descend on me. You must leave before that happens. What I can do, if you can pay, is arrange to have a car drive you to Chhapra, my home town. I know a doctor there who'll take care of you until your injuries heal to the extent they will.'

'Dr Varma, I have my own vehicle. I just need a driver to ferry me out of the city.'

Dr Varma made the arrangements in forty-eight hours. Garcia and he had decided it would be better to have someone come to Calcutta from Chhapra and drive Garcia there. He'd spoken to his brother and made arrangements for Garcia's treatment and accommodation. In the meantime, Garcia had to do what he hadn't wanted to: get in touch with his old associates. He'd wanted to remain incognito so that the risk of being detected by the police remained as low as possible. But now he had to call in some favours, because he needed the cash that his future programmes would require. He called a couple of people he knew were still out of jail. People who owed him big time. They came to meet him in Dakshineshwar, where Dr Varma ran his illegal practice. It was in the neighbouring district of North 24 Parganas, but a part of greater Calcutta. Prabhash and Hashim organized the money in a day. And in seventy-two hours, Garcia was on his way in his taxi, which now had new Bihar number plates. For all the help he got, Garcia forbore from telling either of his old associates exactly where he was going.

In Lalbazar, Tanya and her team members had questioned scores of doctors with shady practices. They had in turn been cajoled and threatened, but none of them had owned up to any knowledge of the man whose sketches they were shown bearing the kind of injuries described. It was always going to be Ramadhar who would crack this one. Out on a raid, he came across the name of Dr Shivshankar Varma, who lived in Dakshineshwar, but ran a practice in a place called Hatibagan, a congested area in north Calcutta famous for its old cinemas and theatre halls, now stripped of their old colonial-era grandeur.

The more Ramadhar enquired about him, the more his name came up in criminal circles. Finally, Ramadhar discovered that like himself, Dr Varma was from Bihar. The difference was that Ramadhar had been born in Calcutta and had lived in the city his whole life, while Dr Varma had been born in Bihar, had come to study medicine in

Calcutta, married a Bihari girl from Calcutta and settled down in the city. After speaking to Tanya about his discoveries, he paid Dr Varma a visit, accompanied by Talukdar.

Ramadhar could be a scary man to deal with, which Dr Varma discovered when the two policemen arrived at his clinic unannounced. Talukdar kicked off the proceedings with some routine questions about his practice until Ramadhar suddenly broke in. 'What part of Bihar are you from?' he asked abruptly in their shared native tongue, Bhojpuri. Disconcerted, the doctor answered, 'Chhapra.'

Ramadhar brought out a slim folder from which he extracted the three sketches of Clayton Garcia. He thrust them at the doctor and asked, 'Ever seen this man?'

Dr Varma inspected the sketches and said, 'No.' Ramadhar extracted three more sketches, showing Garcia as he was likely to look with the injuries that had been inflicted on him, and asked, 'Ever seen this man?'

The doctor inspected the new set of sketches and said, 'No.'

Everyone remained silent for a while. Then Ramadhar said with a deliberate casualness, 'Dr Varma, we know that apart from this practice you run, you also treat criminals who cannot afford to go to hospitals or legitimate doctors. We've heard from many such criminals. That's why we're here.' He stopped speaking for a while and precisely at that moment, Dr Varma started sweating profusely. Ramadhar continued. 'I've got a caseload that's breaking my back. You think I have nothing better to do than sweat you without knowing that you know something. I'll give you a choice, doctor. Either you tell us what you know right now, or I'll haul your sorry ass all the way to Lalbazar. I guarantee you that with the evidence we produce, the court will give us custody for at least a week. Just think of what's going to happen to your practice when I have notices pasted outside your clinic saying: "Closed: Doctor in Police Custody."'

Dr Varma kept sweating, but didn't speak a word for some time. Then he said, 'Yes. He came to me late at night about a fortnight ago. He was in bad shape. His nose was broken. His face was slashed. And he had a couple of broken ribs. I cleaned his face, stitched and dressed his wound and taped his ribs. I also reset his broken nose. He was finding it difficult to breathe. I gave him painkillers and a sedative. He slept in my house that night and all day the next day. I dressed his wound again and medicated him. He paid me and left the next day in a taxi.'

'You called the taxi?' Talukdar asked.

'No. He drove off in his own taxi.'

'Right,' Ramadhar said. 'Can I have a look at your phone?' Dr Varma pulled it out of his pocket and handed it over, silently. Ramadhar took the handset, placed it carefully on the floor, stood up slowly and stomped it to bits.

'What the hell? What do you think you're doing?' Dr Varma expostulated.

'Taking you into custody, while we go pick up Garcia from Chhapra, Dr Varma. You think the cops are the idiots and the criminals the masterminds? Reflect while you're in jail. Even ordinarily intelligent people don't take to a life of crime unless forced to by circumstance. We're not the idiots. You, Garcia and your brother, who runs that penny-ante drug-peddling operation in Chhapra, are. Now, come with us quietly, or we'll take you away in handcuffs.'

Dr Varma said in a small voice, 'I want to speak to my wife. And I want a lawyer.'

'We'll inform your family. You can call a lawyer when we get to headquarters,' Ramadhar said. To Dr Varma, everything about the big cop was full of subdued menace. He locked up his clinic, told his patients he wouldn't be around for a few days and followed the two officers.

The cops called Dr Varma's wife and told her that her husband had been called away to Hooghly for an emergency and would be in touch as soon as he was able to. After that, legal formalities completed, he was taken into custody. During interrogation, apart from disclosing the details of what had transpired the night Garcia had the shit beaten out of him and the following fortnight when he had stayed in the doctor's garret, he proved to be a mine of information about sundry criminals and their networks in various parts of Calcutta and its immediate hinterland, especially, North 24 Parganas. But the most important news he imparted was that he had shipped Garcia off to Chhapra, where he'd be under the care of one Dr Jha, whose practice was similar to his own, with the difference that he was able to operate freely because he worked in a small town under the protection of its biggest don, Dr Varma's own inestimable brother.

While Dr Varma was spending a trying weekend in a cell in Lalbazar, Garcia was fretting in Chhapra. He wanted news of what was happening in Calcutta. Garcia was naturally athletic and strong, and proved also to be resilient. His doctor in Chhapra, Govind Jha, kept telling him to relax. But Garcia couldn't. Finally, he decided to call Dr Varma despite the fact that his Samaritan had expressly forbidden him from doing so, in both their interests. Garcia first called the day after he reached Chhapra, a couple of hours after Ramadhar had stomped the Crooked Samaritan's phone into very small pieces. What he heard on his handset was the message, 'This number does not exist.' He kept calling through the evening and got the same message. After spending a restless night, he woke with a deep sense of foreboding. Now that he could hobble around with the help of a walker, though he wasn't supposed to overdo things, he went to Dr Jha and told him that he feared Dr Varma had been picked up by the police.

Dr Jha tried calling his colleague through the morning and kept getting the same message. By lunchtime, he reached the same conclusion as Garcia had. After lunch, he called Dr Varma's brother and told him what was going on. Shivanand Varma was a dynamic and decisive man. He immediately made arrangements for one of his associates to drive Garcia to Muzaffarpur, about a hundred kilometres away, where one of his 'disciples' ran an operation consisting mainly of prostitution, extortion and drug peddling, a smaller version of his own enterprise. By evening, Garcia was packed and gone, being driven in his own taxi with a new set of fake number plates. All this was costing Garcia, but for the while he was safe. He still had some of the money Prabhash and Hashim had provided, but he'd have to be careful with it.

Around the time Garcia left Chhapra, Bengal DGP Roy made a call at Commissioner Chanda's request to his counterpart in Patna, a man called Pratap Narayan Singh. The two men knew each other professionally. Roy gave Singh the background to the Garcia case and told him what Dr Varma had revealed: Garcia was holed up in Chhapra with a doctor called Govind Jha under the protection of the gangster, Shivanand Varma. He requested Singh to get the police in Chhapra to make enquiries and informed him that a team of Kolkata Police detectives led by SI Ramadhar Tiwari would take a morning flight to Patna the next day, disembarking at around 10:30. Kolkata Police would be most obliged for assistance in hiring a car to go to Chhapra. Singh said he would order Chhapra police to make enquiries immediately and a team of the Bihar Police would be at the airport to meet the officers from Calcutta. Roy informed Chanda at once and Tanya began organizing the trip to Bihar for Ramadhar and his team without delay.

Roy got a call from Singh at around 9 p.m. He was still in office as were Chanda, Tanya and her entire team working out the modalities of what the team would do while in Bihar and how it was going to get Garcia back to Calcutta. Singh's phone call was explosive, in context. He told Roy that the police had raided Dr Jha's clinic and home, but no trace had been found of Garcia. They had, however, made enquiries in Chhapra, which wasn't exactly a megalopolis, and discovered that an injured man had indeed been driven into town in a taxi a few days ago. The taxi had driven off with the man who had been staying with Dr Jha, earlier that evening.

The police had then called Dr Jha for questioning to the local police *thana*. He had, at first, disclaimed any knowledge of a man approximating Garcia's description, but upon being threatened with dire consequences, had admitted that a man called Murtaza had come to him for treatment with multiple injuries. Dr Jha had no idea where he was from or how he was injured. He had admitted him to his clinic and treated him. The man had abruptly left that evening in the taxi in which he had arrived. Asked about the man's injuries, Dr Jha said Murtaza had a raw scar on his face running from just above his left ear and curving down his cheek, past his lips, over his chin and ending above his throat on the same side of his face. It appeared that he had been slashed by some sharp object, possibly a knife.

In Dr Jha's opinion, Murtaza had been lucky, because if the sharp instrument, whatever it might have been, had gone just a little further downward his windpipe would have been severed. Apart from that, his nose had been broken, but had almost healed, though it would remain substantially crooked in the absence of a kind of corrective surgery that he himself could not provide. In addition, he had two cracked ribs which an X-Ray showed were healing nicely. He had offered to show the police the X-Ray plates. But the most grievous injury had been a smashed patella, the right kneecap, in fact. That, too, was healing. But given the fact that it had been shattered, it would never knit together properly again and Murtaza would have to walk with a limp and possibly the aid of a walking stick, unless the knee was operated upon soon, with the bone fragments being extracted and replaced by an artificial patella made either of metal or fibreglass. Dr Jha admitted that he knew Dr Varma, but only slightly. He had met him in Chhapra once when he had come to visit one of the prominent businessmen of the town, Shivanand Varma. He denied receiving any calls from Dr Varma at all, whether about Murtaza or any other matter. He claimed that they did not know each other well enough to speak to each other telephonically. Dr Jha made this claim vehemently, secure in the knowledge that he had actually not spoken to Dr Varma and that he was technically being absolutely truthful when he told the police he barely knew Dr Varma. His acquaintance with Dr Varma was, in fact, slight. The entire Garcia deal had been arranged through Shivanand.

When asked where his patient had gone after leaving his clinic, Dr Jha had said, truthfully again, that he had no idea. In this case, Garcia had been working on the need-to-know principle, again. The only people who knew where he had gone were Shivanand, one of his henchmen and the man who had driven Garcia off. But since Shivanand was not in the frame and since he was a pretty big fish in Chhapra, he wasn't questioned. And Garcia got away, secure in the knowledge that he wouldn't be pursued there.

Roy called Chanda and gave them the gist of the conversation. What it meant was that the plan of sending a team to Bihar stood cancelled. Tanya would have to go back to the drawing board. She also concluded that a Plan B would have to involve interrogating Dr Varma further and the fresh round of interrogation would have to be led by Ramadhar, because it had become abundantly clear that Dr Varma was terrified of the big bad SI whose ancestors had settled in Calcutta but came from the same neck of the woods as him and who broke into Bhojpuri with expletive-laden tirades threatening physical violence and worse.

Tanya assembled her team and passed on to them what she had just heard herself. There were audible groans all around. She ploughed ahead. 'Since Garcia's given us the slip again, we have to prepare another plan. Let's look at what we have. Most probably, Garcia is still somewhere in Bihar. He's on the mend, but still unable to move around freely, mainly because the kneecap on his right leg was shattered by his assailant and will never properly heal unless Garcia gets proper surgery, of which the chances are on the low side. He will walk with a pronounced limp and will be easier to capture. Finally, the chances are that his days of preying are over, though we could never be sure of that. Are we agreed up to here?' There was silence in the room, Tanya presumed, by way of consent. So, she continued. 'Whatever Plan B we have to come up with will have to involve another round of interrogation of Dr Varma, because we now know that he's been distorting the truth and holding back on small, but important, details. The interrogation will be headed by Ramadhar and he will be assisted by Jadunath and Talukdar.' Two bad cops, though Jadunath was not in Ramadhar's class when it came to inspiring terror, but he could be pretty scary as well, accompanied by a mild-mannered good cop, Talukdar.

'Garcia used the name Murtaza in Muzaffarpur. Gopal, Piya and Mrinal will find out everything possible about Murtaza, in case, of course, he was using the name here. I don't have to tell you what to do, but search especially for taxi registration and accommodation. Sushila and Ishita will go back to the survivors to see how they are doing. A bit of hand holding to try and find out whether they remember anything that can help us. They'll also get in touch with Nilanjan Chatterjee and Soumitro Saha to see if they remember anything useful.'

Back on the road, Tanya thought, as the team members dispersed to go about their tasks. All of them looked downcast, some a little more than others. Only Ramadhar and, unaccountably, good cop Talukdar looked happy, broad smiles splitting their faces as they left with Jadunath to prepare for the fresh round of interrogation.

Dr Varma was brought from his cell into an interrogation room, where he had to cool his heels for about three hours. With each passing minute, the panic level kept rising in him and reaching a crescendo when, Ramadhar, Jadunath and Talukdar entered the room and sat on three chairs; Ramadhar was facing him. The sweat had begun to trickle down Dr Varma's scalp and over his forehead. When the first bead of sweat was half way across the doctor's cheek, Ramadhar said in an even tone, 'You've been lying to us and holding out. In other words, you've been trying to mislead.'

'No, no,' Dr Varma said. 'I've told you everything and I haven't lied to you.'

'You motherfucker, you didn't tell us that Garcia's kneecap was smashed and that he'd never be able to walk normally. You didn't tell us that you had no direct conversation with Dr Jha. Now you're going to tell us exactly how badly Garcia was injured, what name he's been using since returning to the city and how you managed to inform him that he would have to get away from Chhapra.'

Dr Varma protested. 'I told you everything, except for the fact that Garcia's right kneecap was smashed. Anyway, unless he checks into a proper hospital and has the correct surgery, he'll never be able to walk properly again. He told me he was driving a taxi for a living, but he had access to funds and would be able to pay whatever I charged. He was using the name Murtaza. He paid me off after two old associates of his gave him the money for my fees and the escape to Chhapra. Their names are Prabhash and Hashim.' He paused. 'It's true that I don't know Dr Jha well, but I've met him. I got in touch with him through my brother, who made all the arrangements. And I have no idea where he could have gone after he left Chhapra. But Dr Jha should know, whatever he may be claiming now.' Little honour among these particular thieves.

That was quite a long speech, all three interrogators thought. Dr Varma was taken back to his cell and Ramadhar reported Dr Varma's revelations to Tanya, who said, 'Okay, so now we have to locate Prabhash and Hashim and sweat them. Get cracking on that immediately. And I'll have to try and persuade the DGP to get the Chhapra police to sweat Dr Jha, who, as of now, claims he has no idea where Garcia is.'

As soon as the trio of detectives left, Tanya called Commissioner Chanda, summarizing Dr Varma's testimony, outlining all measures taken since the phone call from the Bihar DGP, promising a full written status report on the rapes once the ongoing enquiries had been completed, and requested Chanda to ask the Bihar cops to have Dr Jha sweated. Chanda, not pleased, said he'd do his best, but insisted the Calcutta angles should be wrapped up soon.

On Monday, the entire team met early to report to Tanya. Gopal, speaking for his team, kicked off the proceedings. They'd pretty much nailed the Murtaza identity down. 'Garcia must have come to Calcutta in March, ma'am,' Gopal began. 'Perhaps towards the end of the month. He got his taxi registered in mid-April as Murtaza Baig. The licence-plate number is WB 04 T 3741. The documents he'd shown were a voter identification card, a ration card and a driver's licence. He had taken a room in the slums near the Entally market from 1st April. Paid his rent on time. Wasn't in his room for most of the day. Basically, returned to sleep in the early hours when everyone else was asleep. Left home around noon. Started wearing a skull cap and keeping a beard in June. That would be after he raped Aparna Das. Not much else, ma'am.'

Tanya gestured towards Jadunath, who began promptly. 'Located both Prabhash and Hashim, separately. Ramadhar and Talukdar found Prabhash and I found Hashim. Neither tried to be too smart and both came clean, so we didn't bother to take them in. They're partners now. Own a leather unit together, which was bought from the proceeds of their profits from extortion, prostitution, human trafficking and drugs. Both started out under Garcia, so they owe him. Both claimed that they are now legit businessmen, who've paid their debt by serving time. Their separate stories are corroborative. Both claim Garcia called them and asked for money. They organized Rs 1 crore in cash, believe it or not. They knew Garcia was on the run. Both thought this was still the story from the time when Garcia and Shila took off. Both claimed that Garcia told them they didn't need to know where he was headed; the need-to-know principle saved hassles. They agreed and split. Nothing much there, we're afraid, ma'am.'

Piya reported on the survivors. 'First met Gloria, ma'am. In a café. She's been back at work for quite a long time. Seems to have adjusted, ma'am. I mean, got over the trauma. Said she didn't remember anything new. Seemed reluctant to revisit the assault. Mrs Das is another story. We met her at her home. Was reluctant to talk about the incident, ma'am, we both got the impression, for exactly the opposite reason. She hasn't got over it. She's working because she doesn't have a choice. Her ex doesn't pay enough maintenance to run the household comfortably. She's holding herself together. Finding it tough, psychologically. Practically told us as much. She's meeting a counsellor. But can't remember anything that will help.'

Ishita chipped in. 'Chitra's parents have taken her back home. No mobile number for her.'

Tanya said, 'That's okay. I wouldn't feel great about pestering her.'

Piya resumed her report. 'Nilanjan doesn't remember anything new either. Soumitro Saha, ditto. Can't help with half-remembered impressions or anything else at all. It's strange. Everybody in the Gloria Stevens case seems to have moved on.'

'All this is part of the routine. I didn't think we'd get something. All we can do is wait. And get on with the rest of our work. It's up to the Bihar cops, now.'

For the next few days, Tanya concentrated on running her department, trying not to think of Clayton bloody Garcia. On a Wednesday, however, Commissioner Chanda summoned her to his office. Even before Tanya had taken a seat, Chanda started speaking. 'Good news and bad news, I'm afraid,' he said. 'They sweated Dr Jha, who finally admitted that he'd learned later that Garcia had been spirited away to Muzaffarpur. The police promptly detained him and alerted the police in Muzaffarpur, who made enquiries and found out that a man answering to Garcia's description had indeed stayed in a flat for a day and taken off. Showed the sketches and got confirmation. Now, we really don't know where he is and we don't have any leads.'

Tanya almost swore, but controlled herself. 'So, we console ourselves that there won't be any of these nocturnal rapes in the city, until Garcia returns. Women will start feeling safer. Things will return to normal, then Garcia will assume some new identity, some new profession that will give him good reason to roam the city at night, then he'll find a new target. He's going to return, sir, not just because he's a psychopath, which I suppose he is, but because whatever way his warped mind works, ultimately, it's aimed at me specifically and the police department in general. I'm the target because I've destroyed him. There wouldn't be any point for him to do what he's doing in Patna or Lucknow. Or Muzaffarpur for that matter.'

Chanda considered Tanya's analysis in silence. 'You're right,' he said after a while. 'He's going to return.'

'And then we'll nail his hide to the front door of the HQ,' Tanya said.

Back home early, Tanya found the flat empty. Shaman was playing football at Central Park, very close to their home. He favoured it over cricket because it involved more energy, pace and physicality. Shaman wasn't a big boy for his age, but he had plenty of stamina. Tanya showered and decided to cook away her blues. There was some minced beef in the refrigerator and spaghetti. She made a tangy meat sauce. Shaman and Moni came in while she was cooking. By the time he'd showered and changed, Tanya was through, leaving Moni to boil the spaghetti and make a salad. Tanya caught up with her son, who assured his mother that he'd completed his homework. Then the three dined together—a rare occasion. And wound up the day.

The subject of many discussions in Lalbazar was at that moment in a clinic just outside Kathmandu with a new passport and a new identity, hoping to have surgery to fix his shattered knee. His new name was Alex Coelho, a flautist from Pune, who played for a rock'n'roll band called

Western Ghats. Garcia was actually quite an accomplished flautist and had played in a band called Energy in his younger days. And there really was a band called Western Ghats. So, his cover was pretty good, especially considering that it was unlikely that anyone in Nepal would think to check. At best they'd ask him to play the flute, which he'd be able to do because he was carrying a flute he'd bought in Muzaffarpur.

The doctor in the Kathmandu clinic, Roshan Bahadur, inspected Coelho's knee the day after he'd checked in. He had bad news for Coelho. 'If the operation I was thinking of doing had been done soon after the injury, it should have been successful. When did you sustain the injury and what have you been doing since?' he asked, abruptly.

'The injury was sustained almost three weeks ago. Since then, I've been touring with the band. The doctor who plastered my knee told me I should have immediate surgery, but I had a packed schedule, so I thought I'd get it done later. We were doing a concert near Darjeeling when the pain started getting excruciating and someone suggested we come here because the orthopaedics department here is very good.' The story, Garcia was well aware, was thin, but it might just about hold. The flattery might take it across the line, he thought.

'You've been extremely reckless, Mr Coelho. You should have been confined to bed until the surgery. Now there's been further damage to the muscles, ligaments and tendons that support the patella. Even after surgery and the replacement of the patella, your damaged muscles, tendons and ligaments will probably not be able to provide enough support for you to walk properly and unaided. You'll walk with a limp and you'll have to use a walking stick.'

Garcia looked at the doctor, dismay writ large on his face. Shit, he thought. Fucking whore, I'll get you. I'll get both of you, Tanya fucking Samanta and you, pint-sized fucking cunt. I'll find out who you are, I'll rape you and kill you. He forced himself to swallow his rage and said in a voice choked by fury, 'Do your best doc. I trust you.' Dr Bahadur thought, however, that Coelho's voice was choked by disappointment and sadness. He was touched. 'I'll do my best,' he said. 'But looking at the bright side, it won't affect your flute-playing. After the surgery, we'd be happy to hear you play.'

~

Over the next few months, Calcutta regained its stride. Single women resumed taking cabs after dark. And Tanya and her team went about their other investigative businesses, which included orchestrating another round of raids against criminal networks even remotely connected to Clayton Garcia or Shila Nandi. But one thing kept bothering Tanya. Garcia had surfaced, but where in the blazes was Shila Nandi? She didn't really give a flying about the quondam MLA, who had been suspended from the legislative assembly in the interim, but it had occurred to her and the team that locating Nandi could be one way of locating Garcia. Talukdar and Sushila had reverted to Shila's parent *thanas*. Tanya sent Piya and Ishita to speak to Shila Nandi's children, who were being looked after by Debal Nandi, Chhoton Nandi's brother, an unexceptionable retired university professor with no connection to crime. They came back and reported that Shila had not been in touch with her children, who were anxiously awaiting word from their mother.

Meanwhile, Tanya and the team held their breath for what they thought was inevitable. Tanya warned Ghazala that though she'd won one round, she should be extra careful at all times. Even an injured Clayton Garcia was dangerous because he was trained, tenacious and resourceful, and because he was a psychopath, whichever way you sliced it.

Part Five

Salt Lake, Greater Calcutta, January

On a chilly mid-January night, Tanya got a call from Commissioner Ajoy Chanda, asking her to go straight to the Bidhannagar women's police station and get the members of the Garcia hunt team to meet her there. It was around 9 and Tanya had just finished dinner with Shaman and was chatting with him about the possibility of Liverpool, the club he supported, winning the English Premier League, which was distinctly on the improbable side, prior to sending him to bed.

Bidhannagar was the official name of Salt Lake, which was not under Kolkata Police's jurisdiction. 'Bidhannagar?' she asked, surprised she was being sent out of her bailiwick. But even before Chanda could speak, the penny dropped. 'Garcia, sir?'

'Yes,' her boss answered. 'Has his metaphorical fingerprints all over it. Dipanwita Hom. A twenty-six-year-old software engineer, working for an IT firm in Sector V. Lives in Kankurgachi. Left office for home at around 6. Was seen lying unconscious in a pool of blood in Salt Lake Central Park by four teenagers—all boys—at around 8. They were shit scared, but managed to keep it together and find a police officer. A posse from Bidhannagar Women Police Station (WPS) reached the spot in about ten minutes after calling an ambulance that got there at roughly the same time. Took her to Columbia Asia straightaway. I think she's in critical condition. There's a team at Central Park, but you should go to the WPS first. The OC is a woman called ... let's see ... Rupali Mahapatra.' The hesitation with the name was, Tanya knew instantly, a way of registering disapproval of all-women police stations and the necessity of appointing women as their OCs. Tanya thought regretfully that few women had ever been appointed OC of a general *thana*. She pushed the thought aside and said, 'I'm on my way, sir.'

'Is the office car with you?'

'No sir. I'll drive my own.'

'Better not. Call your driver and PSO. At this point, it doesn't matter whether you get there half an hour later than you would have had you taken your own car. There might be mobility issues.' Chanda sure was a shitbag in many ways, but he was very articulate. Not a comma out of place, even when he was speaking.

'All right, sir.'

Tanya called Sheonath. 'Organize a car and come straight to my house as fast as possible. I need to go to Salt Lake.'

'Yes, madam,' Sheonath said. 'I'll be there in half an hour.' That's optimistic, Tanya thought, but she knew he'd get to her place faster than anyone else in the force. She called the members of the Garcia team and told them to proceed to the Bidhannagar WPS immediately. Sheonath and her official car arrived punctually in half an hour.

At 9:30 on a winter night, traffic was thin. Calcutta

hardly has a winter to speak of. Even at its coldest, it's pretty mild. Minimum temperatures of around 9°C are considered harsh by most Calcuttans, especially when the maximum temperature falls below 20°C. Neither happened very often. This year, the minimum temperature had dropped to 9°C, the lowest in hundred odd years, and the maximum had touched 19.3°C. Calcuttans were wearing layers even during the day. After sundown, they scurried home to electric heaters, layers of woollens, and thick blankets and quilts. At this time of the year, Bengalis, like the English, didn't have sex lives, they had hot water bottles. Tanya was in Salt Lake just after 10:15 that night.

Jadunath and Piya were already there when she arrived. Piya had spoken to Ishita five minutes ago; she'd reach in another ten minutes at the outside. She told them to wait and went to see Inspector Rupali Mahapatra. The OC was, in fact, waiting for Tanya outside her chamber. She was all set to give Tanya the details and the state of play. 'Ma'am, the lady who was attacked is in a coma,' she said. 'All the doctors are willing to say now is that the next twenty-four hours are crucial. They can't make a prognosis before that. But from what the first responders and the doctors are saying, the attack was exceptionally brutal. Cracked her head, broke several ribs and her left hand. Also left her with injuries all over. The doctors are pretty sure that rape was involved, though the last time I talked to them they had not done a rape test yet; the priority is saving her life.'

'I was told that there were two teams in place: one at the hospital and one at the spot,' Tanya said.

'Ma'am, there are two constables and an armed sub-inspector at the spot and one constable in the hospital. I haven't really got the investigation going, because I thought you'd be here soon and I should wait for you.'

'Which IT company did she work for? Do you have an address for her? Has her family been informed?'

'Her bag was found next to her. I'll have someone bring it. She worked for Solutions Software ma'am. I've got the number and address for the office and the mobile number of the managing director, who is also the sole proprietor of the company. His name is Alok Rajpuria.' She gave Tanya the number, who saved it on her mobile. 'She lives with her parents in Kankurgachi. Her Aadhaar card was in her bag, so we have her address. I sent a sub-inspector to inform her parents. They must be at the hospital by now. She was found by four boys at around 8. I've let them go home, but they'll come in in the morning for questioning and to sign statements.'

Tanya had heard those details. The one that had stood out, as with the other rapes, was that nothing seemed to have been stolen. 'I want one officer from your PS on my team. Someone who knows the area, the issues, the habitual offenders. You know what I mean. She'll work from here and liaise between DD and your PS when necessary. I'll sort out the paperwork.' It would be necessary. Bidhannagar WPS was under Bidhannagar City Police, which was part of the West Bengal Police. Kolkata Police had been called in after jurisdictional issues had been sorted out at the highest level only because it had been assumed that the attack was part of the ongoing 'cabbie rape' case.

'I'll have to speak to our commissioner to clear it, ma'am. I'll depute Shreya Daga. She's smart and knows the area and the history-sheeters well,' Rupali said. Tanya called her boss, who, anticipating it, had stayed awake. 'I'm in Salt Lake, sir,' she began. 'Getting the whole team together because I don't want to lose any time. I'll line up interviews as and when. I'll also wake people up, if I have to. The victim is in ICU in a coma. The doctors are not committing themselves on anything in the next twenty-four hours. I suspect that could become forty-eight hours. There's a possibility that we'll have a rape-murder on our hands. Garcia was a cop. He'll know if the woman dies and he gets caught, he'll face four counts of rape and one of premeditated murder. He's crossed the Rubicon, sir. He'll swing if Dipanwita Hom dies.'

'Yes,' was all her boss could manage under the circumstances.

'Sir,' Tanya continued. 'I'd like to pull Sushila and Talukdar back into the team. Can I do it right away? You'd have to give retrospective sanction for the fresh deputation. I'm also worried about the jurisdictional issues.'

Chanda said, 'Don't worry about jurisdiction. It's been cleared. If anything comes up I'll talk to DG Roy, who'll have a word with the Bidhannagar police commissioner. I'll clear the deputations.'

Tanya called the two of them immediately and summoned them to Bidhannagar WPS.

While Tanya had been making her calls, OC Rupali Mahapatra called the Bidhannagar Commissioner of Police and asked for his permission to depute an officer to Kolkata

Police in the matter of the rape victim found raped and seriously assaulted in Central Park. Since jurisdictional questions had been sorted out and Kolkata Police DD allowed to take over an investigation that normally would have been conducted by Bidhannagar Police, he green-lighted the deputation verbally, pending paperwork. He knew, unlike Rupali, that the prime suspect in the string of rapes that had remained unsolved for over six months was a rogue cop.

Shreya waited patiently while Tanya worked her phone. It was only after all she had finished making her calls that she noticed a young woman in uniform standing to attention. Rupali introduced her. 'Ma'am, ASI Shreya Daga.' Tanya didn't have to be introduced. Everyone in the PS knew that JCP (Crime) Tanya Samanta of Kolkata Police had come to take over the investigation into the most sensational crime that had taken place in Salt Lake in recent times. Not that the police could be sure it had taken place in Salt Lake at all.

'Hello,' Tanya said. 'Organize enquiries into the incident through your grapevine. See if you can pick up any buzz. Need help?'

'It would be faster, ma'am, if someone helped.'

Tanya called Ishita and told her to work with ASI Shreya Daga. Shreya would explain.

Jadunath and Piya got the job of interviewing Alok Rajpuria. 'Get the names and numbers of every employee of Solutions Software. Then you break up into pairs and go and interview every employee. It doesn't matter if people have to be woken up in the middle of the night,' Tanya instructed them. Sushila and Talukdar had both arrived. She noted that and resumed. 'While Shreya and Ishita, and Jadunath and Piya get down to their tasks, Mrinal will go to the hospital, and the rest of us to Central Park. Mrinal will join us later.'

Jadunath and Piya had disappeared, as had Shreya and Ishita. Mrinal headed off for Columbia Asia, while the rest went to Central Park, which was being guarded by personnel from Bidhannagar WPS and Bidhannagar North police station. Lights had also been set up so that the area could be better examined. When she arrived at the spot, she realized there was no point in tapping the department's forensic resources. Garcia had been a cop; an exceptionally competent one. All the women he had dumped, he had dumped in places where forensic examination would yield nothing: the heavily frequented Minto Park and Lake areas; the densely vegetated area around the pond/lake in Santoshpur; and now Central Park. Not that it mattered, forensics would only and maximally have confirmed the identity of the perpetrator. Which they already knew. Unless this was a copycat. She didn't even entertain that thought for the moment. If it was, they were in big trouble. One Garcia was bad enough, but there was a glimmer that they'd get him. If copycats got in on the act, they were lost.

They examined the area, but there was nothing really to note except the dried blood that stained the spot where Dipanwita had been dumped. Still, they poked around for a while until Tanya realized that going through the motions was farcical and called the whole thing off. Mrinal arrived just when they'd started to pack up. Tanya told the sentries to leave and the park attendants that they could lock up. The DD team went to the women's police station to await word from Jadunath and Piya.

~

Luckily for Jadunath and Piya, Rajpuria lived in Salt Lake, Sector III. His residence was just a ten-minute drive from Central Park through the deserted streets of a dead-at-night Salt Lake. And they made it under ten, the driver speeding down the streets. When they called Rajpuria, it was just past 11. He sounded sleepy. Jadunath introduced himself and told Rajpuria that he wanted to see him now, as in right now, on important police business. 'Are you crazy?' Rajpuria asked.

'No, sir. You will appreciate that crime doesn't follow strict schedules. We have to see you. It's about one of your employees.'

'One of my employees?' Rajpuria said, like an echo chamber. 'Why? What?'

'Sir, we can't discuss his over the phone. That's why we have to see you right now.' Jadunath sounded like he was doing Rajpuria a huge favour.

Rajpuria capitulated. 'Okay. Come quickly.'

They arrived at the house at around 11:15 p.m. Rajpuria opened the door himself and led them in. He looked to be in his late thirties or early forties. His drawing room was tastefully and expensively furnished. Solutions Software was obviously not doing too badly. Jadunath introduced Piya, who, it had been agreed, would break the news and ask for the information they wanted. 'You have an employee called Dipanwita Hom, sir?'

Rajpuria nodded with an air of mystification. 'Yes,' he said. 'Has something happened to her?'

'Yes, sir. She's been attacked, raped and assaulted brutally. Right now, she's in a coma. In Columbia Asia. We need to plot her movements once she left office. At the moment, it seems obvious that she was assaulted on her way home. Or, maybe she was going somewhere else. Do you know when she left?'

Rajpuria had blanched and seemed incapable of speech. Jadunath prompted him. 'Sir.'

'Raped? Coma? What are you talking about?'

'Sir, you have to pull yourself together,' Piya said, not unkindly.

Rajpuria shook his head. 'I don't know when she left. I must have been in my room.'

'How many employees do you have, sir?'

'Twenty.'

'Including odd-jobs people and drivers?'

'No drivers. Only one man to make tea and fetch water. And a lady, who comes in the morning, cleans and leaves.'

Jadunath broke in. 'Sir, we need a list of all these employees and their addresses and phone numbers. Now.'

'Now? How can I give you a list in the middle of the night?'

'By taking us to your office and having it opened. There must be a list in office. Sir, you want this man caught, don't you? Let me tell you. The first twenty-four hours is the most important period for us. Most cases are cracked in the first forty-eight hours. The ones that aren't don't get cracked at all.'

Rajpuria shook his head vigorously. Like he was drunk and was trying to snap back to sobriety. 'Okay. Let's go.'

They went to Sector V. He booted his computer, pulled out a file and asked, 'How many copies do you want?'

'Seven,' Piya said, with abundant caution.

Rajpuria printed out the copies and said, with sudden vehemence, 'What kind of sicko would do this? She's such a nice, bright girl. You have to get this man. Kill him. He doesn't deserve to live.'

'Thank you for your cooperation, sir. We'll get him,' Jadunath promised, before taking off with their list. He dropped Rajpuria home and headed off to the Bidhannagar WPS, where Tanya and the team were waiting. They'd done well, though. Back well before 12:30 a.m., which meant they'd taken just over an hour. They handed over all the copies of the list to Tanya. Four teams, eighteen employees. Spread across the city. Tanya mulled the logistics. North, south, east and west. Two of the employees lived in Salt Lake, one in Baguihati and one in Dum Dum. One team was going to take that lot. Since Jadunath and Piya had already been traipsing around Salt Lake, she allotted this beat to them. 'Okay, Jadunath and Piya, you're taking these four.' She marked out the names and handed a copy of the list to Jadunath, saying, 'Start working the phones. Don't take no for an answer. If someone doesn't answer, just land up on their doorstep and bang on their doors. This goes for everyone.'

There were five addresses in south Calcutta: Bhabanipur, Gol Park, Garia, Tollygunge and Park Circus. 'Ramadhar and Ishita will take the south Calcutta addresses.' She marked the names and handed the list to Ramadhar. There were four addresses in north Calcutta: Shyambazar, Baghbazar, Beadon Street and Amherst Street. Tanya marked those names out and handed them to Sushila. 'You and Talukdar take the north Calcutta addresses. Same rules.' There were three addresses in Behala, New Alipur, Khidirpur, which landed on Mrinal and Shreya's lap. Gopal got two addresses in Theatre Road and Central Avenue; and Tanya went home and awaited developments. The four teams and Gopal started working the phones and set off.

Jadunath and Piya headed at around 1 a.m. to one of the Salt Lake addresses, where an extremely pissed-off young lady, Rajpuria's secretary, was waiting for them, having been woken up from deep slumber. There was nothing gracious in her reception. But it was past 1 a.m. and they hadn't told her why they'd disturbed her sleep. Ananya Chakrabarti ushered them into the flat. Her husband and infant were sleeping. The first thing she said in a stage whisper was, 'Speak softly. Don't wake up my daughter.'

Jadunath spoke in a low tone and without ceremony, 'We want to ask you a few questions about Dipanwita Hom. She was raped and badly assaulted last evening. At the moment, she's in ICU. She might not survive.' He got the effect he had wanted. Ananya's mouth fell open, her face was drained of colour. 'What? What are you saying?' she asked.

'Did you know her well?' Ishita asked her.

'Not really,' Ananya answered. 'I'm Mr Rajpuria's secretary. I handle all the employees' files and they come to me if they want something that Mr Rajpuria has to clear: leave applications, offsite work, etc. So, I know everyone in the office, but I don't really mix with any of them.'

'When did Dipanwita leave the office yesterday?' Jadunath asked.

'I have no idea. I left at 7 and she'd left before that because she wasn't in her seat. Anyway, she usually leaves at around 6-6:30.'

'Was she troubled about anything? Do you know whether something out of the ordinary was going on?' Ishita asked.

'I rarely have conversations about private matters with any of the staff. I'm seen as an extension of the boss. So, nobody is really informal with me and I keep it that way.' On that note, the detectives said their good nights and left for the next Salt Lake address. There, too, an extremely sleepy 'sales executive', Suman Hazra, was waiting for them with bleary eyes. The questioning went more or less along the same lines. Finally, they made it to their northernmost destination, to meet Kallol Sur, who was involved in 'hardware maintenance'. They reached his bachelor pad around 3:30. They had to ring the bell a few times before Kallol opened the door. He apologized, 'I reckoned it would take you some time to get here, so I went to sleep.' He was the only one they'd met that morning who had let them in without rancour. 'So, what's this all about?' he asked. 'It must be pretty serious. I called home, which is in Burdwan, hoping nothing had happened.

Nothing had. And if it's not family, it must be friends or office.' Innocence or pretence?

'How well do you know Dipanwita Hom?'

'Quite well, actually. Why? What's wrong?'

'There's some bad news, Mr Sur,' Piya said. Kallol's forehead creased. 'She was abducted after she left office, and raped and beaten very badly. She's at the hospital fighting for her life. The problem is we don't know when she left, where she was going and how she was commuting. We were hoping you could shed some light on these.'

Kallol had a look of incomprehension on his face. 'Raped? Beaten? Fighting for her life? What the hell are you talking about?'

'Sir, we understand you are in shock. But the faster we get a lead, the better the chance of finding the perpetrator.'

Kallol walked to the fridge, extracted a bottle of water and took a long swig. 'Want some?' They nodded assent. Kallol gave them water. Then he said, 'Dipa and I are good friends. In the context of office, of course. We frequently go out for a cup of tea. We've had lunch together many times. Dipa left at 6 o'clock sharp. I was still in office. She was going home and had plans to go out for dinner with her fiancé. His name is Cyrus Poonawallah. He's a Parsi, which is why there was some opposition to the marriage in her family. But all that got sorted out. I have no idea what kind of transport she took. Shefali, who is also a software developer, left with her. That's Shefali Sinha, she lives somewhere in south Calcutta.'

Jadunath whipped out their copy of the list and located the name. She lived in Tollygunge. He called Ramadhar, who answered immediately. 'A woman called Shefali Sinha, who lives in Tollygunge, left the office with Dipanwita. Have you got to her yet?'

'On our way. She didn't sound very happy.' They'd scheduled Tollygunge as the final stop.

'We're headed home. See you in the morning.'

'It's already morning.' Ramadhar hung up.

Ten minutes later, Ramadhar and Ishita were with Shefali. She was really pissed off, but trying, at least, not to show it. Ramadhar took the direct route. 'We've heard that you and Dipanwita Hom left office together yesterday?'

'Yes, we did. Is anything wrong?' Shefali answered.

Ishita cut in. 'Somewhere between Sector V and Salt Lake Central Park, Dipanwita was abducted, raped and brutally beaten. She's in a coma.'

'What? Are you joking? What's this?' Denial showing up as outrage.

'It's true, Ms Sinha,' Ishita said. 'You need to tell us exactly what happened after you left work.'

Shefali burst into tears. 'It can't be true,' she said, through her sobs.

Ishita gently reminded her, 'You have to pull yourself together. Every minute that passes makes it more difficult for us to catch the person who did this to your friend.'

Shefali managed to get herself under control. Still sniffling, she said, 'We went to the bus stop. Though we go in different directions, we catch a bus from the same stop. I get a direct bus here, but Dipa has to change. But yesterday she was supposed to go out for dinner with her fiancé, so she took a taxi at the bus stop.'

Ramadhar asked very quietly. 'Did you see the driver?'

'Yes. He was leaning against the taxi when we approached him.'

'What did he look like?'

'Thin and fair. Long hair at the back, but balding at the top. Long beard and light eyes. I noticed that. Had a limp and a scar on his face.'

'This is very important, Ms Sinha,' Ramadhar said. 'Can you accompany us to Lalbazar? We'll show you three sketches and drop you back. This is very, very important. We want you to make an identification.'

'Fine,' Shefali said. 'Anything to catch the man.'

By the time Ramadhar and Ishita got back to Lalbazar with Shefali at around 4:30, everyone had gone home except Tanya. 'We brought Ms Sinha here to look at the sketches, ma'am. Confirmation to rule out a copycat,' Ramadhar told her.

'Good,' Tanya said. 'Please take a seat. Thank you for coming here at such an outlandish hour.' She pulled the three sketches out of her drawer and handed Shefali the first one, made with Soumitro's help. Shefali examined it and said, 'Looks familiar, but I can't be sure.' Next, Tanya showed her the photoshopped sketch created with Ghazala's help. Shefali immediately said, 'It's him. For sure, that's the man.'

Tanya exhaled slowly. Small mercies, it wasn't a copycat.

It was 5. A car would drop Shefali home and then Ishita to her place in Garia. Ramadhar remained in the room, fiddling. 'Anything wrong, Ramadhar?' Tanya asked.

'Yes, ma'am,' he said.

'What's it?'

'Ma'am, the attack on Tapan. I'm sure who the leak is. Or the leaks are.'

Tanya stared at him. 'Someone on the team,' she said. It wasn't a question.

'Mrinal, communicating with Garcia through an ASI called Debraj Banik. In Jadavpur PS, ma'am. After the attack on Tapan, I decided to look around. First, I studied our team members. I ruled out Talukdar and Sushila straightaway. Also Ishita because she joined us recently. Piya is new to DD too. Jadunath and Gopal had worked with Garcia, but also with me. I thought it was unlikely they would be in cahoots. Still, I watched them. And Mrinal. For months. The more I watched, the more Mrinal seemed the likely culprit. So, I started following him quietly. A week ago, I shadowed him to a tea shack near Metro cinema hall. I think he figured he'd be anonymous in Dharamtala. He chatted for half an hour with a guy, whom I followed. He went to Jadavpur PS on a motorbike. Turned out to be this Banik guy. I made discreet enquiries about him. He was suspected of being involved in Shila Nandi's rackets. That clinched it for me. But I still ran a test. Without telling you, ma'am. I went out for tea the day before yesterday with Mrinal and told him that Tapan's security cover was being withdrawn from the next day. That is, yesterday.

'I followed Mrinal and he met Banik at the same place. Yesterday, I went to Bhabanipur early in the morning, concealing myself. I was carrying my personal, licensed Smith and Wesson. At 6:45, I called Tapan and told him to leave for his walk, but turn back and go home in two-three minutes. As if he'd forgotten something. He did that. I saw a bike start, rev and take off. I'd already identified the riders as possible shooters and my gun was drawn. I'd have shot them, before they could do anything. I noted down the number of the bike. I told Tapan he should stay home for the day.' Ramadhar paused.

Tanya looked at him and he resumed his story. 'I checked out the bike. It was registered to a punk we'd picked up during our first round of raids on Garcia's establishments: Jibon Sen. He's out on bail. I had his home address. A shack near Picnic Gardens. I'd seen him because he was driving the bike and he'd taken his helmet off for a few minutes. I kept watch on his house to make sure he was one of the would-be shooters. He was. So, we know Mrinal's the leak. Mrinal met Banik for lunch at a cheap roadside eatery in Kasba. My cousin went there and sat at the same table with a recorder in his pocket. We've got our smoking gun. They talked about the message I gave Mrinal. They think they're both compromised. Mrinal wants out and Banik tells him that's not possible. Mrinal agrees and says he wants more money and Banik pays. They decide to keep closer watch and inform Garcia. Before leaving, Banik tells Mrinal there's nothing to be scared of, I must have picked up some wrong information. Mrinal says that's possible, I'm not a very bright guy.' Ramadhar smiled and handed over a pen drive to Tanya.

Tanya rested her chin on her palms and thought: I have two options. One, I allow him to stay on the team and feed Garcia disinformation. But that would be difficult.

Two, I bust him. I'll decide tonight. Before leaving, Tanya chalked out a campaign plan. She wrote herself a memo: We'll have to work shifts to keep the investigation alive twenty-four hours. That means twelve-hour shifts for some time. Ramadhar and Talukdar will be on from 8:00 p.m. to 8:00 a.m. Jadunath, Sushila and Ishita will work from 8 a.m. to 8 p.m. Gopal, Shreya and Piya will work from 11 a.m. to 11 p.m. Today, morning shift can't start at 8 a.m. obviously. It's 5:30 already. So, morning shift shows up at 11 a.m. The new shifts kick off from tomorrow.

Tanya reached home at 6. She was up at 9:30 and at Lalbazar by 10:45. The moment she stepped into her room, she called the hospital to enquire about Dipa. The doctor had some good news. Dipa had stirred, sometime in the night. Her parameters seemed to be stable. He wouldn't say anything definitive till another day had passed or the patient regained consciousness, whichever came first. Relieved, Tanya told her boss, 'I have some good news. It's definitely Garcia. A colleague of the survivor who was with her when she took the cab identified him from the sketches.' She went on to give a clear account of the previous night and that morning's activities. 'It's incredible, sir,' she said. 'He knows his cabbie identity has been blown. He must be aware that we know he has a scar on his face and a limp. He is noticeable. Yet, he's come back to prey again. Sir, we'll have to launch a manhunt. All police jurisdictions need to participate. We must catch him before he kills. As things stand, some more good news is that Dipanwita Hom might survive Garcia's attack.' She didn't mention Ramadhar's story.

'We have to catch him, Samanta. But can we spare personnel from all police stations? I'm not sure. Let me discuss this with the secretary.'

As Tanya hunkered down for a manhunt, her quarry was stretched out on a bed in a small room in a slum-like settlement in Naihati, an industrial town north of Calcutta, where Garcia could live in relative safety but from where he could comfortably commute into Calcutta, by train, getting to Sealdah station in under an hour. He'd chosen the slum settlement because it was a little off the arterial roads, but just a fifteen-minute walk to the station. He'd sold his taxi in Bihar to Shivanand Varma, the man who was responsible for the fact that he was still enjoying his freedom.

He'd settled down in Naihati in November, under the assumed name of Aakash Tripathi. The legend he'd created for Tripathi was a little complicated, but flexible and backed by good documentation: he was from Bihar, but his family had settled down in Calcutta, where he'd gone to college, dropped out and later worked as a driver with various employers. He'd started frequenting tea shops in different parts of Naihati and making friends, passing on the word that he was looking for a job. Most people found this disfigured man grave but courteous. His knowledge of a wide range of topics was much appreciated in tea-stall chatter sessions.

Towards the end of the month, an acquaintance who

was also a driver, introduced him to a wealthy trader, who wanted someone to drive his son and daughter to and from school in the mornings and afternoons, and be around for the rest of the day to drive his wife wherever she wanted to go. He took Garcia's forged references at face value having obtained verbal assurances of his would-be chauffeur's reliability. Garcia started working at the beginning of December, and promptly started making plans for his next assault on JCP Tanya Samanta.

Lying in bed in his small room, Garcia felt the black rage wash over him again. It was getting more and more frequent with every passing day. As the rage built, he'd start fantasizing about raping and mercilessly beating Tanya Samanta and the slip of a fucking bitch-whore who'd beaten and slashed him. Once he calmed down, he'd realize that until he discovered the identity of the girl, he'd have to find substitutes who would provide the sexual gratification that came with rape and the bloodlust that was satisfied only by violent sex and assault. That was the rush he craved. The high he felt when he'd got that bitch in Sector V. They'd never get him. He'd entered Sealdah, after taking a day off on the pretext of wanting to see his ailing daughter, and started walking down CIT Road. He was wearing the blue uniform that yellow-cab drivers were required to.

Close to the spot where he'd turned into a lane with Ghazala on the backseat, he saw a parked taxi with no driver in sight. In seconds, he'd jimmied the door, hotwired the taxi and taken off. He'd picked up Dipanwita from

Sector V in it. After that, it had been a walk in the park, almost literally. He'd raped and beaten her in a quiet spot in the gathered gloom of the early evening that Calcutta's winter brought with it, imagining she was Tanya Samanta. He'd dumped the unconscious woman in Central Park and driven the taxi to the exact spot he'd taken it from and scooted, leaving it unlocked. Then he'd returned to Naihati. Mission accomplished.

Garcia felt he was getting back into his stride. He had a job. It wasn't badly paid. He had a place to live where no one even remotely suspected him of not being who and what he was supposed to be. He was on the run, but didn't really feel like he was, as he had felt in the seven months or so since July last year. The run to Chhapra, the all-too-brief stopover, followed by the run to Muzaffarpur and then Nepal, had exhausted him physically. The long, and enforced, stay there under the watchful treatment of and rehabilitation supervised by Dr Bahadur had almost exhausted the money Prabhash and Hashim had given him. Still, he felt that the Nepalese doctor had done a pretty good job with his right leg.

The constant dull ache was gone and though he still had an unmistakable limp, he could move around reasonably well. He still had money in his Nepal accounts, but he'd decided to keep that untouched for his final run, after he had raped and killed JCP Tanya Samanta and the bitch-whore who'd disabled him. Which reminded him that he'd have to start making enquiries to establish her identity. Not now though. He knew they'd launch a manhunt, especially if that stupid cunt died. He would avoid Calcutta completely. When he got tired of Naihati, he could go someplace else. Possibly north. Perhaps the hills.

~

Tanya had returned to her room a little downcast. Confirmation of the necessity of apprehending Garcia was a no-brainer. She hadn't needed to go to her boss for that. She'd wanted cooperation in launching a manhunt involving all police stations in Calcutta. Still, she thought, she'd have to devise a strategy. But nothing came to mind as a feasible way of going forward. They knew it was Garcia. They knew his cab's licence-plate number. The problem was that they were clueless about what name he was using now, where he was staying and what taxi he was driving, or, for that matter, the new licence-plate number of his registered taxi, which had never been located. So, where did they start?

They couldn't trawl the slums and dives for a man with no name or a random assumed name. What they could do to prevent another attack was to tell women in the city, through a press briefing, not to ride a taxi driven by a man with a scar running from over the left ear and ending just above the windpipe on the same side of the face. They could also ask the public to report a man with such a scar and a limp, possibly driving a taxi. That wasn't a bad idea, she thought. And called her boss again. 'We can't not inform women in the city that they are in danger from the cabbie who terrorized the city last year, can we?' Tanya asked, with a rhetorical flourish. 'The danger is, of course, that he'll simply go underground and surface in guises we know nothing about and continue preying. But, sir, I think we have to take that risk.'

'We'll wait for a few days. If nothing breaks, I'll have Rath hold another press conference. You can tell him what he'll have to communicate to the media.'

Disappointment again. It was almost 11 o'clock. She went to the meeting room and found everyone there, except Ramadhar. 'There's nothing we can really do,' she told them. 'We know it was Garcia. That's it. We can hit his associates, including Dr Livingstone, for more information.' She turned to Jadunath and Gopal. 'See what you can get.'

Mrinal looked a bit mystified, 'Dr Livingstone?' he asked.

'Forget it, Mrinal,' Tanya said and left the meeting.

Soon after she returned to her room, her landline rang. The operator told her that the OC, Entally police station, was on the line. She asked him to be put through. 'Ma'am, good morning. Myself Tirtho Samajpati, OC, Entally *thana*,' a voice said.

'Good morning,' Tanya responded.

'Ma'am, I want to report a case that may be connected to last evening's rape. Yesterday, a taxi driver came to the *thana* and reported that his taxi was missing. He'd parked it near the Ananda Palit bus stop and gone to buy some things. When he returned to the spot, his vehicle, number WB 04 M 2922, was missing. This morning, he returned and reported that he had gone back to the Ananda Palit area to see whether anyone had noticed anything, and he found his taxi parked exactly where he'd left it, unlocked.

Totally surprised, he came to report the matter.' The OC stopped to take a breath. 'One of my officers found this incident so odd that he thought about it for a long time and made a connection between the rape and the stolen taxi. He then reported his conclusions to me. And I called you immediately. Ma'am, do you think there could be a connection?'

'I think there's a chance that the perpetrator stole the taxi to commit the crime. Thank you for getting in touch with me immediately and tell your officer he's done a fine job,' Tanya said. She called the commissioner again. Thrice in the space of just over an hour, Tanya thought. Must be some kind of record. She told him about her conversation with OC Samajpati. She pointed out, 'This means that Garcia has disposed of his vehicle. If we assume that he's going to follow this pattern of stealing cars to commit his crimes, he'll be even more difficult to trace. I think it is our duty to inform the public, sir. I'd like to circulate all three sketches through the media.'

'I'm meeting the HS this afternoon. I'll run both ideas past him then. I'll call you when I'm back.'

Datta had always struck Tanya as a competent and commonsensical man. She also decided to make a full disclosure about the Mrinal angle. 'Sir,' she began nervously, 'I have a big problem on my hands, which I can't sign off myself. It's for you to take a decision.' Chanda nodded absently. And Tanya gave him a blow-by-blow. His eyes widened, the breath went out of him with a whoosh and he seemed to crumple by the time Tanya finished the story. She gave him the two options on hand.

Chanda glared at her. 'Suspended, pending investigation. I'll issue orders,' he said.

Tanya was glad her boss had finally taken a tough decision. She knew, of course, that while most people in the force thought that the commissioner was a weak-kneed, political type as well as a real bastard, there had never, ever been any doubts about his personal integrity. He bowed to politicians, but he wasn't corrupt and never took personal advantage of his position. 'Can I interrogate them after the order comes through. Before they are taken into custody?' she requested.

'All right. Make it the day after.'

Tanya went back to her room with a sense of optimism. She tried to find patterns but couldn't. Not geographical, not occupational. None of them knew each other. Random, opportunistic crimes; the only motives being the desire to take revenge on his former boss, herself, for dismantling his criminal network; and severe psychopathology of some kind, possibly. She just couldn't get into Clayton Garcia's head. Most people don't think that paperwork is a big part of police procedure. But the fact was that a cop could go through his/her whole career never being involved in a car chase or a murder investigation, but paperwork? That was an unavoidable part of their daily lives. So, Tanya busied herself catching up with the paperwork on which she always seemed to be behind.

At the end of the working day, Chanda summoned her. 'Met the HS. He doesn't agree that a manhunt on the scale you have suggested is feasible, or wise. His choice of words. The good news is that he agrees that the public must be informed. I'll have Rath hold a press conference; we'll give the press copies of all the sketches, the extent of the injuries, etc. Brief Rath. The orders on ASI Mallik have been passed. You'll have to serve them on him tomorrow.'

Tanya balked, but said, 'And Debraj Banik of Jadavpur PS, sir?'

'OC Mishra will serve the same orders on him, tomorrow.'

She went ahead and organized the press briefing with Rath. The text was a reworked version of the one Rath had released after the attack on Chitra. They also wrote a caption: *Three good likenesses of the taxi driver. He has a scar on his face (sketch 3) and a pronounced limp, because of an injury to his right knee. If you spot this man, call the police immediately on dedicated lines. The numbers you can call are:* ***1800 9231 899/100.*** *The man is dangerous armed or unarmed. Do not engage in any way. Call the police at once.*

The press briefing was the starting point. The warning and the sketches were telecast that night and printed in all the papers the next morning. Some of the brighter and cannier reporters, including Raina Aqeel, made the connection between a rape and serious assault that had happened the night before last but had not been reported in full because of time constraints. Taxi drivers who heard the news realized that they'd have a hard time getting fares after sundown.

~

Garcia was an early riser. Had always been. That gave him one more life. He'd already used up four. The first in Madhyamgram, where the alert from his accomplice had hastened his getaway. Then, in Calcutta, where Dr Varma's alertness, quick thinking and adroit organizational work had enabled his departure to Chhapra. The third in Chhapra, where his intuition, which had kicked in when he had been unable to get through to the doctor, allowed him to escape to Muzaffarpur. What had caused him to run from Muzaffarpur was the news that the police were asking questions about him in Chhapra.

Garcia was wedded to routine. He couldn't maintain it perfectly because a policeman's life is unpredictable. But he tried to minimize chaos. In Naihati, upon waking up, he would wash and go to a nearby roadside tea shop, read the papers and drink tea, before heading back to his room. On this morning, however, he was filled with horror when he looked at the front page of *The Times of India*. He didn't linger for a cup of tea, but went straight home, where he slowly and carefully read the three-odd stories that bore Raina Aqeel's byline. Much before he finished reading, he realized he'd have to flee. There was no way that a significant section of the general newspaper-reading or television-viewing public would fail to connect him with the sketches. And they wouldn't miss the limp. He had to admit they'd done a remarkable job of producing a likeness, which his long hair and beard wouldn't hide.

Garcia completed his ablutions quickly, packed his meagre belongings and went to the bus station, thinking instinctively that he'd have more flexibility. All he wanted was to hightail it to somewhere much further away from Calcutta. He boarded a bus leaving right then for Krishnanagar, the headquarters of the neighbouring district of Nadia. Reaching his destination, he first went to a barber's shop and got a standard haircut: neither the shaven style, nor the long locks. He also had his beard trimmed closely. Then he checked into a small, affordable hotel. His room was small, but reasonably clean. It had running water. And, being close to the station, it was pretty anonymous. He had a bath and changed into his clean, but threadbare clothes. He had some money on him. Whatever he'd brought back from Nepal and his salary, mostly intact. He cursed himself for not having robbed the woman he'd raped and dumped in Central Park. He decided he'd rape, batter and rob Tanya Samanta when he finally got her, and that slip of a girl too.

In the meantime, he had to plan where he would run from his temporary refuge, Krishnanagar. First thing he crossed out was any further help from Shivanand Varma, who had told him categorically when he couldn't and wouldn't help him anymore. Jharkhand? Garcia thought. There were many small towns and pretty backwaters. The fuck-up was that there were too many Bengalis there, both residents and tourists. Someone could spot him.

Bihar thrust itself forward as the only real option. Close enough to raid his home town, but not interested enough to keep track of what was happening in Calcutta. So, Garcia stayed in Krishnanagar for a few days, cooped up in his room during the day, leaving only for meals after sundown, limping his way around town. He studied maps of Bihar to identify a safe destination and finally chose Katihar, a small town near the Bengal border, up north. He could be in Calcutta overnight. It would be tough to plan the Tanya project from that distance, but once he decided on something he felt better. He'd figure out a way of getting back to Calcutta for a week and setting up shop. He tried to call Prabhash. No reply. Tried Hashim. Ditto. He called four more former associates. Shut out. Then he called Banik, his point man in the force. No reply. Now that he was a fugitive accused of raping four women and almost killing one of them, he'd become a pariah. His associates were mobsters. They'd kill if absolutely necessary, but no wanton rape and murder. That was beyond the pale for run-of-the-mill criminals.

The only person who loyally answered his call was Suleiman. 'Stay away from Calcutta, Kali*da*,' he had warned. 'If you come to the city, they'll catch you.' Garcia had thanked him and hung up.

The next morning, Garcia left for a town called Raiganj in the district of North Dinajpur, which bordered Bihar. After stops and dodges, just in case, he was in Katihar in thirty-six hours. He rented a similar kind of room in a similar kind of place and immediately set about looking for a driving job. He also started using his phone again, getting a reply again only from Suleiman.

~

The morning Garcia was forced to flee, Tanya held her customary meeting with her team to be updated on their achievements in the day that had just passed. Before they began, she gave them the dope about the stolen taxi and the likelihood that Garcia did not have his own taxi anymore. Then she dropped the bomb. 'You will have noticed that one member of the team isn't here.' Everyone looked around; Ishita blurted out the name: 'Mrinal.'

Tanya nodded. 'We all know there was a leak somewhere. Turns out Mrinal Mallik had been working with Garcia, with an ASI from Jadavpur.' Ishita looked stunned and then she started to cry. No one said anything, for a while. Then Tanya asked her, 'You never suspected?'

Through her tears, she said, 'I can't believe this.'

'It'll take some time to get over this. Just concentrate on work.'

Jadunath had been working on picking up the pieces, with the help of Ramadhar, Mrinal, Shreya, Talukdar and Sushila. He rushed in to fill the silence. 'Ma'am, first, Dr Varma has left Calcutta. He's given up his clinic in Hatibagan and sold his house in Dakshineshwar. He's gone back to Bihar. We couldn't find out where. We picked up Prabhash and Hashim. But they haven't seen him or heard from him since he left for Bihar. It didn't seem like they were lying. They gave us names and numbers for several other associates who are still out of jail, but running really minor rackets, including Kalua and Lyangda. We picked them up and put them inside. We can take our time grilling them. We've pulled in five others and shut down twelve small establishments: prostitution and drugs, mainly. We can wrap this up in a couple of days. But it doesn't seem like anyone knows anything about Garcia. He's just dropped out of sight. Prabhash told us that no one will touch Garcia because rape is not appreciated.'

'Ma'am, we've circulated the three sketches to relevant *thanas*, owners' associations and unions. We also interviewed some taxi owners with the three sketches, using the old list. No luck, ma'am. If he stole a vehicle, he's not renting one…,' Gopal piped up.

'Keep at it till tomorrow,' Tanya ordered. 'If nothing turns up, I'll give you other assignments. Garcia must be on the run again. I don't think he'll risk being in Calcutta.'

Right after the meeting. Vivek Singh, ACP, EOW, was on the line. 'Ma'am, got a call from Tahir Hussein. Remember him?'

'Your senior Bangladeshi *thulla*.'

'Right,' Singh said. 'After Garcia and Shila Nandi sold their farm in Rajshahi, it remained empty for some time. The new owners moved in a couple of months ago. When they started farming the land, they discovered, hold on to your armrest, a body. Later established to be that of a woman. Tahir just called asking for either dental records, we all know how many people have those, or, DNA samples, unless Shila Nandi had some really distinctive mark on her body.'

'Fuck!' Tanya was so overcome by astonishment that the expletive was forced out of her. 'How could that have happened? Hussein told us that the Shaikh brothers had helped the two of them—'Alamgir' and 'Farzana'—find a flat in Dhaka.'

'I asked Tahir the same question, ma'am, which had occurred to him as well. His officers talked to the landlord, who said he'd never seen Farzana, Alamgir had conducted all the negotiations. They talked to the neighbours as well. Most hadn't seen either of them. Some had spotted Alamgir, but no one had seen Farzana. I think we can safely assume that Garcia killed his lady love for unfathomable reasons, buried her in Rajshahi and moved to Dhaka, a free bird. Maybe he thought that she'd be a liability.'

This was big. Tanya met Chanda, along with Singh, who repeated his conversation with Hussein. Tanya asked, 'Should we send someone?' Chanda maintained a gnomic silence for a long time, with the two officers sitting there, trying to conceal their impatience, and, in Tanya's case, irritation. Finally, Chanda said, 'I can't clear a Dhaka trip. I'll let you know.'

The two officers left. 'It must be her. We'll have to send a DNA sample from one of her children, I suppose,' Singh said.

Tanya dismissed the Garcia case from her mind and got through a whole lot of work, before texting the doctor about Dipanwita, who called back. 'For the first time, I am optimistic she'll pull through without any lasting damage. Our concern was brain damage. The blow the man delivered cracked her skull. She's lucky. There has been no brain damage. She'll be in the ICU for some days and have to undergo surgery, but, as I said, I'm optimistic.'

'That's good news,' Tanya said. 'Thanks.' She felt lighter after a disappointing day and started preparing to go home, when the phone rang and Chanda summoned her. 'The HS agrees,' Chanda informed her. 'Someone must go to the Nandi home and pick up something from which the Bangladesh Police can extract DNA. I'm taking up the case with the police there, through the good offices of Mr Datta.'

Tanya returned to her room and asked Singh to inform the Bangladeshi officer that the needful was being done, expeditiously. At the meeting the next morning, Jadunath reported major progress. They'd talked to Suleiman, who had spoken to Garcia on the phone. He'd stored the number, though Kali*da* had asked him not to. He also told the police that he'd warned Garcia that the police were looking for him, which wasn't exactly top-secret, classified information. Jadunath produced the number on a slip of paper and said, 'Ma'am, it's a mobile number, possibly registered in Bihar. I'll get the details.'

'Well done,' said Tanya. 'I've got news for you as well.' She shared the Shila Nandi story with the team. 'Gopal will go to Dhaka,' she said. 'But we'll first have to check whether her dental records exist. It's unlikely; we'll have to get samples for DNA testing, probably from her children. But the thing has to be handled sensitively. Which means, through the uncle who is now their guardian. Sushila or Piya will do that. Jadunath will track down Garcia's telephone number. Gopal will do his homework on the Dhaka end and prepare to go. Ramadhar will continue with the mop-up operations helped by Ishita, Shreya and Talukdar. I can smell the end.'

The team dispersed to tackle their tasks. Tanya steeled herself for the interrogation of ASIs Mrinal Mallik and Debraj Banik, to be conducted in the presence of Commissioner Ajoy Chanda. She called her boss. 'Sir, if you are free, we can finish the interrogations. They are currently being held in the cells. Shall I have them brought to the interview room?'

'Just the two of us. Interrogations to be videographed.'

In just under an hour, Tanya and the commissioner walked into the interrogation room in which Banik and Mrinal were sitting. In civvies. They sat down, and out of habit, Tanya let the silence build up to a tense crescendo. Finally, she said, 'Mrinal, what made you sell out? Didn't Gopal teach you better? Don't bother to deny it, we have absolutely incontrovertible evidence.'

Mrinal and Banik remained silent.

'Where's Garcia now?'

'Ma'am. We can't call him. He calls Banik, when he wants information or something done. He always calls from a public phone, ma'am.'

'What are his plans? You must know something.'

'Nothing,' Banik said.

'I'm sure he's headed out of Calcutta. He was staying in Naihati. I found out. But my feeling is he'll get out of Bengal. You should talk to Suleiman, ma'am,' Mrinal said. Banik shot him a baleful look. 'I'm sorry, ma'am. I let myself down, I let Ishita down. My family, you, Gopal*da*, I let everybody down. Apologies, ma'am.' He wasn't in tears, but had a look of utter desolation on his face.

'Both of you are suspended without pay until enquiries are completed,' Tanya said. The two men were taken away. Mrinal reached the door and looked back once, at Tanya, with what she thought was a beseeching look.

Tanya went back to her room, unsettled, to do yet another spell of paperwork, having remembered that the Garcia file was quite a bit behind developments. She was almost finished, when Chanda called her to his room. 'Have you nominated someone for the Dhaka trip?'

Nominated? Supercilious bloody idiot, Tanya thought. 'Yes, I've told Gopal he should go.'

'Wouldn't it be better if you went?'

'Too much to do here, sir. Supervision, coordination. A couple of major cases. Gopal is efficient, most of them are, and urbane, which the seniors on the team aren't all the time. He'll handle it competently, diplomatically.'

'What about the preparations?'

'Sushila or Piya will approach Shila Nandi's children through her uncle. At this point of time, they should not be given cause for anxiety. The uncle is a retired university professor. Apparently, very sensible. He's, for all practical purposes, their guardian, though he doesn't live with them. He'll find a sample for DNA testing. If he can't find anything of Shila's, it will have to come from her children. We'll have to lift something of theirs—both—for comparison.'

'All right. Once the DNA samples are with you, inform me. Barui will have to report to Additional Inspector-General Police (IGP), CID, Bapan Mollah. He'll tell Gopal whom to liaise with. Mollah is the second-most senior police officer in Bangladesh.'

'All right, sir. There's another lead, which Jadunath is chasing. While his team was tearing down the last vestiges of Garcia's network, he spoke to Suleiman, who was Garcia's gofer. Garcia helped him set up a tea stall close by. Appears Garcia trusts him. He called Suleiman, possibly after all his old associates gave him the brush-off. Suleiman told him that word on the street was the police will get him if he came into town. Jadunath got Garcia's number from him. It's being traced.'

'Fine,' Chanda said, in dismissal.

Before leaving, Tanya got an update on Dipanwita. 'She's stable. We'll operate tomorrow,' the doctor told her.

The next morning, Tanya began the meeting by bringing her team members into the loop. Then Sushila reported. 'I met Professor Nandi, ma'am. And we explained the situation to him. He was horrified, but agreed that until we were certain about the identity of the body, we should shield the children. We told him we needed something of Shila's from which her DNA could be extracted. He told us he'd retired as a professor of molecular biology from Calcutta University. We could trust him to find something appropriate. He'll call us tomorrow.'

'Good,' Tanya said. 'Jadunath?'

'Good news, ma'am. Progress. It's a Bihar number as we suspected. I asked for details, but was told I'd have to make an application through my boss, you, ma'am, after which they'd have to process it and so on. I know someone, ma'am.' Everyone smiled, Jadunath knew 'someone', practically everywhere. Jadunath continued, 'I told him what I wanted. He found out that the connection was taken in Patna. I'd also told him about the call I wanted traced and given him Suleiman's number and the time of the call. Turns out it was made from Katihar. We need to go and pick him up.'

Tanya smiled a broad and truly heartfelt smile, after a long, long time. 'I'll get it done,' she said, and ended the meeting. Then she went to her room and worked it out. Of the eight remaining members in the team, four were women. First, she thought she wouldn't send them unless someone really wanted to go. Then she thought, hell, that wasn't fair, even though Garcia was dangerous enough by himself and she had no idea what kind of scum he'd collected during his travels. Provisionally, she thought, Jadunath would lead the team. Ramadhar would have to be there; Talukdar was a tough guy in his own way; and, she thought, maybe, Piya. Gopal would have to stand by for the trip to Dhaka. Which would leave her with Sushila, Ishita and Shreya on duty in Calcutta. Having sorted that out in her head, she met Chanda. After recounting Jadunath's discoveries, she said, 'I've picked my team, sir. Jadunath, Ramadhar, Talukdar and Piya. We should hit Garcia as soon as possible. We've already seen that he tends to disappear the moment we get wind of his whereabouts.'

Chanda looked at her with a flat expression. 'Fine,' he said. 'Talk to the Crime Investigation Department (CID) in Patna and keep me informed.' She found Jadunath and Gopal waiting outside her door.

Jadunath asked, 'Ma'am, how soon can we go?'

'I've picked my team. You, Ramadhar, Talukdar and Piya will go. I'll lead. I'm sure Bihar Police will provide back-up. Gopal will be on stand-by for Dhaka. He'll head the investigation till we're back.' That settled, Tanya called up the Patna CID. The officer at the other end said, 'IGP CID Jyotirmai Upadhyay.'

'Good morning, Mr Upadhyay,' Tanya began, 'I'm Tanya Samanta, JCP (Crime), Kolkata Police. Can I speak to you for a few minutes?'

'Please, Ms Samanta. Go ahead.'

'We've been on the lookout for a rogue cop for just

over a year. He absconded with an MLA, who was his lover. You may have read about the case.'

'Yes, I have.'

'Now, we want him for four rapes. Two of them also involving brutal assault. The last one almost resulted in the woman's death. Luckily, it looks like she'll survive without lasting physical consequences. The other assaulted woman was a DU student from Patna. Information from Bangladesh suggests he killed his MLA lover, god knows why, before fleeing back to Bengal. We believe he's holed up in Katihar now. I'm heading a team that will go there to pick him up. Would you like to provide back-up or should we make it on our own?'

'When you reach Katihar, please get in touch with the SHO of the Katihar police station. He'll provide back-up and logistical support. When do you think you'll be here?'

Tanya knew SHO meant station house officer, the north-Indian equivalent of Bengal's OC. 'Probably taking the late flight to Bagdogra and driving there. If we miss that, we're taking an early flight tomorrow. Either way, I'll talk to your SHO before or around noon tomorrow. What's his name?'

'Hang on,' he said. And a while later he confirmed, 'Nalin Singh. I'll call him right away. Good luck, I hope you get Garcia.'.

Tanya thanked him. She handed over organizing the trip to Jadunath. Jadunath suggested that they should pull into Raiganj first, dump their stuff in a hotel and then go to Katihar. The distance was eighty kilometres, just over a couple of hours by car.

'You're right,' Tanya said, 'we'll be less conspicuous that way. The four of you go home, pack and get to the airport on time. Get handguns from the armoury, I'll sign off on that. When's the flight?'

'8:30 p.m., ma'am. We should all be at the airport by 7.'

'I'll have to be there by 6 because I'll have to talk to airport security about the guns and ammunition in our check-in luggage.'

Then she went to meet her boss. Tired of pussyfooting round him, she shot from the hip. 'Sir, we're off to Katihar on an 8:30 flight. Could you countersign the forms for withdrawal of handguns and ammo—we'll be carrying the Glock 17s. There are five of us.'

'We? What the hell does "we" mean?' he exploded.

'Sir, I'm leading this operation. It's too big to leave to Jadunath, even though he's a very competent and experienced officer.'

Chanda goggled. 'Who will head the investigation here?'

'Sir, nothing's happening here. We should be back in a few days. We reach tonight. It might take us a day to figure out where he's staying. We move in the day after. Another day to get transit remand. At night, we fly back, with Garcia in handcuffs. Three days. Say, four. Gopal will hold the fort. He's not going to Dhaka in a hurry anyway. I'll leave instructions. He'll report to you every day, via email.'

Fait accompli and Chanda knew it. He countersigned the forms with an air of resignation.

By lunchtime, they'd collected their guns. Tanya's

was at home. All the members of the team assembled in her room after that. 'We'll get to Raiganj by 2 a.m., latest. Have a good rest before we move. That's essential. You don't want to be unfocused during a shootout. Let's say, we leave for Katihar at 11 a.m. after calling the SHO. I have his number. Go home, relax and reach the airport on time.' They left, wound up tightly. Jadunath and Ramadhar had been on operations during which they'd had to carry guns. Jadunath had never fired his outside the shooting range; Ramadhar had, once, but in the air, to announce his arrival. He hadn't had to fire it after that. Piya and Talukdar had handled guns only on the range. Only Tanya had fired a gun during operations. She'd hit her target both times, smashing one person's femur in Bankura, when she was superintendent of the district, and one person's shoulder when she was deputy commissioner in North Calcutta. Those were the breaks, but Tanya was fully confident of her team.

~

All the members of the team were up by 9 a.m., having gone to bed just before 2 a.m. They'd arrived at the hotel Jadunath had booked unexpectedly early because the roads were empty and the driver of the hired car was driving like a maniac. Doesn't matter, thought Tanya. She called SHO Nalin Singh at 9:30 a.m. 'Good morning, Mr Singh,' she'd started in a bright, morning voice. 'This is Tanya Samanta of Kolkata Police.'

Thankfully, the voice that responded was just as cheery.

'Good morning, ma'am. Myself Nalin Singh, SHO Town Police Station, Katihar. Upadhyay sir has informed us of your visit and purpose, ma'am. I think we've also located your target. Please come over and we'll make the plan.'

'Thank you, Mr Singh,' Tanya said. 'We'll be there around lunchtime.'

'Yes, ma'am. I'll be waiting.'

They left the hotel at 10 and were in the Town Police Station a little after 1:00 p.m. SHO Singh welcomed them effusively and invited them into his room. 'Ma'am,' he said, once everyone had settled down, 'is this who you are looking for?' he pushed a photograph across the table at Tanya. What she saw was a snap of Clayton Garcia. Sporting the kind of haircut she'd seen him with in the force. But also a well-trimmed beard, which she'd never seen on him. And, of course, the scar, partly hidden by the beard. But nothing really disguised him. It was Garcia, without a doubt. Suddenly, she thought of a Katihar cop tailing him and getting that snap. Garcia's antenna would have picked him up right away. Dismay registered on her face; Singh read it easily.

'Don't worry, ma'am,' he said. 'Your quarry has not been alerted. I did not have him followed. I made discreet enquiries about new people in town under my own PS. And I came to know of this man, who has been staying at the Jagat Hotel for the past few days. Looking for a job as a driver, I was told. I thought it would be indiscreet to send a plainclothesman to track him. So, I sent my nephew who lives with me and works in the local branch of the State Bank of India. He shot Garcia on his mobile phone, when he left for dinner. The light was not good, so the picture is not clear. But you recognize him, ma'am?' Tanya nodded. 'Ma'am, are all of you armed?'

'Yes,' Tanya said.

'The man is dangerous, I was told, but is he armed?'

'He's very dangerous. I don't know for sure, but he must be armed.'

Singh nodded. 'I'll tell you my plan. Then you tell me what you think. I'll provide an armed four-man back-up team, including me. Is there anyone in your team the man doesn't know?'

'Talukdar.'

'Then, ma'am, I'll have lunch brought into the *thana*. None of you should go out so that there is no gossip in town about five strangers. Somebody from outside the *thana* will take Talukdar sahib to the tea shop, which is excellent for surveillance, where he can read the papers and drink tea after the sun sets. Garcia will leave the hotel to have dinner. When he returns, Talukdar sahib will call you and find an inconspicuous place to wait. He should also have dinner after Garcia returns to the hotel. He will be shown all these places. Garcia is on the third floor. Top floor. His room is at the rear side, away from the main street. It faces a narrower, parallel road, which passes into residential neighbourhoods on both sides. It is connected to the main road on one side of the hotel by a road, little more than a lane. On the other side of the hotel is a kind of service alley, bricked up on all sides, accessible only from the hotel reception. We will approach the hotel at around 2 a.m. Three officers will be at the back of the hotel, where there is an exit. One will be stationed in the connecting lane, to which there is no separate access from the hotel. And one pair and Talukdar sahib will guard the main entrance. Two people, ma'am, will knock on the door and get him. And call the others, who will rush there. Just three calls. I'll make two, you'll make one. Talukdar sahib will give us a couple of minutes and follow us in. He'll wait at the reception to guard the door to the alley, just in case. Everyone will be in plainclothes and everyone will be carrying his or her gun, but it should not be seen from outside. We will leave in pairs, an officer from my *thana* and one from your team, since you don't know the layout of my town. I will go up to the room and you'll choose the person from your team who'll go with me.'

'I'll go with you. I suppose you want to go at 2, because he'll be sleeping and will wake up groggy and unprepared.'

'Exactly, ma'am, unless he sleeps with a gun under his pillow. That is possible?'

'If he has a gun, you can be sure it'll be under his pillow. Or by his side.'

'Okay, ma'am. I'll send someone to get your lunch. You are all Bengali?'

Tanya nodded.

'Should I get fish curry? Many Bengalis in Katihar, living here for generations. You can have a good Bengali *thali* (platter) if you want.'

'We'll eat whatever you get, it doesn't matter. We eat Bengali food every day. Wouldn't mind something else.'

When the food arrived, Singh, three officers of Town PS and the five Kolkata Police officers lunched together, after the introductions. 'Inspector Pramod Kumar, SI Divya Yadav and SI Ismail Altaf.' Singh did the introductions. 'And JCP Tanya Samanta.' Tanya introduced the others. After the meal, they sat around, while the others went off to work. A little after 8:30 p.m., Talukdar called to report that Garcia had returned to his hotel after dinner. Tanya conveyed this message to Singh. 'I know already, ma'am. This is my town.' At 9 p.m., dinner arrived. Tanya and her team had dinner and chafed, ready for action. At around midnight, SHO Singh, Kumar, Yadav and Altaf arrived. Singly. They held a conference, to go over the ground. By 12:30, they were primed for action. Tanya called Talukdar, who said, 'He's inside. His room has been dark since 11:30, ma'am, I checked from the road at the back. He must be asleep.'

***

Garcia had been busy as well ever since he arrived in Katihar and checked into the hotel. On his first day, he wandered up to the roof. It was locked. His hand forced, he asked the sleepy desk clerk for the reason. 'It's open during the day,' the man had said. 'And locked after dark.' That wasn't good news for Garcia. He refused to be stuck in a building with only one way out. In this case, the stairs leading down to the reception area. From where, of course, he had only the option of the front door really. The back door was used to bring in supplies, otherwise it remained locked. The side door stayed locked. Even if it had been open, he had for all practical purposes only one way out when he was in his room: the stairs leading down. So, he'd gone back up and opened the door to the roof with the help of one of the simplest of instruments in his toolkit. No sweat. First thing in the morning, on awakening, he locked the door again. Stage one complete, he thought.

Stage two was a recce of the roof, which he carried out that morning. It was dominated by two big platforms on which stood two big concrete structures. Water tanks obviously, but leaving nothing to chance, Garcia had climbed on top of both, opened the hatches and made sure. Apart from these, overhead nylon ropes were tied to a number of stanchions. Clotheslines, Garcia thought. He'd check later in the day. Then came the crucial bit. Escape routes. He walked to the front and checked, leaning over the parapet. Nothing. He walked to the back of the hotel and found two stout-looking pipes. Water pipes or drain pipes. Didn't matter. As emergency escape routes they'd do. Then he walked across to the side of the roof overlooking the lane connecting the two roads at the front and back of the hotel. Two more stout pipes. He kept scanning the place, trying to formulate rapid-action plans. JCP Tanya Samanta wouldn't give up easily. A midnight knock couldn't be ruled out. He walked to the other side of the roof and found two more pipes leading down into an alley that was bricked up. He nodded, satisfied.

Then came stage three. He went back to his room at a leisurely pace. Once in, he sat down on the only chair in the room. Okay, he thought, the roof has possibilities. But if there are cops outside the door, how the fuck do I get there? He went to the only window in the small room, opened it and leaned out to take a look. The water pipe on that side was too far to reach. The good news was that the other one was ideal. Then, with the hairs prickling at the nape of his neck, he looked down, and exhaled with relief. There was a narrow ledge on to which he could easily lower himself and from which he could reach the pipe. Garcia was a cop. He knew that if there was a knock on his door, there'd be cops on the roads in front of the hotel, at the back, and the side with the connecting lane. They would be in the reception area as well. He was a big fish, he thought, proudly. When that passed, he told himself that he'd have to do a dry run that night from his room to the roof, checking out the lights.

That night, he quietly unlocked the door to the roof. Back in his room, he went to the open window, closed the shutter on the side of the pipe he wanted to use and lowered himself down to the narrow ledge. Carefully, he reached out with one hand and grasped the pipe. Using his considerable upper body strength, he heaved himself towards it and grasped it with his other hand, his thighs locking into position. Then he climbed the short distance up to the roof and went over the wall. It was a picnic. The upper half of the building was in darkness; the lower half, somewhat lit by two streetlights at either side of the road. For him, this lighting was good. He went down, passing the sleeping reception clerk on the way, picked the lock on the back door, and stepped out. Standing outside the hotel, he looked up. The top of it was bathed in darkness. He walked a few paces in both directions, but looking up he could see nothing, especially because the lights were off in all the rooms. Satisfied, he went back in, shut the door as quietly as he could and set to work on stage four.

He unlocked the door to the alley and went out of the reception area, leaving the door ajar. He walked over to the wall at the rear. As he had suspected, the top was studded with glass shards. Whipping out his penknife from his pocket, he made an incision on his forearm. From the other pocket, he took out a piece of fabric he'd cut from one of his trousers and soaked it in the blood that was oozing from the surface wound. Then he reached up to the top of the wall, making sure not to cut himself, and manoeuvred the piece of fabric to get it snaggled in the shards. That done, he mopped up the blood from his left hand and smeared it on top of the wall, near the spot where the fabric was lodged. Then he wiped his wound with another piece of cloth and stuck a plaster on the cut. He stepped away from the wall and examined the scuffmarks his boots and legs had left on it. Finally, satisfied, he went in, shut the door quietly and walked to his room.

Normally, Garcia slept well. Lightly, but well. That night, musing on his options, sleep eluded him. As the night deepened, Garcia fell into a semi-conscious reverie. And the memories of that fateful night in Rajshahi crowded his mind. It had been business as usual when he and Shila had gone to bed. Garcia was sick with anxiety. Surprisingly, Shila was less anxious, perhaps because she had been leaning on Garcia. Depending on him to get them out of danger. When Garcia wanted to make love, Shila said she wanted to talk. 'About what?' Garcia asked. 'Details,' she answered. What was he was planning for the two of them in the next couple of months? Why not just leave Bangladesh and go somewhere where they couldn't be found? Garcia snapped, 'We just can't go anywhere we want to go. Visas have to be organized, which isn't easy. You can forge a passport, but a visa is tougher.' From there the argument had turned into a flaming row. Shila not letting go, Garcia getting angrier until he totally lost it. Garcia and Shila had never fought before this. But as matters escalated, Garcia felt a wave of violent rage build up inside him. Most of his relationships with women had been casual. And Garcia had no compunctions about hitting a partner, or a whore, if he lost his temper. With Shila the question hadn't arisen. But suddenly, he hit her with the back of his hand. She was sitting on the bed and the heavy blow sent her flying, ramming her head against the corner of the bedside table before her body hit the ground. Garcia remained on the bed, breathing heavily. Then he walked up to her. Her head was bent at an unusual angle. Garcia had been a cop. He knew right away that she was dead. A thrill ran through his whole body. His first thought was, 'Good. I'm free now.' He lifted her by her hair and battered her head in with a stout stick she'd used for cross-country treks. Then, under cover of the darkness, he buried her. He threw away the stick at a spot far away from their house. And cleaned up the room thoroughly.

Khaled and Mudassar hadn't asked about Shila. Though Garcia didn't really feel remorseful, he started to miss her. Then she started haunting his nights, whether he was asleep or awake.

***

The minutes seemed to drag for everyone. Jadunath briefly tried to persuade his boss that he should go up with Singh. Tanya waved him aside. The clock kept ticking. 'He's very resourceful. Thinks fast and moves fast. We'll have to be careful,' Tanya said, just to break the tension.

After an eternity, it was 1:50 a.m. 'Time to go,' Singh said. The pairs were: Singh and Tanya; Kumar and Piya; Yadav and Jadunath; and Altaf and Ramadhar, who had been very quiet, even by his standards. They took different routes. By 2, there were three cops at the rear of the hotel, guns drawn. One on either side of the door—Altaf and Piya—and Kumar, a little further away, backing them up; Jadunath in the connecting lane. On either side of the front door were Ramadhar, looking menacing with his gun drawn, and Yadav. Singh and Tanya entered the hotel. Behind them, Talukdar waited, looking at his watch. He followed, a moment behind, and stood guard at the door to the service alley.

Singh walked up to the man at the desk, who was nodding off. He shook him roughly. 'Get out of the hotel, now,' he said. The man scrammed like he had a firecracker under his ass. The two of them drew their guns and went up the stairs. Tanya and Singh walked up to the door and stationed themselves on either side. Garcia could start shooting through the flimsy plywood door. Singh stretched out and rapped on the door hard, thrice. Garcia had cultivated the habit of snapping out of his sleep instantly, which he did, the moment he heard the first knock. He reached under the pillow for his gun, an old, but reliable Colt that he acquired many years ago and never registered. By the time he heard the second and third knock, he was fully awake. He scooped up the shoulder bag in which he'd packed everything he had, wore it like a bandolier and headed to the window. In seconds, he was on the parapet, heading up to the roof. He'd have to wing it from there.

When Garcia grasped the parapet to haul himself over, Singh blew the lock to smithereens with his Glock. 'It's over, Garcia. Surrender. You're smart and you've been there,' Tanya shouted. 'You're surrounded. You'll never get away.'

Singh fired a couple of shots and Tanya went in at a crouch, also firing. The room was empty as she had feared. Singh bustled in. 'He must have left through the window,' Tanya said. She leaned out and told the three at the back to hold their positions. Then she called for back-up—Talukdar and Ramadhar, leaving Yadav to guard the front door. When the reinforcements arrived, the four of them went to the roof, stopping in the landing in front of the open door, which, they'd heard, was supposed to be locked after dark. The roof was in darkness, because Garcia had turned off the lights when he'd unlocked the door and the moon was hidden behind a thick bank of clouds.

By then Garcia had adjusted to the darkness and in minutes, he could hear the squeaking of the stairs as four pairs of legs came up them, trying to make as little noise as possible. While going up to the roof, Garcia had figured out that going down wasn't an option, which conclusion was borne out when he looked down from there. He spotted three cops, guns drawn, on the road. Garcia knew he didn't have to look out into the road in front or the connecting lane. That meant he had to go down to the narrow alley, where he'd be trapped. No way, really. He crossed over to the nearer of the two water tanks, climbed atop it, opened the hatch and gingerly lowered himself in, gun in his hand. The water came up to his chest. He pulled the hatch down.

There was nothing wrong with Ramadhar's hearing. He was the first to hear shuffling noises and he took out his powerful torch with his left hand and played a beam through the door. Nothing. He snapped off a couple of rounds as Talukdar, gun in hand, ran into the roof at a crouch and loosed off a few rounds, while Ramadhar fired again, to cover for Singh and Tanya. They moved in at a crouch, heading in different directions. Ramadhar was the last one in, but only after he'd turned the roof lights on. The roof was empty. Talukdar went to the alley side. There were two lights down there, but no one to be spotted. Tanya and Singh worked the phones. Front, back and lane-side, no one had seen Garcia. But, as they all admitted, they hadn't been looking up. And as all of them realized, even if they had been, it wouldn't have made a difference. Which meant that either Garcia was on the roof, or he hadn't come up at all. Or, he'd climbed down alley-side. And probably entered some other room, empty or occupied. Singh called the owner, Rahul Tripathi, who, having been informed about the operation, had been unable to fall asleep. He answered the phone as soon as it rang, to hear Singh barking, 'Get to the hotel fast. As fast as you can.' He was on the roof in ten minutes having sprinted to his scooter, dashed to the hotel and run up to the roof, taking the stairs two at a time.

'How many rooms do you have for guests?' Singh asked him.

'Twenty-seven, Singh sahib,' Tripathi said. 'Three are for storage. One on each floor.'

'How many are occupied?'

'All twenty-seven. Long holiday in Bengal because of Republic Day and Netaji's birth anniversary.'

'Stay at the reception desk. We'll need to check every room. You'll have some unhappy guests on your hands, but it can't be helped.'

Garcia was freezing in the cold January night, but he had no option but to stay put. Was Tanya dumb enough not to check the water tanks? He hoped so. Would I have checked? he asked himself. Maybe, maybe not. They'll have people on the roof, he thought despairingly. Either I'll freeze to death or get caught.

Cold or not, he would have to stay in the water tank. Ramadhar was elected to guard the roof. He chose a spot from which he could survey the whole roof without being charged, gun resolutely in his hand. They'd checked to make sure Garcia was not crouching on a parapet, hanging on to one of the pipes or windows, or otherwise concealed somewhere along the walls of the hotel. The others left to search the hotel. Jadunath remained in the alley, Altaf out in front and Kumar at the rear of the hotel. Piya and Yadav joined the others to search the hotel. Tanya and Singh searched the top floor, Piya and Yadav the second, and Talukdar the first. The store rooms on each floor were checked first. Empty. Then they went about waking up the guests, but Garcia was nowhere to be found. He was literally freezing his ass off, still standing in the water tank, with the cold water lapping against his chest.

Finally, they searched the ground floor: the common areas, the kitchen, the laundry room where bed linen and clothes were washed by hand, the staff loo and the recreation room boasting an ancient television set used by the staff. Zilch. Out in the alley, Talukdar and Yadav found the piece of cloth snaggled on the glass shards, the scuff marks on the walls and the other evidence of a hasty escape over the wall. They called in the heavy artillery. A ladder was fetched and SHO Singh climbed it to retrieve the piece of cloth and inspect the area surrounding it. In the light that was available, including that of the dawn beginning to break, he took some photographs. More could be taken later in proper daylight. Tanya and Singh questioned Piya and Kumar. They had been vigilant and had not seen anyone emerge over the wall. But that area had been dark, the illumination poor because, as in most small towns, low voltage meant dim lighting. Still, Jadunath stayed in the lane, Kumar joined Yadav at the rear of the hotel, while Talukdar joined Altaf at the front door. It seemed like a belated bolting of the stable door, but it couldn't be left open either. The rest went to the police station, but not before Singh called the station and dispatched two officers each to the railway station and main bus stop, with orders for them to familiarize themselves with Garcia's photograph, which was on his desk, and detain the rogue cop if he tried to escape.

The first thing Tanya did back in the *thana* was call Gopal, who was fast asleep. He was woken up and told to find out Garcia's blood group (from whatever possible source) and get back to her. Singh said he'd have one of the pathology labs do the test on the piece of cloth, on which the blood was congealed, making it stiff. No one would be able to tell on casual inspection that it had been snaggled on top of the wall for many, many hours.

On hearing a cell phone ring, the sound penetrating the walls of the tank, Garcia guessed that whoever had been left to guard the roof was being summoned downstairs. He waited ten minutes after hearing the ring and slowly pushed the hatch up. Then he pulled himself up with frozen arms and looked around. The roof was empty. He climbed out of the tank and took off his sodden clothes, wrung them out and changed into another outfit. He repacked the wet clothes into the shoulder bag, did some silent freehand exercises to get his circulation going and climbed under the other tank to wait. It was lucky for him that Singh had ordered the hotel sealed. No one to step in or out. And, despite their loud protests, the guests had to stay in their rooms till the all clear was sounded. The staff members were to remain wherever they happened to be, which was mostly home, except for some kitchen hands who were sleeping in the recreation room. And Tripathi, who was sitting morosely at the reception desk.

Singh and most of the other officers went home to eat and change. The officers from Calcutta had food brought to them at the station. Ramadhar, Piya and Yadav relieved Jadunath, Talukdar and Altaf, who too went home.

By 10, however, everyone was back at the station and reinforcements were sent to the hotel for keeping watch. Singh was as good as his word. Punctually at 10, he sent Altaf to the best lab in town to get the piece of fabric tested. Soon after Altaf left, Gopal called to say that Garcia's blood group was AB negative, the rarest one. If it matched the blood on the piece of cloth, Tanya thought, they'd have to conclude that Garcia had, against the odds, managed to slink away. Tanya did not underestimate Garcia. He'd been a very good officer. These kinds of skills had helped him become one. She sat and brooded, waiting for the results to come back. Singh had told Altaf to stay at the lab, get the work done immediately and return with the report. While they waited, they also began to consider the possibilities.

'It's been eight hours since we knocked on his door. Assuming he left then, and not before that on a hunch, where could he have got to?' Tanya asked Singh.

'There are no trains at that time of the night that stop at the Katihar station, so he couldn't have left then. A few buses go through, but I don't know of any that make night halts here. I'll find out. It is possible that he's walked around the town and familiarized himself with it. In which case, he could have sneaked into the residential neighbourhoods and made his way to the station or the bus stop. I'll find out,' Singh replied. And promptly called the officer from his *thana* who was on duty at the bus stop. One officer was assigned to cover the bus stop every night anyway, just in case something happened. One bus had indeed stopped at Katihar, but no one had boarded it from there. It was a quick stop to let people get off and stretch their legs. Garcia hadn't been seen in the area. Singh told Tanya that in Bihar, few buses ply at night because of security reasons. The ones that do, make a minimum of halts. And passengers are never allowed to take a bus mid-route. He also called someone at the railway station and confirmed that no trains stopped at Katihar at night.

'That means he'll be in the area,' Tanya said, with a suggestion implicit in her voice.

'He's got a good lead on us. He could have walked out of the town by now. Looking for him at this time will not be possible,' Singh replied. 'We'll put together a search soon. I'll have to coordinate with other *thanas*.' Singh started making calls to *thanas* in the neighbourhood, circulating verbal descriptions, followed by scanned versions of the sketches and the indistinct photograph taken by his nephew. 'Let's see what happens,' he told Tanya. 'I think he must be hiding someplace.' Little knowing that Garcia was a few kilometres away from the *thana*, sweating and on the verge of panic as he lay prone under a water tank.

At around noon, Altaf returned with the blood report, which he handed over to Singh. It said AB negative. The conclusion everyone reluctantly reached was that appearances had not deceived them and Garcia had indeed managed to escape. Still, Tanya requested Singh to keep the hotel under wraps till the next morning. Singh agreed. Garcia remained under the tank fearing imminent discovery, without knowing that his adversary had just thrown him another lifeline.

Ramadhar and Jadunath stayed in town to keep

watch on the hotel, with the help of Singh's men. Tanya reluctantly left for their hotel in Raiganj with the rest of the team to shower and change. After resting for a while, they started out for Katihar at 4 p.m. They were at the police station by 6:30. The bad news they got from Singh was that there was no news. They'd brought Ramadhar and Jadunath's stuff. They went off duty and headed to a guest house. Tanya took over the reins, but there was nothing she could do. Singh told her that the word had been sent out and if Garcia surfaced, he would be apprehended. When night was about to fall, at Singh's suggestion, the Calcutta team headed back to Raiganj. Ramadhar stayed back, in case something broke.

Night fell on poorly-lit Katihar. Garcia remained under the tank. He'd decided to make his move at midnight by which time Katihar, like other small towns across India, would have definitely gone to bed. He waited and sweated, though the darkness had brought with it the usual nocturnal, end-January chill. Precisely at midnight, he crawled out from under the tank and stretched his cramped muscles. Kinks ironed out, he headed to the rear of the hotel, got down on his knees before getting to the parapet and cautiously looking out over it. A uniformed cop was standing guard. He checked the front and the open side and saw the same thing. No doubt, he thought, other members of the constabulary were at hand. With no other option in sight, he went across to the alley side and looked out. The alley was deserted. Garcia began to climb down the pipe. After a brief pause to compose himself, he climbed the wall. The sentry was looking at the door.

Garcia silently dropped on the other side, having packed his heavy boots into his shoulder bag because climbing the wall was an easier proposition barefooted and because he would make less of a noise when he jumped. He made practically no noise as he dropped into a pool of darkness. Straightening, he walked away from the hotel hugging the walls of the shops strung out beside it. When he was far enough away, he crossed the road and moved into a residential neighbourhood. He paused to put on his boots and headed out of town. As Singh had guessed, Garcia had indeed scoped out the town during his stay. His sense of direction was excellent, so he headed straight out of town into open land, hoping he could find his way to a village of some sort before dawn.

Garcia kept walking at an even pace, knowing that his damaged leg would not be able to withstand speed. It was better to keep moving at a regular pace than have to stop for an unforeseeable period of time. He guessed he had six to seven hours before it was fully light and before the bustle of people starting their day in earnest began. And he was right. In the course of his nocturnal ramble, he saw settlements—hamlets or villages—but he didn't stop, wanting to put as much distance between himself and Katihar as possible. The sky started to grey, but Garcia pushed on. At around 6:30 in the morning, he saw smoke. And where there was smoke, he reasoned, there must be human habitation. Garcia headed towards it. He had some money and a debit/ATM card. He had fake ID papers in the name of Aakash Tripathi, the name he'd been using since his run to Naihati. And he had his gun. That was it.

The police kept vigil till daylight. Extensive searches were made but Garcia just could not be located. Tanya and her team returned to Katihar in the morning and spent the whole day in town. Tanya wanted to take control, but she knew there wasn't much she could do. It was better to let Singh handle it. He'd been invested in the operation far beyond what protocol demanded. He was still trying his best. 'We must get him,' Singh told Tanya. 'He's not a good example.' That, Tanya thought, could be Garcia's epitaph. But they returned to Raiganj that night, knowing not much would be gained by hanging around. Singh assured Tanya that he wasn't closing the case. He'd keep pushing the hunt for the 'bad example'.

The next day, they took a flight for Calcutta from Bagdogra, the taste of failure embittering their journey home. How the hell? Tanya kept thinking. It was like a Houdini act. The bastard had vanished without a trace. Back in Calcutta, she wrote a report and sent it to the commissioner, who summoned her. She was expecting a roasting. Surprise! 'Samanta, this kind of thing happens. It's not your fault. The plan was good, but Garcia got away. Look ahead. Get him next time,' said the commissioner.

Tanya went to her room feeling a little less downbeat. The next morning, she actually felt she had the energy to go ahead. She reassigned the team members to other cases, until something broke. While they'd been away, Gopal reported, Debal Nandi had delivered several strands of hair from his nephew and niece's head. He in turn had dispatched the package to Dhaka. About a month after Tanya had returned to Calcutta, she got a call from

Additional IGP Bapan Mollah, who told her that the DNA tests had been done and shown a relational match. The autopsy had proved that the dead woman's skull had been battered in and the victim had to be Shila Nandi. A couple of days later, Gopal went to Dhaka, getting a fast-track visa on arrival because of the nature of his visit. And returned to Calcutta with the DNA and autopsy reports, and whatever remained of Shila Nandi's body.

Tanya had to orchestrate the handing over of the body to the family and felt obliged to break the news to the children herself, in the presence of their uncle. It wasn't easy, but it had to be done; and it was.

Tanya was seething, but she returned to work and calmed down as routine took over. One positive outcome was that the rapes stopped. And Dipanwita recovered both physically and psychologically, turning out to be a tough cookie. Along with Ghazala and Gloria, Dipanwita took the initiative in starting a counselling centre for rape survivors, a few months after being released from hospital.

Part Six

Ballygunge Place, Calcutta

Even though her uncle and Tanya had warned her to be careful, Ghazala was too much of a free spirit to remain weighed down by the fear of this creep, Garcia. She'd been careful for a couple of months; getting home at reasonable hours; watching her back for someone trying to shadow her if she was out late; and, always, always carrying her knife in a sheath at the small of her back and a pepper spray in her tote bag (right at the top). But as Calcutta returned to normal, she, too, relaxed, though she always carried her knife and spray. And from habit, remained constantly alert to danger. But this was part of her training, not a concession to Garcia.

After the attack on Dipanwita, Ghazala had kept herself informed about her progress, mainly through Tanya. When she was moved out of the ICU, Ghazala had visited her and told her the story of thrashing Garcia. One day, Gloria, too, had dropped by and the three had become friends, forming a survivors' bond. In the beginning, their group just met up for tea or coffee and a chat.

One evening in early August, when the monsoon rains had arrived, Ghazala went to Pritha's house to study. Pritha was exceptionally good at Maths unlike Ghazala. Pritha cajoled her to come over and work on problems. They studied all evening, in all seriousness. After dinner and a chat, it was almost midnight. Pritha and her parents tried to convince Ghazala to stay back.

'I'll find a taxi,' said Ghazala. 'I'm late pretty often. I'll call my parents and tell them I'll be home in an hour.' Her parents were used to Ghazala's hours and seldom worried. She left Pritha's house and headed into College Street, thinking she'd walk to Wellington Square, bang in the centre of town, where she was sure to find a taxi. Maybe she'd get one at the Bowbazar Street crossing. It was pleasant walking at night. It had rained a bit in the evening, so the city had cooled down. She walked down Amherst Street, turned into Mirzapur Street and a little while later, into College Street. Her university, Presidency, was off to the right. She turned left, passed Calcutta Medical College and Hospital and walked towards the Bowbazar Street crossing, where she thought she might get a cab.

She'd almost reached the crossing when she heard the distinctive sound of a taxi engine. And she knew. She sprinted to the crossing and turned into Bowbazar Street, just as a taxi ploughed into the pavement on College Street. She heard a crash, but kept going, knife in hand. She concealed herself at the first opportunity and called Tanya, who was fast asleep. She woke up startled. Ghazala's number was flashing on her screen. At 12:20 a.m. 'Where the hell are you calling from?' Tanya asked, rattled.

'The College Street-Bowbazar crossing, Tanya. Someone just tried to run me down with a taxi half way between Medical College and the Bowbazar crossing. Missed. I'm in a recessed doorway on Bowbazar Street, away from Lalbazar.'

'Stay where you are,' Tanya told her. She called HQ immediately and gave them the information. And told them to dispatch a couple of cars. She changed in record time and drove to the College Street-Bowbazar crossing, breaking every possible traffic rule. On the way, she called Jadunath and Ramadhar and told them to get to where Ghazala was waiting as soon as they could. Both owned motorbikes and lived close to where Ghazala was. Jadunath reached the spot in fifteen minutes and Ramadhar in less than ten. By the time a patrol car from Lalbazar was tearing down Bowbazar Street, the cabbie, presumed to be Garcia, had disappeared into the warren of lanes and by-lanes in the area.

Tanya reached HQ and discovered that two cars were prowling around the area as was Ramadhar on his Bullet. Tanya reached the spot from where Ghazala had not budged. Keeping her company was Jadunath. As soon as he saw Tanya, he roared off on his Bullet. Tanya was furious. 'You're the absolute limit, Ghazala. Didn't I warn you to be careful?'

'Relax, Tanya,' Ghazala said. 'That was a long time ago. I didn't even think he was alive after your Katihar operation. But my outing today has brought Garcia out of the woodwork. He was probably driving a stolen taxi again. I don't think he'd smash his own car. What I want to know is how he discovered my identity. And how he knew where I'd be. I guess, I should be careful...But Tanya, I can't hide all the time because of a mutilated asshole like Garcia. That isn't me. He could be out there for years. He could die, without us knowing about it. I'll take it easy for a while and drift into my old patterns. Maybe I should get firearms training. Can you expedite a licence for me?'

Tanya just nodded slowly. Either in disbelief, or frustration. 'We'll see.'

The hunt for Garcia petered out. Everyone pushed off, some going home, some back to work. Tanya dropped Ghazala home. Before they said their goodbyes, Ghazala promised Tanya that she'd be careful. At least, she'd get home by a reasonable hour. Luckily for her, her parents were sleeping and had no idea when exactly she returned. In the morning, she didn't enlighten them, either, about what had happened.

Ghazala called her uncle and went over to visit him. She described in graphic detail the events of the previous night. Aftab listened gravely and said, 'You were smart in not chasing him.' He didn't berate her for being out in the streets after midnight. Didn't tell her she should have taken a cab right away, instead of walking at that late an hour. Instead, he asked, 'Do you really want to learn how to shoot?'

Taken aback, Ghazala had no reply. After a while, she regained her composure and said, 'Jyatha, of course.'

'We'll go to a shooting academy. I'll teach you to shoot both handguns and rifles. But before that you have to listen to a lecture.'

'Sure.' She'd listen to a hundred lectures for this.

'Pay attention.'

'Right.'

'Okay. Firearms are deadly weapons. Never, ever point a gun at someone unless you intend to shoot. To injure or kill. Never shoot to injure or kill except in self-defence or in the defence of people in danger. Always keep your gun oiled, cleaned and ready for action. A malfunctioning gun is worse than no gun at all.'

Ghazala nodded.

'Why?'

Ghazala replied after a pause. 'Because when you're drawing your gun, you are completely reliant on it. You're not thinking of back-up options. If your gun malfunctions, you have to switch to something else and you lose valuable time. That gives your adversary an advantage.'

Aftab smiled. 'Full marks. Don't you have college today?'

'No. University's closed. Some religious holiday.'

Aftab smiled again. 'Okay, then let's get the process of getting a licence going. Tanya should be able to help.'

Over the next few days, Ghazala filled up forms and submitted the application. Her uncle wrote a reference, as did Tanya, with some foreboding. About a month later, the licence materialized. Aftab called Ghazala to his place and gave her a gun. He said, 'I've been handling all kinds of firearms since I was in my late teens. The first thing is that you must be comfortable with the feel of the gun. Heft it, feel its weight. Feel the butt in your hands. I'll give you a gun. Use it only if, and when, you are completely comfortable holding and pointing, arms outstretched. The trigger can always be adjusted. But your shooting finger must also be completely comfortable inside the trigger guard. If you don't feel comfortable with it, we'll go shopping.'

He fetched a gun from his room, wrapped in oil paper. Even the uninitiated would know it had been looked after lovingly. Aftab said, 'This is a Colt .45. Takes eight cartridges. One in the chamber, seven in the magazine. A balanced, reliable gun, with a maximum range of around forty metres. That's the maximum. For certain effectiveness, budget for thirty. That's good enough. I've fired the gun many times. I got it as a present from an American friend, just after I joined the force. It was my first personal gun. It's yours now. We just have to register it in your name. Learn to shoot a handgun first, then I'll teach you to shoot a rifle.' From the next day, Ghazala would leave home early after her morning workout and head to her uncle's house, which was under ten minutes away on her bicycle. The two would leave for the shooting range together. She'd keep her gun at her uncle's place because, as with the hand-to-hand combat training and fighting with knives, her parents had no idea what she was doing.

~

Garcia, as everyone suspected, had indeed, disappeared into the warren of lanes in the Bowbazar area. He'd holed up in an empty warehouse till after dark, when he left his safe haven to return to the slum where he'd found a place to live. In Titagarh (again a town in the neighbouring district of North 24 Parganas), around forty kilometres to the north of Calcutta and easily accessible. Trains on the north suburban section left for Titagarh every fifteen minutes at peak hours on weekdays and were pretty regular generally speaking. Garcia made his way to Sealdah station, thinking he'd walk the whole way, which wasn't a humongous distance. Garcia had pegged it for around three kilometres, under an hour, factoring in his damaged patella. After a while, he realized he wouldn't make it. He'd injured himself when he lost control of the taxi and crashed into a wall trying to run Ghazala down. Shit, he thought, I'll get those two whores, whatever it takes. So, he limped his way to a bus stop. And, despite the danger involved, took a bus to Sealdah, where, losing himself in the crowd, he felt safe.

He made it to the station, got a train and made it to Titagarh, and his one-room abode, without detection. It helped that he had learned to disguise the scar with some expertly applied make-up and the beard. But he couldn't disguise the limp. Burning with barely controllable fury, he limped home. If he could make contact with his first victim, Gloria Stevens, she could have taught him the Serenity Prayer: 'God, give us the serenity to accept the things we cannot change/The courage to change the things we can/And the wisdom to know the difference.' It may have helped; then again, it may not.

Garcia washed at the common tube well, went to his room and changed the sheets on his meagre bed. Then he drank a glass of Horlicks. Feeling a little better, he lay down to think matters through. First, he told himself, he'd have to hole up for a while, to rest his aching lower body. He'd go out and get some chicken, eggs and vegetables and cook himself a healthy broth. He needed to eat properly to recoup his strength. Once that was done, he'd have to start working out. He could maintain his not inconsiderable upper body strength at least. And he'd have to start doing the exercises for his lower body that his physiotherapist had taught him in Nepal. The exercises were not a part of his daily routine because he'd been on the run and obsessed by plans to rape and wreak mayhem on Tanya Samanta and the girl who pulverized his patella.

These thoughts took him back to Katihar and his miraculous escape. It wasn't a miracle. He'd saved himself, helped by courage and endurance, quick thinking and the assembling of a feasible plan. His presence of mind had helped him slip away from the hotel in Katihar, hugging the walls and seeking the shelter of the shadows, before darting across the street and slowly walking out of town, Garcia had been thinking of only one thing: clearing the town's limits and getting on to a bus. But he'd jettisoned the idea, because it was too dangerous. So, he'd just kept walking and, sure enough, he reached a village, where he found a group of men huddled around a fire, drinking tea on a chilly end-January morning. He told them that he had been abducted in a car and robbed by some men on the outskirts of Katihar town. They'd thrown him out of the car in an unconscious condition. He'd recovered half-an-hour or so ago. After washing his face in a pond, he'd walked till he reached the village. Garcia had taken the precaution of burying his gun and wallet at the base of a tree and memorized the spot before making the approach. He had no money, he told them, he was hungry and cold. Could they help him to reach Calcutta, from where he'd come?

'Are you a Bengali?' a bald man with magnificent sideburns asked him.

'My parents are from Lucknow. They moved to Calcutta when I was a kid. I grew up in Calcutta. My name is Aakash Tripathi,' Garcia said. His idiomatic Hindi, he was hoping, would take his story across the line. The men nodded.

'My name is Beni Prasad,' his interlocutor said. 'You are injured, *bhai* (brother). Come to my house. You must rest till you are better; then we'll send you off to Kalkatta.'

It was, thus, that Garcia stayed in a village called Teligaon, in Katihar district, Bihar, for five months. To all intents and purposes, he didn't have the money to pay for any treatment, or food, or shelter, or clothes, including woollens. No one asked him for money. One of the villagers, a doctor who practised at a government primary health centre in Munger town, about 170 kilometres away, was home on vacation. He treated Garcia for superficial injuries. He was given a bed and blankets. And he washed himself on the banks of a lake, to which he hobbled with the aid of a stick. He was given simple, but tasty and nutritious food. In a month or so, he had regained his strength and could even manage to walk around without a stick.

In the village, in return for clothes, boarding and lodging, he had to do menial chores that did not require bucolic skills. He swept cowsheds, courtyards and barns; manned the shack where tea and snacks were sold; accompanied villagers on bullock carts to the wholesale market nearby when they went to sell produce or buy essentials. In Beni Prasad's house, he also washed dishes and clothes; fished in their pond, which he was good at; and did a variety of odd jobs. He also helped his host set up an efficient system of keeping household accounts, which was adopted by many others. Though in some ways he felt content, thoughts of Calcutta, Tanya Samanta and the girl with the karate chop never quite left him. He craved to go back to extract his revenge. But he knew the longer he stayed away from the city, the more they'd forget about him and the stronger and healthier he'd get.

Working under the baking sun from March to June gave him a deep tan that disguised his scar to some extent. The simple life, in an environment not completely fucked up by air pollution, along with a healthy diet and regular physical activity, supplemented by a daily regimen of exercises consisting of upper body routines and the ones his physiotherapist in Nepal had taught him, allowed him to get better and stronger. When he decided to return to Calcutta, citing work and friends and home, Beni Prasad put him on a bus to Siliguri, the largest town in North Bengal and the third largest in Bengal. Anonymous, he took a bus to Calcutta, reaching the Esplanade terminal at 7:30 a.m. Without delay, Garcia headed for Sealdah station. For no discernible reason, he decided he would go to Titagarh and after having breakfast, boarded a train. Half an hour later he was sitting in a tea shop, a place where gossip is picked up and deals made, drinking tea and munching on a biscuit. He began to enquire about places to stay and in a couple of hours had organized a room in a slum, where he was to base himself. The next day, he started looking for a job. He found one soon enough, driving a car for a businessman, starting 1 July.

It was only after he had started working that Garcia gathered the courage to make an exploratory trip to

Calcutta. He hung around in the Esplanade-Dalhousie Square area, listening to tea-shack gossip and reading as many newspapers as he could borrow. Especially the Bengali ones, which gave him a better idea about what was going on in the city than the English rags. He knew there would be no report on Clayton Garcia, because the ex-cop had featured in the news only as an anonymous rapist cabbie several months ago. As far as the media was concerned, he was a back number. It made him feel both relieved and angry. Relieved because he would be able to move around town on Sundays, his off day, without having to watch his back. Angry because he craved attention. He wanted his life, if not celebrated, to be constantly in the limelight. He'd have to do something about that. In the late afternoon of that first day of checking his city out, he went slinking around to Golf Green. It was a dangerous game, but he was like a junkie: obsessed with the idea of raping, beating and killing Tanya. It was just after 5 in the evening. Even though the gloaming was upon him, Garcia found the place too thinly populated. People were still having their Sunday afternoon nap or preparing to have tea, after having just woken up. Keeping the building in which her flat was in view, Garcia half-hid behind a car—a tallish SUV—and watched. Hoping Tanya would emerge at some point of time before he had to head back to Titagarh.

After about an hour later, by which time darkness had descended upon the city, a woman came out of the building in which Tanya lived. It wasn't Tanya was the first thing that struck Garcia. But once she was on the street, under the glare of the halogen lamps, his heart started racing. He screwed up his eyes and rubbed his temples. It was the girl who'd thrashed him. Gotcha, fucking bitch-whore, he thought. He started trailing her, using every trick he knew. He boarded a bus that was leaving right after the one she had hopped on, selecting a seat that would give him a clear view of the road ahead. As the two buses took off, a minute within each other, Garcia hoped that the bus he was in would stick within viewing distance of the other. It did, in the thin Sunday evening traffic. And Garcia got off at Ballygunge Post Office, the stop he'd seen Ghazala get off at (though he didn't know her name was Ghazala). He followed her at a discreet distance down Ironside Road all the way to the end. She disappeared into the compound of a multi-storeyed building called 'Hemchhaya'. Garcia watched her go in, pretty sure this was where she lived. He couldn't give a fuck what her name was and what she did. He had her, he'd get her. And then he would gun for JCP Tanya Samanta.

In just over an hour, he was back in his slum in Titagarh. Lying down in his spartan refuge, Garcia felt thrilled. He'd got the bitch, now, he needed a plan of action. He got off work at 6 p.m. and he could be at Ironside Road by 7:30 every day. Sundays, he could shadow her all day. On weekdays, he could station himself at a location from where he could keep watch on the entrance to Hemchhaya to time her return. The problem was that after she'd beaten him up, he'd started to stand out. And opposite Hemchhaya was a housing complex for senior government officers—mostly those of the Indian Administrative Service (IAS). The place was crawling with cops. The roads in the area were deserted all day long because it was an upper-middle-class area. Anyone hanging around for hours or days on end would easily be spotted and dragged away to Karaya Police Station. A person as noticeable as him would be made in a couple of hours. How was he to form an impression about his quarry's daily routine—at least, find out when she got home in the evenings—without being caught?

The answer came to him in his sleep. Fully formed. Every evening, he'd go to the Ironside Road area in the garb of a Muslim mendicant, pick a spot from where the Hemchhaya gate was visible and sit there. He'd already let his hair and beard grow, which would help. After that, it was mainly a question of fixing his attire. That wouldn't be a problem. He'd sit at the chosen spot till his quarry returned home. Give it a little time and then wander off and crash somewhere. Living rough. In the morning, he'd go back and watch for the girl to leave home. By 8 a.m., however, he'd have to head back. To wash, eat and report for duty at 10 a.m.

He started his new routine the next day, with astonishing ease. In a fortnight, he discovered that the girl almost never returned home before 9:30 p.m. Six days, she got back between 10:15 and 10:30 p.m. and twice, at around midnight, both on Saturdays. She left home for a jog at around 5 a.m. She'd leave again, before he quit his surveillance, at 7 a.m., on a bicycle. On the two Sundays that he tailed her all day, she left home at around 7 a.m. and stayed out all day, getting back home by 10 p.m.

Come next Sunday, Garcia got up early as usual, and

after completing his morning routine in a reasonably relaxed fashion, left for Calcutta sans the mendicant disguise. He reached Ironside Road, his hair tied into a ponytail and beard trimmed, at around 6:30 a.m., hoping his quarry wasn't the 'let's-go-bird-watching-to-the-Santragachhi Jheel' type. She wasn't. At 7 a.m., Ghazala left home and walked to her uncle's house. Without realizing she was being shadowed by an expert. After a while, Aftab and Ghazala left in his car and Garcia, wrong-footed, drifted around in the Park Circus area. Had a couple of cups of tea, lunched on beef *bhuna* and *paratha* and finally headed to the house he'd seen the girl enter. The garage was shut, so he couldn't make out whether they were back home and so he decided to stretch his legs and limped to Ironside Road. It wasn't far. In better days, it would have taken him around twenty minutes to walk there. But now it took him almost half an hour. He wandered around in the vicinity, without attracting attention, making sure the Hemchhaya gates were visible.

Garcia's decision to not hang around in Colonel Biswas Road, where Aftab lived, had been the right one. Aftab and Ghazala had gone to meet some relatives and later for a relaxed lunch at the Lake Club in the Dhakuria Lake area, involving the consumption of small quantities of beer and large amounts of mutton and pork. After dinner, Aftab dropped her home. He had a cup of tea and a chat with his brother and sister-in-law before leaving. Providentially for Garcia, he'd spotted Aftab's car enter Hemchhaya. As a former cop, he'd obviously memorized the make, model, colour and licence-plate number. He'd also spotted the car being driven out and away. He hunkered down, sure that the girl would go out later in the evening. That was when an opportunity would present itself.

Ghazala left home later in the evening and headed for north Calcutta on a bus. Garcia had to board it as well. He didn't have the money to hail a cab. In any case, by the time he found one, the route 240 bus would be long gone. Luckily, buses had a couple of seats reserved for the 'handicapped'. Both were occupied by people without any obvious disabilities. One of them surrendered his seat to Garcia. So, he travelled inconspicuously with his quarry until she got off at the Amherst Street bus stop. Garcia remained seated. Just after the bus started to move, he said, 'Brother, I want to get off at Amherst Street.' The conductor grumbled and the bus stopped a second time.

'Sorry, *dada* (elder brother),' Garcia said. No one protested. Fringe benefit of being a fucking cripple, Garcia thought. He got off, spotted Ghazala and followed her. She went into a building and stayed there for hours. Garcia drank a cup of tea and got something to eat. He was planning frantically. He'd use a car to run her down. No Marquess of Queensberry rules. Not with him banged up the way he was. If she left the place really late, would he find an orphaned cab to hotwire? Would she find a cab first? Questions buzzing round in his head, Garcia finally gave up. He had been a good enough cop to know that you couldn't plan down to the last detail all the time. That's why you had ears to play by.

Ghazala emerged from the building around midnight, by which time Garcia had snoozed and freshened up. But he knew this would be tricky. The streets had emptied out. Only the occasional passer-by hurried down the street. Ghazala was a quick walker; Garcia struggled to keep pace. But he managed to keep her in his sight and realized she wanted to walk a bit. Good for you, Garcia thought and immediately saw an unattended cab parked by the side of the road. He walked up to it cautiously and looked around. Safe, he thought. Then he sprung the lock, hotwired the cab and set off at a sedate pace behind Ghazala, following her as she turned into College Street. He followed for some distance and then idled. Giving himself distance for a murderous assault. Garcia's ruminations crashed into the reality of the denouement. He'd been unlucky, he thought. But he knew where she lived. He'd get her.

~

Having survived a bollocking from Tanya, Ghazala changed her routines significantly to accommodate concerns about her safety. She'd jog to her gym at the crack of dawn and jog back. No compromise there. After that, she cycled to her uncle's place from where they'd leave for the shooting range, usually after a quick coffee. From there, she went home to shower, change, eat and leave for university. Having done all she wanted to by way of attending classes, studying and hanging out with friends, she'd be at her judo/karate/kung fu club for an evening session, but would make sure she was back home by 9:30 p.m. Her weekend treat was a crack-of-dawn hand-to-hand combat session. For being a good girl, Aftab had promised to try and sneak her into some kind of commando training programme for a week or so. It would be tough and could well fail to transpire. But the promise was enough to make Ghazala heed security concerns.

Chafing under a security regime she considered wholly idiotic, Ghazala wanted to 'do something' that would do justice to her normally high levels of adrenaline. One restless evening, she met up with Gloria and Dipanwita for coffee. From where they sat in the café, the trio could see some punks harassing girls or young women passing by. That was enough to set the fuse off for an already disgruntled Ghazala. She turned to her friends and said, 'Want to have some fun?' They nodded. 'Come along,' she commanded them.

'See those pricks there?' Gloria and Dipanwita nodded. 'We're going to walk past them, chatting among ourselves. Walk provocatively.' As they passed the group, one of the men asked, 'Sleep with me?' Two men sniggered; the rest laughed uproariously. Ghazala walked up to the man, still provocative. 'Where will you take me, sweetie?' she asked. For a moment, he was taken aback, but regained his composure. He cracked a wide grin and said, 'Why should I take a whore like you anywhere? We can do it right here. Any problems?' Ghazala's mouth formed a moue. 'Why not?' she responded. Most people on this benighted planet are idiots to varying degrees. But men who hang around the streets harassing women generally occupy the lower rungs. The man leaned forward, arms outstretched to grab Ghazala, who first rabbit punched him to stun. Then she caught him by his right hand and twisted it till his elbow snapped with a sharp crack. She turned him back towards herself and kneed him in the groin. He dropped to the ground like a sack of coal. In less than a minute.

There was a stunned silence. Passers-by hadn't even registered the assault. Ghazala turned to the rest of the men. 'Anybody else wants to sleep with me? Or any of my friends? Please feel free to put in an application.' One man stepped up. 'I'll get you bitch,' he said, as he whipped out a knife. Before he gained any control over it, Ghazala whipped out her own knife and slashed him across the face, Garcia-style. Then she kicked him in the balls. Another sack of coal down! 'Anyone else?' They stood still. 'Okay,' Ghazala said, 'here's what happens now. You kneel down on the ground in a row, facing away from the street, holding your ears. Until I tell you to get up. Now.' They wouldn't move. 'Fucking *now*,' Ghazala said. And they did. Then she called for an ambulance on her phone. A knot of people had gathered. It dissipated as the sound of a wailing siren drew near. Everybody likes a free show, but nobody wants to get involved.

Ghazala had signalled to Gloria and Dipanwita to beat it. Which they did, going back to the café with misgiving writ large on their faces. By the time the ambulance arrived, the crowd had melted away. Ghazala, too, made her exit, heading back into the café. They had another cup of coffee each, paid their bills and left unmolested and unsuspected. The ambulance had left with the injured and the genuflecting men seemed to have discovered that they were free to leave and split, not wanting, like the general public, to answer any questions.

Ghazala was her usual composed self. Dipanwita and Gloria's responses were mixed. They were aghast and excited and couldn't stop chattering to dissipate their nervous energy. It was then that Ghazala had an idea. 'Guys,' she said, 'why don't we start a weekend club teaching self-defence to women? Especially the older ones. I can book an hour's slot at my judo club during the off-peak hours at reduced rates or free of charge. The sessions, from me and a couple of other women, will be free. You two can be the first recruits.'

No one knew whether this was just a heat-of-the-moment idea. But the more the three thought about it, the more sense it made. Ghazala mooted the idea to Shibaji Sanyal, the amiable man who ran the club and owned the building. He agreed to let them use the space on Saturday and Sunday afternoons, when the club was closed anyway. Initially, it would be just the three of them. Luckily, Gloria was off on Saturdays and Sundays, a luxury not many enjoyed in the hospitality trade. She spent weekends with her family, but from now on, in the afternoon, she'd be at the club, as would Dipanwita, who was footloose on weekends. After much persuasion, Pritha agreed to join in. Within a month, there were fifteen recruits. Friends, mainly of Gloria and Dipanwita's, who knew what had happened to the two. The whole thing was only half-serious, however. Ghazala and another black belt taught them basic techniques, but also warned them that these would not equip them to repel serious attacks. The aim, as Ghazala put it, was to stun and run. After classes, they'd all go for tea or coffee, before dispersing. Sometimes, Tanya would drop by to give them moral support, and to help out with the training, being a pretty good judoka herself.

Little did they know that one person was following them around. Garcia had disappeared after the failed attempt to run Ghazala down. He'd hunkered down for a while, recovering from his newest set of injuries and building up his strength by eating well and working out. He was making decent money driving his businessman boss around. His boss turned out to be a contractor and supplier of building materials, and a small-time crook involved in 'protection' and drug-peddling. He also supplied muscle to those higher up the food chain. His name was Anadi. 'Just Anadi,' as he liked to tell those he considered his equals or betters. Those he pegged as subordinates called him Chhorda—youngest older brother, if you enjoy your oxymoron. Within days, like had called to like. Anadi had guessed that the battered man who called himself Aakash was not all that he appeared to be. And Garcia, combining his instincts as a policeman and a crook himself, made Anadi out in hours. A fruitful relationship was born.

Apart from driving Anadi's car and massaging his not inconsiderable ego, Garcia ran errands that no law-abiding chauffeur would. Anadi rewarded Aakash handsomely for his pains. Garcia moved to middle-class accommodation after his botched attempt on Ghazala. In effect, Garcia went from cop-cum-crime lord with an MLA for a squeeze, to a sidekick for a two-bit gangster. But after a long time, he started making enough money to live comfortably. In small-town Titagarh, once a flourishing industrial centre with a paper mill and jute mills, where he was attached to a nominally important man, he could not satisfy his craving for rape. He indulged in another kind of sexual assault: very rough sex with cheap whores who needed the business desperately and had so little protection from their pimps that they submitted to Garcia's violence.

Garcia stayed put in Titagarh for a couple of months, making money, getting stronger and serving his master. The comedown bothered him, but the thought that it was a means to an end kept him going. Garcia didn't venture into Calcutta for a couple of months. But as October came along and the festive season, kicking off with Durga Puja passed, he began to get restless. It wasn't just that Titagarh was a crummy, small-time, post-industrial town, affording no avenues of extra-curricular entertainment, it was also that he wanted to visit the big city to tail his quarries and chalk out the final plan that would deliver them into his hands. So, in mid-October, he took a week's leave of absence from his boss and headed into Calcutta on a warm, sticky day.

Garcia travelled to Calcutta early on Monday, preparing mentally and otherwise on his day off, to make sure he arrived at Ironside Road before the girl who'd kicked the shit out of him left home for the day to do whatever it was she did. When he realized he didn't know what she did, he knew he was slipping up. The first objective of surveillance should have been establishing her daily routine, which would have told him what she did and where she went to do it. He decided while on the train that he would shadow her all day. He'd done that on weekends, which is why he hadn't been able to establish her workday routine. Now, he had a whole week. She'll be easy meat before the week's out, he thought. JCP Tanya Samanta will be next, before year-end, he hoped.

Living a relatively comfortable life fuelled by good nutrition and exercise had filled up his gaunt frame. He looked fresher and healthier. Garcia sometimes thought his limp was less pronounced, which was complete horseshit. He had shaved his head again, partly because he wanted a change of look and partly because he thought it went better with his cheap 'hood' status. He had swiftly risen to become Chhorda's favourite two-bit enforcer. He was dressed in a cheap, checked shirt and dark trousers. Clean. He had shaved before he left home. And he was wearing a baseball cap—the right way round. He looked like one of the thousands of respectable people, if in his case just a touch down-at-heel, who went to Calcutta every working day to make some sort of a living. He could have been mistaken for a clerk in a small office, or even, in fact, the driver he had actually become.

Garcia reached Sealdah station at 6:15 and hopped on an empty bus, getting down at the Ballygunge Post office stop. He was there by 6:45. Looking around the practically deserted street, he started limping down Ironside Road. Half way down the road, he saw a jogger pass him by on the other side, ponytail bouncing on her back. Though she sped past before he had really had the opportunity to register her, Garcia knew from her figure that this was his quarry. Much before Garcia could draw abreast of the Hemchhaya gate, Ghazala had disappeared inside. Her routine seemed to be the same. But he had to make sure.

Excitement and anticipation mounting, Garcia looked around for a safe vantage point from which he could watch the gate of the compound. Garcia turned left when he reached Hemchhaya because that was the only way he could watch the gate. The only problem was that if he stationed himself there, he'd never be able to catch Ghazala when she left for the day. Nevertheless, he stayed where he was, trapped in indecision. Less than half an hour later, Ghazala emerged on a cycle and pedalled away furiously. Garcia realized he would just have to take his chances and wait. Hoping she'd return before really leaving home for the day. When she did that, Garcia reckoned, she'd take a bus, like she'd done before. So, Garcia limped back to the main road, a 150-metre walk, to wait for the girl who'd upended his life. Better than hanging around a housing estate for IAS officers, guarded by cops.

Reaching the main road, he wondered whether he should remain on the southbound flank of the arterial road or cross the street. After wracking his brains for some time, he decided to stay put, taking up position at the bus stop in front of the shuttered Ballygunge Post Office. Years of police work had taught Garcia to be patient. You couldn't be a decent cop without that quality. Running a criminal enterprise also required patience. So, Garcia waited. He wished he could sit down and wait but that option was not open to him. The morning got warmer. Sweat streamed down his face and his shirt was soaked. But he kept looking around, hoping he would be able to spot the girl on her way back home. If she was getting back. If she didn't return, he'd find a cheap hotel, which he'd have to do at some point anyway, and go back to the drawing board. But Garcia had read the situation correctly. At around 9:30, a bicycle whizzed past and turned left into Ironside Road. Then, following his instincts, he crossed the road and took up a discreet position near the bus stop on the northbound flank, a few paces to the left and practically in front of the white, gleaming monstrosity known as Birla Mandir.

Garcia's instincts had not failed him. Almost an hour later, the girl crossed the road and reached the bus stop. She didn't notice Garcia, who had turned his face away to stare in the opposite direction. Or maybe she didn't recognize him. She waited and got on a crowded route 240 bus, headed ultimately for north Calcutta. Garcia just managed to nip in keeping a few people between them. Even though the bus was crowded, he bagged a seat reserved for the 'handicapped' again. He could not keep an eye on Ghazala, however, on account of the crowd; he could not even see her, in fact. Being a tallish man, however, he kept an eye on the street every time the bus stopped to see who was getting down. It wasn't a perfect strategy, but it would have to do. The crowd in the bus increased, thinned and increased again, until there was a rush of people getting off at Sealdah station. Garcia managed to spot the girl. She was still standing, just a few paces behind him. In under ten minutes, the bus reached College Street. She got off there, and pulling the old dodge,

Garcia alighted a few metres further up and followed her. It wasn't tough because Garcia's disadvantage was offset by the crowds. Ghazala had to move slowly; Garcia kept a few people between them. She entered the Presidency University campus. Must have some work there, Garcia thought. He hadn't pegged her for a student.

He stationed himself on the other side of the road, watching the gate. A person could hang around College Street for days on end, as Garcia would eventually, without anyone noticing. Even a twenty-foot tall, green extra-terrestrial probably could pull it off... They'd reached College Street at around 11. Minutes grew into hours. There was no sign of the girl, but Garcia waited, manfully. He couldn't leave his post, so he couldn't grab a bite. By 3, he was hungry, though. His last meal had been an early breakfast before leaving Titagarh. But he was used to it.

Ghazala, in the meantime, was busy with classes, and working in the library to prepare a term paper. The night before, she'd lost sleep worrying about her studies. She'd been studying, but not enough. This was her penultimate undergraduate semester. Till now, her grades had been good. She didn't want to mess that up. During a break, Ghazala and a few of her friends went out to grab a bite, not feeling like sampling the same old college canteen fare. There were four of them and they headed to the Indian Coffee House, though the thick pall of cigarette smoke that always fogged the huge hall despite its incredibly high ceiling put Ghazala off. Still, as her friends always told her, the Coffee House was the stuff of what legends were made of and, thus, *de rigueur*. She shouldn't mind a bit of smoke to buy into immortality. Besides, the Mutton Afghani was pretty good. Garcia spotted Ghazala the moment she left the campus. His boredom and discomfort disappeared. He didn't follow her because he didn't need to. The entrance to the building housing the Coffee House was directly across the street from the Presidency gate and Ghazala disappeared into the doorway. Garcia waited for forty-five minutes, after which his quarry and her companions crossed the road and re-entered the university campus.

Garcia had to wait till 5:30. He was a patient man, but even his patience was wearing thin on this lonesome stakeout. Finally, Ghazala and a few other students emerged in a group and stood chatting outside the gate. Ghazala headed off in the direction of Amherst Street. Garcia followed. Down Mirzapur Street and a few paces into Amherst Street, Ghazala entered a building with a small signboard outside which said, Mirzapur Club of Martial Arts. Shit, Garcia thought. That's why she caught me. But now that he knew, he'd be careful. Problem was that though Garcia had been a karate black belt himself, pressures of work had prevented him from practising hard enough to make it to the top level. And now, with a broken leg, walking was fine. But martial arts? Ha!

Ghazala left the club at 8 and went home, Garcia following her. That night, Garcia checked into a cheap but reasonably clean hotel near Sealdah station and, headquartered there, kept up his surveillance to make sure this was Ghazala's unvarying weekday routine. But Garcia was curious about her morning bicycle ride. On Wednesday, after two days of dogging Ghazala's steps, he hired a bicycle with the help of the desk clerk at his hotel and waited on the northbound flank of Gariahat Road, the arterial thoroughfare off which Ironside Road pushed eastward. He was at the bus stop, south of the intersection, which, he hoped, would prevent him from running into his quarry. At around 7:15, Ghazala emerged on her cycle, turned right—northward—keeping a pretty punishing pace. Garcia took off. He had been a good cyclist, back in the day. And after his injuries he did, in fact, feel more comfortable cycling than walking, because the badly-knit patella somehow hurt less than when he walked. Garcia followed Ghazala, not being excessively mindful of keeping a distance. In the early morning, cyclists were thick on the ground. Milkmen with enormous canisters hanging from both sides; chicken vendors carrying trussed-up birds on handles and carriers and their shoulders; fish vendors with their metal pots filled with fish, some thrashing about in water; people generally out and about; and, of course, people going to work, usually those for whom a cycle ride meant a meagre but crucial saving on the bus fare. For Ghazala, this cycle ride was not just about getting to Aftab's house as fast as possible, it was also an extension of her exercise regimen. She was going flat out and Garcia, now handicapped by injury, just couldn't keep up. But as long as the bouncing ponytail was in sight, he was more than happy.

Ghazala whizzed past the Gurusaday Road crossing, no lights to speak of that early. Garcia kept going. When she crossed Modern High School, Garcia realized she was going to the house on Colonel Biswas Road to meet the middle-aged man she'd met the other day. Garcia got there just in time to see Ghazala and the man shoot off in a car. Frustrated, he got back to the hotel, returned the cycle, had breakfast and headed out towards College Street, to keep tabs. Garcia also decided he'd have to find out where she went in the morning. The solution, he thought, was simple. He'd steal a taxi, by now his favoured mode of transport. Lots of taxis parked by the roadside that early in the morning, waiting for the drivers to start their day. Nicking one wouldn't be a problem.

On Thursday, he left the hotel at 6, walking down to Moulali and turning left into C.I.T. Road towards the spot where he'd nicked the taxi he'd used to abduct, rape and nearly kill Dipanwita Hom, though he hadn't known her name at the time. He walked slowly, scoping out his surroundings until he reached the Ramlila Maidan, just before the Phillips bus stop and the right-angle turn. And he spotted a taxi: locked, no driver in sight. Garcia stopped for a moment and limped ahead. After fifty paces or so, he stopped and looked around. When he was reasonably sure he could swing it, he hobbled back to the cab, sprung the lock, hotwired the vehicle and was gone. He was going to fit another piece of the jigsaw in.

Garcia drove from the Moulali area to Beck Bagan, easing past the tram depot and swanky Quest Mall, turned right, rolled on for a hundred-odd metres and stopped in front of the Park Circus market, metres from Aftab's house.

At 7:30, the car he was waiting for, with the girl and the middle-aged man, came out of Colonel Biswas Road and turned left heading for Lower Circular Road. Garcia had to execute a U-turn and ease behind them. They turned into Lower Circular Road and kept going straight. People would hardly suspect they were being followed this early in the morning, especially by a cruising taxi. Aftab's car was an SUV, a Mahindra Scorpio. It went past the Exide crossing, Garcia not far behind, and finally came to a stop in front of a place Garcia knew well—the Kolkata Police shooting range. It was open to the public for shooting lessons and this was where Ghazala went to learn to shoot from her uncle, with the occasional tip from the trainers there. Jesus, Garcia thought, she's also learning to shoot. Does she pack a gun? But he was not nervous. He was packing as well. I just have to be careful, he thought.

He headed back to his hotel, dropping the cab near the spot he'd taken it from, but on the opposite flank of the road, reckoning parking it there was safer. At the hotel, he worked out in his room, had lunch, rested and headed to the university. Fuck, he thought again, this was a dangerous girl, he'd have to be careful. It never once crossed his mind that there was plenty of 'prey' in the city, and he should give this one a miss. Garcia established that the girl he was following had a pretty unvarying routine. The only change came one day, when she went from the martial arts club to the house she'd left the day he had almost run her down.

By Friday evening, Garcia was sure he'd figured out the girl's weekday routine, though he was still rattled by two things: the discovery that she was learning to shoot guns; and, the presence of a big, burly man by her side, who looked more than capable of taking care of situations.

Garcia could tell, because he'd seen plenty of men who had the look. What he couldn't tell was what relationship the two shared. It could be important, keeping in mind the plans he had for Miss Karate Chop. What remained to be done to make the trip a success was to confirm her weekend schedule. He'd turn up bright and early at Ironside Road on Saturday to follow her around all day.

In the meanwhile, however, fate, in the combined shape of Lakhan Kumar, ASI Barin Laha, OC Tirtho Samajpati and JCP (Crime) Tanya Samanta, was about to intervene. When Lakhan strolled out one Thursday morning to start his day plying the cab which he'd parked bang in front of Ramlila Maidan as he did every day, he found it was gone. Panicked, he ran up and down the road, unsure if he'd parked by mistake at a different spot. When he realized it had been stolen, he was shattered. It wasn't his vehicle. The man from whom he rented it was a local politician—a hard man. What would he do? Lakhan couldn't even begin to imagine the consequences. He rushed to the Entally police station to lodge a complaint. A GD entry was made by ASI Laha, a relative greenhorn who had a good memory and remembered the curious case of the taxi that was stolen and returned to the same spot near Ananda Palit. So, he went to his boss, OC Samajpati, who immediately put through a call to Lalbazar and asked for JCP Tanya Samanta. He re-introduced himself, 'Ma'am, myself Tirtho Samajpati, OC, Entally *thana*.'

Tanya obviously remembered him. 'Hello,' she said. 'Any more taxi thefts?'

'Yes, ma'am, that's exactly it,' Samajpati replied. 'A taxi

driver came in just a while ago and reported his vehicle missing. He'd parked in front of Ramlila Maidan. As you will recall, ma'am, the last time, the vehicle was stolen from near the Ananda Palit bus stop, less than a kilometre away. ASI Barin Laha took the complaint, remembered the last case, detained the driver and immediately came to me.'

'Good work!' Tanya said. 'Congratulations to both of you. Tell ASI Laha to be discreet. You might want to post some people in plainclothes in the area. He might try returning it to the spot like last time.'

'Yes, ma'am, absolutely,' said Samajpati.

Tanya made three calls in quick succession. First, to Aparna Das. 'Tanya Samanta. Where are you?'

Aparna was surprised as much by the call as by the abrupt question. 'I'm at home,' she said.

'Remain there until I tell you that you can go out.' Tanya suddenly realized she was scaring Mrs Das. She added, 'I'm sorry. I don't want to scare you, but we have reason to think that your assailant is back in town. So, as a matter of abundant caution, I'd like you to stay at home. I'll send a car with a couple of men as security until we've cleared this up.'

'Thank you,' Aparna said. 'You must be under a lot of pressure.'

'Occupational hazard, Mrs Das. I'll manage,' Tanya said, and hung up.

Then she called Dipanwita. 'Where are you?' she asked.

'In office,' Dipanwita replied. 'What's up?'

'Your assailant is probably in town. Be a good girl and stay in office until I send a car to take you home. Stay there until I say so. Take leave if necessary.'

'I hope you get him. Or Ghazala does.'

Tanya then called Gloria.

'Hi, Tanya,' Gloria said. 'What's up?'

'We think Garcia is back in town.' She heard a gasp, and continued. 'Remain wherever you are until I send officers to escort you home. A car will be parked outside your home until this crap is cleared up.'

'Okay. I'm in office. Send your boys to Park Street.'

Where it all began, thought Tanya, as she hung up. For a while, after getting OC Samajpati's call, Tanya had mulled putting tails on each of the victims, without telling them. But she couldn't make herself do it.

She called Ghazala. 'Hi, where are you?'

'At the univ,' Ghazala said.

'Stay there and don't do anything out of the ordinary. Just follow your normal routine. I'm sending you a mail.'

'What's up, Tanya?' Ghazala asked.

'I'll mail, right away,' Tanya said, and hung up. She opened her mail account and sent a message to Ghazala:

Garcia is back. Someone stole a taxi from in front of Ramlila Maidan, not too far from Ananda Palit bus stop where he stole the taxi he used to abduct Dipanwita. The MO is too similar for us to take chances. I've grounded Aparna, Dipanwita and Gloria. But I'm not grounding you because I think he's following you. After what you did to him, you'll definitely be at the top of his psychopathic, homicidal rage list. I'm probably next. You can just go home and stay in. But if you are willing to take a risk, we may get him. I'm going to speak to Aftab and to my boss before I lay the trap. Mail or call. Till I call, be super careful. Carry your gun.

Ghazala called in ten minutes. 'Up for it, Tanya. You speak to Jyatha first, then I'll speak to him. I shouldn't try to spot him, should I? That'll give the game away.'

'Act normal, Ghazala. It's not a game.'

Finally, she called Aftab and filled him in on everything that happened in the past hour or so. It wasn't regular, because Aftab was a civilian. But what the hell, thought Tanya, he could really help and she was using his niece if not exactly as bait, at least to draw Garcia out. Then she said, 'Would you want to provide back-up?'

Aftab was a measured man. He thought about the proposition for a while. And then replied, 'If Garcia has been following Ghazala to establish a routine, he'll have somehow followed her to my house in the morning, because she comes here every day. We leave for the range from my place. So, he'll have seen me. If he has, I'll have to shadow him, shadowing Ghazala. I'll carry a gun. I think she should as well.'

'I've already told her to,' Tanya said.

'So,' Aftab said, 'let's get the show on the road.'

~

Tanya called Commissioner Chanda, who seemed almost to have forgotten about the Garcia case. Or, the multiple Garcia cases spanning, prima facie, various forms of criminal enterprise, rape, grievous assault and murder. The last in Bangladesh, but still. 'Sir,' she began. 'We have reason to think that Garcia has shown up in town again. I mean to get him this time.'

'Garcia?' he said.

'Clayton Garcia, sir,' Tanya replied.

'Oh, Garcia,' Chanda said, as if he was visiting from a different planet. 'Come by in fifteen minutes.'

In exactly fifteen minutes, Tanya was filling her boss in on all that had transpired in the past hour and a half, editing out her call to Aftab. Then she told him about her plan. 'Sir, Ghazala is going to go about her business absolutely normally. We'll have a team of three tailing her all the time. They'll watch the house. Follow her to her uncle's place and the shooting range, then back home. Also follow her to the university, the martial arts club and back home. If she makes an unscheduled visit—to a friend's place, or to see a film—they'll follow her. I think we should be able to pick out Garcia if he's following her as well. I think he will after the hammering she gave him.'

'You want to use Ghazala as bait?' Chanda asked.

'No, sir, she'll follow her normal routine, which she would have done anyway, and we'll give her adequate security. One member of each team will have to pack a gun, because Garcia is probably armed. We'll need permission for that.'

'And what if a bystander gets hurt or killed? What if something happens to Ghazala?'

'Sir,' said Tanya, trying desperately to sound ultra-rational. 'We have to get Garcia. He's a psychopathic time-bomb. In the process, we'll have to take some risks, like we did in Katihar. If he's in town, we have a chance to get him. I can assure you that we will only take acceptable risks.'

Chanda didn't move a muscle. For a while, it seemed

he wasn't even breathing. 'Bring me a detailed plan,' he said, finally. Tanya took off. She knew this would go to the home secretary first. Chanda wasn't going to put his ass on the line. No way. Tanya knew that if she made Ghazala sound like bait, HS Datta would simply torpedo the plan. She started having doubts herself. So, she called Aftab again. 'Hi,' he said. 'Having second thoughts?'

'Yes. And if I don't pitch this right, it'll be blown out of the water.'

'Don't have second thoughts. We'll get him,' Aftab said. 'As for convincing your bosses, I'm confident you can do it.'

The conversation beefed up Tanya's resolve and she put her mind to writing a proposal:

We have reason to believe on the basis of a report about a stolen taxi that Clayton Garcia has returned to Calcutta after trying to run down Ghazala Alam in Bowbazar. The taxi was stolen from the Ramlila Maidan area. We have good reason to believe that Garcia had earlier stolen a taxi from the Ananda Palit area, which is nearby, and used it to abduct, rape and assault Dipanwita Hom, before returning the taxi where he'd found it. Garcia had earlier tried to do something similar to Ghazala Alam, who inflicted a severe beating on Garcia in self-defence, leaving him with a slashed face and a broken kneecap, which has, it is believed, given him a permanent limp. This happened in the Ananda Palit area as well. Ghazala's assault on Garcia, already a fugitive, has made him noticeable and unable to operate freely in Calcutta. We believe he will target Ghazala. We propose to let her go about her business and have her, and Garcia, if he's shadowing her, followed twenty-four hours by teams consisting of three officers each, working eight-hour shifts. At least one of the officers will be armed, since it is likely that Garcia is carrying a gun. Care will be taken to avoid collateral damage of any kind. We can pick him up right away, but I don't think we have a watertight case against him, other than in the Ghazala incident. And since Ghazala forestalled the attack, we can only get him for attempted assault. If we can catch him in the act, we'll be able to put him away.

The following are the teams proposed and their hours of duty.

Team A:	SI Sushila De
ASI	Abir Talukdar
ASI	Piya Kanungo
Team B:	Inspector Jadunath Majumdar
SI	Jayanta Nag
ASI	Shreya Daga
Team C:	Inspector Gopal Barui
SI	Ramadhar Tiwari
Constable	Ishita Pal
Team A:	6 a.m.-2 p.m.
Team B:	2 p.m.-10 p.m.
Team C:	10:00 p.m.-6 a.m.

Tanya Samanta
Joint Commissioner of Police (Crime)

Tanya e-mailed the proposal to the commissioner and then called him. 'Sir,' she said 'Forgive the cliché, but time is really of the essence. It would be very good if we could start at 6 a.m. tomorrow.'

Chanda grunted. 'Let me see what I can do.'

Tanya summoned all the members of her team who were 'in-house' and told them the plan, but warned them it could get shot down. In the middle of the briefing, the commissioner called. 'Go ahead,' he said. 'The HS is going to mail me officially and I'll mail you officially after that. If a situation develops, shoot to kill. Don't mess around. Lives are at stake.'

Tanya was stunned, but managed to say, 'Thank you, sir. We'll need to get Talukdar, Sushila and Shreya back in the team.'

'Call them in fifteen minutes.'

From Tanya's beaming face, her team had no difficulty in figuring out that the plan was on. Tanya first called Ghazala and got a sketch of her weekday and weekend schedules. Then she told the team, 'Team A reaches Hemchhaya on Ironside Road at 6. Ghazala won't be there. She'll be back around 7 from her jog. You'll have to find ways to keep track of her. Once she leaves for the university, it's going to be much easier for Teams A and B. Team C will follow her home from the martial arts club, or maybe a friend's place, if she goes somewhere after practice. Anyway, I won't lecture you on how to conduct a surveillance operation. Keep in touch with each other at the time of changing over and with Ghazala. And with me on a regular basis. Concentrate on Garcia. Don't get distracted.' That was Tanya's way of protecting Aftab, in case one of the officers noticed another man hanging around too close for comfort.

Friday went smoothly. Even though Ghazala knew she

was being followed by teams of detectives and her uncle, she never made them. That was partly because she had to act normally, instead of looking around all the time. But Garcia didn't make them either. In part, probably, because he was so obsessively focused on Ghazala. But all the three teams made Garcia. It wasn't that difficult.

Back home, Tanya suddenly remembered her boss's injunction: 'If a situation develops shoot to kill.' Tanya wasn't exactly an idiot. She knew that Garcia couldn't have run a vast criminal network without other cops and political leaders being involved. His network spanned several police jurisdictions: in Calcutta and the neighbouring districts of South and North Parganas. He recruited and collaborated with local hoods and used local muscle, patronized by political leaders. It was inconceivable that none of them knew about Garcia's involvement. It was very likely Garcia paid them off. That was possibly how he'd come to know Shila Nandi in the first place. So far as the cops were concerned, Tanya was absolutely certain that other officers were involved in Garcia's operations. Capturing him alive would open a reservoir of worms. Which was why Chanda was so concerned about lives being at stake. He wasn't corrupt, but he didn't want to preside over an inquisition of his force. Tanya was, nevertheless, determined to try to bring Garcia in alive.

On Saturday, Ghazala went for a jog and then to the shooting range via Aftab's place. Four people were tracking her movements. Three were tracking Garcia's as well. Team A had broken up. Sushila had gone directly to the shooting range. Talukdar was at Aftab's. Piya was tracking

Ghazala and Garcia on a bicycle. When Ghazala returned from her jog, Piya was chatting with the security guards at the gate of the IAS quarters, resting on a bicycle. The idea was that if anybody noticed her at all, she'd be taken for one of the numerous domestic workers, who worked for the middle-class families in the neighbourhood. Garcia hadn't worked with her so there was very little chance of him noticing her.

Piya tracked in behind Ghazala when she emerged from the Hemchhaya compound and followed her to Beck Bagan, but kept going till she reached Karaya Road PS, practically next door, where she ditched her bicycle and called Talukdar. She said, 'Couldn't spot Garcia. Be extra watchful. See you at the range.' Then she called Sushila. 'Sushila*di*,' she said. 'Couldn't spot Garcia. He may have gone straight to the range. Be watchful.' She hitched a ride to a point near the shooting range and proceeded on foot.

Talukdar was on a bike. His own. Petrol paid for by the department, since he was on duty. He picked up Aftab's car after it had turned out of Colonel Biswas Road. Taking it easy, trying to pick out Garcia, which he couldn't. Aftab and Ghazala hit a red at the Exide crossing, not very far from their destination. Talukdar was a few cars behind. When the light turned green, Talukdar finally spotted Garcia, who pulled in behind Aftab's car as it eased past the crossing. Smart, Talukdar thought, but not smart enough. He followed the two cars to the range, drove some distance away, parked and lit a cigarette. Waited. Garcia parked his taxi, which he'd stolen from the Dharamtala area, well away from the range. He too lit a cigarette and waited. Sushila was already there, concealed in a doorway. Her car parked a good distance away. Piya arrived and sat down on the footpath. The tableau was set.

Ghazala's shooting slot was 8-9 o'clock. She left the range at 9:15 with her uncle. A cavalcade followed. First off the blocks was Garcia, followed by Talukdar. Piya had strolled up to his bike and was riding pillion. A little after them came Sushila, in an unmarked police car, with a board leaning against the windshield which said, 'On Government Duty, Department of Fisheries'. Aftab and Ghazala drove to the Lake Club, where they had breakfast.

'What do you think this creep is going to do, Jyatha?' Ghazala asked.

'I think he's going to make his move this weekend. He's been stealing cabs and returning them. He must know, or guess, that the thefts are being reported. The more this cycle repeats itself, the more likely he's going to get caught. Garcia's not a fool. We'll have to be alert, especially you. I'm betting he'll make his move when you are returning home at night. After you get home, disassemble your gun. Clean it, put it back. Make sure it's firing perfectly.' Aftab paused for a while, lost in thought. Then he said, 'On second thoughts, we'll do that at my place. We're going there in any case because you'll have to pick up your bicycle. After you're done and after you've checked, I'll check too. Close the stable doors before, if you know what I mean.' Ghazala didn't say anything. They left at around 11:30, getting to Colonel Biswas Road around noon. The cavalcade followed. Garcia still had no clue.

At around 1 p.m., Aftab and Ghazala left Beck Bagan

and went to Hemchhaya. The plan was that Sushila and Piya would stick with Ghazala, and Talukdar, who was packing, would stick to Garcia. One of the problems was that too many guns were in play. Garcia, the cops were correctly assuming, had a gun. Talukdar had one. And Aftab and Ghazala had one each. If it came to a shootout, this would be a disadvantage for the cops, because they couldn't just spray bullets. Garcia would have an advantage because he wouldn't give a damn about who was injured or killed, except himself. Moreover, he didn't know how the situation was playing out. But Aftab's assumption was shared by the police. They also thought that if Garcia made a play, it would be at night, when Ghazala was returning home, from her Sunday afternoon-to-night jaunt.

As Aftab pulled into Hemchhaya, Garcia cruised past with Talukdar tailing him. Sushila parked near the gate of the IAS housing complex. Garcia rounded the corner on which Hemchhaya stood, circled the block and parked at the Ironside Road-Gariahat Road crossing in front of the Ballygunge Post Office, secure in the knowledge that Ghazala would have to pass his taxi on the way to the bus stop. Talukdar stopped on the northbound flank near the bus stop, secure in the knowledge that Ghazala would have to be at the bus stop, on the way to the martial arts club. A series of calls were made to ensure that no glitch in coordination occurred. Jadunath arrived at the bus stop at 1:50 p.m. on a motorbike, carrying a gun; Talukdar took off. Jayanta and Shreya reached Ironside Road at 1:50 p.m. and parked behind Sushila's car. Their vehicle displayed an identical board through the windshield. The Department of Fisheries was on a Saturday overdrive. Sushila drove off. Everyone waited.

At 2 p.m., Aftab dropped Ghazala at the bus stop and went home. He parked his car in the garage and picked up a motorbike borrowed from a friend and zoomed off toward the Amherst Street martial arts club. He knew the police were in position. He was the ace in the hole. Ghazala got into a bus and headed off to Amherst Street. Garcia followed with Jayanta and Shreya trailing after them in their car and Jadunath bringing up the rear. Instead of getting off at the Amherst Street bus stop, Ghazala went two stops ahead and got off at the College Street stop, because she wanted to stretch her legs before the judo session. College Street was one-way and could not be accessed from Harrison Road, where the bus dropped Ghazala. So, the vehicles following her had to execute a U-turn before going back to the Amherst Street bus stop to take a right turn toward the club. It could have made the cavalcade look conspicuous and prompted the cops and Aftab to curse the object of their protective surveillance. It didn't bother Garcia though. He knew where she was going. He took the U and turned into Amherst Street. The others had to overshoot College Street and make U-turns at various points and follow Garcia. But all of them knew where to go, so they all landed up near the club and took up appropriate positions from where they could watch their respective quarries.

***

At Lalbazar, Tanya got a call from Hare Street PS. 'I'm Debabrata Lohar, OC, Hare Street, speaking. Am I speaking to JCP Samanta?' he asked.

'Yes,' Tanya said.

'Ma'am,' OC Lohar said, 'we have just received a complaint of a taxi stolen from Dharamtala. It was parked near Loreto Day School.'

'Thank you,' Tanya said, feeling a frisson run down her spine, as she noted the number of the cab and messaged it to all the teams. The game was afoot. Later, she got the first report from Team A informing her that Garcia had been spotted in a cab. Her day was made.

***

When the self-defence session ended, fourteen women walked out of the building, among them Ghazala, Dipanwita, Pritha and Gloria. They congregated at a roadside stall for tea and biscuits. They didn't go to a café, because some, including Ghazala, were in a hurry. She had to submit a tutorial by Tuesday and wanted to finish it that day so her Sunday would be relatively free. After tea and biscuits, they split up. Pritha ambled home and Ghazala went off in the direction of Harrison Road to take a bus. She was followed, but the return journey was uneventful. After she reached home, Aftab called her. 'Work?' he asked.

'Yes, Jyatha,' she replied. 'Have to finish a tutorial, which is due on Tuesday.'

'So, you'll be home?'

'Yes. Not going anywhere, unless I have to step out to get something. It's unlikely.'

'Stay in. We'll wrap this up tomorrow, I'm hoping.' He hung up and called Tanya. 'Hi,' he said. 'Ghazala's studying this evening. She's not leaving the house.'

'Good,' Tanya said. 'We'll see what happens tomorrow. But the surveillance will be on.'

'Maybe you can find out where Garcia's putting up.'

'That's right. I was thinking whether we should pick him up. The case against him is weak. Gloria doesn't remember; Aparna is not sure; and the severe assaults on Chitra and Dipanwita have made their recollections vague. The only identifications in the ballpark are those of Soumitro, Shefali and Ghazala's. But in Ghazala's case we can't pin anything on him other than 'attempted'. And Shefali and Soumitro's testimony are not conclusive. A smoking gun would nail him. We know he's guilty.'

'Don't have second thoughts, Tanya,' Aftab said. 'We'll get him.'

Tanya first called Jadunath and then Gopal. She delivered the message: when Garcia abandoned his surveillance, one member of whichever team was on the scene should follow him and find out where he was putting up. And she should be informed, whatever the hour.

Garcia stayed in place till 8:30, by which time a smooth change of guards had taken place. Ramadhar was tasked with following Garcia. He was parked in front of the post office on his Bullet. Gopal and Ishita pulled in behind Jayanta and Shreya's car near the IAS officers' housing compound. Gopal, who was an okay shot, had a gun, as well as Ramadhar. Garcia drove the taxi up to Beck Bagan and parked it in front of the famous sweet shop called Mithai.

Then he took a route 45 bus, with Ramadhar purring along behind him. Garcia, oblivious to the surveillance, got off at the foot of the Sealdah flyover and proceeded on foot. He checked into his small hotel. Ramadhar parked near the hotel, with an unhindered view of the doorway and prowled around. Having made sure that there was no way Garcia could leave the building other than by the front door, he settled down to wait the night out.

At around 5 a.m., the team members called each other to coordinate the change of guard. Talukdar reached the Sealdah hotel and Ramadhar left at 5:55 a.m. Sushila and Piya arrived in their department of fisheries car and Gopal and Ishita left. Just after the changeover, Garcia emerged from the hotel and started off towards Moulali. Talukdar guessed he was going to take a bus. He eased in behind Garcia just when he was about to go out of sight. Garcia took a bus from the foot of the flyover and Talukdar called Sushila and gave her the alert. Then he followed the bus. Garcia got to the post office bus stop and, though he wasn't anticipating trouble, activated his back-up in the shape of the transferred and much-aggrieved Gautam Biswas, formerly OC Park Street, now posted to the boondocks. Garcia called him. 'Reached Calcutta?' The answers was a yes. Satisfied, he went on, 'Be at the Amherst Road-Mirzapur crossing as soon as possible. You'll find the Mirzapur Martial Arts Club there. Keep an eye on it discreetly and watch out for me. Don't make contact, but follow me unobtrusively wherever I go. Be armed. Use a bike if you have one. Remember to be inconspicuous and don't lose me.' He rung off and settled down to wait.

After Ghazala emerged on her bike, he crossed the road and took a bus, with Talukdar following him on a motorbike. The department of fisheries car waited at the Ironside Road-Gariahat Road intersection until Garcia had boarded the bus. Then it followed Ghazala. After they were through at the range, Aftab dropped Ghazala home. She left for the martial-arts session after lunch, at around 2 p.m. What followed began as a rerun of the previous day, except that Aftab went straight to Amherst Street from his place; Garcia was on foot; and the police team was careful to turn straight into Amherst Street. Biswas was lolling in a tea shop that was shut for the afternoon, looking suitably down at heel and, he hoped, inconspicuous as instructed, with a borrowed bike parked not too far away. He saw Garcia, waited for a while and moved away to get closer to his bike.

After the session was over, the self-defence group walked to College Street. They hung around having street food, tea and letting their hair down. The Indian Coffee House opened at 5 p.m. on Sundays. As soon as it opened, the group headed in. They were not the only people hanging around waiting for it to open. A whole procession trooped into the premises, once known as Albert Hall. Garcia followed the group, with the police team in tow in its two vehicles. Nobody had noticed Biswas, who waited for Garcia to leave, before following him. When Garcia saw that the women were not going anywhere in a hurry, he took off towards Bowbazar Street. Jadunath followed on foot, guessing Garcia was looking for a taxi to steal. Difficult, at this time of the hour on a Sunday. But Garcia was in luck. Just a short walk from Presidency University, he found a taxi parked opposite the Calcutta Medical College and Hospital and approached it cautiously. The street was practically empty. The shops closed. In minutes, Garcia unlocked the cab and started it. Jadunath waited. Garcia eased the cab past the University of Calcutta campus and parked at the corner of College Street and P.C. Sarkar Street, on which stood the Eden Hindu Hostel, a 125-year-old institution for boys studying in government colleges under the University of Calcutta. Jadunath walked back to his bike. He had to be extra careful because Garcia knew him well. Biswas was in the mix, his bike parked while he browsed at one of the famous second-hand bookshops on the pavement. Aftab was fiddling with his motorbike near the entrance to the Coffee House and the department of fisheries car was parked near the Presidency University gate, between Garcia's taxi and Harrison Road. They'd all have to head in that direction.

The gang stayed in the Coffee House for almost two hours. The Sunday crowd was thinner as was the usual pall of smoke. They began straggling out at 6:45. By 7, they had congregated on Bankim Chatterjee Street, outside the Coffee House building. In ones and twos, they headed off. Ghazala, Pritha and Gloria were the last ones left. Aftab had also taken off, apprehensive that Garcia would spot him. He wasn't far away though, waiting near the bus stop from which Ghazala would board a bus. He had his helmet on, which, he guessed was adequate protection. Ghazala and Gloria went to the bus stop, four vehicles following them. Ghazala had already called her uncle to tell him that she was going to a friend's place in Gol Park, a few kilometres south of Ballygunge Post Office. From there, they'd probably head out. This information was passed on to Tanya, who informed the members of Team B. Ghazala boarded a route 240 bus to Gol Park. Four vehicles followed.

Ghazala and her friend, Mohitosh Sengupta, left his house at 9. They strolled down Southern Avenue, past the Dhakuria Lake, past, in fact, the spot where Garcia had dumped Chitra Srivastava, and finally turned into Lansdowne Road. They took the second right turn and stopped in front of Xrong Place, a cross between a pub and a club. Three women and two men joined them. They had been classmates in school and met once every two months to have a good time. They went in around 9:45.

Garcia passed them and went further up the road. To everyone, except Biswas, the members of Team B, Aftab and Ghazala, who'd also made him, he was just a cruising cabbie. As you turn into Dr Sarat Banerjee Road from Lansdowne Road, Xrong Place is on the left. You can't park on that side of the road. And you have to pay a parking fee of Rs 10 an hour, if you park on the right. Cabbies either don't use paid-for parking zones or make sure they aren't charged. That worked at off-peak hours. Around 10 p.m. on a Sunday, in an area full of hospitality establishments, no chance. Garcia knew that Ghazala and her gang wouldn't be out till late. He took a right turn and returned to Southern Avenue, with Ramadhar, who, with the rest of Team C, had replaced Jadunath and Team B, on his tail, turned back into Lansdowne Road, went down the road, took a U-turn and parked on the main road, just before the turn into Dr Sarat Banerjee Road. Ramadhar parked about ten metres behind, dismounted and settled at a roadside tea stall for a cup of tea. He was itching for action. Aftab parked practically across the street from Xrong Place, dismounted and wandered off. He didn't mind paying the parking fee, which was chickenshit for two-wheelers. Gopal and Ishita parked their car a little down the road. A parking attendant came over. Gopal mulled for a while the wisdom of telling him they were cops on duty. Thought better of it. Forty-odd bucks was what they'd have to pay. No sweat. Garcia had still not made any of his pursuers, or his back-up. Biswas had been intent on keeping track of Garcia. He wasn't a fool and had figured out that Garcia was following a young woman about whom he knew nothing. But he hadn't realized that others were on the trail as well. Like Garcia, though, Biswas was more than competent. He'd blended into the background enough not to be noticed by anyone.

Aftab had eaten while he was waiting for Ghazala to exit the Coffee House. The members of Team C had dined; Biswas had had a substantial lunch; which left Garcia out as the odd, hungry, man. The place was littered with restaurants (not cheap ones), but he couldn't go into any of them in case the gang left early. He wandered off in search of food, keeping an eye on the Xrong Place doorway. Ramadhar abandoned his bike and followed. Near Xrong Place, on a parallel road, was a joint called Go Lebanese. Its Lebanese antecedents may have been dubious, but it was cheap. Garcia ordered hummus and pitta bread for

Rs 120 and ate it standing on the pavement across the road from Xrong Place. Which, he thought, made him an inconspicuous diner. He was being watched, of course, by Ramadhar, with back-up a few paces away concealed in a doorway, in the shape of Aftab, which he didn't know, and a few metres down the road, in a car, in the shape of an armed Gopal and Ishita.

It was a long wait. Xrong Place closed at 11:30. And it was then that the gang emerged. They went their separate ways. Ghazala, Mohitosh and two others went towards Southern Avenue. That made it two women and two men. A distance behind them was Garcia in his cab, followed by a motorbike and a car. This was where Biswas was in danger of being spotted, but he evaded attention by taking the wrong side of the carriageway. Since there was a wide strip of land dividing Southern Avenue, dotted by trees and at one point, a structure containing a swimming pool, he went unnoticed. Aftab had eased past the group and took a detour to Gol Park. After Ghazala had come out of the club/pub and the foursome turned into Southern Avenue, strolling, Gopal had given Tanya an update. 'Ma'am,' he said, 'They're on foot. I think they'll walk it to Gol Park and then take a taxi.' Tanya was in a car at the Gol Park roundabout, near Wise Owl, ready to move.

Though Southern Avenue wasn't the safest of places to walk down at that time of the night, it was okay for four people, especially with two men and Ghazala in the group. The two men would deter would-be harassers and if it didn't, they'd regret it. The second man in the group, Ashani Chowdhury, was big, good in a scrap. Being a fitness freak, he didn't drink. Ghazala generally drank sparingly—a glass or two of beer—but on that day, she had stayed sober. One of the women lived in a high-rise on Southern Avenue. She left the group first. Mohitosh hived off at Gol Park. Ghazala and Ashani continued toward the big Gariahat crossing, swarming with people during the day, but now practically deserted. Gopal gave Tanya another update as soon as Mohitosh had gone his way. Tanya spotted Ghazala and Ashani the moment they came to Gol Park and turned left, moving clockwise toward Gariahat Road. Tanya waited for them to go some distance and followed, noting Aftab's motorbike rolling past the two pedestrians. Biswas stepped onto the right side of the road at the roundabout but at a good distance. He was getting jittery.

Ashani lived on Mandeville Road, which branched off from Ekdalia Road, which in turn branched off the main road a few metres north of the Gariahat intersection. After that, Ghazala would be on her own. It was past midnight. Ghazala didn't get a cab; the few parked near the intersection refusing to go the roughly one and a half kilometres to Ironside Road. What they wanted was one long-distance passenger, who they could charge some impossibly high fare. Then they'd head for their garages.

Finally, Ghazala told Ashani to go home. She'd walk back. 'Ghaz,' he said, 'it's well past midnight. I'll walk you home or you can crash at my place. Jog home early in the morning. You'll be there before your parents wake up and call the cops.'

Ghazala smiled. 'It's cool, Ash,' she said. 'You know me. I can take care of myself. I'm carrying my knife.'

'It's still not safe. I'll go with you'

'Ash, go home, your parents will be angry if you're too late. Tell you what, I'll walk with you upto your place. From there, I'll hoof it alone. Ballygunge Place is safe.'

~

Ashani went home, leaving Ghazala to walk down the one-odd kilometre from Mandeville Gardens to her place, with misgivings. But Ghazala was so confident he had no choice but to agree. Ghazala looked around, but couldn't spot a single vehicle. After Ashani had entered the gated compound, she spotted a motorbike making its way down the road. She knew it was her uncle. She turned right into Swinhoe Street and a little further, left into Ballygunge Place, practically into the home stretch. If anything was to happen, she thought, it would happen soon.

As Ghazala turned right into Swinhoe Street, Aftab gunned his engine, sweeping past her and turning into Ballygunge Place. Some way in, he parked in the shadow of a balcony and hid in an alcove. Tanya was just behind him. Sheonath went a little further and parked. In minutes, Ghazala had turned into Ballygunge Place and had taken out her gun from her tote bag. She held it at her side and kept walking, not being able to decide whether she'd prefer Garcia to attack and get the whole thing done with or walk back home peacefully.

Then Garcia turned into Ballygunge Place, crawling. He saw a parked bike, but thought nothing of it. He saw a car parked a little way ahead, but it was unoccupied.

Tanya was prone on the back seat, head raised just enough to see out of the window. The door was cracked open by an inch. Sheonath was PSO and chauffeur for the night. He was in the same position. He was as good a shot as Tanya, Jadunath and Ramadhar, if not better.

Garcia crawled, he wanted to get her half way down the road. Get out of the taxi, shoot her legs, smash her on the head, scoop her into the taxi and scoot. It would take no more than a couple of minutes, he reckoned. As he crawled, a car, also moving slowly, passed him and continued up the road. Garcia was furious. Why were these cocksuckers taking it easy on an empty road in the middle of the night? Anger and the single-minded focus on Ghazala, so near to damnation, blunted his instincts. He wasn't thinking clearly. In fact, he was hardly thinking at all. Behind them, Ramadhar turned into Ballygunge Place, parked and started strolling down the pavement, keeping to the shadows. Biswas stuck close to Garcia from the point he turned into Ekdalia Road, ignoring the one-way restriction, right until they turned into Ballygunge Place because for that stretch Garcia could have gone in several directions at several points. Into the long Ballygunge Place stretch, he slowed down to a crawl.

Ghazala reached a dark stretch. Garcia stopped as he drew abreast of her. He pushed open his unlocked door, gun in hand, and hopped out. And Ghazala turned, with her gun pointing at his head. It was a standoff, Garcia thought, but he'd shoot the gun out of her hand before she could shoot. It wasn't easy for ordinary people to shoot at other people. But Tanya, who was just behind them, jumped out of her car, gun pointed at Garcia's head. Aftab had heard the car and emerged from the shadows, gun in hand, looking around. And Ramadhar had sneaked in close, on foot, gun drawn. Garcia was corralled, but he didn't realize it until a gunshot from Biswas, who was furthest behind and had no idea how many people and guns were in play, shattered the silence. Tanya went down on her knees, clutching her upper arm, where she'd taken a bullet.

Then, everything seemed to happen simultaneously. Ramadhar barked, 'Drop your gun,' and shot Garcia at the base of his spine, blowing his coccyx to bits. He collapsed. The crack of two gunshots also rang out, followed by two quick sounds: a metallic clang, followed by a dull thud. Standing by, taking everything in, Aftab had seen a muzzle flash and shot at it twice, hitting Biswas. The two sounds were those of a gun hitting the pavement followed by a body landing on top of it.

Gopal calmly called the two police ambulances, which had been waiting at Ballygunge Phari, very close to the scene. They arrived in minutes. Tanya got into the first one. The second stretchered Garcia in and took off.

Gopal called another ambulance and personnel from Gariahat *thana* to deal with the dead man. Aftab had left. Ghazala was with Ishita. And Ramadhar and Gopal were standing over the body, which had fallen face down. They were waiting for the Gariahat cops. In minutes, two police cars arrived from Gariahat PS, with a team led by OC Taranga Haldar. He walked up to the body and exchanged nods with the two detectives before bending down and turning it over. Ramadhar clicked his tongue.

'You know him?' Haldar asked.

Ramadhar nodded. 'Gautam Biswas. Former OC of Park Street PS.'

'Holy shit,' Gopal and Haldar said in unison.

Gopal followed the ambulance. Ramadhar gave Ishita a lift home on his bike. The Gariahat cops dropped Ghazala home.

Ramadhar and Jadunath, notified of the night's events by Gopal, joined him at the hospital, until officers arrived to keep watch over Garcia. Tanya would be in the hospital for the day according to the doctors. Just a flesh wound, but she could do with some rest. Garcia wasn't going anywhere, anytime soon. A couple of hours later, a doctor arrived. 'He'll live. But he'll be on a wheelchair all his life,' the doctor said.

'Where he's going, he won't get a wheelchair,' Ramadhar told the perplexed doctor before leaving, with Gopal and Jadunath in tow. Tanya would have to file a full report when she recovered.

The Garcia squad would get into work late.

Epilogue

A trial court gave Garcia a life sentence, convicting him for four rape-and-assault cases as also three attempted murders in the cases of Chitra Srivastava, Dipanwita Hom and Ghazala Alam. He was also convicted on various charges relating to his criminal network. Instead of allowing the sentences to run concurrently, the court stipulated that they were to run consecutively, which practically amounted to a life in jail. Unable to hire top lawyers, Garcia failed to get the sentence overturned in a higher court. The trial court granted the harshest possible sentence, convinced by the prosecution argument that not only were his crimes heinous, the fact that they were committed by a man who was supposed to be a guardian of the law made them worse. The defence counsel's attempt to depict him as a man of unsound mind who could not be held accountable for his actions failed because that kind of argument rarely washes in Indian jurisprudence. The fact that he'd pursued a long and 'distinguished' career as a police officer with no indication that he was psychologically imbalanced also weighed with the judge. The higher court—the Calcutta High Court—possibly keeping the same considerations in mind, upheld the conviction and sentence. Garcia lacked the means to move the country's top appellate court—the Supreme Court. He also figured, as he made clear to his lawyer, that life in a wheelchair outside jail, without the means to support himself, was not worth fighting for.

Garcia refused to reveal a single detail about his network, even when he was offered a lighter sentence. He knew that if he squealed, he wouldn't have lasted more than a few days in prison, because, incapacitated, he wouldn't be able to defend himself. And many people outside jail wouldn't want him to remain alive. The politicians as well as all the other cops involved stayed untouched. Except, of course, Gautam Biswas, who had two motives for being a back-up for Garcia that night. First, he had been significantly involved in Garcia's network and had been promised a big pay-off. And, second, he hated the Kolkata Police brass for pulling him out of Park Street before he'd recouped his investment and making a scapegoat of him. And Tanya Samanta for being assigned his case and solving it.

Gloria, Aparna and Dipanwita proved to be extremely resilient and returned to their lives with renewed vigour after Garcia's conviction. The news also reached Chitra, who after taking a year off to recover from her injuries, mental and physical, returned to her doctoral work. Gloria continued to attend AA meetings as often as she could and spent a great deal of time with Nilanjan. Dipanwita broke up with her Parsi beau, Cyrus Poonawallah, who couldn't handle being in a relationship with a rape survivor. She was distressed at first, and then relieved. She realized she was better off without him. She got a promotion not long after Garcia was shot and apprehended, which cheered her up.

Ghazala was persuaded by her uncle to enrol for a Master's degree before taking a decision about making a career out of combat. She agreed that it was a good idea, because she found herself increasingly enjoying her academic work. Pritha, too, played a role in convincing her. Nevertheless, Ghazala continued with her shooting lessons, martial-arts training, and hand-to-hand combat, sometimes involving the use of knives, sometimes not. As she rapidly approached the status of a crack shot, she took another step towards becoming a formidable fighting machine.

Of the members of the Garcia squad, only one wasn't completely satisfied. Having dinner at home all by himself the night after the shootout, Inspector Gopal Barui was an unhappy man. He had mentored Mrinal Mallik and known him to be a capable, thoughtful man with ambitions and ideals. Where and when had he crossed the tracks? It troubled Gopal that he had failed to see a single sign. He still thought of Mrinal as a fundamentally decent man. And bad though he felt, he felt worse on Ishita's behalf. But despite his schoolmasterly mannerisms, Gopal was a tough guy. He'd get over it, as would Constable Ishita Pal.

JCP (Crime) Tanya Samanta had been worried about being posted out of DD because her pursuit of Garcia had flown in the face of the chief minister's spur-of-the-moment statement, (publicized first by her boss, Commissioner Chanda), that Gloria's accusations had been fabrications, designed to malign the administration and the chief minister herself. Combined with the fact that her relationship with her boss wasn't exactly perfect, she was expecting a letter any time transferring her to an irrelevant post, even though her report, copiously supported by witness statements, had not been faulted by anyone in the bureaucratic or political hierarchy. Just because you did good work didn't mean you were going to be rewarded, however. Bureaucracies didn't work that way.

So, when Tanya got a summons from Chanda, who was due to be elevated to the soon-to-be-vacant post of DGP, she went to his office fearing the worst. After she was seated, Chanda said, 'Good work, Tanya. Keep it up. The new commissioner's a good fellow.' The last statement was a touch oracular, but Tanya didn't notice it. Nor did she pay attention to her boss's unusual reversion to her given name.

All that registered, all that really mattered at that moment, was that she was still heading her beloved Detective Department.

Acknowledgements

A loud shout-out to Atri Bhattacharya, IAS, for tutorials on police procedure and for saving me from what would have been an embarrassing error; to Dr Arindam Ganguly for advice on shattered patellae; and to Sunip Sen and Tapas Ghosh for coming to the rescue late on matters legal.

Thanks are also due to several people who read the manuscript and offered encouragement: Subhas Ranjan Chakraborty, Jishnu Dasgupta, Debashish Ghosh and Moushumi Roy Chowdhury. Thanks also to Shantanu Datta for helping me in making a crucial connection.

Special mention, too, of Samita, my sister, and Seshadri, my brother.

Extra-special thanks to Srinandan Das Mahapatra for his illuminating and typically prompt comments.

I am grateful to Ravi Singh of Speaking Tiger Books for having faith in my book, and to Vineetha Mokkil for her insightful editing and sage advice.